**Celie ran her fingertip over the rim of her glass,
then licked the salt off.**

John's gaze followed her movements.

"Feenie warned me about you, you know," Celie said.

"I'm aware of that."

She propped her elbow on the table and rested her chin on her hand. "She's usually right about stuff like that."

John tucked a strand of that honey blonde hair behind her ear. "Celie, honey?"

"What?"

"Why don't you forget about what Feenie says, and find out for yourself?"

Also by Laura Griffin

ONE LAST BREATH

And look for

THREAD OF FEAR

Laura Griffin

One Wrong Step

POCKET STAR BOOKS
New York   London   Toronto   Sydney

Pocket Star Books
A Division of Simon & Schuster, Inc.
1230 Avenue of the Americas, New York, NY 10020

Copyright © 2008 by Laura Griffin

First Pocket Star Books paperback edition May 2008

POCKET STAR BOOKS and colophon are registered trademarks of Simon & Schuster, Inc.

For information about special discounts for bulk purchases, please contact Simon & Schuster Special Sales at 1-800-456-6798 or business@simonandschuster.com

Designed by Lisa Litwack

Manufactured in the United States of America

10 9 8 7 6 5 4 3

ISBN-13: 978-1-4165-3738-0
ISBN-10:   1-4165-3738-4

ACKNOWLEDGMENTS

I owe many people a huge thanks for their help and support. Thank you to Dmitry Zhdanov, Eric Zipkin, Barbara Castillo Noyes, Bill Sharpe, CJ Lyons, Mary Buckham, and Rae Monet for patiently answering my pesky questions. Any mistakes, technical or otherwise, are mine.

Thanks to Liz and to Sheryl, who have my deepest respect and admiration.

I am grateful to the team at Pocket for all their hard work, especially Abby Zidle for her editorial insights and sense of humor. Thanks to Kevan Lyon for being the best agent possible. And also, thank you to my ever-amazing book club, my sisters, and my parents.

And finally, a special thanks to Doug, who supports me always and never complains about eating McDinner.

ONE
WRONG
STEP

PROLOGUE

Mayfield, Texas
8:35 A.M.

John McAllister slid behind the wheel of his black Jeep Wrangler feeling grateful for beautiful women, strong coffee, and clean getaways.

Swigging caffeine, he sped away from the Stop-N-Go parking lot and tried to decide which route to the newspaper office would make him the least late for work. Fortunately, Melanie—or was it Mallory?—lived in one of the nicer parts of town, not far from the business district where the *Mayfield Gazette* was headquartered. John had left her bed moments ago, jotted a quick note, and heard her shuffling in the bedroom as he'd slipped out the front door. He didn't like mornings after, and the combination of too much tequila and not enough sleep had made this one a narrow escape.

John glanced in the backseat, and, hot damn, his luck was holding. The dry cleaning he'd picked up on his way to happy hour yesterday hadn't been stolen, rained on, or mutilated in the bar parking lot or Melinda's—that was her name—driveway. If he avoided traffic snarls and changed shirts on the fly, he might actually show his face at the staff meeting before it adjourned.

As he pulled up to a stoplight, John stripped off the T-shirt he'd worn last night. He ripped open the plastic dry cleaning bag, shrugged into a crisp white shirt, and buttoned up. He was about to unzip his jeans and tuck in the shirttail when he noticed the young brunette in the red Mustang convertible pulled up beside him. Her mouth hung open as she stared at him with naked admiration. It was a look he usually enjoyed, but the light had turned green, so he settled for giving the woman a friendly wink before shifting into gear.

Mayfield had a lot going for it. Warm weather. Hot women. A fresh flock of tourists migrating to the beaches every summer. The sun wouldn't hit full, skin-scorching intensity for a few hours yet, and on mornings like this, John was almost glad he lived here. Almost. If it weren't for the increasingly serious shit going down along the border, this place would be paradise.

As he shifted into fourth, he heard the familiar howl of an approaching police cruiser. Check that—two police cruisers. Check *that*—three or more.

What the fuck? John pulled over and watched *five* black-and-whites race by. In the distance he heard yet another emergency vehicle, this one coming from the direction of the closest fire station.

John followed in the cruisers' wake, cursing himself for leaving his police scanner on his desk overnight. His editor would be pissed. His only shot at redemption would be getting whatever this story was and hoping nothing important had transpired last night while he was burning up the sheets with Melinda.

The cruisers turned down a street lined with King palms and, set farther back from the curb, expensive brick-and-stucco homes. This was an upscale neighborhood, and many of the houses had waterfront views, three-car garages, and boat slips. Whatever this emergency was, it wasn't your typical liquor store holdup.

The police cars screeched to a halt in front of a white stucco residence, and five pairs of officers hopped out, guns drawn.

John parked across the street from the house, a Mexican-style three-story with a red tile roof. A gray Volvo SUV was parked in the driveway with one of the back passenger doors open. The cops surrounded it. John climbed out of his Jeep and saw a young officer—the first responder, most likely—already kneeling on the driveway next to, holy shit, a *body*. It looked like a woman in a dark dress, but it was hard to tell for sure. A pool of blood surrounded the mutilated mass that had once been her head.

John scanned the area for any sign of the gunman, but all he saw were neighbors in bathrobes and warmups who had been lured outside by the commotion. Not far up the block, a silver-haired man with a Chihuahua bouncing around his ankles talked to a cop and gestured wildly down the street. John caught the words "black

Hummer" and "bat outta hell." His gaze shifted back to the Volvo. A spray of bullet holes perforated the rear fender.

Shit, a drive-by.

In this neighborhood? This wasn't gang-on-gang violence. More like someone gunning down a judge or a city official. Not that most city officials lived around here. The mayor had some money, but even he lived several streets over.

John caught the neighbor's eye. "Hey, you know who lives here?"

The cop glared at him, but Chihuahua Guy was eager to help out. "The Prices," he said. "Pam and Barry."

"Thanks." John walked off before the cop could get territorial.

Pamela Price. The assistant U.S. attorney was currently prosecuting some midlevel members of the Saledo drug cartel. Her murder would spook every law enforcement official in the Rio Grande Valley.

A shrieking ambulance skidded to a halt in front of the house, and two paramedics dashed up the driveway. John approached the crime scene, which was already being secured by several uniforms with rolls of yellow tape. As John watched the paramedics kneel down beside the victim, he realized she wasn't alone. Lying next to her, in a second pool of blood, was another body.

A little boy. In blood-covered overalls.

Beside the back tire lay a blue-and-red Spider-Man backpack. Pamela Price must have been buckling her kid into his car seat when the Hummer came by, and the fuckers had shot them both.

One of the medics strapped an oxygen mask over the boy's face while the other scrambled to stanch the bleeding. Blood was everywhere, turning the paramedics' latex gloves scarlet and forming an ever-expanding puddle around the mother and child.

John's stomach turned. He spotted a cluster of trash cans and raced over just in time to puke his guts up. He crouched down, leaning a hand against the neighbor's house. The smell of vomit and garbage filled his nostrils, and the humidity closed in on him. He was going to hurl again if he didn't get some air.

A low hedge separated the Prices' property from their neighbors'. John walked into the adjacent backyard and plunked himself down on a patio chair in front of a weathered boathouse. He took a deep breath and tried to spit out the vile taste in his mouth.

Damn, what was wrong with him? He'd covered the crime beat for nearly a decade now. He'd been to countless homicide scenes; he'd seen corpses.

He thought of the Spidey backpack and shuddered. He needed a cigarette.

Something mewed, and John glanced around, expecting a cat. No cat, but the noise continued, growing louder every second. The mewing gave way to something vaguely human, and John stood up. Low, keening noises were coming from the boathouse.

The tide was out, and the wooden decking surrounding the boat slip stood several feet out of the water. Four pilings supported the structure, which had a sundeck on top. The boat slip was empty except for two nylon straps flapping in the wind.

A flash of pink behind the nearest piling caught his eye.

"Hello?" he called.

The noises stopped. John glimpsed some brown hair a few feet off the ground. A child.

He stepped closer. "Anyone there?"

The hair didn't belong to a child, but to a doll. The doll came into view and, attached to it, the white-knuckled hand of a little girl. She was slack-jawed, trembling, and staring at John with huge brown eyes. Her little body was shaking so violently, the doll looked like it was having a seizure.

It took him a second to notice the blood splatters all over her pink dress. He rushed forward.

"Are you hurt?"

She lurched back, nearly falling off the dock.

Shit.

He didn't want to scare her into the bay. Slowly this time, he stepped toward her. She stepped back again, not even noticing she was inches from the edge.

Could she swim? He had no fucking idea. She looked about four, maybe a tall three. She was about the same height as one of his nieces, and she had long brown pigtails. He studied the blood on her dress. It didn't seem to be coming from her. More likely it was her mother's blood, or her brother's.

What should he do here? He knew jack shit about kids.

He needed to get help. But what if she fell in while he was gone? What if she couldn't swim? What if that wasn't her mother's blood and this girl was injured?

She moved closer to the piling, wrapping an arm around it and squeezing her eyes shut. She started the freaky animal sound again.

Cautiously, he stepped onto the dock. A plank creaked under his foot, and her eyes flew open. She looked at him, then over his shoulder at what was probably her house. John hoped she didn't have a line of sight to the ambulance.

She clutched the doll closer to her chest.

He'd seen the doll before, or something like it, at his sister's place. His niece's doll carried around a purple backpack and spoke Spanish. What the hell was its name? Dyna. Dyna the Adventurer or something like that.

"Is that . . . Dora you've got there?" Dora the Explorer. Damn, he'd pulled that out of his ass.

She looked from him to the doll and nodded. The noise stopped.

John crouched down. "My niece has a doll like that. Her name's Hannah. What's your name?"

She didn't answer. But she didn't move toward the water, either, so he took that as encouragement. Sweat slid down his temples, and his jeans and boots were streaked with vomit. He probably looked pretty frightening to this kid.

"Hey!"

John whirled around. A cop was jogging toward him, reaching for his holster. John held up his hand.

"Don't come closer!"

The cop drew his gun anyway. John darted a look at the girl. Her eyes bugged out, and a trickle of fluid ran down her leg. She started keening again.

"You're scaring her!" John yelled. "Put that away!

Please? I think she's hurt, and I'm trying to get her off this dock."

The cop hesitated a moment, then holstered the weapon. But the kid still looked terrified, and John wanted the cop out of her sight.

"We need a paramedic," John told him.

He wanted the officer to trot back to the house to get one, but instead he said something into his radio and stayed right where he was, his hand twitching on his holster. John didn't blame him. If he'd come upon a strange man and a freaked-out little girl at a murder scene, he probably would have done the same thing.

John took a deep breath and held out his hand to the kid. "Can you and Dora come closer?"

She shook her head.

Shit. But okay. Communication was good. He beckoned her with his fingers. "Please? See, that's some deep water there, and I'm worried you might fall in. Maybe Dora can't swim."

She glanced from him to her doll and back to him again. John blinked the sweat out of his eyes.

She stepped forward.

He nodded slightly, and she took another step. She wore black shoes with silver buckles and lacy white socks. Her socks and shoes were splattered with some sort of bloody tissue.

John snapped his gaze back to her face. He held his breath.

She took another step. She stretched out her hand.

John took it. And something twisted inside his chest as her cold, clammy little fingers closed around his own.

CHAPTER

I

Austin, Texas
Nine months later

Celie Wells dropped the fire extinguisher on the floor and gaped at her kitchen through the cloud of yellow dust. How come they never showed scenes like this on the Food Network?

Her lungs tickled. Coughing, she waved away the superfine particles that floated around her. God, she'd made a mess. And a racket. She should probably notify the building super about her little accident.

She eyed the disemboweled smoke detector on her kitchen floor and decided against it. If anyone from the building's management saw her luxury unit in its current state, she could kiss her hefty security deposit good-bye.

And her ceiling wasn't permanently damaged, nothing a little spackle and touch-up paint couldn't fix.

She picked up the portable phone, battling the urge to do what she normally did when disaster struck, which was call her mom. Virginia Wells was great in a crisis, and she would be delighted to learn that her domestically challenged daughter was baking, though she'd never approve of the reason.

But Celie wasn't in the mood for a lecture, and that's just what she'd get if she told her mother she'd set her kitchen on fire while baking goodies for the Bluebonnet House Easter party. It wasn't that her mother disliked battered women's shelters *per se*; she just didn't believe it prudent for a thirty-one-year-old divorcee to work at one.

Celie wasn't up for the debate tonight. Her self-esteem had taken a hit already when the cheerful, scrumptious bunny cake she'd lovingly created had morphed into a charred, inedible pancake inside her oven. *Throw together a festive Easter party in six simple steps!!* the glossy magazine had proclaimed from the check-out line. Celie's radar should have been on red alert when she read step one: *Create a tasty bunny cake that doubles as a fun centerpiece!*

Celie dumped the nontasty, nonfun bunny cake into the sink. Even her disposal rejected it.

Celie sighed. Her uselessness in the kitchen was just one more sign that the Suzie Homemaker gene had missed her. It was ironic, really, considering that her lifelong ambition had been to settle down, make a home, and raise a family.

She was being hormonal again.

She fetched the broom from the hall closet and began sweeping up the snowy mess all over her floor. She'd made it through this entire hellacious week without a meltdown, and she wouldn't lose it now, not over a stupid rabbit cake. If Feenie were here right now, she'd be laughing, not on the verge of tears.

The phone rang. Celie glanced at the caller ID and confirmed for the umpteenth time that her best friend had mental telepathy.

"Hi, Feenie, what's up?"

Feenie Juarez lived five hours away down in Mayfield, but she and Celie talked so much, she may as well have lived next door.

"Just calling to see how your meeting went. Did you get the director to recommend drug treatment for your kid?"

Feenie always called the children at Bluebonnet House "her kids," and Celie hadn't gotten around to mentioning that it bothered her.

"No." Celie leaned her broom against the counter and took a clean mixing bowl out of the cabinet. "But I *did* get roped into being in charge of the Easter party tomorrow."

"You're kidding. Don't tell me you have to cook."

"You got it." She started measuring ingredients again. Darn it, she was out of baking soda. She'd borrowed that first teaspoon from her neighbor across the hall, but she dreaded the thought of going back there. That woman could talk the ear off a cactus.

"Hey, you know anything about cake baking?" she asked hopefully. Feenie was no domestic diva, but she'd come a long way in the months since she'd been married.

Just last week, she'd been making tamales for her husband.

"I know two things," Feenie said. "Betty and Crocker."

Celie sighed, and then explained what was going on, omitting the part about the four-foot flame that had leapt out of the oven and scorched her ceiling.

"I can't believe you're making something from a magazine," Feenie said. "Are you masochistic or just nuts?"

She eyed the April issue of *Living* sitting open on her counter. The photograph showed a rabbit-shaped cake with jelly bean eyes, licorice whiskers, and fur made of shaved coconut, tinted pink of course. Her gaze shifted to the singed heap in her sink.

"A little of both," she answered, glancing out the window. Even if she hadn't been wearing threadbare plaid pajamas and waiting on a take-out delivery, she didn't relish the thought of braving west Austin's hilly streets in a driving rainstorm.

Especially at night. Celie steadfastly avoided going out alone after dark.

"The good news is I figured out where I went wrong," she told Feenie. "The bad news is I don't have any more baking soda, and I want to give this recipe another whirl. Is there something I can substitute?"

Feenie snorted. "You're asking me for cooking tips?"

"Well, you mentioned the tamales, so I thought—"

"It was a nightmare. I was up to my elbows in corn husks all day, and the final product tasted like soggy Fritos. Next time Marco wants homemade Mexican food, he can hit up his mom."

"Oh." Celie felt deflated. In the morning her boss expected her to put on an Easter party for twenty-two kids, some of whom had never even received a birthday present. She wanted to do something special and memorable, but the prospects were growing dimmer by the minute. And the thought of picking up a package of generic, grocery-store cupcakes depressed her. Celie's mother never would have resorted to such a thing.

"Get over it," Feenie said, reading her mind. "The kids'll be fine. Bring 'em some chocolate bunnies, and they'll think you hung the moon.

"So what are you doing home, anyway?" Feenie asked. "I thought you had a hot date with that grad student."

And there it was—the real reason for the call.

"I'd say 'hot' is an exaggeration," Celie said. "Think Will Ferrell without the jokes."

"Well, didn't he ask you out for coffee tonight? What happened?"

Celie plopped down on the couch. "I told him we'd take a rain check. With this party tomorrow, I didn't have time."

Actually, she'd gotten cold feet. Celie hadn't been on a date since before Google was invented, and she felt woefully out of touch with modern standards. What if this guy wanted more than coffee? What if, say, he wanted to come back to her apartment afterward and jump into bed together? Celie didn't do recreational sex. Even when she'd been married, the recreation part had been pretty lacking.

"Celie."

"Hmm?"

"That's chickenshit, and you know it. Who doesn't have time for coffee?"

Celie heard cooing on the other end of the phone and decided to change the subject. "Olivia's awake?"

"Yeah." Feenie's tone mellowed. "We're having one last feeding before bedtime. At least I hope it's bedtime. Last night we were up every hour between midnight and six."

No wonder Feenie sounded crabby. "You must be exhausted."

"I'm okay. Liv's just colicky, bless her little heart."

Feenie could hit the kill zone of a paper silhouette from forty yards away with her .38, but motherhood had turned her into a complete softy. Celie had spent a few days down in South Texas after Olivia's birth, and had actually caught Feenie getting misty-eyed over reruns of *Seventh Heaven*.

Celie felt a pang of envy, and then hated herself for it. Feenie deserved to be happy. She'd been to hell and back over the past few years.

Feenie must have sensed what the silence meant. "So, this cake thing. Here's my advice: toss the Martha Stewart mag in the trash and stop by the grocery store on your way to work."

The buzzer sounded, and Celie got up to grab her checkbook off the kitchen counter. "My dinner's here. Lemme let you go."

"I mean it, Celie. Pick up some Easter candy and quit torturing yourself. Those kids adore you, with or without cake."

Celie punched the intercom button. "Yes?"

"Ms. Wells, we have a delivery down here—"

"Send him right up!" And then to Feenie, "All right, I'll talk to you tomorrow."

Celie got off the phone and wrote a check to Shanghai Garden. On her way to the door, she glanced in the bathroom mirror to make sure she looked halfway decent. She didn't. Her dark blonde hair was dusted with flame retardant, and globs of batter decorated her pajama top. Plus, she wasn't wearing a bra. She grabbed a denim jacket off the hook in the foyer and shrugged into it just as a knock sounded at the door. Out of habit, she patted her pocket to make sure she had her pepper spray handy before going to work on her numerous locks. As she flipped the first latch, she peered through the peephole, expecting to see a stranger in the hallway holding a carton of Chinese food.

But the man who stood there looked all too familiar.

Celie's hands froze. She backed away from the door and darted a frantic glance around the apartment. Where had she put the phone? He knocked again, and then the doorknob rattled. God, was it possible he had a *key*? She took out her Mace.

"I hear you in there, Celie. Open up, okay? I just want to talk."

Yeah, right. Did he think she was crazy? She held her Mace in a death grip as she bit her lip and tried to decide what to do.

"Celie, please?" The familiar voice made her chest tighten. Guilt, anger, regret—the emotions battled inside her.

"I just need to talk to you," he repeated.

Guilt won out.

Instead of locating her phone and calling the police, she moved toward the door. Methodically, she undid all the locks until only one deadbolt remained. She waited a beat, giving herself one last chance to heed the warnings blaring in her head. Then she turned the key and pulled open the door.

Her ex-husband stood before her holding a drooping bouquet of flowers and a baseball cap. He wore a tattered UT windbreaker, sneakers, and wet jeans that clung to his gaunt frame. He desperately needed a haircut.

And, from the look of it, a methadone fix.

"Hello, Robert. Rumor has it you're dead."

CHAPTER

2

Robert glanced over his shoulder, then back at her. A smirk spread across his face as noticed the pepper spray clutched in her hand. "You'd like that, wouldn't you?"

Sighing, she stepped aside to let him in. "Can't say it hasn't crossed my mind."

He walked through the doorway and immediately created a puddle on her Saltillo tile floor.

"Nice place you got here. I thought students were supposed to be broke."

"I've got a job. What is it you want?" she asked, trying to hide her jangled nerves. Not only was he *here* in her apartment when she hadn't so much as lain eyes on him in nearly a year, but he'd been checking up on her, too. He'd found out she was enrolled at UT.

Celie had selected this overpriced apartment complex specifically for its security. It had a gated perimeter, enclosed parking, and a round-the-clock guard in the lobby. Didn't do much good if she buzzed the crazies up herself.

Robert thrust the yellow carnations at her as he strode into the kitchen. The arrangement was tied together with cheap ribbon, and he hadn't bothered to remove the price tag. "Special delivery.

"You got anything to eat around here?" He paused in front of the sink. "What's all this?"

Unbelievable. He'd abandoned her, emptied their bank account, and fled the country. Now he shows up wanting a meal? Celie slammed the flowers onto the kitchen counter with a *thwack*. She wasn't scared anymore, just royally pissed. She pocketed her pepper spray and crossed her arms over her chest.

"I should call the police, Robert. You're a wanted man."

He shot her a dismissive look as he opened a cabinet. "You won't do that."

"How do you know? You think you know anything about me anymore? You think you have a right to even *be* here?"

He tossed his grimy cap on the counter and began rummaging through her cupboard, knocking over soup cans and boxes of mac-n-cheese.

"What are you looking for?"

He ignored her question. "If you really wanted to rat me out, you would have done it after your PI came to visit me in Antigua."

Celie bit her lip. He was right. She *had* had a chance to turn him in, but she hadn't done it.

Instead, she'd divorced him.

After enduring weeks of grueling interviews with the FBI, constant surveillance, and phone taps, Celie had decided her marriage was undeniably over. Her seemingly innocuous husband, the mild-mannered accountant who opened doors for blue-haired ladies at church and didn't have the nerve to send back an undercooked steak, had been laundering money for the Saledo drug cartel.

After overcoming her initial shock and inertia, Celie had asked Feenie's husband for help. Marco Juarez, a talented private investigator who made a habit of steering clear of authorities, conducted a quiet search. He located Robert, informed him that Celie had filed for an ex parte divorce, and told him it would be ill-advised for him to contact Celie or her family ever again.

Knowing Marco, he hadn't been too subtle about driving that point home.

So why was Robert standing here now, foraging through her pantry like a wet raccoon?

"You still get migraines?" he demanded. "You have any of those pills?"

Aha. He needed drugs. Marco had spared her the details of his visit with Robert, but he'd made a few key points: Robert was living the high life, partying hard, and availing himself of the services of numerous local women. It had also been Marco's opinion that Robert was just a few months shy of a crash. Apparently, he'd been pretty strung out.

"Yes and no," Celie said firmly.

"Huh?"

"Yes, I still get headaches, and no, I don't have any meds for you."

He scowled and opened another cabinet. Celie noticed the tremor in his hands. She had to get him out of here.

"Prenatal vitamins? You never give up, do you?" He plopped a fat plastic bottle on the counter. "Who's the lucky guy this time?"

Okay, she'd had enough. She spotted the portable phone on the counter and lunged for it.

He grabbed her arm. "Oh, no, you don't. We're not done talking."

"Then *talk*!"

His fingers bit into her skin, and she caught a whiff of beer. He'd been drinking, and clearly he was jonesing for something stronger. She'd have to ratchet things down a notch and *persuade* him to leave her apartment. She'd had enough experience with drug addicts at the Bluebonnet House to know they could be unpredictable and dangerous, especially when they needed something they didn't have.

God, he looked awful. His skin was tinged yellow, and he hadn't showered or combed his hair in days. He had a goatee now, too, which just emphasized his underfed junkie persona. Had she actually been *married* to this guy? For six *years*?

She took a deep breath and steeled herself for a conversation she really didn't want to have. "All right," she said. "What is it you want to talk about?"

He smiled wickedly. "Money, honey. What'd you think?"

• • •

Kate Kepler hated panty hose. Ditto for heels, purses, and any other accessory that made her feel like a wannabe Barbie doll. She steered her Volkswagen Beetle down the winding road, trying to strip off the too-tight nylons without having a wreck. The elastic waistband had been cutting into her skin all night, and the control top made her desperate for air. Finally a stoplight appeared, and Kate wrestled the damn things off.

"Free at last," she muttered, taking her first real breath in hours.

Never again would she jump at an assignment before nailing down the details. When Irene, the political editor, had told Kate she needed someone to cover a campaign event, Kate had literally leapt to her feet in eagerness. The political beat at the *Austin Herald* was her heart's desire, the coveted news job Kate had been pining for ever since her first journalism class. Reporting on democracy in action, scrutinizing the activities of elected officials, relaying critical information to the public—this was the work Kate fantasized about.

But tonight she'd done none of those things. Instead, she'd donned her only matching skirt and jacket, moussed up her brunette pixie cut, and—at Irene's insistence, the old-fashioned witch—shimmied her body into a suffocating pair of panty hose. All so she could spend three hours rubbing elbows with snooty, overdressed socialites who had gathered at some minimansion in the hills to hear a state senator give a ten-minute speech. And what had been the inspiring content of the senator's talk? Money, of course. And why wealthy Austinites should break out their checkbooks to make sure he got reelected.

The light turned green, and Kate gunned the engine. She had two hours to get back to the newsroom, write up tonight's event, and transmit her copy to the night editor. Normally, she'd have no problem making the deadline, but rain was coming down in buckets, and she couldn't ignore the speed limit like she usually did.

"Oh, come *on!*" she huffed as a blinking yellow light turned red in front of the fire station up ahead. She slid to a stop and waited while a man in a fluorescent yellow poncho helped a red fire engine reverse into the driveway. Between tonight's lightning storm and the slick streets, Kate predicted the men of Station 33 would be summoned back into action in a matter of minutes.

Finally the light changed. Kate hit the accelerator and snaked her way up Ranch Road 2222, one of the steepest, curviest streets in town. As she neared the crest of a hill, she looked out over the precipice to her right, but the typically breathtaking view of Austin was obscured by clouds and sheets of rain.

Something appeared in the road. "Omigod!" she screamed, yanking the wheel left. The Beetle fishtailed and spun, skidding to a stop on the shoulder.

"What the hell?" She whipped her head around to see what she'd nearly run over. Something shiny. A hubcap? A bumper? In the darkness, it was impossible to see.

Her heart thudded in her chest along with the *swish-swish* of the wiper blades. She'd stopped just inches shy of the guardrail that prevented cars from careening over the cliff.

She looked through the windshield and saw a pair of red lights on the opposite shoulder. It was an SUV, its taillights tipped up at an odd angle.

Kate threw the Beetle into park and jumped out. It looked as if the driver had crossed the yellow line and slammed into the cliff. The wreck looked bad. Deadly, even. The left-front side was crumpled like an accordion, and the headlamp on the right stared straight ahead, spotlighting the striations in the limestone wall in front of it. The passenger door stood open, and Kate wondered whether someone had managed to walk clear of the wreckage.

Rain pelted her face as she dashed across the highway to check it out. The car turned out to be an Explorer, dark blue. She approached the open door and peered inside.

"Oh, God," she muttered. A man was slumped over the steering wheel. "Are you okay?"

The question was absurd. Clearly he wasn't okay. He probably wasn't even alive, given the head-shaped indention in the windshield. Kate noticed the flaccid airbag. It had deployed, evidently, but hadn't managed to protect him from the wall of rock he'd crashed into.

Kate heard an engine start and glanced up the hill in time to see a pair of taillights glowing red in the distance, not fifty yards up the shoulder from her Beetle. It was a pickup truck, and its interior light was on, illuminating two people in the cab.

"Hey!" she yelled. Had they witnessed the accident? Maybe they could help.

The passenger pulled the door shut, and the light switched off. Then the pickup's back tires spun, kicking up a rooster tail of mud and gravel. Were they *leaving*?

"Hey, wait!" She waved frantically, but the truck disappeared over the crest.

She turned back to the SUV. The driver still wasn't moving. He wore a windbreaker in that hideous UT orange and a baseball cap. She guessed he was young, maybe even a college student, but it was hard to tell because his face was concealed by blood-matted hair.

"Hey, can you hear me?" she yelled over the rain.

No answer.

Kate scrambled back across the highway, feeling pinpricks in the soles of her feet. She was barefoot, her heels tossed in the backseat along with her ridiculous panty hose. She yanked open the car door and snatched her cell phone from the drink holder.

No signal. Kate sucked in a gasp as the message flashed on the screen. Of course. Ranch Road 2222 was carved out of the hills. She was standing beside a hundred-foot wall of limestone.

"Damn it to *hell!*" She stuffed the phone in the pocket of her rain-soaked suit and shifted her attention to the highway. On a normal night, this would be a well-traveled route. But with the rain . . . The driver was in bad shape. She couldn't wait for a Good Samaritan.

The fire station.

"I'll be right back, okay? Hold on!" she yelled across the road, hoping against hope that she wasn't talking to a dead man.

"And did you get the license plate of the vehicle, ma'am?"

The rain had let up, and Kate sat shivering beneath a Mylar blanket on the hood of her Beetle. Across the highway, paramedics loaded the accident victim into the back of an ambulance. He wasn't conscious, as far as Kate could tell, but she took the paramedics' hurried movements as an indicator that he still had a chance.

"No," Kate explained for the third time. "The truck was only there a few seconds."

"And could you describe the passengers? Are you sure it was two of 'em?"

The tobacco-chewing cop was getting on Kate's nerves. He'd called her "little lady" twice now and kept telling her she should get someone to look at her cuts.

Kate shrugged off the blanket and stood, trying not to wince as her feet made contact with the pavement. She'd stepped on some glass at the crash site, and chips were embedded in her soles. She probably did need first aid, but she'd be damned if she'd admit it to a patronizing redneck. "I told you. I couldn't *see* them. It was dark and rainy. But they were parked at the top of the hill and then they took off. I'm pretty sure it was a hit-and-run."

Officer Skoal looked her over skeptically and spat on the gravel. Kate shuddered. Chewing tobacco was high on her list of repulsive male habits.

"But you didn't actually *witness* the accident?"

She fisted her hands at her sides. "No. I told you before. When I got here, the Explorer had already crashed."

Kate glanced at her watch. She was so screwed. She had barely an hour to get back to the newsroom with her story, and she hadn't had a chance to call the night editor yet about the accident. He'd probably want it for tomorrow's metro section.

"I can't believe he had a pulse," Kate said, watching the

ambulance pull away. Its siren was on, which she interpreted as a positive sign.

Officer Skoal turned and followed her gaze. "Barely. He was tore up pretty bad. Wasn't wearin' a seatbelt."

Kate shuddered again and for a moment thought she might lose the cheese bites she'd eaten earlier.

At the senator's cocktail party.

The one she was supposed to have written a story about more than an hour ago.

Kate watched as a fireman directed the intermittent traffic around the cones he'd set up in the lane nearest the wreck.

"Excuse me," Kate said. "What did you say your name was again?"

The cop's chest expanded. "Don Poole."

"Officer Poole, did you see any indication that a dark-colored vehicle bumped into the back of that Explorer?"

He glanced at the SUV. Aided by the light of orange street flares, several workers were measuring skid marks and investigating the wreckage.

"Not so far," Poole said.

Kate hadn't seen anything either, but she'd thought she should at least ask. Several things about the accident scene didn't make sense to her, starting with the fact that the passenger's-side door had been open.

"What I *did* see was some cans of Bud in the front," Poole continued. "Looks to me like this kid got liquored up and lost control of the car."

"You say 'kid.' Did you get an ID?"

Poole frowned. "What's with all the questions? You're not some kinda reporter, are you?"

"Actually, I work for the *Herald*. I'm pretty sure we'll be running an article about the accident, especially if it turns out to be fatal."

Poole scowled. "Shoulda known. If it bleeds, it leads, right? I'll tell you, what we really need is a news article about this here road. Kills more people every year than all your serial killers combined. People speed, irregardless of warning signs and weather conditions. Why don't you put *that* in your paper?"

He spat out some chaw juice for emphasis.

"It's a good point," Kate said, not bothering to explain that she didn't personally oversee the editorial content of the entire paper. "So, is that it for the accident report? I really need to get downtown."

He passed her his clipboard. "Sign at the bottom there."

"Thank you."

"You're welcome, little lady. And lemme call a fireman over to take a look at your feet."

Kate sat in the *Austin Herald* newsroom the next morning with her bandaged feet elevated on a stack of phone books beneath her desk. She'd worn flip-flops to work, which was pushing the envelope, even in Austin. But it was Saturday, so she figured no one would care.

She shuffled through her notepad, trying to find the phone number for Brackenridge Hospital. At pressrun, the hospital still hadn't released the crash victim's status, and Kate had been hoping that meant he was in surgery.

"Any more where that came from?"

Kate glanced up to see John McAllister looming over

her. He sported his movie-star smile and a Widespread Panic T-shirt. He, too, was wearing flip-flops, which made Kate feel better about her attire.

"Any more . . . ?"

"Krispy Kremes." He nodded at what was left of her chocolate-iced doughnut. "No fair keeping 'em all to yourself."

"Sure, uh, over by the copier. I brought in two dozen." Bringing doughnuts to the newsroom on Saturdays was a quick way to make friends. Kate had recently supplanted McAllister as the newbie on staff, and she needed all the friends she could get.

"Kate, you're the love of my life." He winked at her. "Can I top off your coffee while I'm up?"

John McAllister was offering to fetch her coffee. Forget that she refused to touch the tar they concocted in the break room and had filled her travel mug at the doughnut store on the way over.

"Thanks." She took a big gulp and handed over her cup.

"Sugar?"

"What?"

"You take sugar?"

Oh. For a second there she'd thought he was calling her "sugar." He called women things like that all the time, which should have been offensive, but somehow he managed to get away with it.

"Um, sure. Sugar's good. Or black's fine, too."

He looked amused. "Which is it?"

"Sugar. If they have it."

He smiled and walked away before Kate could come

up with more scintillating conversation. What was it about him? Every time she opened her mouth in his presence she lost IQ points. It was pretty embarrassing considering the man had joined the *Herald* with more journalism awards under his belt than any other reporter on staff.

She stared after him, admiring the way his jeans fit. He had that long, tall Texan thing going on, and even in a state full of Texans, he stood out. He was well over six feet, athletically slender, and had just enough drawl in his voice to charm the pants off of even the most clear-thinking woman. Kate had seen him in pickup mode over on Sixth Street, Austin's hub for nightlife, and somehow *still* managed to have a crush on him.

"I need that car wreck update five minutes ago, Kepler."

The weekend editor stopped at Kate's desk, effectively ending her daydream. Bruce Schaffer was the anti-McAllister, short and skinny, with a receding hairline. He favored polyester pants with gray snakeskin boots.

"You need it now?" Kate asked. "I just got started. I haven't even called the hospital yet—"

"Don't bother. I already called. Guy was DOA."

Kate swore under her breath.

"And I just got a call from Shel," Bruce said. "He's coming in to take a look at your story. So get your notes together ASAP."

Bruce loved to talk in acronyms.

"Why is Shel involved?" Kate asked. The editor in chief never showed his face on weekends unless something major was going on.

"You must have been right about your hit-and-run theory," he said. "Something's weird, and suddenly the FBI's calling."

"The FBI?"

McAllister strolled over with her coffee cup and several doughnuts hooked to his long pinky.

"Yeah," Bruce said, "apparently the victim's someone important, but they won't tell us who. You checked out the vic's car with the DMV, right?"

"Thanks," Kate said as McAllister passed her her mug. She reread her notes. "Just got a call back. Vehicle is registered to a Cecelia Wells, but—"

"Wait, *what*?" McAllister seized her arm, sloshing coffee all over her desk. "*Who?*"

Whoa. Kate double-checked the name. "I said Cecelia Wells. Owner of a blue Ford Explorer. Why? You know her?"

The color drained from McAllister's face. It was remarkable. Two seconds, and he was white as chalk. "She was the *victim*? You mean she's . . . ?"

"Victim was a guy," Kate clarified. "Looked like maybe a college student out joyriding in her car."

"You know this girl?" Bruce asked McAllister.

"Yeah." He closed his eyes briefly. "She lives in my hometown. Mayfield."

"Not anymore." Kate scanned her notes. "Looks like she's here in Austin. Three-thirteen Grand View Drive."

McAllister snatched the notepad away. "Fuckin' A," he muttered. "She didn't tell me she'd moved here."

Kate rolled her eyes. What an ego. She looked him over as he read through her notes. Okay, so he came by it honestly. He was gorgeous—*People*'s Sexiest Man Alive gorgeous. Kate watched his wavy, blondish-brown hair fall over his eyes as he stroked his stubbled jaw.

"We need a follow-up on this," Bruce was telling her. "We need to find out what the deal is with her car. Was it stolen? Did she lend it to somebody? We got some FBI hotshot calling Shel about this, and he wants to know why. Get your butt down to police headquarters and find out what they know about this victim."

"I'm on it," Kate said.

Bruce turned to McAllister. "You want to lend a hand here? Is this woman married?"

McAllister looked up. "Huh?"

"Is she married? Any chance her husband was behind the wheel? Maybe she's got a teenager?"

"Uh . . . she's divorced," he said. "No kids."

"Well, call her up and see why someone else was driving her car last night."

"That's not necessary," Kate said. "I can cover this."

If this story turned into something big, Kate didn't want McAllister stealing it out from under her. He had a competitive streak.

"No, this is important," Bruce said. "I want both of you on it. Shel wants answers, pronto."

Kate picked up her keys.

"And hey, Kepler," Bruce said, "before you go, I've got a number for some FBI agent who wants to talk to you. Tell him what he needs to know, but don't make any promises about what we will or won't print. Remember who you work for."

Kate froze. "Couldn't *you* talk to him?" There were

few things Kate would enjoy less than talking to an FBI agent.

"Sorry, Kepler. He wants you."

Cecelia Wells was hiding something. Special Agent Mike Rowe had a gut feeling about it; he just hadn't figured out what the something was.

"And you're sure about the timeline, ma'am?" his partner asked. Nick Stevenski was young, charming, and nice to look at, and consequently their standard operating procedure was for him to interview any female witnesses. Stevenski had been sitting across from sweet little Ms. Wells for nearly an hour now, and she'd been extremely cooperative.

But something was off. She was holding back. Rowe knew it as sure as he knew that her ex-husband was at this very moment laid out in the morgue.

"He left around ten," she told Stevenski for the second time. "I remember because right afterward I took a half-hour bubble bath to relax, and when I got out David Letterman was on."

A half-hour bubble bath. Nothing like an indisputable time line.

Cecelia pulled another tissue from the box on the coffee table and blew her nose in that dainty way only women can pull off. She looked different than she had down in Mayfield the last time Rowe had seen her. Her blonde hair was longer; maybe that was it. Her eyes looked greener than usual, but that was just because she'd been crying. Then he figured it out. She'd gained weight. Her cheeks were plump, and the rest of her body seemed slightly fuller now than it had eight months ago. Probably the stress, Rowe decided. Lots of people put on weight when they were under pressure, and Cecelia Wells had been under plenty of pressure since her husband became a fugitive last summer.

"And can you remember anything else you talked about?" Stevenski asked. "Anything besides money and your idea that he should seek rehab?"

Rowe wandered into the kitchen as the interview dragged on. Another strategic reason for Stevenski to take the lead was that he'd never met Cecelia before today. Rowe was interested to see whether his partner could elicit new answers to some of the questions Rowe had asked a few months ago.

So far, no luck.

Cecelia had cooperated fully and given a convincing performance as the bereaved-but-not-overly-so ex-wife. Everything she'd said thus far had checked out, right down to the wilted yellow carnations in the bottom of her trash can, the flowers she claimed Strickland had used to get past the doorman downstairs.

So what was bothering him?

"And about the money again," Stevenski continued, "you say Robert asked for a few hundred bucks to tide him over, and that's when you told him you only had a twenty in the house?"

"That's right."

Bingo.

Rowe pretended to be looking out the window while he waited to hear whether Cecelia would realize she'd changed her story.

"I told him I didn't keep cash like that lying around, but he could have the twenty," she said. "I hoped he'd use it for a meal. I guess deep down I knew he'd try to buy drugs, but I felt guilty, you know? He looked so skinny and awful, I didn't want to send him away empty-handed." Her voice faltered. "I guess I was wrong, huh? If he hadn't been on something, he might not have had the wreck."

Stevenski refrained from assuaging her guilt, and Rowe waited for him to pick up the thread of inconsistency in her story. At the start of the interview, she'd said Strickland asked her for a few *thousand* bucks, not a few hundred. She was lying about her conversation with Strickland, at least about the money part. And now Rowe had a lead.

"Okay, so that's when you told him to wait while you got him an aspirin?"

Stevenski had switched topics again. Damn it, this was why Rowe liked to conduct interviews himself. But females didn't open up with him like they did with Stevenski. At six-one and 210 pounds, Rowe tended to intimidate women, especially shorter-than-average ones like Cecelia Wells. Plus, other agents had told him that his eyes put people off, that there was something cold about them.

"—and when I came back in, he was standing by the door," Cecelia was saying now. "I didn't realize he'd taken my keys until I was getting ready for work this morning."

"At the Bluebonnet House, right?"

"Right. We were supposed to have an Easter party today, but we're doing it tomorrow now because I couldn't make it. The police asked me to come to the station. . . ." Her voice trailed off as she reached for another tissue.

Rowe strolled back into the living room and stood behind the sofa where Cecelia was curled up, her legs folded under her, hiding the shiny pink toenail polish he'd noticed when they'd first arrived. With her long blonde hair and soft southern accent, this woman radiated "sorority chick." But Rowe knew better, even if Stevenski didn't. This woman was sharp. He wanted to signal his partner to get back to the subject of money. Rowe had reason to believe Robert Strickland was indebted to the Saledo drug cartel for a quarter million in stolen drug profits, money he hadn't been in possession of at the time of his death. If his ex-wife had some knowledge about the money, it might mean a break in the case.

Manuel Saledo wouldn't turn his back on a debt like that—not because of the amount, which was chump change to him, but because he had a reputation to uphold. If Cecelia knew the money's whereabouts, Saledo would damn sure try to collect. And when *that* happened, Rowe and his task force might get a chance to collar some high-level operatives in Saledo's enterprise, hopefully someone who could help them develop useful intelligence on Saledo himself.

"Are you almost finished with your questions, Mr. Stevenski? Like I told you before, I have plans for the evening."

Rowe shifted his attention back to Cecelia, who had just reminded him of the other thing bugging him—this lie she'd obviously concocted about a date coming over. Rowe didn't know a woman alive who would go out on a date with bloodshot eyes and a runny nose. And she was wearing gray sweats that didn't exactly make a fashion statement. He'd bet money Cecelia's only plans for the night included a bottle of Chardonnay and another one of those bubble baths. Which meant she was trying to get rid of them. Which meant—despite her seeming cooperation and polite, thorough answers—she was uncomfortable being interviewed. Which confirmed Rowe's suspicion she was hiding something.

A buzzer sounded, and Cecelia sprang off the sofa.

"Excuse me." She rushed across the living room and punched a button on the intercom by the door. "Yes?"

"Ms. Wells, you got a visitor here. A John McAllister?"

She went still. Rowe would have liked to see her face, but her back was to him.

"Thank you," she said. "Please send him right up."

CHAPTER

3

John stepped into the elevator and immediately noticed the fancy brass NO SMOKING sign posted beside the door.

Jesus, he wanted a cigarette. He rode up the three floors to Celie's apartment, desperately wishing for just one drag, or even a piece of freaking Nicorette gum. Quitting smoking sucked, and he couldn't have picked a worse month to do it.

He'd spent all afternoon trying to talk to Celie, but her number wasn't listed and she'd spent the day away from home. John had dropped by her building three times since noon, and each time the burly guy in the lobby had said she was out. Finally at 5:15, when the doorman or security guard or whatever the hell he was had called up to her apartment yet again, she'd picked up.

John tried to imagine what she'd do when she saw him. Would she invite him in or tell him to get lost? He figured his odds were pretty evenly split.

The last time he'd seen Celie had been just after Feenie's wedding reception last summer down in Mayfield. Celie had left her car at the church, and John had offered her a ride home. He'd known she was going through a rough time, and he'd meant to play it cool, to give her plenty of space. But his noble intentions had evaporated after that first kiss on her front porch.

She'd been backed up against the front door, looking flushed and tousled and sexy as hell. He still remembered her mouth, all red and swollen from where he'd nibbled on it. God, she'd tasted so sweet, and not just her mouth either. Her skin had tasted sweet, too, that pretty stretch of it from her neck all the way down to the top of her party dress. He remembered kissing her there, listening to her uneven breathing, getting revved up for all the things he'd been waiting to do with her for ages.

And then she'd shut him down.

"You have to leave," she'd said, reaching for the doorknob.

"*Why?*"

She'd fumbled with her keys, finally shaking them loose from this ridiculously tiny black purse. Then she'd turned and looked at him, and he'd never forget her face.

She'd looked appalled.

"I can't sleep with you. Don't you understand?"

"I understand we both want each other. What else—"

"Don't you *get* it? I can't do this. I'm *married*, for crying out loud!"

Now he stood in front of her door again, wondering if he should expect another brush-off. She was no longer married, which was definitely good. But the fact that she'd moved all the way to Austin and neglected to call him wasn't what he considered a positive sign.

He couldn't focus on that right now. Celie was mixed up in some kind of trouble, and he needed to help her.

He took a deep breath and lifted his hand, and the door swung open before he could knock.

"McAllister!"

And then she was in his arms, all soft and warm. He stood there, amazed, as she melted right into him, instantly reminding him how good she always smelled, like woman and strawberries and some kind of soap. He glanced inside and noticed the two men standing in her living room.

"Got company?" He shifted her so she was standing beside him, his arm wrapped firmly around her shoulders.

"Oh, um, yeah." She tried to step away, but he kept her planted right where she was.

John didn't like the idea of men, period, lounging around Celie's apartment, but these guys were especially bad. They both wore suits, which in Austin usually meant you were headed to a funeral or to the state house. These guys were headed to neither, which made them feds.

Both men stepped forward. One was young, maybe late twenties, with dark hair and a smarmy smile he probably practiced in the mirror a few hundred times before going out on a date. The other one was older. His dark hair was gray at the temples and he had crinkles around his eyes. He was ripped, though.

Something about the older agent seemed familiar. Then John placed him: he'd been on the scene at Feenie's house the night Robert Strickland skipped town.

John looked down at Celie. She'd been crying, over her dead ex-husband, no doubt. He gave her what he hoped was a reassuring squeeze. "Care to introduce me?"

"Oh . . . yes. I'm sorry," she said, regaining some of that southern gentility she'd been raised with. "John McAllister, this is Special Agent Nick Stevenski and Special Agent Mike Rowe. They're with the FBI."

John shook hands with both men. *Back the fuck off,* he telegraphed mentally. Rowe raised his eyebrows, clearly getting the message.

"I was just apologizing because we'll have to postpone the rest of our interview." Celie turned to John with a plea in her eyes. "I'm running a little behind. Can you give me ten minutes to change before we go?"

Go?

"No problem," he said. "Take your time."

Rowe cleared his throat. "We'll talk tomorrow, then. How about ten A.M.?"

"I'm working tomorrow," Celie said quickly.

Rowe looked perturbed. "Any chance you could get the day off? We need to go over a few more details."

John felt her tense. She did *not* want to talk to these guys, and he couldn't blame her. The FBI had practically set up camp in her front yard for weeks after her ex's disappearance. It had been a nightmare for her. And now here they were, back for an encore.

"I'm in charge of the Easter party tomorrow. There's no

way I could disappoint the kids again." She smiled weakly. "I'm sure you understand."

"Fine," Rowe said. "We'll come by in the afternoon. Four o'clock."

He made his way toward the door without waiting for a reply. Stevenski trailed behind him, smiling as he walked past Celie.

"Nice meeting you, Ms. Wells." He gave John a curt nod. "Mr. McAllister."

"Later, fellas." John slammed the door behind them. He turned back toward Celie, who was staring at the door and looking dazed.

"You okay?" he asked.

"No."

Right. Dumb question. "You want to talk about it?"

She gave him a wobbly smile. "You wouldn't believe me if I told you."

Cecelia Wells lived in a fortress. Rowe scrutinized the place—for the second time that day—as he made his way across the visitor parking lot. The building was composed of white limestone and stucco, the type of architecture Rowe had seen everywhere since he'd come to Texas. The sprawling complex perched atop a cliff overlooking some hills or greenbelt or some sort of park. Cecelia's unit faced west, and during the hour-long interview Rowe had noticed she had a spectacular view.

Knowing what he did about Cecelia, though, he doubted she'd picked the place for the scenery.

Rowe unlocked the Buick and squinted up at the third floor, counting the units until he located Cecelia's.

The apartment was nice, but small compared to the other luxury units at The Overlook. Hers was the smallest unit available, in fact, just eight hundred square feet. Rowe had garnered these and other details from the well-heeled young leasing agent at The Overlook's front office on the way out.

"Quite a place she's got there," Stevenski said, following Rowe's gaze.

"Yeah," Rowe agreed. "Pricey, too. For Austin, at least. How do you think she affords a place like that working at a battered women's shelter?"

Stevenski shrugged. "Dunno. Maybe she's got a rich family."

She didn't. Rowe was thoroughly familiar with Cecelia's background, having done some of the original legwork on her over a year ago when her husband's name had cropped up in connection with the Saledo cartel. Rowe knew everything about Cecelia's past, including the fact that her mother, a widow, lived in Mayfield and was comfortable, but by no means wealthy. Cecelia's late father had been a chemical engineer.

"Nah," Rowe said, "she doesn't come from money. You read her file?"

"I skimmed it."

Rowe slid behind the wheel. The car was a piece of crap, but budgets were tight throughout the Bureau, and the San Antonio field office wasn't high on the list when it came to spreading money around. Making matters worse, San Antonio's current SAC, or special agent in charge, wasn't much of a diplomat. At a time when most of the Bureau's money and talent was being thrown at the antiterrorism campaign, George Purnell had been banished to Texas to deal with drug traffic and money laundering. Apparently, the SAC had had some sort of falling out with the top brass in Washington. His situation was similar to Rowe's, actually, only Rowe's previous home had been Chicago.

The car felt like a sauna inside, and Rowe flipped on the air-conditioning. A blast of hot air shot from the vents.

"She's not at all like I thought she'd be," Stevenski said.

Rowe knew what he meant. Based on Cecelia's file, his partner had probably expected to meet a real ballbuster. Instead, he'd met a weepy, pudgy-cheeked blonde.

"She really claw a guy's eye out?" Stevenski asked.

"Yep, she really did." Rowe paused at The Overlook's wrought-iron gate, waiting for it to open.

"And that was, what, ten years ago? She would have been a kid at the time."

"Yep," he said again. Cecelia Wells had been twenty-two, definitely a kid in Rowe's book, when she'd been raped, beaten, and left for dead behind a bar in downtown Austin. She'd been a senior at UT, just one semester shy of graduation, when she'd decided to go out drinking with some girlfriends on Sixth Street. She'd peeled off from the group early, then been accosted in an alley on the way to her car. Rowe had read the police report, and the attack had been horrific. Cecelia Wells was a mere five feet three, 110 pounds at the time. The man ultimately convicted of assaulting her was six feet tall and 200 pounds, almost exactly the same size as Rowe. For a woman that small to actually *claw* the guy's eye out . . . Well, suffice it to say she must have been experiencing some serious panic. The rapist had been unarmed, thank God, or he almost certainly would have killed her.

And the eyeball thing wasn't even the most impressive part. After the trial, Cecelia had made a few public statements, becoming somewhat of a spokeswoman for sexual assault survivors. In subsequent years, she'd dropped off the map, though.

"She's tough," Rowe said. "She may have been shaken up today, but she'll get over it. She just feels responsible."

She felt that way because Stevenski and Rowe hadn't been entirely candid with her. Yes, her ex-husband had had a few drinks when he lost control of the Explorer, but he hadn't been on drugs. And some black-on-blue paint transfer on the rear fender indicated he may have had a nudge into that rock wall.

Rowe turned onto the highway and glanced at the clock. He needed to track down that reporter from the crash scene. He definitely should have talked to her by now, but she hadn't returned any of his phone calls.

"You ever hear back from that woman at the *Herald*?" Stevenski asked, reading his mind.

"No, and I'm beginning to think she's dodging me." Rowe checked his phone, but still no messages. "Looks like I need to pay her a visit."

Celie sat across the table from McAllister and wondered how the heck he'd talked her into this. One minute she'd been thinking up a tactful way to get him out of her apartment, and the next minute they were in his Jeep on their way out to dinner. Forget that she felt—and looked—like roadkill, and that going out was the very last thing she wanted to do tonight. Somehow McAllister had convinced her that whatever her problems, she'd feel better after a stiff margarita and some Mexican food.

And, just like that, she'd said yes.

So now here they were, at a loud Mexican dive sandwiched between a Laundromat and a Goodwill shop. McAllister claimed it was the best Mexican food in town, but Celie had her doubts. The place was wall-to-wall kitsch, down to the Elvises-on-velvet and neon beer signs decorating the walls.

She snuck a glance at McAllister over the top of her menu. Austin agreed with him. His skin was tan, his hair streaked gold from the sun. Clearly, he'd been spending time outside, probably water-skiing, or rappelling, or practicing one of the many daredevil sports he was so fond of. Whatever he'd been up to, he looked good. Better, even, than he had last summer back in Mayfield. How was that possible? How was it that as time ticked by, men got better and better looking, while women just looked more and more used up?

That's how Celie felt these days. Exhausted by an endless series of trials and disappointments. And with each passing day, the things she wanted most for herself seemed to move further and further out of reach.

"You're not going to cry, are you?" McAllister asked, not looking up from his menu.

"Huh?"

"Your chin's quivering." He laid his menu aside and met her gaze. "And you can cry all you want, honey, but just let me know ahead of time so I can change your margarita to a double."

"I'm not going to cry," she said, meaning it. "I spent most of the day at the police station and on the phone with my former in-laws—who hate me, by the way. I'm all cried out."

He watched her for a long moment. "I'm sorry about Robert," he said.

He didn't really look sorry about Robert, but he seemed genuinely sorry she was upset.

"Thank you."

"Don't look so guilt-ridden. It's not your fault."

Hello, Robert. Rumor has it you're dead.

You'd like that, wouldn't you?

She wished, for the hundredth time that day, that their last conversation hadn't been so awful. She shook her head. "I just keep thinking if I'd said something different, he never would have taken off like that."

McAllister frowned. "You didn't lend him your car?"

"God, no! That's the last thing I would've done. He swiped my keys while I was in the bathroom getting him some aspirin."

"Why would he steal your car?"

"Transportation, I guess," she said. "Our conversation wasn't real friendly, and he left in a big huff."

A waitress stopped by to drop off their drinks and take their orders, and Celie was grateful for the interruption. She didn't really want to get into all this, especially with McAllister. She'd learned he was a reporter first and foremost, and anything she said might later become fodder for a news story. It was uncanny, really, that whenever something traumatic happened in her life, John McAllister seemed to be standing around with his notepad. It was one of the reasons she didn't trust him.

That, plus Feenie's repeated warnings that he was a chronic playboy incapable of a serious relationship.

Celie picked up her fishbowl-size margarita. She hadn't had one in forever. She hadn't had any alcohol, in fact, in months. It was all part of her health kick, the health kick that now seemed utterly pointless.

Celie plastered a smile on her face, like she always did when her mood bordered on maudlin.

"So, congratulations on your new job," she said, taking a sip. Wow, that margarita packed a punch. She needed to watch herself or she'd be under the table in nothing flat. "I guess the *Herald* is a big step up from the *Mayfield Gazette*, huh?"

He shrugged. "It's a step."

"And how do you like Austin?"

He hesitated a moment. "I like it. It's scenic. Sunny. Everyone's friendly and easygoing." He leaned back in his chair and watched her. "What do *you* think of Austin? You've been here, what? A couple months now?"

"Eight."

He flinched, and then covered it with a carefree smile. "Damn, I wish you'd called me. I could've helped you settle in."

Now there was a loaded statement.

"Actually," she said, "I settled in pretty quick. Enrolled in a few classes, got a job. You know, the usual."

But his blue eyes were perceptive, and she could see he knew there was nothing "usual" about it, at least not where she was concerned. Reenrolling in school had been a major milestone for her, something she'd spent years gathering the courage to do. Luckily, her credits with the university hadn't expired. She supposed she had the special circumstances surrounding her withdrawal to thank for that.

He leaned his muscular forearms on the table. "I'm glad you're finishing your degree. What do you have left now? One semester?"

"That, plus a six-month practicum in social work."

He smiled. "That's great. You're almost there."

Celie looked away. This was a bad idea. She shouldn't be out with McAllister. No matter how attractive he was, he knew way too much about her, and her defenses vanished around him.

With Robert, it had been different. She'd met him down in Mayfield about a year after the trial, and, although he'd heard about it vaguely through the grapevine, he wasn't clued in on all the details. Nor did he want to be. Celie had liked that about him. That and the fact he seemed safe, secure, harmless. He was courteous and nice, and he had a good job at an accounting firm. He liked to barbecue and play golf once a week. The very blandness of it all had attracted Celie to him.

"Celie? You listening?" McAllister was watching her intently.

She wondered what it would be like to sleep with John McAllister. Probably anything but bland. It might be fun, actually. Imagine that.

She had. Too many times to count.

"Celie?"

"I'm sorry. What?" From the way he was staring at her, she wondered if he knew the direction her thoughts had taken.

"I said, do you want to get this to go?"

The waitress had delivered their entrées. The scent of grilled onions wafted over from McAllister's fajita platter, and steam rose up from Celie's enchilada plate. Her stomach rumbled. She hadn't eaten all day.

"No. Thanks." She took an icy gulp of margarita. Warmth radiated through her system, and her shoulders relaxed a smidgen. "This is great."

He lifted an eyebrow. "You sure? You seem distracted."

"I'm fine. Really. Why don't you tell me what *you've* been up to?"

John watched her nibbling on her enchilada while she skillfully evaded his questions. He'd had her there for a minute, the real Cecelia, the woman behind the thousand-watt smile. It seemed like every time he caught a glimpse of her, she retreated behind an impenetrable wall of polite conversation.

"And have you seen any good movies lately?"

Fuck. "Not really. You?"

And with that witty remark, they started down the predictable path of first-date banter. John would have been ready for a nap, but the mindless exchange gave him a chance to look at her. Really *look*.

She seemed different now than she had back in Mayfield, less polished somehow. John couldn't decide whether he liked it or not. Her hair had changed, for one thing. He'd never realized it before, but that straw blonde color must have come from a bottle. Her real color was darker, more like honey.

Pretty.

And her body was different, too. Last time he'd seen her, she'd been thin, like a woman addicted to her aerobics class. She still looked good, but she was softer now, a little fuller through the hips, he'd noticed. His gaze strayed southward as she sipped her drink. Fuller in the breasts, too.

She looked sexy. Womanly. And not in the obvious, over-made-up way he was accustomed to. Most women he dated put everything on display, but Celie was different, and it worked for her. Even in faded jeans and a T-shirt, she held his attention. She seemed natural, confident. It was fucking attractive. He wanted to go home with her tonight so they could finish what they'd started back in Mayfield.

But they were in Small Talk Land, which meant she planned to keep him at a distance. He needed to change her mind.

"Hey, not to rush you, but you mind if I get the check?"

Her smile faltered. "Not at all." She looked down at her bare plate and the empty glasses. She'd ordered a second margarita halfway through the meal. "Sorry, I didn't mean to keep you."

"You didn't." He signaled the waitress. "It's just their bar's getting crowded, and I can barely hear you. You care if we leave?"

"No, that's fine, but"—she glanced around the restaurant, then back at him—"could we get another drink somewhere or something? I don't really want to go home just yet."

And neither did he.

Wanting to stay the hell away from Sixth Street, John drove to a quiet pub north of campus. The place was frequented by grad students and some literary types from the faculty. John steered Celie to a dimly lit corner and found a table.

"This is nice," she said, pulling up a stool made from a converted whiskey barrel. "Kind of homey."

He smiled. He'd never heard the Ale House referred to as "homey," but it sort of fit. She probably liked the candles scattered around the tables.

"Can I get you a beer?" he asked.

"Hmm . . . You think they have margaritas?"

Her cheeks were tinged pink, and she had the vaguely happy look of someone well on her way to being toasted.

Fine with him. She'd had a crappy day and deserved to toss back a few drinks.

"Coming right up. It'll probably be on the rocks, though. I've never heard a blender in here."

She smiled. "That's fine."

"Back in a sec."

He made his way to the bar, fielding greetings from regulars and smiles from some of the women. As soon as he got the drinks, he returned to the table.

Celie was just where he'd left her, but the empty stool beside her was occupied now by Austin's very own celebrity scribe, Andrew Stone. The guy had perfect hair, perfect clothes, and perfect teeth. Despite being vertically challenged, he probably could have made it as a TV anchor. But he had a Woodward-and-Bernstein complex, so instead of talking to the camera he wrote pseudo-investigative pieces for *Lone Star Monthly*, the state's version of *Vanity Fair*. In reality, Stone didn't investigate stories so much as he *read* stories written by newspaper reporters, then regurgitated them with better photos.

John watched as Stone leaned close to Celie, said something, and brushed his hand down her back.

John plunked the drinks on the table, sloshing Guinness on Stone's designer pants.

Stone looked up, startled. "McAllister! Long time no see, bud." He toweled himself off with a napkin. "Once again, you've cornered the market on beautiful ladies."

To Celie's credit, she rolled her eyes.

"You're in my chair, *bud*."

Stone stood up, all manners. "Sorry there, pal. Couldn't stand to see a pretty girl sitting alone." He looked down at Celie and cocked his head to the side. "You sure we haven't met before? You look so familiar."

She smiled. "I don't think so."

John sat down and scooted his stool right beside Celie's.

"But you said UT, right? We must have had a class together or something. I swear I recognize you from someplace."

Okay, game over. John looked up at Stone. "Hey, I'm surprised to see you here. Don't you usually hang out at the Hobbit Hole?"

Stone's face reddened. The Hobbit Hole *was* an actual bar, but John doubted Stone had ever set foot in the place. He was sensitive about his height.

"Not really my scene," Stone said tightly. Then he

nodded at Celie. "I need to get going. Nice meeting you, Cecelia."

After he left, John glanced over the rim of his beer glass and caught Celie's reproachful frown.

"That was mean."

John shrugged. "Guy's an asshole."

She crossed her arms and looked around, taking everything in. "Do you really hang out here?"

"Yeah. Why?"

"It's not at all what I expected."

"What did you expect?"

"I don't know," she said. "College girls, maybe? Or at least a little more silicone."

"Thanks a lot."

She looked down and ran her index fingertip over the rim of her glass, then licked the salt off. His gaze followed her movements.

"Feenie warned me about you, you know."

"I'm aware of that."

She propped her elbow on the table and rested her chin on her hand. The margarita buzz seemed to be overriding her need for small talk. "She's usually right about stuff like that, too. She's a good judge of character."

He raised an eyebrow. "Yeah, that first husband of hers was a real winner."

Celie smirked. "Are you saying she's off base about you?"

John tucked a strand of that honey blonde hair behind her ear. "Celie, honey?"

"What?"

"Why don't you forget about what Feenie says and find out for yourself?"

CHAPTER

4

John had miscalculated. Badly. That third margarita had done way more than take the edge off Celie's bad day. And the fourth one she'd insisted on had made her good and sloshed.

"Sorry," she said, grabbing his arm as she stumbled from the elevator. "I'm over here. Last one on the left."

John guided her down the hallway, cursing his stupidity. This woman weighed about a buck twenty. He should have known she wouldn't be able to hold her liquor.

"Stop!" She halted in her tracks.

Here we go.

"Is the hall tilting?"

"That's just the tequila."

She clasped his arm. "But it feels *tilty*."

He sighed and tugged her forward. "Come on. We're

almost there." Her pink fingernails dug into his skin. He was going to have claw marks tomorrow, and not the fun kind.

When they finally reached the door, she just stood there, staring up at him. He reached for the purse at her side, and she flinched.

"Relax," he said, unzipping it to look for her keys.

"Oh. Here." She produced something from her front pocket. It was a single key, not a key chain, and she folded it into his palm.

He unlocked the door and flipped on the light. Her apartment was messy, just as she'd left it. There were shoes on the floor and wadded tissues scattered across the coffee table. The entire place smelled like burned sugar, which John attributed to whatever mysterious event had put the scald mark on her kitchen ceiling.

Celie crossed the room purposefully and opened the refrigerator.

"You want something to drink?" she asked. "I don't have any beer, but I could make us some caffee. *Coffee.*"

John closed the door behind him and locked it. He didn't expect to be here long, but he wasn't taking any chances with her safety. Her ex-husband had been mixed up with some extreme lowlifes.

"I'm fine, thanks." He followed her into the kitchen. "Why don't you have some water, though? You'll thank yourself tomorrow."

She narrowed her eyes at him. "Are you implying that I'm drunk?"

"I'm implying that you're thirsty. You just don't know it yet."

Maybe she recognized the futility of argument. Or maybe she was just too wasted to give a shit, but she got a glass down from the cabinet without further comment and poured herself some ice water. She turned back to face him and tipped her head to the side thoughtfully.

"You know, you'll never be truly happy," she said, sighing. "You're much too good looking."

Spoken like a true drunk. "Is that supposed to be a compliment?"

"No." She took a sip of water. "So, there's this question I've been wanting to ask you."

"Let's hear it." This could actually get interesting.

"Why'd you offer me a ride home from Feenie's wedding last summer?"

He knew better than to answer that honestly, but he doubted she'd remember this conversation in the morning.

He leaned back against the counter. "I wanted to sleep with you."

Her expression didn't change, so he guessed she knew this already. Hell, it hadn't been much of a secret at the time.

She held the sweaty glass to her neck and gazed at him for a long moment. "And now? Do you still want to sleep with me?"

Fuck.

"At the moment," he said carefully, "I'm more concerned with getting you tucked in before you get 'tilty' again."

A gleam came into her eye, and his body responded before his brain could. She placed the glass on the counter and sauntered over to him. Then she settled herself against him and slid her hands up around his neck. Those pretty fingernails combed through his hair, and he took a deep breath.

"That wasn't a challenge," he said, resting his hands on her ass. She felt good. Much too good. And he fully intended to leave in the next five minutes.

She stood on tiptoes and kissed his neck. "Stay with me tonight," she whispered. "Please?"

"Celie—"

She touched his lips with hers, and he lost track of whatever damn thing he'd been about to say. Her mouth was tart. And warm. And tempting in a way that was painful to think about right now. He pulled her closer, just to torture himself, and heard a faint little moan.

How had he gotten into this predicament? *Four* freaking margaritas. A rookie mistake.

She was the one to pull away. She gazed up at him, and he wondered what she was thinking. Then her hand dropped down and reached for his belt.

"Don't." He grabbed her wrist. Her eyes widened, and she drew back.

Shit, now he'd hurt her feelings.

"We'll try this again tomorrow," he said, wrapping her in a hug. He had two minutes, tops, to get out of here before she got watery and apologetic. And after that he'd be in for an endless stream of sob stories about Robert.

"You'll come back tomorrow?" Her voice was muffled against his chest.

"Sure. How about lunch?" If she was even functional by then.

"Um. Lunch." She squirmed out of his arms and stared

off into space, frowning. "I have something to do . . . the Bluebonnet House!"

She looked up at him. "You want to come to an Easter party?"

An Easter party. She'd mentioned that to the feds earlier, but he'd thought she was bullshitting. "Sure. Just tell me when and where."

"The Bluebonnet House," she said, sighing. "Bring your basketball shoes. Enrique will love you."

O-kay. Who the hell was Enrique?

John wrapped an arm around her and steered her out of the kitchen toward the door. Her breast pressed against his side, and he told himself he was doing the right thing, leaving now. He suspected she'd be asleep or puking by the time he made it to the elevator.

She slouched against him, and his suspicions were confirmed. "Thanks for dinner," she mumbled.

"Anytime."

A relentless hammering jarred Celie awake. Who was *hammering* something at—she checked her clock—9:45 in the morning?

She shot out of bed, and her head imploded.

Boom, boom, boom!

"Just a *minute*!" The noise was coming from her front door, which meant either the building was on fire or Dax was home from vacation. She stumbled across the apartment and checked the peephole.

Dax. Decked out in athletic gear. She undid the locks and pulled open the door.

"Was I hallucinating, or did Matthew McConaughey deliver you home from a bar last night?"

Celie stepped back to let him in. "It was a Mexican restaurant." Followed by a bar, yes, but so what?

Frowning, Dax stepped closer and pressed his palm against her forehead. "You okay, sweetie? Don't take this the wrong way, but you look like shit."

"Thanks." Coming from a guy who worked with sick people all day, this comment didn't do much for her mood. Celie glanced down at herself. She'd slept in her clothes, apparently, and she looked like a pile of laundry.

She staggered into the kitchen and opened a cupboard. "You want some coffee?"

"I'm already wired, thanks. Just on my way to the weight room. Thought you might wanna come walk on the treadmill and hear about my trip."

She measured out the coffee, adding an extra scoop for her hangover. "Can't do it today. I've got an Easter party at the Bluebonnet House in"—she glanced at the clock—"forty minutes. But I'm dying to hear about Australia."

Dax set his iPod on the counter and pulled up a bar stool. "Australia was fabulous, the outback was breathtaking, and I have a whole new appreciation for my Sleep Number bed. Now tell me about the hottie."

Celie smiled. Dax had finally realized his lifelong dream of going to Australia, but apparently her going on a date was bigger news. "His name's John McAllister. I know him from home, and it wasn't a date."

Dax combed a hand through his peroxide blonde locks, freshening up his trendy, just-out-of-bed hairstyle.

"Are you wearing mousse to the *gym*?" Celie asked. He had more elaborate grooming habits than most women she knew.

"I'm recovering from civilization withdrawal," he said defensively. "Spit it out, Celie. What's up with this guy?"

"Do you mind if we don't talk about my non–love life? I've already got a screaming headache."

"I can see that." His brown eyes grew concerned. "And I'm guessing since you were out on a drinking binge last night, your appointment didn't go well."

Dax was referring to the results of her latest round of in vitro fertilization. Celie had gone to her doctor two weeks ago so a blood test could confirm what she already had suspected: this latest round of IVF had been a failure, just like the two before it.

She tried to smile. "Guess it wasn't meant to be."

"Oh, sweetie." He came around the counter and pulled her into a hug. She never would have guessed her twenty-eight-year-old neighbor would become her fertility coach as well as her closest friend in Austin. Dax had been with her through all the ups and downs of the past eight months. As a physician's assistant, he'd talked her through the medical jargon, helped monitor her numerous prescriptions, and even administered the injections she couldn't handle by herself. He'd done everything short of donating DNA to her endeavor.

Dax had been a godsend, and he knew more than anyone else in the world the incredible lengths to which Celie had gone trying to have a baby.

Celie stepped out of the hug and dabbed her eyes. "Sorry."

"Don't be ridiculous."

She got a mug down from the cabinet. "I'm having kind of a rough patch."

"I understand," Dax said, although, really, he had no idea. "Let's look forward. When's your next cycle start?"

She poured some coffee. "I think this was it for me."

"Really?"

"Yeah. I've given it a lot of thought, and I think I'm tapped out. Financially and emotionally."

"You sure? You're only, what, thirty-one? God, in IVF years you're a *child*. There's still plenty of time—"

She held up a hand. "I've been at it four years now." After three years of more conventional attempts, she'd decided to cross the high-tech threshold. She'd even uprooted her life and moved to Austin to be near a world-class fertility clinic. The clinic had helped thousands of women become mothers, but it hadn't helped her.

"I just don't want to beat myself up over this anymore. It feels like it's taken over my life." She sipped her coffee and looked at Dax. Just having him in her kitchen was a comfort, even if he didn't know what to say.

"Well," he said, "I admire your efforts."

She scoffed. Her efforts hadn't amounted to anything more than a series of insanely high medical bills. Oh, and fifteen excess pounds, a wonderful side effect of all the drugs she'd been taking and her doctor's periodic exercise bans. But, hey, Celie believed in looking on the bright side. Thanks to all the prenatal vitamins, her hair and nails had never looked better.

Too bad she couldn't care less.

"I'm serious," Dax said. "If there's anything I can do—"

"Actually, there is." She glanced at the clock. "Could you give me a ride to work? I still really want to hear about your trip, and my car was stolen, so I'm stranded."

"It was *stolen*? When?"

"Right after my ex-husband came to visit me Friday night."

Dax shook his head. "I leave town for two weeks, and your life becomes a soap opera."

Celie topped off her coffee. "You don't know the half of it. Take me to my party, and I'll fill you in."

"Thanks." The brunette smiled sweetly. "But I'm actually in a hurry this morning."

"Don't be too hasty, ma'am. If you blow off recommended maintenance, you're liable to end up on the side of the road with a breakdown."

Rowe stood in the parking lot of the lube shop and watched the woman he was fairly certain was Kate Kepler talk to a mechanic about her car.

"At a minimum, we recommend you change out all your fluids," the guy continued, shoving a list under her pretty, turned up nose. "The sooner the better."

She took the list and folded it neatly, then slipped it into the back pocket of her jeans. She wore them low on her hips, showing a strip of toned, tanned stomach. Rowe tried not to stare because she was practically a teenager.

"Thanks," she said, "but I'll take a pass."

"You sure, ma'am? You should at least change the air filter. We're running a special—"

"Look." She squared her petite shoulders and planted her hands on her hips.

Rowe leaned back against his car to enjoy the show. Nothing about Kate Kepler was what he'd expected, starting with the fact that she was so damn young.

"I realize you guys are running a business here. I also know a lot of these mantras you chant come down from corporate." She edged closer, not seeming at all put off by the mechanic's greasy gray coveralls. He frowned down at her. "I can appreciate that. But what I *don't* appreciate is your trying to scare me into buying ninety dollars' worth of services I don't really need."

"Ma'am?"

She crossed her arms. "There's nothing wrong with my fluids. Or my filter, for that matter, and we both know it. I came here for an oil change, just like the two *men* you serviced before me. How come you didn't try to up-sell them with all this crap?"

The mechanic backed away, belatedly deciding he didn't want a confrontation. She whipped out her wallet.

"I'd like the bill, please," she said. "And my keys."

Rowe intercepted her a few minutes later, just as she was opening the door to her black Beetle. "Kate Kepler?"

She shot him a glare. "What now? You want to sell me some snow tires?"

Rowe slid his hands into his pockets. "Do I look like a tire salesman?"

Her brown eyes skimmed over his dark suit. "Hmm, not really. But let me save you some time here. I'm also not in the market for life insurance or Amway."

He smiled. "I'm not selling anything. I just want to talk."

Her eyes became wary suddenly, adding years to her age. Now she looked old enough to vote.

"Who are you?"

"Special Agent Mike Rowe, FBI." He extended his

hand and watched the lightbulb come on. "The guy you've been dodging the last twenty-four hours?"

She glanced at his hand but didn't take it. "How'd you find me here?"

"I talked to your roommate."

"How'd you get my address?"

"I talked to your editor."

She slid behind the wheel, muttering something about the Patriot Act. When she started the engine, Rowe's easygoing mood disappeared.

"I'm in a hurry," she said. "You'll have to make it quick."

He didn't *have* to make it anything, but he decided to use finesse instead of force. "This shouldn't take long. How 'bout I buy you a cup of coffee?"

She squinted at him, as if deciding what to do. What was it with this girl? Most people—the innocent ones, at least—jumped at the chance to be interviewed by a federal agent. It made them feel important. Kate Kepler was different for some reason, and Rowe wanted to know why.

"There's a Java Stop on Twelfth and Lamar," she said. "It's mostly joggers and cyclists, though. You'll be the only suit."

He shrugged. "I don't mind." Actually, he did mind. Wearing a coat and tie every day was one aspect of his job he'd never liked. Typically he dressed down on weekends, but he'd been to mass earlier.

"You know how to get there from here?" she asked.

"No, but I have a feeling you do."

"Follow me." She put her car in gear. "And I'm not kidding, I only have a few minutes."

CHAPTER

5

Celie stood in the Bluebonnet House kitchen and dumped a giant envelope of orange Tang into about four gallons of tap water. She felt a tug on her dress and looked down into a pair of glistening blue eyes.

"Miss Celie?" Three-year-old Kimmy Taylor's cheeks were wet with tears.

Celie scooped the little girl up onto her hip. "What is it, sweetheart?" She braced herself for what might come out of the child's mouth. Given Kimmy's background, the possibilities were daunting.

"Miss Celie, why'd we have to kill all the eggs?"

"The eggs?"

Kimmy toyed with the tiny white buttons on the front of Celie's dress. "The *Easter* eggs," she said. "Why did Miss Chantal and everybody kill 'em yesterday?"

Kill them . . . ?

"You mean *dye* them? Why did we *dye* them yesterday?"

Kimmy nodded sadly, and Celie gave her a hug.

"Oh, sweetheart, dyeing the eggs is like painting them. We didn't hurt the eggs. We just made them pretty colors, that's all. After a while we'll have the egg hunt!"

Kimmy frowned. Clearly, the concept of an Easter egg hunt was foreign to her.

"But first, we're having cupcakes!" Celie pointed with false enthusiasm to several large boxes from the grocery store.

Kimmy's face perked up. "Can I have pink?"

"I think we can manage that." Celie kissed her soft brown hair, and couldn't resist inhaling the wonderful scent of baby shampoo. When Kimmy had first arrived at the Bluebonnet House last week, she'd smelled like urine and cigarette smoke.

Celie set Kimmy back on her feet. "You want to help me serve the juice?"

Kimmy nodded gamely.

"All right then. I'll carry the cooler, and you can get the paper cups, okay?"

She followed Celie into the backyard, where several long picnic tables had been set up with paper napkins and plates. Chantal, the center's slender, uber-efficient director, was placing a cupcake at each place. Like Celie, she had forgone the typical Bluebonnet House uniform of T-shirt and jeans today. Instead, she wore a sleeveless orange tunic and flowy orange pants that showed off her dark complexion. Her boyishly short haircut was contradicted by a pair of bronze chandelier earrings. Spotting Celie, she cleared a space for the cooler at the end of one table.

"We don't have enough cupcakes," she observed.

"I've got more in the kitchen," Celie said. "And more plates, too."

Thank goodness she'd thought to bring extras. Word of the party had spread, apparently, and a number of families Celie hadn't seen in months had materialized out of nowhere. Now the playground was overcrowded, and Chantal was short a few Easter baskets. On the upside, many of the kids and their mothers looked healthier than when they'd last visited the center.

Kimmy plopped the stack of cups on the table and ran off to play in the sandbox. Celie watched her go, her heart aching just a little. Celie had taken Easter mornings for granted growing up. The holiday always meant new dresses for Celie and her sisters and festive egg hunts in her grandparents' backyard after church. Easter was a happy time. Celie's entire childhood had been happy, really.

It was adulthood that had thrown her for a loop.

Tom Gilligan sidled up next to her. The minister had changed out of the robes he'd worn for the prayer service into khakis and a golf shirt. "Nice turnout," he said.

"Looks like." Celie gave him a warm smile. Tom represented one of the many local churches that contributed to the center's operating budget. "I can't believe all these children. We've got at least three dozen."

"Thirty-eight," Tom said. "I bet you all can't wait for the new rec room. When will it be done?"

"Last I heard, end of summer." At least the crew didn't work Sundays. Celie's throbbing head couldn't have withstood any hammering today.

"I'd better go help Chantal bring out more food." Celie turned toward the house and nearly collided with her boss.

Who did *not* look happy.

John McAllister trailed behind her looking perfectly at ease in gym shorts and basketball shoes.

Shoot. An uninvited, unregistered visitor. An uninvited, unregistered *male* visitor, whose presence would explain the just-ate-a-lemon expression on Chantal's face.

Celie's gaze skimmed over McAllister's tan, muscular legs, the pecs bulging beneath his T-shirt. She saw his mouth quirk up at the corner and realized he'd noticed her checking him out.

"Hey, there." He strolled up and kissed her—right on the lips, right in front of Tom and Chantal and thirty-eight kids.

"Uh, Chantal." Celie forced a smile. "I'd like you to meet John McAllister. A friend of mine."

"We met inside," she said coolly. "You didn't tell me you'd invited a guest today."

"Sorry. I forgot to mention it."

Tom cleared his throat.

"Oh, and this is Tom Gilligan. Our minister. Well, not ours, exactly, but sort of—"

"Nice to meet you," McAllister said, shaking Tom's hand. Then he turned to Celie. "Looks like you're on your way in. Need a hand with anything?"

"Yes, thank you."

She led him inside and pulled him into the hallway leading to the administrative offices. "*What* are you doing here?"

A grin spread across his face. "You don't remember inviting me, do you?"

"I didn't invite you."

"Remember?" He leaned closer, flattening his palm against the cinder-block wall behind her. "Back at your apartment? Right before you kissed me good night?"

She'd *kissed* him? God, she had no memory of that. Or of inviting him to the Easter party. Of course, everything after that third margarita was kind of a blur.

"How'd you get in, anyway?" she asked. The Bluebonnet House was surrounded by an eight-foot security fence, and the only entrance was through the electronically locked front door.

"I told Janice you asked me to come." He smiled. "She buzzed me right in."

Of course. The college senior working reception today would have been starry-eyed at the sight of him.

With the tip of his finger, he brushed her ponytail off her shoulder. "I like this dress you're wearing. You didn't tell me this was formal. Fact, I distinctly remember you telling me to bring my Nikes. I'm supposed to shoot hoops with someone named Enrique?"

Celie closed her eyes, remembering now. Vaguely. God, why did she ever drink tequila?

She opened her eyes, and McAllister was still staring at her, clearly enjoying her discomfort. He trailed a finger along the neckline of her dress, which scooped low in the front. Celie had always thought the long skirt and tiny floral print made it look demure, but McAllister obviously didn't.

And that thing he was doing with his finger was making her skin tingle.

"Miss Celie?"

She jumped, bumping his chin with her forehead.

Kimmy stood in the hallway, grinning and holding an empty Easter basket. "Look what Miss Chantal gave me! She said I can put candy in it!"

"That's pretty, sweetheart." Celie pressed her back against the wall, wishing McAllister weren't standing so close. "You go on outside now, okay? It's almost time for cupcakes."

Kimmy smiled and skipped off, swinging her basket beside her.

Celie took McAllister's hand and dragged him into her office. It was barely larger than a broom closet, but it was out of the traffic pattern. She flipped on the light switch and crossed the tiny room so they were separated by the cheap metal desk.

He wandered over to the file cabinet and picked up a framed photograph of Feenie holding Olivia. "This your office?"

"Yes." She cleared her throat. "I'm sorry I didn't remember inviting you. I think I had too much to drink last night."

"Ya *think*?" He was laughing at her now, and she felt her cheeks flush.

"I apologize. I don't usually have three margaritas in one evening."

He crossed to the window beside her desk and peered through the dusty miniblinds. "Four."

"What?"

He pulled the blind cord, and the room suddenly dimmed. Then he turned around. "You had four." He took a step toward her, and her stomach tightened.

"Why did you do that?"

The corner of his mouth curved. "Why do you think?"

He edged closer, and her heart started to race. She stepped back, bumping the desk and plunking her bottom onto it. He gazed down at her with that look she recognized, the one she'd seen on his face the night of Feenie's wedding.

"What are you doing?"

"What I wanted to do last night." His voice was low and intimate, as if they were in a bedroom together instead of an office.

"We can't do that here."

He glided his hands up her bare arms and laced his fingers together behind her neck. "Why not?"

She was eye level with his chest, and she tried not to think about how good it looked as she floundered for a reason. She tipped her head back and looked up at him. "Someone might walk in."

"I locked the door."

She glanced frantically over her shoulder and saw that the door was indeed locked, the little thumb latch in the horizontal position.

"Still, we can't."

Instead of backing off, he eased closer, nudging her knees apart with his body.

"McAllister—"

He kissed her, slowly, sending a sharp thrill right through her, straight down to her toes. Angling her head slightly, he parted her lips and licked into her mouth, and before she knew it she was kissing him back with every cell in her man-deprived, frustrated little body. His hands moved down to circle her waist, and she felt their warmth through the fabric of her dress. His thumbs rubbed over her hip bones, and she started to feel intoxicated, like she'd been last night, only much, much better. He was way too good at this, and that fact alone should have been a wake-up call, but it wasn't.

Suddenly she felt a whisper of cool air and his palm sliding over her knee. *That* was a wake-up call.

"We can't," she said, pushing her hem down.

His mouth moved to her temple as his fingers slid up her thigh. "You're not seeing someone else, are you?"

"What? No, but—"

He kissed her neck, just below her ear. "And you're attracted to me, right?"

She held on to his shoulders, trying to catch her breath as his lips moved against her skin. This situation was wrong. And inappropriate. It was wrongly inappropriate. Her ex-husband had just died; she was coming off an IVF cycle; and here she was, at her *workplace*, making out with the very last person who would ever be interested in the things she wanted in her life. Babies. Parenthood. Responsibility for another human being.

McAllister was interested in getting laid and getting a scoop, period.

His teeth nipped her. "Don't lie, honey. I know you are."

"I am, but we can't just—"

He kissed her mouth again, and in a fit of bad judgment, she let herself enjoy it. His kisses were like him—leisurely and confident and persuasive, all at the same time. She wrapped her arms around him and pulled him closer.

A knock sounded at the door. "Cecelia?"

Chantal! Celie gave McAllister a firm shove and hopped off the desk. She whirled toward the door, which was shut, thank heaven. "Yes?"

"We need your help outside." Her boss's voice oozed disapproval. "We're about to start the egg hunt."

"I'll be right there!" She shot McAllister a glare.

Sighing, he leaned a shoulder against the wall and crossed his arms. He watched her adjust her dress and smooth her hair. Then she scurried for the door, but he didn't move to follow her.

"Are you coming?" she asked. "Or was the basketball thing just a ploy?"

He shook his head. "I'm going to pretend I didn't hear that. You invited *me,* remember? Hell, I even wore my basketball shoes."

"Good. You're going to need them."

"I doubt it."

She popped the lock and yanked the door open, motioning for him to lead the way out.

"You might be surprised." She checked her dress again and tried to sound normal, like someone who hadn't nearly had sex on her desk. "Enrique's got a pretty good game."

McAllister paused in the doorway and gave her ponytail a tug. "I'm starting to think the only one with any game around here is you."

CHAPTER
6

Kate emptied another sugar packet into her latte and concentrated on stirring so she wouldn't have to look at the agent.

"You want some coffee with that?" Rowe asked.

Kate looked up, not acknowledging his lame attempt at humor. She stared at him, smileless, wanting to see if he'd squirm.

He didn't. Instead, he reached over and grabbed another tray of sweeteners from a neighboring table. He pushed them toward her, and she gave in to the childish urge to add a *third* packet of sugar to her coffee, successfully ruining it.

Why did she do this? All her life she'd had problems with authority, so she acted out whenever anyone older tried to tell her what to do.

She sipped her coffee, trying not to gag. Rowe grinned suddenly, and Kate had to look away.

"So, why didn't you return my calls?" he asked.

"I've been busy."

He raised his eyebrows, clearly waiting for more.

"I'm new on the paper," she elaborated. "So I'm stuck covering weekends twice a month. It got pretty hectic yesterday."

"Low man on the totem pole, huh? How old are you, exactly?"

She stiffened. "What does that matter?"

"It doesn't, really. I'm just curious." He smiled, and the skin gathered at the corners of his gray eyes. He had nice eyes, but only when he smiled. The rest of the time they looked icy. "Hey, come on. You're too young to get offended by that question."

She crossed her arms. "How old do you think I am?"

His gaze dropped, and she couldn't tell whether he was reading her T-shirt logo for clues or trying to guess her bra size.

"Thirty-two B," she told him.

His lifted his gaze, and a flush crept up his neck. She'd embarrassed him. Good. Now she had the upper hand.

"I'm twenty-four," she said, taking pity on him for some reason. "How about you?"

He cleared his throat. "Thirty-eight."

She took another sip of the ruined coffee and glanced at her watch, hoping he'd get the hint.

"I spoke to Officer Poole. He says you told him you came upon the accident on the way back from a party."

"It was a campaign event. I was on assignment."

"And you just happened to drive past this wreck? You weren't responding to the police scanner?"

She recited the details of the incident and was relieved when he didn't ask her the same questions over and over like Officer Skoal had.

Rowe leaned back in his chair. He hadn't interrupted her, just jotted down a few notes about the truck.

"Did it strike you as odd that the Explorer's passenger's-side door was open?" he asked.

She felt flattered he wanted her opinion, but then wondered if that was just a tactic he used to make people loosen up.

"Yes," she said. "Especially since the driver was unconscious when I got there."

He nodded. "Seems to me like someone else opened the door, maybe to get out? Or maybe to retrieve something? Think back to those two guys. Can you remember anyone holding something or tossing something in the truck bed right before the door slammed?"

Kate closed her eyes, trying to replay the scene. "I don't remember that. But I really only got a brief look." She opened her eyes, and he was watching her closely. "Sorry."

Rowe drummed his fingers on the table and looked off into the distance. Obviously this mystery truck was important to him, and Kate wished she'd noticed more about it.

"So, you think there was foul play involved?"

His gaze veered back to her, and she waited for him to say something evasive.

"Looks that way," he said. "As of this morning, it's a homicide investigation."

Wow, candor. Kate decided to push her luck. "What do you have besides the mystery car and the open door?"

He hesitated a beat, watching her. "A number of things. Like skid marks up the road indicating the Explorer was involved in a high-speed chase just before it crashed into the cliff. After that, it's possible someone opened the door and took something from the vehicle."

"Someone like one of those guys I saw?"

He nodded.

She leaned forward on her elbows. "What did they take?"

He smiled slightly, and she knew she wasn't going to get anything else, at least not right now. She'd have to hit him up later. Maybe she could catch him off guard somehow.

"I appreciate your time today, Miss Kepler." He pulled out a business card and scribbled a number on the back before handing it to her. She noticed the San Antonio area code. "Here's my cell number. I'm staying at La Quinta downtown, but I'm never there, so that number's the best way to reach me. Call me if you think of anything else."

"You're from San Antonio?"

"I'm part of a joint task force operating out of there, yes."

"Investigating . . . ?" McAllister had filled Kate in on Robert Strickland's fugitive status and his connection to the Saledo cartel, so Kate had some idea what this was about. But she wanted to hear what Rowe would say.

"Lots of things," he replied. "That's why there're multiple agencies involved."

Okay, so he wanted to be vague. Maybe she should track down Officer Skoal and see if he'd gotten a clue yet.

Rowe's cell phone buzzed, and he dug it out of his pocket. "Rowe," he snapped.

Kate looked him over as he took the call. He must be sweltering in that navy suit. She wondered if he always dressed like this on weekends, or if he'd specifically worn it for her. He probably thought it made him look official. Intimidating, even. Plus, it gave him plenty of room to hide his holster.

Kate hated guns. She hated feds, too, but this one had been okay so far.

And he was in decent shape for a thirty-eight-year-old. His wide shoulders strained the fabric of his jacket, and instead of the predictable middle-aged paunch, his abs looked flat beneath his starched white shirt.

"When?" He flicked a gaze at her and checked his watch. "Okay, thanks." He shut his phone, and his eyes were cool again. "I need to go."

"I should get going, too." Kate shoved his business card in her pocket, right next to the list of maintenance recommendations from the lube shop. The ones she'd never use. "If I remember anything else, I'll get in touch."

Celie rode in McAllister's Jeep with the wind whipping around her face.

"This the one?" he asked, as they neared a roadside storage facility.

"A few more miles," she said. "It'll be on the right."

Her voice sounded calm, which was unbelievable considering how rattled she felt. She'd been a bundle of nerves ever since McAllister had shown up at the Blue-bonnet House. And that had merely been the first big surprise of the day.

The second big surprise had been the party's success. McAllister, it turned out, was better than a bunny cake. The kids loved him, especially after he got a game of basketball together and coached them on their free throws. He even won over Enrique Ramos, a scrawny eleven-year-old who frequented the shelter and carried a boulder-size chip around on his shoulder. Enrique tended to be sullen and belligerent, and didn't play well with others. But McAllister had overcome his attitude by treating him like an equal and not letting him win at basketball just because he was a kid.

Enrique would never acknowledge it, but Celie could tell it meant something to him to be treated with respect by a grown man.

"Thanks for coming," she said earnestly. "Everyone loved you."

McAllister shot her a look. "Not everyone."

He was referring to Chantal, who'd pointedly ignored him for three hours.

"Don't mind Chantal. She's like that with everyone."

"She's like that with *men*," he corrected. "It was pretty obvious. She even gave the minister the cold shoulder."

It was a fair assessment, so Celie didn't argue. But Chantal was an excellent advocate for abused women and children, and she ran a quality program, particularly considering that all their funding came from churches and private donations instead of government subsidies.

"It's right up here," Celie said, pointing to an orange

Public Storage facility just up the road. They were here to deal with the third surprise of Celie's day: someone had vandalized her storage unit during the night. The manager had called Celie's cell phone and asked her to come by to fill out a report, and Celie had had to ask McAllister to take a detour on the way home. First thing tomorrow, Celie needed to talk to her insurance company about a loaner car.

McAllister pulled off the highway into the minuscule parking lot. He slid into a space beside a police cruiser.

"So, you talk to Agent Rowe this morning?" he asked.

Uh-oh. "No. Why?"

He cleared his throat. "I heard from one of my co-workers. She told me they're investigating Robert's death as a homicide."

A *homicide*? "But . . . I thought he died from head trauma. . . ."

"They think he was run off the road," McAllister said. "And that whoever did it took something from his car."

Celie stared at him.

"Now they're looking for the truck that was seen fleeing the scene."

"What truck?" Why hadn't the FBI told her all this? What else was going on that she didn't know about?

"You read the news brief we ran yesterday?" he asked.

"No."

"Our reporter saw a dark-colored pickup leaving the scene. She also noticed the door to your Explorer was open, even though Robert was unconscious."

Celie shoved open the door and got out of the Jeep. She turned her back on the Public Storage office and walked down the shoulder of the road a little ways, until she got to a wire fence separating the highway from a cow pasture. McAllister's footsteps crunched on the gravel behind her. He stopped beside her but didn't say anything.

She looked out over the landscape, blinking back tears.

Robert was dead. Murdered. He'd be buried this week, and his family didn't even want Celie coming to the funeral. She hadn't realized it before now, but, in the back of her mind, she'd always thought she and Robert would have a chance to forgive each other. Not to reconcile, but to at least put all the ugliness behind them.

She couldn't think about it. It was just too awful. And she did *not* want to unravel right here in front of McAllister. She could do that later, at home, far away from the prying eyes of reporters and investigators and anyone else who might be watching her.

She forced herself to turn around and walk back toward the rental office.

"I really appreciate this," she said over her shoulder. "You don't have to come in or anything. I just need to talk to the manager and check out my unit."

Celie hoped he wouldn't come in. She had a terrible, sinking feeling about this whole situation, and she didn't want McAllister standing around picking up on her uneasiness.

To her dismay, he followed her to the office, reaching past her to open the glass door. She was hit by a wall of frigid air as she stepped inside.

"Hi, I'm Cecelia Wells," she told the attendant, a teenager who had numerous tattoos and a shaved head. "I got a call about a problem with my unit? Two-twenty-nine?"

The kid nodded toward the lot. "Just go on back," he said. "The manager's out there now with the cop. Looks like your unit was the only one with any trouble."

John caught Celie's arm as she walked down the sidewalk and turned her to face him. "What the hell's going on, Celie?"

She looked up at him and bit her lip. "I don't know," she said, obviously lying.

He took a deep breath and tried to reign in his temper. "You know, you're a terrible liar."

"I don't *know,* okay?" She tugged her arm away and started back down the sidewalk.

"*Wait,*" he said to her back. "We need to talk. We can do it here or in front of the cop. Your pick."

She turned back around. "I really don't know what happened. But if I had to guess, I'd say this isn't some random act of vandalism."

"No shit."

Her cheeks flushed. "Look, if you're going to be crude—"

"Sorry," he said. "But I'm getting a little pissed off here. Your ex was involved with some very dangerous people. I'm concerned about you, and I can tell you're not being straight with me."

She gazed up at him, that worry line appearing between her brows. She was scared, and for this woman to be scared did funny things to his heart.

"Someone lifted a business card from my wallet," she

said. "It was a Public Storage card with little blanks on the back for my gate code and unit number. I'd filled the blanks in so I wouldn't forget. I think Robert took it."

"Celie, listen to me. Do you know why I moved to Austin?"

She rolled her eyes. "You got a better job?"

"That wasn't the only reason. I came up here to get away from all the shit going on down at the border." John could still see Pamela Price lying in a pool of blood in her own driveway.

"Look," he told Celie. "I know you're familiar with some of the shit Robert was involved with, but you have to believe me when I tell you it can get much, *much* worse. You can*not* get mixed up with these people. You have no idea how low these guys will go—"

"Oh, no?" She stepped back. "Well, that's where you're wrong. And if you think I *want* to be involved in any of this, you're wrong about that, too. Now, do you mind? I need to go talk to the police and find out what happened."

Goddamn it, she was walking away again. And he hadn't gotten through to her. He followed her across the lot, deciding the least he could do was to eavesdrop and possibly learn something.

A uniformed officer and a middle-aged woman with frizzy brown hair—presumably the manager—were standing at the end of a row next to an open unit. Celie introduced herself.

"We're sure sorry about this," the manager said.

"When did it happen?" Celie asked.

"The computer says your gate code was used real early Saturday morning, right when we opened for business. No one noticed anything funny until this afternoon, though. One of our tenants reported your door was up a couple inches. You think you left it open?"

Celie stepped into the unit. "I haven't been here in months."

John followed so he could take a look inside. The space smelled musty. When his eyes adjusted to the dim lighting, he saw a splintered chair turned on its side and the remnants of what had once been a comforter, but was now merely a heap of feathers and shredded fabric. Toward the back of the space, he saw some dining room furniture, a baby crib, and some cardboard boxes labeled BOOKS and CHINA. The boxes had been ripped open, and the cement floor was littered with paperbacks and shards of white porcelain.

"Wow." Celie knelt and picked up a broken teacup.

"We'd like you to go through everything," the officer said. "Make a list of what's damaged or missing."

"Has anyone checked the security tapes?" John asked. He'd noticed cameras mounted by the gate. Maybe they could get some vehicle tags, or, hell, even a shot of the perpetrators. John made a mental note to buddy up with the bald kid on his way out.

"We'll go over those," the cop said.

John glanced at the padlock dangling from the metal door of the unit. It looked as though someone had used a key to open it.

"Where do you keep the key to this padlock, ma'am?" the officer asked, voicing the question in John's head.

"I've got one in my dresser and one on my key chain." Panic spread across Celie's face as she said it.

"Where's your key chain, Celie?"

She glanced at John. "I lost it." Then she looked at the officer. "Right along with my purse, just Friday night. Whoever found my purse and keys must have found my Public Storage card."

John watched her lie to the officer, who of course bought everything she said. Who wouldn't? She looked like a freaking Sunday school teacher in that flowery dress with the little buttons up the front.

"Would you mind helping me move this box, Officer?" she asked. "I want to see if the rest of my china's still intact."

John watched as she deftly diverted the cop's attention. Why didn't she just tell him what was going on?

Maybe she didn't want to make things more complicated by involving the local police. Or maybe she was hiding something, something she didn't want to talk about with cops or anyone.

Including him.

John stepped out of the unit, wishing for a cigarette. He heard sandals snapping against the concrete as Celie poked around, taking inventory of her stuff.

"Well," she said finally, "nothing's missing that I can tell. It's just a big mess. Why don't you give me the paperwork to take home, and I'll return it later when I come back to clean this up? I don't really have time to do this right now."

The manager looked concerned. "Are you sure? I've got a push broom in the office. I'd be happy to help you."

"No, don't bother." Celie smiled and ushered everyone out of the unit. "I'll take care of it later."

She pulled down the metal door and fastened the padlock. Then she collected the paperwork from the manager, all the while chatting pleasantly. John watched her, wondering if she fully realized what it meant that someone had her keys. And he'd left her alone in her apartment last night. The place wasn't safe. She needed her locks changed, soon, and she definitely needed to give her security guards a heads-up.

Hell, what she needed to do was vacate her place altogether. She could stay with him.

CHAPTER

7

John had figured out years ago the most important part of being a reporter was listening, plain and simple. Most times, if you just gave a person the right prompt, they'd start telling you their story. John was the king of going back again and again until his source got comfortable with the idea of talking. Almost always, his persistence paid off. Most people *liked* to talk, whether because they had a guilty conscience or they wanted to feel important or sometimes just because they were lonely. The key was to wait them out and then be there when they finally decided to spill.

Celie was no different. And John intended to wait her out, just like he would a news source.

She'd been a source for him before, both during the rape trial and then again in Mayfield when he was covering the Josh Garland scandal. John had never actually met Celie during the rape trial, though. Back then he'd been a lowly intern, so his job had consisted of sitting in the courtroom and taking notes for the veteran courts reporter.

He hadn't met Celie, but he'd sure as hell watched her. She'd been riveting up there on the witness stand. He'd never seen anyone so brave. And he'd been harboring something like awe for her ever since.

Meanwhile, she hadn't even known he existed. They didn't meet until years later in Mayfield, just after Feenie dropped the Josh Garland story in his lap. Garland had been Feenie's husband before she figured out he was running around on her and gave him the boot. When Garland wasn't busy committing adultery, he'd been using some family businesses to launder money for the Saledo cartel. Feenie uncovered his operation, setting in motion a chain of events that eventually led to Feenie's near-murder, Robert Strickland's implication in the money-laundering scheme *and* the murder attempt, and eventually Robert and Celie's divorce. John had covered the entire saga for the *Mayfield Gazette*, his hometown paper. He'd won numerous awards for the series, including a national journalism prize that had garnered him the respect of his editors and the job in Austin.

Which had brought him back to Celie.

John had spent the past ten minutes sitting on a bar stool in her apartment pretending to be absorbed in a decorating magazine—did she actually read this shit?—while he did what he did best.

Which was listening.

"You told me my keys were sent to a *crime lab*, when actually, they were in possession of a suspected murderer." Celie told Special Agent Stevenski for the third time. The guy had been waiting in the lobby when she and John had returned from the storage place.

"Again, I apologize for the oversight," he said meekly.

"It might be just an 'oversight' to you, but to me it's much more than that. I take my personal safety very seriously."

"I understand."

"What if it were your mother or your sister? Would you have been this sloppy concerning the whereabouts of *her* house keys?"

"Ma'am, I really do apologize."

"Fine," she said. "Let's get this over with. You said you had some questions for me? I really don't know what else I can tell you besides what we've already talked about."

McAllister heard Stevenski shuffling through his notepad. She had him flustered, apparently.

"Uh, so there seems to be a gap between the time you say he left here and the time of the accident. About an hour, we think. Are you *sure* he left at ten?"

"Yes."

"And you're certain he wasn't meeting anyone nearby?"

"I'm not certain at all. But if he was, he didn't tell me about it."

"And you're sure you only gave him twenty dollars? Even though he asked for several thousand?"

He'd hit her up for several *thousand* dollars? What a dickhead.

"That's right," she said. "That's all I had in the house."

"Do you have a habit of keeping large amounts of cash at home? Say, more than a hundred dollars?"

"No." Her voice had become wary now.

"See, here's the thing. For him to even ask that seems pretty unusual. I mean, most people are like you. They don't keep big sums of cash lying around. So I'm wondering why Mr. Strickland even thought to ask."

Silence.

"Ms. Wells?"

"I don't know."

"Can you remember, back while you were married to Mr. Strickland, being in the habit of having large sums of money around?"

"No."

"Do you know if your ex-husband might have kept money hidden anywhere?"

"I've been through all this before, with Agent Rowe. When Robert and I were married, I knew next to nothing about our finances. He was an accountant, for heaven's sake! It seemed perfectly logical to me that he wanted to be in charge of all our money stuff. I was *not* involved with any of his illegal activities!"

"Over the past ten months, has Mr. Strickland ever asked you to give him money?"

"No."

"Not even a loan? Maybe a small wire transfer?"

"No."

"If he had, would you have given him one?"

Stevenski wouldn't let it go. He evidently believed Celie had been funneling Strickland money while he was a fugitive.

"No," Celie said firmly. "I'm sure you remember that he cleaned out our bank account before he left. I wasn't feeling very generous toward him after that."

Another pause while Stevenski shuffled papers.

"Well," he said. "I guess that's it for now. I'll call you if anything else comes up."

From the corner of his eye, John watched her walk him to the door. The agent gave Celie a big smile, and John got another one of his brief nods.

"*Adios,*" John said, waving.

Celie closed the door and turned around. John got up from the stool and walked over to her. She looked tired, and he wanted to rub her shoulders, but the look on her face told him that might not go over well.

"He doesn't realize you're a reporter. All that's off the record."

John shrugged. "I'm not writing about this, so it doesn't matter."

Celie watched him, and he could tell she was debating whether to trust him.

"Someone's probably writing about it, though, right? Someone at the *Herald*?"

"Probably," he admitted. "Depends how much the homicide has to do with something bigger. Like the Saledo cartel."

Celie looked away.

"Do *you* think Robert was murdered by someone working for Saledo? Maybe over an unpaid debt?"

It was a gamble, asking her point-blank like that. But he got the sense she was ready to open up.

"I have no idea."

Or maybe not. Shit, maybe she needed more time.

"Celie, look. I've been thinking. You obviously can't stay here tonight, so—"

Someone knocked on the door. She checked the peephole and immediately pulled it open. "Hi! I was just about to call you."

A stocky guy walked in wearing jeans and a black T-shirt that looked like it had been ironed. He slipped off his sunglasses and kissed Celie's cheek. "Hey, beautiful."

John's defenses went up until he noticed the guy's eyes. Brown. Friendly. And definitely giving him the once-over.

"And who do we have here?" her friend asked, tilting his head John's way.

"Dax Gillespie, meet John McAllister," Celie said. "John's a friend from home."

Friend. Great. Only five o'clock, and already he had a strike for the evening.

"Dax is my neighbor," Celie explained. "He lives just down the hall."

John shook hands with Dax, taking the opportunity to slide an arm around Celie's waist. "Good to meet you. I was just asking Celie to come get some dinner with me. Can you join us?"

Dax's eyes twinkled. "I'd love to, but I've already got plans." He grinned at Celie, like they were sharing some sort of inside joke. "You two enjoy."

Celie stepped away from John's arm. "Sorry, but I can't do it either. I've got some reading to do tonight for one of my classes."

Strike two.

"Hey, Dax," she said, "I need a favor."

"Sure. What's up?"

John was pretty sure he knew what the favor was.

"Can I sleep on your sofa?" Yep. "Just for tonight? I've got to get a locksmith up here tomorrow, and until I do, I don't really want to be here."

Dax looked from Celie to John and back to Celie again. "Sure, no problem."

Strike three. Just like that, he was out.

Celie stuffed clothes into her overnight bag and darted her gaze around the room. Someone had been here. She could feel it. She wasn't sure what had tipped her off, but someone had definitely been in her apartment. Her hands felt clammy as she zipped the bag.

"May I say, just once, that you've lost your *mind*?"

Dax stood next to her closet. She scooted him aside so she could grab her Nikes off the floor. Not that she intended to exercise, but it looked like she'd be stuck taking the bus to campus tomorrow morning, and her classes were a good hike from the bus stop.

"Are you listening? Mr. McConaughey just asked you out!"

She glanced at Dax, who looked horrified by her apparent lapse in judgment.

"He didn't want to take me out," she said.

Dax crossed his arms. "Hmm, as a matter of fact, I *did* just hear him. And he *did* ask you out to dinner."

Celie rolled her eyes. "He didn't want to take me *out* out. He wanted to take me home. So he could talk me into sleeping with him."

Where had she put her prescription? She was almost guaranteed to get a migraine tonight. It was probably in the bathroom.

She glanced at Dax, who was staring at her like she was nuts.

"What's wrong with *that*?" he demanded. "The man is gorgeous. And *nice,* I might add. Not a homophobic vibe for miles. And yet totally, 100 percent manly man. His confidence level is off the charts."

"That's his ego."

"And you know him from home," Dax plunged on, undeterred, "so he automatically passes the crazy-psycho background check. And he's totally into you."

Celie brushed past him and went into the bathroom for her pills. As she walked through the door, the smell of nail polish nearly knocked her over.

"Oh, my God."

Dax leaned against the door frame. "What?"

"Someone's been here." She stared at the traces of L'Oréal Gypsy Rose in the grout between the floor tiles. "They were *here.* See?" She pointed at the floor.

"Who was here?"

Celie felt woozy. She had to sit down. She flipped shut the toilet lid and sank down onto it. She buried her head in her hands. This was so out of control. What was she going to do?

"Are you okay?" Dax picked up her wrist and started taking her pulse. "Here, put your head between you knees."

Celie did. She opened her eyes and found herself staring at the nail polish on her floor grout. She was so, so dead.

"Do you need an Imitrex?"

"No." She sat up and tried to smile. "I'm fine, really. Sorry. I just . . ." What could she say? She didn't want Dax involved. "I had a roach yesterday and I asked the building to send the exterminator up. I think he broke a bottle of nail polish in here, and the fumes are getting to me."

Dax looked around. "Well, somebody definitely broke something. They should have left you a note."

Celie stood up. Her gaze landed on the medicine bottle sitting beside her toothbrush. She grabbed both off the counter and strode out of the bathroom.

"Almost ready!" Her voice was surprisingly chipper considering she could hardly breathe.

Oh God. Oh Lord. What was she going to *do*?

Rowe looked up from his laptop as Stevenski walked into the break room Monday morning. "You're not gonna believe this," he told his partner.

"What?" Stevenski refilled his Styrofoam cup with coffee and walked over.

As of Saturday, Rowe and Stevenski had been working out of the Bureau's satellite office in Austin. It wasn't nearly as big as the field office in San Antonio, which was why Rowe's laptop and files currently occupied the better part of a table in the lunch room.

"Here, take a look." Rowe pivoted his computer so Stevenski could read the e-mail he'd just received.

A DEA agent in Mexico who was part of the task force had sent Rowe a transcript of a recent phone conversation he'd recorded. Saledo and his operatives were constantly switching landlines and cell phones to throw off investigators, but every now and then the surveillance guys caught a break.

"Whoa," Stevesnki said. "Where'd we get this?"

"Mexico. Zapata's crew just sent it over. I think they recorded it last night." Rowe scanned the e-mail again. "Yeah, the call came in about ten-thirteen. They traced it back to a San Antonio pay phone."

"You listen to the tape?" Stevenski asked.

"Nope. Caller was Spanish-speaking. Male. Zapata translated it for us and typed this up."

The call had lasted only about three minutes, but it had revealed some crucial information. One, a couple of guys had taken out Robert Strickland, and two, they seemed to be looking for something that belonged to Saledo, but they hadn't found it yet and neither had the cops.

The most startling part of the call was Saledo's reaction to this news.

Surprise. Followed by outrage that someone was stealing from him.

Meaning whoever murdered Strickland hadn't done so on Saledo's orders. The killers were working for somebody else, someone who knew Strickland had "something" that belonged to Saledo.

"Damn, this is big," Stevenski said. "It confirms your informant theory."

Rowe nodded, feeling both vindicated and unsettled at the same time.

He *knew* he'd been right about a mole. Over the past three years nearly every sting operation the task force had undertaken had turned into a disaster. Three federal agents had lost their lives trying to bust Saledo. Many people at the Drug Enforcement Agency and the Bureau were convinced someone on the inside was feeding tips to Saledo and his network. Personally, Rowe believed it was someone on one of the local police forces who was supposedly "helping" with operations. Several years ago, an FBI agent had been planted on the San Antonio police force to try and root out the mole, but he and his SAPD partner, Paloma Juarez, had been killed by people with ties to Saledo.

Clearly Saledo still had someone on his payroll, and it looked like that person was in San Antonio.

"Zapata know what they're referring to here?" Stevenski pointed place in the transcript about the killers looking for something.

"Nope," Rowe said. "Most likely money or drugs. I'm thinking money, especially given the rumors Strickland had a stash somewhere. The guy went to his ex's place looking for something, and I don't buy it that she'd keep drugs around, at least not knowingly."

"Yeah, me neither."

"So I'm thinking Strickland ran out of money and returned to the U.S. to recover his stash from his ex. She'd probably socked it away somewhere or spent it. If she still had it, maybe he got it back from her."

"And then what?" Stevenski asked. "If the killers already found the money, why stick around?"

Rowe shrugged. "Maybe they didn't find it. Maybe Strickland put it somewhere before his car crash."

Stevenski looked skeptical.

"I wish we knew where Strickland spent his last hour." Rowe leaned back in his chair and scanned the e-mail again. "We need IDs on these two guys, find out who they were working for."

"You hear anything more from that gas station clerk?"

Rowe sighed. "Not yet. But there's somebody else who might be able to help."

Stevenski smiled. "That reporter? You planning to interview her again? I heard she's hot."

Rowe frowned. "Where'd you get that?"

"Hey, I'm an investigator. I check out anyone and everyone connected to our case. The girl's one of our only witnesses."

"Yeah, too bad she works for the media," Rowe said. "Anything useful she knows'll probably end up in the goddamn paper before we hear about it."

"And are you sure you won't be needing our supplemental collision policy?"

Celie forced herself to smile at the woman behind the Hertz counter. She wore a taxicab yellow golf shirt and had little pink and lavender Easter eggs painted on her fingernails. She was entirely too perky for Monday evening rush hour.

"No, thank you."

The woman handed her a key with a Hertz tag attached. "Looks like you're all set then!" She nodded toward the glass door. "That's your car right there. Full tank of gas."

Celie gathered up her purse and backpack and exited the office. "Car" was stretching it. The tiny orange Aveo sedan looked more like a Sunkist can on wheels. No wonder this one had ended up in the rental fleet. Celie stowed her things on the passenger seat, already homesick for her SUV. Oh well. This was only temporary.

Celie pulled to the edge of car lot and sighed. The five o'clock traffic was heavy, but a black pickup was nice enough to let her in. She waved a thank-you and glanced in her rearview mirror.

"Oh my God!" She slammed on the brakes. A man was watching her from the backseat.

CHAPTER
8

"Drive, bitch."

Shrieking, she grasped for the door handle.

"*Drive!*" Something jabbed the back of her neck.

Celie froze. He had a gun. It felt hard against her skin. And warm, like he'd been keeping it close to his body. She could barely breathe, but she forced herself to replace her hands on the steering wheel. She looked in the mirror.

He nudged her with the shiny silver pistol. It looked fancy, like maybe it was plated with nickel or something. "Go straight for a while. I'll tell you when to turn."

"You can have the car," she croaked. "I've got some money, too. You can have whatever you want."

"Shut up and move."

She obeyed.

She glanced at the mirror. The man was young, probably early twenties. Was he Robert's killer? He had close-cropped dark hair, olive skin, and brown eyes. He was scowling, which made it look like he had one thick eyebrow stretched all the way across his forehead.

Her palms felt slimy on the steering wheel. Had anyone noticed she'd been carjacked? She looked around, but everyone around her was creeping through traffic, immersed in their own little worlds.

Where was he taking her? The black pickup was still behind her, and it was following too closely. It stayed right on her bumper through three traffic lights, until they'd almost reached the edge of downtown. Celie thought about ramming into a utility pole, but she wasn't wearing a seat belt. And what if the gun went off?

"Turn here." The tip of the gun caressed her neck. "Left."

Celie's heart hammered. She turned left down a narrow alleyway—barely wide enough for two cars to pass. There wasn't a person in sight, just potholes and Dumpsters. Thank God it was daylight. But where were the *people*? The alley was empty. No pedestrians, no vagrants, not even a stray dog.

The black pickup turned in behind her, effectively trapping her in. Now the only way out was straight ahead.

"Stop here."

Celie's throat constricted, and suddenly she felt dizzy. This could not be happening again. It could not. She'd rather take her chances with a bullet than go with him behind one of those Dumpsters.

"I said *stop!*"

Her knuckles whitened on the steering wheel as she put her foot on the brake. *Oh God. Please, please, please . . .*

Suddenly the passenger door opened and another man got in. He shoved her backpack to the floor and then yanked a big, black gun out of his pants and pointed it at her face.

Her blood turned to ice.

"Here's how this goes." His voice sounded calm. Celie struggled to listen, but all she could think about was the gun just inches from her nose. If he pulled the trigger, would she feel anything?

She tore her gaze away from the gun and looked at his face. He resembled the guy in the backseat, except his head was shaved and he had a black goatee.

". . . give it to us, and we don't hurt you," he was saying. God, she'd missed the rest of it. Give them what?

Celie opened her mouth, but nothing came out. She nodded dumbly.

"Where's the money?"

The money. She gulped. Robert's money.

"I don't have it."

Pain seared through her as the pistol butt connected with her cheekbone.

"Wrong answer."

Something wet trickled down her face. She choked back a sob.

The goatee guy leaned over the console. She pulled back as far as she could until her head was pressed against the glass window. "I s-swear. Robert had the money. He had it in Antigua. Then he brought it back to the States so he could return it to someone."

"Fuck, man." This from the back.

Celie glanced over the seat. The man there looked agitated now. Sweat beaded on his upper lip, and his hands were shaking. Thankfully, his gun was on the seat beside him, not pointed at her neck.

She slid her attention back to the man in front. *His* gun was still aimed right at her face. Some kind of strange graffiti covered his knuckles. His hands were steady, and he looked eerily calm.

"He had the money *with* him?"

Celie swallowed. "Yes. He . . . he smuggled it back here."

"She's lying, man. She's fucking *lying!*" The guy in back was bouncing on his seat now. "We searched the car."

Celie darted a glance at him. His gray T-shirt was dark with perspiration, and his eyes were bloodshot. He looked about ready to blow a fuse.

"I'll tell you everything I know," she said. "I swear. Just listen, okay? Robert had a stash of money. He told me that. He'd been living on it in Antigua. He came to visit me Friday night, but he'd called me earlier. From a motel."

She locked eyes with guy in front. He seemed like the leader. Maybe if she could convince *him* to believe her, she'd have a chance.

He nodded slightly. He was listening.

"He told me he was in trouble." Her voice shook, and her chest hurt. "He said he owed money to someone, but he didn't have everything he needed to pay him back. I think he owed a lot. He said he had to return all of it soon or he'd be killed."

Goatee Man was watching her intently with those brown-black eyes. He had a diamond stud in his ear. No tremors, no sweating. He seemed like a professional, but a professional *what* she was scared to contemplate.

She couldn't tell whether he believed what she was saying.

The guy in back pounded a fist on the window. "Man, she's *lying!*"

"*Shut up!*" Goatee Man swung his gun toward the backseat. "Did I tell you to talk?"

Celie bit her lip, praying a shootout wasn't about to erupt.

"Where did he call you from? What motel?"

The gun shifted back now, and her attention locked on the black tunnel pointed at her face.

"I don't know. He didn't say, just that he'd checked in and he planned to stay a few days."

You know, you're a terrible liar. McAllister's words came back to her, and her stomach clenched.

"So why'd he come see you if you didn't have the money?"

She licked her lips. They tasted coppery, like blood. She was bleeding somewhere. "I think he thought I could lend him what he needed. To pay back this guy."

"How much did he need?"

"Fifty thousand."

Goatee Man stared at her. Celie held her breath.

"And what'd you tell him?"

"I told him I didn't have that kind of cash. But maybe I could get it. A loan or something. If he'd just be patient." She cleared her throat. "But then he died, so . . ."

He glanced at his partner in back. Celie felt her heart thundering. Was he actually buying this? She had no idea. Maybe he planned to kill her no matter what she said.

Oh, God. She could describe him. *Both* of them. They hadn't bothered to conceal their faces.

She had to think of something.

"This money," she sputtered. "Saledo's money? Robert said he thought someone might try to take it, so he was keeping it somewhere safe. Until he could pay it all back. He didn't say where. Maybe his car or his motel or something."

Her voice was so wobbly now, even she could barely understand herself. Sweat streamed down her neck, between her shoulder blades. She looked at the gunman, pleading with him with her eyes. "He took my car, too. I swear that's all I know."

"She's fucking with us, man!" The man in back was practically vibrating now. "I say we cap her."

The gun swung toward the backseat again. A flurry of angry Spanish ensued, and Celie knew she was about to die. They were going to shoot her. Right here in this alley. She thought of her mother and her sisters. What would they do when someone told them she'd been murdered?

She watched them arguing. Goatee Man's head had been shaved recently. Short black bristles covered his scalp, except for a jagged, crescent-shaped white scar above his right ear. Was the scar from a knife? A beer bottle? Celie knew with certainty his haircut was meant to show off the scar, to make him look more menacing.

A horn blared behind them, and everyone turned in unison. A delivery truck was trying to get by, but the black pickup was blocking its way. The driver opened his door and climbed down from the cab.

"*Fuck,* man!" The man in back snatched his gun off the seat.

"Hey!" Goatee Man nodded at the weapon. "Chill the fuck out."

He turned his attention back to Celie. "We're not done with you. We'll be back."

Celie's gaze flicked to the rearview mirror. The truck driver was striding past the pickup now, and he looked peeved. Celie prayed he wasn't about to get shot.

"Hey!" Her attention snapped back to Goatee Man. His gun had disappeared, but the look on his face was every bit as threatening. "Talk to the cops and you're dead. We'll be in touch, bitch."

Celie nodded.

An instant later, both men were out of the car. Celie watched in the rearview mirror as they approached the truck driver. Their hands were empty, and she could tell by the driver's indignant expression that he had no idea he was confronting two armed men. After a brief exchange, the driver returned to his truck, and the other two got into their pickup.

She was free.

The breath she'd been holding whooshed out of her lungs. Her hands were trembling all over the place, but she managed to lock the doors and put the car in gear. She raced down the alley, bouncing over potholes, nearly sideswiping a Dumpster. When she reached the first cross street, she made a sharp right turn and stomped on the gas.

• • •

John perched atop Celie's stepladder with a metal trowel in one hand and a tub of spackle in the other. He hadn't repaired Sheetrock in years, but this little patch of ceiling had been a breeze. Now all he needed was a can of touch-up paint, and it would look good as new.

"You know if she keeps any of this paint around?"

Dax looked up from his *Entertainment Weekly*. "She doesn't, but I do. Got it from maintenance after my last party."

John climbed down from the ladder. Flecks of spackle dotted his army green T-shirt. "You burned up your kitchen, too?"

Dax smiled. "Red wine stain on the wall. But these units are 'matte ivory' top to bottom, so the paint works anywhere. I'll go get some."

He slid off the bar stool and headed for Celie's front door, stepping back suddenly when it swung open.

"Hey, it's just us," Dax told her, confirming John's suspicion that they were close. Celie's good friends knew she didn't like surprises.

Such as finding two men waiting for her in her locked apartment.

Dax kissed her cheek and took her backpack.

"Who's 'us'?" Celie peered over his shoulder. She wore sunglasses, so John couldn't see her reaction to his being there.

"Just me and McAllister here," Dax said brightly. "He dropped by to fix your ceiling, and I buzzed him up."

John had come over on a hunch, and he'd been right. Celie had given Dax a spare key after the locksmith had left, meaning for the price of a little chitchat John had access to Celie's apartment whether she wanted him there or not.

His second hunch had been right, too. Judging by Celie's silence and the way she'd turned her back on him, she probably would have found an excuse to avoid seeing him tonight if he'd called ahead to ask.

She and Dax were murmuring back and forth by the door, so John went to the sink to wash his hands. He heard the door shut.

"Give me a minute." Celie's voice faded to the back of the apartment. "I'll be right with you."

I'll be right with you. Like he was the cable guy or something. Like she hadn't had her tongue in his mouth yesterday.

Shaking his head, he opened the fridge and searched for a beer. No beer, so he settled for a bottle of mineral water and leaned back against the counter. His ceiling repair didn't look half bad. After the spackle dried, he'd finish up the paint, which would give him another excuse to come back here. Or maybe he wouldn't need an excuse. Maybe she'd be grateful enough to invite her handyman to dinner. And dinner might lead to a nightcap.

She came into the kitchen and made a beeline for the fridge. Something was up with her face. Was that . . . ?

"What the hell happened?" He reached for her, and she jumped back.

He stopped in his tracks. The look on her face was pure panic, and the bruise on her face twisted his guts.

"What the fuck, Celie?"

"Please don't talk to me like that."

Shit. He took a deep breath. "What happened?" He stepped closer and lifted her chin so he could see better. She had an angry red cut at the top of her left cheekbone, and the skin all around it was bluish-purple.

She averted her eyes while he looked at her.

"Celie?"

"I'm fine." She cleared her throat. "Really. I was coming home from the rental car place and—"

"Yoo-hoo. You decent?" Dax strode into the apartment with a red tackle box. He plunked it on the counter and started rummaging through it.

Celie smiled weakly. "Dax said he'd fix me up. I'll just take a sec, okay?"

Celie seated herself on the bar stool beside Dax. John crossed his arms and looked on while the younger man dabbed at her wound and put some sort of ointment on it. They murmured amicably back and forth over the box of bandages until John was ready to howl.

Finally, Dax packed up his gear and shot John a stern look. He knew something serious was going on. Maybe John's desire to punch a hole in the wall was written all over his face.

"Make sure she ices it," Dax instructed. "And the ointment should be reapplied before bed and then again in the morning."

John nodded grimly, accepting the underlying message not to leave Celie alone tonight. As if there was a chance of that happening.

"*I* will be sure to do that," Celie said, planting her hands on her hips. With ointment glistening off her face, the tough-girl act left a lot to be desired.

"I'm here if you need anything." Dax kissed her uninjured cheek and slipped out of the apartment.

Celie turned to John. "We need to talk."

No shit. "I think that's a good idea."

He followed her into the living room and waited for her to sit down on the sofa so he could take the seat next to her. She wasn't nearly as rattled as she'd been when she first got home, but John could see the nerves beneath the surface. And then there was the way she'd looked at him earlier, like she was scared of him or something.

It made him sick. And angry. And more than a little worried about what she had to tell him.

She sat cross-legged on the sofa and put a throw pillow in her lap. Her eyelids were puffy, and he could tell she'd been crying. He'd never seen her cry, not for herself anyway. The few times he'd seen her shed tears, they'd been for other people.

"Don't look at me like that," she said. "I'm okay."

"You don't look okay to me."

She took a deep breath. "I'm all right now. Dax says it's nothing."

"It's not nothing." He reached his hand out to stroke her cheek, just under the bruise. He barely touched her, but he could feel her tense up. "Tell me what happened."

She cleared her throat. "Some guys carjacked me on the way home from the rental car place."

"You were *carjacked*?"

"Not exactly." She took his hand, which had dropped into his lap. "They made me drive into an alley so they could ask me questions about Robert. They had guns, so I did what they said."

His heart clenched. "Did they hurt you?"

"Not like that." She knew he was thinking of the last time she'd been forced into an alley by someone.

"What did they want?" He hoped his voice didn't sound as out of control as he felt. He wanted to kill somebody.

"They wanted money. I'm pretty sure Robert stole some money before he died. From Manuel Saledo."

Fuck. He'd been afraid it was something like this.

"It was a lot. Two hundred thousand dollars. These guys thought I'd know where it was."

"Why would they think that?"

She squeezed his hand. "Because I do."

Rowe pulled up to Kate Kepler's house and made a mental list of all the things he hated about it. Item one, lack of sufficient exterior lighting. Item two, overgrown hedges crowding entrance. Item three, yard sign touting security system provided by now-defunct company. Item four, shirtless male neighbor smoking home-rolled cigarette on the front porch next door.

Rowe got out of his car. Kate's shiny black Beetle was parked in the driveway, which was nothing more than strip of shale next to her white adobe bungalow. She probably liked living in this eclectic neighborhood so close to downtown, probably thought it was charming. She most likely considered the homeless guy on the corner a "colorful character," and maybe she hadn't bothered to notice her house was five blocks down from a soup kitchen.

Rowe didn't see her roommate's car, but it hadn't been

there yesterday either. He walked across the weedy lawn to the entrance. The front steps were covered with blue and yellow Mexican tiles.

Item five, fake rock on top step containing hide-a-key.

Rowe rang the bell.

"Coming!" a female voice called from behind the door. It sounded like a perky version of Kate.

The door swung open, and there she was, wearing a smile that instantly turned into a frown. "What are you doing here?"

She had on tan cargo pants and a black tank top. No bra.

Rowe looked away. "You always open the door for strangers?"

"You're not a stranger."

"How do you know? I could be anybody. You didn't ask."

She crossed her arms and stared at him a moment, and then she seemed to decide not to get into an argument, which he easily would have won. "Would you like to come in?" she asked instead.

He stepped into the foyer and removed his sunglasses, tucking them into the pocket of his suit jacket. He resisted the urge to loosen his tie, even though she kept her house at a stifling eighty degrees or so.

"What brings you here?" Her bare feet brushed softly against the tile floor as she led him into the main room. After his eyes adjusted, he took in the comfortable brown sectional, the low coffee table. He could hardly see the top of it for all the CD jackets scattered across it—U2, Feist, Green Day. His gaze veered toward the breakfast room, where no fewer than five computers sat in various stages of disassembly.

He walked over to the machines, sidestepping a knee-high stack of *Wired* magazines.

"Hobby of yours?" he asked.

She shrugged and walked to the back door. A mangy-looking tabby pawed at the glass.

Item six, sliding glass door.

"More of a side business," she said, opening the door, which of course was unlocked. The cat darted inside and jumped on the counter. Kate wandered into the kitchen after it and filled a cereal bowl with water from the sink. She placed it on the floor, and the cat jumped down and lapped at it.

"You've got a lot of expensive equipment here," he said. "Ever think about getting an alarm system?"

"I've got one."

"Ever think about getting a real one?"

She smiled and motioned to the table covered with dismantled CPUs. "If someone thinks they can put all this back together and sell it, they're welcome to try. Most people wouldn't bother."

"You seem to know how," he pointed out.

She tilted her head and smiled smugly. "I'm not most people."

This was true. Truer than he'd realized yesterday when he'd first interviewed her, but he'd had a chance to do some digging since then. Kate Kepler had an interesting background, especially for a twenty-three-year-old. She'd lied about her age by two weeks.

In addition to being a recent graduate of Rice University with a double major in political science and computer science, she was the only daughter of James Kepler, the multimillionaire software genius who had designed one of the top-selling computer gaming systems in America. He owned a sprawling ranch on the outskirts of Austin, and he'd lived there like a hermit since a decade ago when he'd been investigated for tax fraud. The indictment never came down, but when word of the investigation leaked to the press, his reputation suffered permanent damage. Rowe was pretty sure James Kepler's experience was the reason for Kate's hostility toward federal investigators.

Her gaze skimmed over him. "Nice suit. Do they, like, *make* you guys wear those things?"

He ignored the question. "I read your article in this morning's paper. Who'd you talk to over at the barbecue joint?" Someone—who of course wanted to remain anonymous—at a restaurant on Ranch Road 2222 had seen a man matching Robert Strickland's description arguing with two guys in the bar just before his car wreck.

Kate smiled. "I'm sorry. I'm afraid I can't disclose my source on that."

Rowe gritted his teeth. This was one of the many reasons he hated reporters. "We had an agent interview everyone on duty there. They all denied seeing anyone resembling the victim at the restaurant Friday night."

Kate tilted her head to the side. "Maybe you guys need to work on your interview technique."

"This is serious, Kate." Shit. "Miss Kepler."

"I agree." She shoved her hands in her pockets. "And so does the waitress who would probably lose her job if she admitted to law enforcement that she served a couple beers to a man who minutes later died in a car crash."

Okay, so at least she'd told him it was a waitress. That was probably the best he was going to get on that topic. Rowe slipped some papers out of his pocket and unfolded them. They were pictures of pickup trucks, various makes and models, all from a rear view.

"We've found a gas station clerk who says a black pickup truck arrived at his store shortly after the estimated time of the crash." He handed the pictures to Kate. "The lighting was good, and the clerk's been able to provide a detailed description of the car. He also got a look at the vehicle's occupants."

Kate looked at the pictures. "Two males?"

Rowe nodded. "One got out to use the phone. They made a quick call, then left in a hurry. Any of those trucks look like the one you saw?"

Kate shuffled through the papers, pausing several times to study them closely. She wasn't wearing makeup today—not that she needed it—and she looked even younger than twenty-three.

"This one," she said, shoving a picture at him.

He cleared his throat. "The Avalanche? You're sure?"

"I'm sure. It's got that distinctive back part. I remember now."

"Thanks." He returned the pictures to his pocket, then slipped on his sunglasses.

"So maybe you can trace the phone call. From the gas station? It'd be interesting to see who they were calling. Seems like they would've used a cell phone, unless maybe they were worried about caller ID."

"We're working on it." He headed for her front door. As he passed the hallway, he caught a glimpse of an unmade bed in one of the rooms.

"Your roommate out?" he asked, then wondered why in the hell he cared.

"I don't have a roommate."

He turned around. "That woman who was here yesterday? Silver nose ring? She told me I'd find you at Jiffy Lube."

"That's Amber. She lives across the street. She just comes over sometimes so she can use my Internet."

Perfect. "And you gave her a key?"

"She uses my hide-a-key, mostly."

He thought of a dozen things to say, and then decided not to say any of them. Kate Kepler's personal security was none of his business.

Except that she was a witness, of sorts, in his investigation. His investigation of one of the most dangerous DTOs in Mexico.

Goddamn it.

"You need to be more careful," he snapped.

"Excuse me?"

"Your house. It's wide open. Anyone could get in here."

She laughed. "Why would they want to? This place is a dump. I mean, it's cozy, yeah. I like it. But it's not like I've got diamonds lying around."

"That's not the point!" He was glad his eyes were covered by sunglasses, because he probably looked a little strange. And it *was* strange, coming over and getting all argumentative with this girl he barely knew. He needed to detach.

He took a deep breath. "Lock up behind me, will you?"

She had a "what's with you?" look on her face, but she didn't say anything. She just nodded and opened the door.

He looked down at her plastic rock and sighed. "And find a new place for your key, okay? You're a smart girl, Kate. Use your brain."

"You *know* where Robert stashed the cash? What, did he tell you?" John wanted to kill that prick all over again for getting her involved in this.

"He didn't tell me," she said. "I found it, actually."

"You *found* two hundred thousand dollars."

"That's right."

"Where was it?" Not that it even mattered now.

"You remember that night down in Mayfield, the night the FBI and everybody came out to Feenie's house?" she asked.

As if he could forget. Celie had found out her husband had helped try to murder her best friend, who'd just become hip to his money-laundering operation. She'd rushed over to tell Feenie. Robert had followed her over there, hoping to shut her up, probably. When Celie told him she'd called the police, he gave her a bloody lip and fled the scene.

"I remember," he said now.

"Well, ever since that night, the FBI's been grilling me about money. Where was Robert getting it? Did he have a stash hidden somewhere that he took when he fled the country? When he was living as a fugitive for so many months, he *had* to have something to live on."

"I thought he emptied your bank account," John said. "That's what Feenie told me, anyway."

"He did. But that wouldn't have gotten him far, and the FBI knew it. They thought he'd taken off with some of Saledo's cash."

"Okay. So Robert took the money. Then what?"

She closed her eyes and rubbed the bridge of her nose. "That's the thing. He only took some of it. The rest he left back in Mayfield."

"Why would he do that?" If he'd taken time to empty their account, why leave behind two hundred grand?

"Because he was in a hurry." She sighed. "And because the money was hidden in a storage unit on the outskirts of town, and Robert's key was missing."

"His key?"

"Yeah, I'd found it in a drawer and put it on my key chain, thinking it was mine."

She leaned her head against the back of the couch and stared at the ceiling. "I think that's why when he came to Austin and went through my purse and saw that Public Storage card, he thought he could find the money there. I had to hide it somewhere, and it's not like you can just show up and put that kind of cash in a bank."

She was right. Banks paid attention to deposits over ten thousand, as did the federal government.

"Then Robert must have met with these guys and told them he knew where the money was," she said. "Maybe he promised to lead them to it in exchange for some. Or maybe he was trying to buy himself off Saledo's blacklist. I don't know."

The pieces were coming together. "So they killed him,

took your keys and the card, and went after the money themselves?"

"That's my best guess."

John brushed a wisp of hair out of her face. "How about some aspirin? You don't look very good."

"It's okay. I want to get this over with."

He tried not to let that sting.

"So," she continued, "Robert flees the country, and I've got this extra key on my key chain. It's to this storage unit where we kept some furniture my grandmother had given me that we didn't have room for. It was baby stuff mostly. A crib and a rocker, things like that." She looked away. "We were saving it for when we had a baby."

Thank hell that never happened. But John kept that opinion to himself. Celie probably wanted to be a mother. She was terrific with kids—her whole personality just lit up around them.

"So I went over there one day. I was feeling sad, I guess. About lots of things." She wouldn't look at him. "I was going through this box of old toys I'd saved. Underneath a few old dolls was just this *stack* of money."

John smiled. "Bet you didn't expect that, huh?"

She scoffed. "Nope. I started opening all the boxes, and it was unreal. The money was squirreled away everywhere. Tens, twenties, hundreds. Little stacks all over the place. He'd hidden it all in boxes of stuff I never use. I guess he figured I wouldn't see it."

John visualized her in a storage unit surrounded by piles of cash. It made a funny picture. She wasn't the least bit materialistic. Other people might have been elated, but she'd probably been terrified.

He took her hand. "You were scared, huh?"

"Heck, yeah! Wouldn't you be?"

"I don't know. I've never run into that problem before."

Her hand was soft in his, and she stroked his fingers with the pad of her thumb. He wondered if she realized she was doing it.

"But you didn't go to the police," he stated.

"No."

"Why not?"

She looked down. "I guess I was in denial. I kept thinking maybe it was legitimate, that he'd earned it and not stolen it, and maybe he was just hiding the money from *me*, or trying to avoid paying taxes on it. I knew he did some off-the-books accounting work for friends, people he never ran through his firm."

This was where everything got sticky, John knew. She'd decided to keep the money. But why? She was a law-abiding citizen. Little Miss Honor Society. The FBI had turned her life inside out looking for evidence connecting her to Robert's criminal enterprise. They'd found zilch. Nada. Celie didn't have so much as a parking ticket. But she *did* have a track record of working tirelessly for bleeding-heart causes—food banks, cancer kids, the Red Cross, you name it. Investigators had struck out.

"Why'd you keep the money, Celie?"

She hesitated a moment, then met his gaze. "Have you ever wanted something so badly, it just knotted you up inside?"

He stared at her. "I don't know," he lied. "What was it you wanted?"

"It doesn't matter anymore, but I was pretty sure I could buy it if I had enough money."

What the hell was she talking about?

"So you spent some," he said.

She nodded, staring down at their hands. "And I can't get it back."

Shit, how much had she spent? And what could possibly be worth risking the wrath of not only the FBI, but a drug kingpin?

"Whatever you did, I'll help you. I promise. But please, *please* tell me you didn't spend all of it."

She bit her lip.

"Celie?"

"I didn't spend all of it."

He released the breath he'd been holding. "Damn, I'm glad to hear you say that."

He kissed her forehead, and she slid her hands around his neck. They felt good there, like they belonged, but he pushed the thought away.

"McAllister?"

He sighed. Just once he'd like her to call him "John," not "McAllister," like they were drinking buddies or something.

"What?"

"Let's talk about something else. I'm getting a headache."

"Fine by me. How about I get you an icepack and we can talk about all the reasons you're not getting rid of me tonight?"

She pulled away from him, her eyes guarded suddenly. "I don't think that's such a good idea. I'm feeling a little . . . freaked out right now. I need some time alone."

He watched her for a moment, trying to read her mind. Was she freaked out about her attack, or merely nervous about him? He knew he'd come on too strong in the past, and he realized now that had been a mistake. She wasn't like the other women he'd known.

"I'll leave you alone," he said. "If that's what you really want. But I'm not leaving you by yourself tonight."

CHAPTER

9

Celie lay beneath her comforter, completely exhausted, yet unable to sleep. The sensation was familiar.

She glanced at the clock. One thirty-four. She'd been trying for nearly three hours now, but sleep wouldn't come, and she knew it would continue to elude her until just before daybreak. Then she'd get a few uninterrupted minutes—an hour, if she was lucky—and start the next morning with kinks in her neck and sandbags under her eyes.

Celie threw back the comforter and rolled onto her back. Sometimes that helped. But after squeezing her eyes closed, she saw the same images that had been plaguing her for hours: the abandoned alley, the rusted blue Dumpster, and the empty black hole at the end of the gun.

Her chest constricted as she relived the helplessness. She'd been at their mercy. They could have done anything to her.

She stared at the ceiling and tried to regulate her breathing. She *wouldn't* panic. She was safe at home, behind a locked door. A security guard was on duty downstairs, and John McAllister was asleep on her sofa.

A soft tapping sounded at her door.

She propped up on her elbows. "Come in," she said, her voice gravelly.

The door creaked open. McAllister stood in the opening, silhouetted against the yellow light of the hallway.

"Trouble sleeping?" he asked.

She sat up and tugged her nightshirt down over her thighs. She'd gone to bed in Robert's old Dallas Cowboys jersey. It had been washed about sixty thousand times, and it was the most comfortable thing she owned. Alluring lingerie, it was not.

"Sorry about my couch," she said. "It can't be nearly long enough for you."

He stepped into the room, and her pulse quickened.

"I've slept on worse."

He walked over to the bedside. "Since you're awake anyway, there's something I need to ask you. Mind?" He nodded toward the bed.

She scooted over, trying to ignore the way her heart was racing. The mattress sank under his weight as he sat down, and she had to catch herself to keep from rolling into him.

"Sorry," he said.

She watched him scan the room. He couldn't see

much in the dimness, but she wondered anyway what he thought about it. He'd probably been in dozens of women's bedrooms over the years. His gaze paused on the rocker in the corner.

"Your grandmother's rocking chair, huh? The one you had in storage?"

Here was the problem with confiding in this man. He filed everything away, no matter how inconsequential. "That's what you wanted to ask me?"

He picked up her hand. "No."

She waited, wishing she didn't like the way his hand felt, all warm and callused. How did he get calluses, anyway? He was a reporter.

A fact she needed to remember.

Moonlight filtered through the window, and she could see his face in the shadows: the strong jaw, the faint stubble, the little white scar just below his ear that he'd picked up somewhere along the way. She knew nothing about that scar. She knew nothing about him, really, which made it all the more unnerving to have him sitting on her bed in the dark.

"I need to ask you something, even though I know you think it's none of my business," he said.

She nodded.

"What did you do with all that money?"

He was right. It wasn't any of his business. And yet she had this insane urge to tell him.

But she couldn't. "It doesn't matter. You wouldn't understand anyway."

"You might be surprised what I'd understand."

What could she say to that? She didn't say anything.

"Okay," he said. "Let me ask you something else then. Are you absolutely sure you can't get it back?"

That was an easy one. "Absolutely."

"Then I think you need to go to the FBI. Tell them what happened today—"

"I can't. I told you, those men threatened to kill me."

He took a deep breath and looked down. He fidgeted with her fingers. "I've been thinking. Maybe you should try to join the federal Witness Protection Program."

Her first reaction was absurd. She felt *hurt*. Part of her was devastated he would suggest that she disappear.

Which just illustrated how screwed up she'd allowed herself to get over this guy. She did *not* have a future with John McAllister. They were complete opposites. And he didn't want her anyway, not for anything serious.

"I couldn't do that." She pulled her hand away and folded it in her lap. "I know it may not seem like it to you, but I *do* have a life. I have a mother, and two sisters. And friends. And a goddaughter. I couldn't just abandon all that."

He touched her calf now. Which was worse than his holding her hand. "Feenie's daughter?"

"Yes," she answered. His hand was giving her goose bumps.

"Don't you think your mother and Feenie and everyone would rather you be safe than anything else?"

"Sure, but what about what me?" she asked, annoyed.

"What do you mean?"

What did she *mean*? It was *her* life they were talking about. Unlike most people she knew, she didn't have a marriage, or a child, or even a career to speak of, but she still had a life. And what she had meant something to her.

"I mean, what about what I want?"

"Okay. What *do* you want? Do you even know?"

Anger welled up in her chest. "Yes, as a matter of fact. I want to finish my degree and become a social worker. I want a family someday. I want everyone to stop worrying about me and pitying me, including you! I want to have control over my goddamn life!"

Whoa. Where had that come from? She was breathing hard, and her hands were fisted at her sides.

His fingers had stilled on her leg. "You think I *pity* you?"

She took a deep breath. She might as well get it out there. "Yes, I do."

"Celie . . ." He shook his head. "You have no idea what you're talking about."

"Oh, really? Let me ask *you* something then."

"Okay."

"When was the last time you slept with someone?"

Silence.

"What does that have to do with anything?" he finally answered.

"I think it has a lot to do with everything, actually. Just answer the question."

"Three weeks ago."

Three *weeks*? He'd been even busier than she thought. She felt a little burr of jealousy in her chest.

"And is she your girlfriend?"

He tipped his head back. "No, she was just . . . Shit. No, she's not my girlfriend."

She waited for him to get it, but he just sat there staring at her. "I haven't slept with anyone in a lot longer than that," she said. It had been nearly a year, but she couldn't bring herself to say it.

"Yeah, so what?"

"So, we're totally different."

"What, because I had sex three weeks ago?"

She rolled her eyes. "Because you have sex *often*. Without strings attached. It's no big deal to you."

"How would you know?"

She laughed. "You tried to have sex with me at my *office*! Sorry, but that's not really normal for me. When I sleep with someone, it's a big deal, but to you it's like tying your shoes or something. We're completely different."

She held her breath, waiting for him to deny it, but he didn't.

"Don't you see?" she continued. "The only thing we have in common is that our pasts overlap. And every time I get hit with some new trouble, you feel sorry for me, like everyone else."

"I don't feel sorry for you. Jesus. That's the last thing I feel."

Yeah, right. If there was one thing she recognized, it was pity. She'd been on the receiving end of it for a decade now, and it pissed her off.

"McAllister, let's be honest, okay? You're here because you want to protect me, right?"

"So?"

"So, I appreciate what you're doing. Part of this is my fault, really, because I keep letting you help me. But you're off the hook now."

"What the hell is that supposed to mean?"

"It means you can stop looking out for me," she said. "I've decided to hire a professional bodyguard. I called Marco Juarez this evening and asked him to put me in touch with someone up here who can protect me until I figure out what to do about this mess."

"Celie—"

She held up a hand. "It's *my* problem. Not yours. You don't need to worry anymore. You can get back to your job and your social life and everything you were doing before you found out I was in Austin."

He stood up. "Is that what you want?" His voice was tight, like he was talking through clenched teeth.

"Yes."

He looked down at her for a moment before walking to the doorway. He paused with his back to her. "When do you plan to hire this person?"

She sighed. "Tomorrow. First thing in the morning."

"Fine. I'll take you to wherever it is."

"It's okay. Dax can drive me." She hoped.

John shook his head. "Great. Terrific."

"McAllister—"

"I'll be on your couch." He yanked the door shut behind him.

Kate found him camped out with his laptop at the Starbucks closest to City Hall. John was battling a cigarette craving and concluding that a double venti espresso was a piss-poor substitute.

She sat down on the arm of his chair. "You haven't been at the office in days. If it weren't for your byline, I'd have thought you walked off the job."

John had spent the better part of the week at City Hall

chasing down stories. Or at The Ale House. Now that Celie had her bodyguard, he limited himself to driving by her building once a night like the pathetic loser that he was. All he'd learned from his reconnaissance missions was that Celie probably had insomnia. He'd caught the bluish flicker of her television in the living room window well after midnight.

And with Celie unable to sleep, John's nights were shot to hell, too. He was running on caffeine and raw frustration. And now he had Kate Kepler in his face looking primed for battle.

John downed his last sip of coffee. "What's up, Kate?"

She was dressed conservatively today in a tailored black pantsuit. Definitely not her usual.

"I've got a meeting with Wozniak this afternoon," she said, referring to the news editor. "I'm going to try and convince him to assign me the Saledo story, including the Strickland homicide follow-ups and anything else that arises."

He noted her rigid posture, the stubborn set of her jaw. Her chin tilted up slightly, like she was daring him to challenge her.

"You sure you want to do that?" he asked. "The drug beat could be hazardous to your health."

Her nostrils flared. "What, you think I should stick to school-board meetings and human interest crap? You don't think a woman can handle crime stories?"

John had a hard time thinking of Kate as a woman. Yes, she had a nice, lithe little body under those unisex clothes she always wore. But she was fresh out of college and totally green.

"So what do you need from me?" John asked, although he was pretty certain he already knew.

"I need you to back off," she said firmly. "Wozniak's dying to let you take over because you're more experienced and you won all those awards when you lived down in the valley. I need you to step aside so he'll give me a chance."

She suddenly reminded him of Feenie Juarez. God save him from feisty young feminists who wanted to prove themselves.

"Fine," he said. "Have at it." In reality, it didn't matter what he said. If the Strickland homicide turned into a series about the Saledo cartel, Kate would be off the story in no time. Yes, it was probably sexism, but Wozniak typically assigned the hardcore news stuff to the men on staff.

But hey, if Kate wanted to think John was doing her a favor, who was he to set her straight?

She looked shocked, then suspicious. "What do you mean?"

"Just what I said. The story's yours. I don't want anything to do with Manny Saledo or Robert Strickland or the whole freaking crew. I'm sticking to City Hall."

She regarded him skeptically for a few moments. "You're seeing that woman, aren't you? You've got a conflict of interest."

He did, but not like she thought. His conflict involved his interest and Celie's complete lack thereof.

He checked his watch. He needed to get going so he could catch the mayor on his way to a late lunch. John had spent half an hour yesterday sweet-talking the man's admin into giving him a peek at today's schedule. The *ac-*

tual schedule, not the one his office normally released to the media. And if he didn't hustle now, he'd miss his shot at an exclusive quote.

He stood up and stretched. "Gotta run, Kate. Anything else you need?"

She stared up at him, not at all intimidated by his towering over her. He admired her spunk. Too bad she was a decade too young for him. Despite what Celie thought, John no longer dated girls just out of college.

She tipped her head to the side. "Are you okay? You don't seem like your usual self."

"Oh, yeah? And what would that be?"

She shrugged. "I don't know. Energetic. Charming. Cocky as hell."

"That's my usual self?" How would she know? He'd met her only a few months ago.

"I just expected you to put up a fight. You know, everyone says you're persistent. The King of Cling."

He sighed. "Yeah, well. Sorry to disappoint you."

"I'm not disappointed. Just surprised."

Maybe that was his problem. The King of Cling had given up too soon. He was exceptionally good at waiting people out, but when it came to Celie, he'd gotten frustrated and thrown in the towel.

He picked up his computer bag and took a long, hard look at Kate. The girl was perceptive. And gutsy. She'd make a good reporter if she could keep herself out of trouble.

"Be careful, Kate. And if you ever cross paths with Saledo's people, be *very* careful."

"I will," she said much too quickly.

"I mean it, Kate. Watch out. Those guys don't fuck around."

T-Bone escorted Celie down the hallway and unlocked her door. In keeping with the routine they'd established, he entered the apartment first, conducted a search of all the rooms, and then nodded when it was clear.

"Thanks, Tom." Celie had made a point of learning her bodyguard's real name. She couldn't bring herself to actually address someone as "T-Bone." It sounded like something from professional wrestling. But he'd come highly recommended by Marco, so Celie wasn't about to complain.

"I'll see you tomorrow then? Ten o'clock?"

"Yup," T-Bone answered in his usual monosyllable.

In the morning he'd pick her up for class in his gray Ford Expedition with tinted windows. The SUV was just right for blending in around town. Unlike T-Bone himself, who had a bleach blond crew cut and looked like an ad for Gold's Gym. His biceps were as big as Celie's thighs and just a *tad* firmer.

"Have a nice evening, then," Celie said.

She locked up behind him. Now she was home. Again. For the third afternoon in a row.

After seeing Celie's face Tuesday, Chantal had given her the week off. Apparently the pistol-whipped look wasn't what Chantal wanted her staffers projecting to the Bluebonnet House clientele.

So for the past week, Celie had spent her mornings on campus with T-Bone and her afternoons and evenings at her apartment, diligently getting ahead on her assignments. She'd also organized her closets, given herself daily pedicures, and logged a zillion miles on the stationary bike downstairs.

She was ready to scream.

Celie dropped into an armchair and checked her watch. It was just after five. She'd spent the afternoon in the library researching a term paper and still hadn't managed to use up the day. She kicked off her sandals and resigned herself to another wasted hour of channel surfing.

The phone rang. It was probably her mother, and Celie wasn't up for a conversation right now. She let her answering machine pick it up and listened as her cheerful voice filled the apartment, telling someone to please leave a message.

"Hey, bitch."

She bolted out of her chair.

"I know you're home, so listen up." It was Goatee Man. Celie's blood chilled as his voice surrounded her. "We haven't found shit, so we're coming to you. Two hundred grand, cash."

Her breath shallowed as his voice droned on. "You have a week. Bring it to me under the Lake Austin Bridge, south side. Next Thursday night at eleven. And come alone. If I see a cop or a boyfriend, you're dead. And then we go visit your parents in Mayfield."

Click.

She glanced at the windows. The blinds were closed, but they were watching her house. She backed deeper into the living room and sank onto the couch.

Thursday night. Two hundred thousand. It was impossible.

They knew about her *family*.

Sort of. Her mom lived in Mayfield, but she'd been a widow for years, ever since Celie's dad had had a heart attack at fifty-five.

Could they be bluffing?

A buzzer sounded, and Celie jumped to her feet. Were they *here*? She went to the intercom, but hesitated. After a moment, she pressed the button and waited.

Nothing.

"Ms. Wells?" Terrance's familiar voice finally crackled over the speaker. "Ms. Wells, you there? I've got a John McAllister down here. Ms. Wells, can you hear?"

John McAllister. Or someone claiming to *be* John McAllister.

She cleared her throat. "Uh, I can hear you. Could you put him on, please?"

A brief pause and then, "Celie, it's me. Can I come up?"

She'd never been so glad to hear a man's voice.

McAllister looked almost comical squeezed into her rental car with his knees folded up near his chest. But the grim set of his mouth told Celie he wasn't feeling amused.

He was angry. Livid. He'd hardly said two words since she'd played back the message for him.

"You really think this is safe?" Celie asked, stopping at a light.

McAllister looked at the side mirror. "They want you to deliver them two hundred grand next Thursday. This is probably the safest you've been all week."

It sounded logical. And Lord knew she was desperate

for a break from her apartment. But it felt strange going out without T-Bone around.

"I've got a gun in my purse," she blurted out.

McAllister's head snapped around. "You're shitting me."

She gave him a look that said, *no*, she wasn't shitting him, and she also didn't like his language.

"Sorry. Jesus. I just never thought . . . Do you even know how to use it?"

Not at all. She'd bought the .38 revolver last summer at Wal-Mart, but for the past ten months it had lived in a shoebox, untouched. "I'm pretty rusty."

He eyed her purse on the floor at her feet. "Is it loaded?"

"Not exactly."

"What the fuck is it, exactly?"

"Please stop cursing."

He rolled his eyes. "Are there bullets inside it or not?"

"They're zipped into the side pocket of my purse."

He shook his head and looked out the window. "You're taking a left here."

Celie turned onto another curvy two-lane road. They passed private drive after private drive—all tucked discretely behind huge live oak trees—until they neared the base of the hill.

"West Hills Marina?"

"I keep my boat here." He gave her a look that dared her to object. "I've had a hell of a week, and so have you. We need to get out on the lake."

She slid through the wrought-iron gate and parked between two Suburbans. She gazed past a row of cypresses and weeping willows and caught a peek of glistening water. "I didn't bring a swimsuit," she said.

"No problem. I've got an extra on board."

She shot him a withering look.

"It's my sister's," he said. "She and her kids were up here a few weekends ago, and I took them tubing. She's about your size. You'll be fine."

Yeah, great. She wanted him to look at her and think of his sister. She'd stick with her jeans and sleeveless button down. At least her shirt was white, which shouldn't be too hot.

McAllister levered himself out of the Aveo, then scooped her purse off the floor and shouldered it. He looked funny standing there in his Levi's and cowboy boots, with a woman's handbag dangling at his side, but he clearly didn't trust her with it.

Celie grabbed her sunglasses from the cup holder and got out. "So, this is a picnic?"

He reached into the backseat and gathered up his purchases from the convenience store where they'd stopped a few minutes before. "I bought sandwiches and chips. And I hope you like beer."

"Water?" she asked hopefully.

He paused. "Shit. *Shoot*. No water. But I might have some stored on the boat."

He led her across the gravel lot, through a gate, and across a patch of grass to the water's edge. The entire marina was shaded by a canopy of trees. A weathered wooden dock stretched the length of the waterfront, with twenty or so boat slips jutting out from it. Most of the boats were tucked neatly under canvas covers.

She trailed him down the dock, and he glanced at her over his shoulder. "How's work going?"

"Chantal gave me the week off."

"Good for her. You could use it."

McAllister stopped in front of one of the boats and placed his bags on the dock. He untied the canvas cover, revealing a sporty red ski boat. A babe magnet, of course. What else would he have? He'd probably taken dozens of bikini-clad women out on this thing. She imagined their coy little giggles as he slathered them with suntan oil.

We are so not compatible, she thought, picking up her purse.

"What's wrong?" He was standing on the bow now, holding a coil of rope.

"Nothing. It's just smaller than I expected."

He smiled. "Yeah, but she's fast."

Of course she was.

Celie stepped aboard and looked for a place to stash her purse. She tried the glossy teak cabinets. The first one was packed with life jackets, and the second held an expensive-looking stereo. She opened the third and found a fully stocked bar.

"Is there anywhere I can put this?"

He finished untying a line. "Sure, here." He hopped down from the bow and opened the cabinet closest to the captain's seat. "Stow it in there."

She crouched down to shove it inside.

"Wait." He took the purse from her, unzipped it, and pulled out the sleek silver .38. With a few deft movements, he flipped the gun over in his hand, checked the cylinder—which was empty—and returned it to her purse. "Here," he said, handing her the bag.

"I was just thinking. Maybe we should—"

"I've got it covered."

"You're *armed*? Where?"

He tugged up the leg of his jeans, and she saw the bulge in his scuffed brown cowboy boot.

"Great," she said. "And here I was wondering why you weren't wearing swim trunks."

"I wasn't planning on coming out here today." He raised an eyebrow. "But I've never been big on swimsuits, so if you want to take a dip later—"

"I'll pass." Definitely. Skinny-dipping was for skinny people.

She settled into the passenger seat and waited as McAllister did some things to the engine. His movements were smooth and efficient, like he'd done this countless times. The process seemed to relax him, and he no longer had that look on his face like he was ready to deck someone.

After flipping some switches near the steering wheel, he turned the key, and the engine hummed to life. He expertly maneuvered the boat backward out of the slip and pointed it toward the sun.

"Hold on," he said, and punched the throttle forward. The bow popped up, and soon they were skimming along on the water at a rapid pace. Celie's hair whipped into her eyes, and she dug a rubber band out of her pocket to secure it back.

"How long have you had a boat on Lake Austin?" she yelled over the noise.

"Since I got here."

Many of the lakes in central Texas had been created by damming the lower Colorado River. Both Town Lake and Lake Austin were long and narrow, like rivers. Towering trees and squatty houses flew by as McAllister overtook ski boats and wave runners. He was going fast and seemed to like it. His face looked serene as he stood at the helm.

The late afternoon sun warmed Celie's shoulders, and she tipped her head up toward the sky. It must be nice to have hobbies. Ever since she'd moved here, her life had been consumed with classes and the Bluebonnet House and endless doctor appointments. She'd had an appointment on Christmas Day, for heaven's sake. And even now that the treatments had ceased, she was still busy with work and school, still spent most of her Saturdays at the library on campus. She couldn't remember the last time she'd done anything to unwind, particularly outdoors.

She looked at McAllister. Ten minutes zooming through the water and he looked like himself again—relaxed, strong, supremely confident. She suddenly felt this overwhelming fondness for him. Where had that come from? She'd been lusting after him since Feenie's wedding, but now she was starting to like him, too. It was a dangerous combination.

He glanced at her and smiled. "What?"

"You look good."

His expression turned quizzical.

"I mean it," she said. "You're a natural out here, and you obviously love it."

His smile faded, and she wondered what she'd said. Probably something that reminded them why they were here. The real reason. Celie knew they were heading west, toward the bridge over Lake Austin.

She dragged her attention away from McAllister, and, sure enough, the giant brown arches came into view. They weren't here to picnic, but to scope out the drop site. The bridge loomed larger and larger until they were nearly under it. McAllister slowed abruptly and shifted into idle. When the engine quieted, she could hear the rush of traffic on Highway 360 above them. The boat drifted into the bridge's cool shadow.

She took a deep breath and tried to keep the emotion out of her voice. "Why do you think they picked this place?"

He scanned the structure, then shifted his gaze to the surrounding landscape. On the south side of the bridge was a concrete boat ramp where a green pickup was inching backward, easing a trailer carrying a pontoon boat into the water. On the bridge's north side, the shore was covered with dense foliage, interrupted by a narrow hiking trail.

"I don't know," he said. "But we need to find out."

He made a slow circle under the bridge, darting his gaze this way and that. Celie looked, too, trying to figure out what had prompted criminals to want to meet here. It was near a major highway, which gave them a rapid escape route. But the boat ramp meant possible witnesses.

Maybe this was to her advantage. They wouldn't actually hurt her in front of witnesses, would they?

McAllister's jaw was set, his relaxed expression long gone. "I don't like this," he muttered.

"Neither do I."

"We don't know if they're coming by boat, or car, or, shit, even on foot. It's too unpredictable."

Celie gnawed on her lip.

McAllister pointed the boat west, toward the gradually sinking sun. He punched the throttle forward and left the bridge behind them. "One good thing, there's lots of underbrush. Plenty of places for the FBI to conceal a sharpshooter."

"A *sharpshooter*? Did you even listen to the message? If I don't come alone, they're going to kill me and my family!"

He gave her a grim look.

Celie's stomach tightened. "You think they plan to kill me anyway. You think this is a setup."

His gaze slid toward the horizon.

"Is that really what you think?"

"I think you'd be crazy to do what they said. I think the only way you're coming out here is with cops hidden all over this bridge. I think what you *really* need to do is let a trained agent, someone who looks like you—"

"Whoa. I am *not* letting some agent come out here to get shot at."

He scowled. "Oh, so *you* should get shot at?"

"I won't get shot at." Probably not. "If I do what they said—"

"Hell no! You're not doing anything they said."

Celie closed her eyes. She knew he was right. Even if she wanted to come out here alone and make the exchange, she didn't have the money. But the alternative . . .

"Do you realize if I turn to the FBI for help, I'll probably go to jail?" she asked. "I stole that money! The FBI wanted it for evidence. They're not just going to scare away the bad guys for me and tell me to live happily ever after!"

"Who says you stole the money?"

She scoffed. "I did. I *told* you, I—"

"I don't remember that. Fact, as far as I'm concerned, your shithead ex-husband blew his wad down in the Caribbean and came back here to hit you up for a loan. You don't know crap about his drug money. Never did. That means the feds owe you *protection* if you're kind enough to lead them to the bad guys."

Her breath caught. It made sense. God, it might work. For the first time in days, she felt like she had a way out. Maybe.

"Don't you think that's a long shot?"

He looked down at her, and his blue eyes softened. "I think it's the only shot you have."

CHAPTER

10

John surveyed their surroundings for the fifth time and decided he was being paranoid. There was nobody out here. He'd found a quiet stretch of shoreline without lake houses or boat docks and a giant cypress that offered shade. It wasn't so much that they needed to cool off—the sun would disappear behind the hills in a few minutes—but the tree's broad shadow gave them an added measure of security. Even in a red boat, they'd be much less noticeable to the casual observer speeding by.

The problem was the not-so-casual observer.

"Don't look so worried," Celie said, reading his mind. She popped the cap off a Shiner and passed it to him. "You said yourself they have no reason to bother me right now. Besides, we've been out almost an hour now, and I haven't seen anyone around but skiers and fishermen."

She had a point. But after listening to that call this afternoon, John felt anxious. Plus it had been his idea to bring her out here, so he needed to keep her safe.

"Here." She passed him a sandwich wrapped in brown paper. She'd arranged all the food he'd bought neatly atop a striped beach towel on the floor of his boat. She looked so wholesome sitting there in that white shirt and those blue jeans, with her legs folded under her. This was definitely a first for him. Usually the women on his boat wore barely-there bikinis.

And usually they didn't waste a whole lot of time on food. Typically, it was knock back a few beers, maybe watch the sunset, take a dip in the lake, and then . . . well, whatever the mood called for.

He looked into Celie's trusting green eyes and suddenly felt like scum.

"What's wrong?" she asked.

Maybe she was right. Maybe he wasn't ready for a woman like her. He knew he didn't deserve her.

He took the sandwich she held out to him. "Nothing."

She smiled. "Hey, would you mind making me another drink? I'm so thirsty today."

"Sure, no problem."

She passed him her empty plastic cup.

Here was the other thing worrying him: she'd gone into his cabinet looking for water and found his nieces' leftover supply of Hi-C. Which would have been fine, except she'd decided to mix it with rum. He'd watched her make the drink, too, and she'd been extremely generous with the Malibu.

He filled her cup two-thirds with juice and added a

splash of rum. The last thing he needed was a repeat of last Saturday night, when she'd gotten drunk and propositioned him.

Leaving her apartment had been the most disciplined moment of his life, his all-time peak in terms of willpower. And he'd been fucking miserable afterward. Walking down to his car had been painful—literally. Did she think he was Superman? He'd been burning for her for years, and he couldn't just keep walking away. Especially when she looked up at him with those lush, pouty lips.

Like she was doing right now.

Fuck.

He passed her the drink. "So how's your bodyguard working out?" He lowered himself down next to her and leaned against the side of the boat. There was a good two feet of space between them. If he concentrated on the conversation and didn't look at her mouth anymore, he'd be fine.

"Okay, I guess."

John had a vision of some muscle-bound meathead camped out at her place. Maybe *that* was who had been watching TV so late at night this week. Not a fun thought.

"Does he stay with you at night?" He picked at his sandwich but didn't feel like eating. He took a pull of his Shiner instead.

She nibbled a potato chip. "No, he just comes with me to class mostly. And out on errands." She grinned. "This afternoon we spent a couple hours in the library. I think he was bored to tears."

So he wasn't sleeping over. That was good. But John was jealous anyway.

"Does he know what he's doing?"

"He seems to," she said. "I'm not exactly an expert, but Marco recommended him, so he must be good."

"I bet Feenie wasn't too thrilled when she heard you needed a bodyguard."

She rolled her eyes. "*There's* an understatement."

What a fucking mess this had turned into. Robert was an idiot. No one stole from Manny Saledo and got away with it.

And what had Celie been thinking? It really bothered him that she didn't trust him enough to tell him what she'd done with the money.

"Feenie's freaking out," she continued. "If it weren't for the baby, she'd be up here right now trying to set me straight."

"What does she think you should do?"

Celie sighed. "Last time we talked, she mentioned New Hampshire."

"New Hampshire?"

"Yeah, my sister Bethany lives in Manchester. She's got four kids, and her husband runs a private school there. After my divorce, he offered me a job as a teaching assistant. Wanted to help me make a fresh start."

New Hampshire. He didn't like the thought of her being that far away, but she'd be safer. At least she'd be far removed from Saledo's turf. "Maybe you should go."

She shrugged. "I've been giving it some thought."

What if she actually did it? Out of nowhere, he'd been

given a second chance with this woman, and now she might leave.

This was so screwed up. He *wanted* her to leave. She'd be safer somewhere else, and his own life would be a lot less complicated.

John reached across her and opened the cooler to exchange his empty beer bottle for a new one. When he settled back against the side of the boat, Celie scooted closer.

"This is nice," she said, leaning her head on his shoulder. "And it's not too hot after sunset."

"Yeah."

She smelled like strawberries again. Maybe if he didn't do anything to encourage her, she'd sit back up. He looked down and caught a glimpse inside her shirt at the pale swell of flesh disappearing into white lace.

"McAllister?"

He swigged his beer and looked away. "Huh?"

"Did I really kiss you Saturday night?"

God help him. "Yes, you really did."

"I don't remember it real well."

"Thanks a lot."

She bumped her knee against his. "No, I mean I remember it, just not like that. It's kind of fuzzy, but . . ."

"But what?"

"I remember you kissing *me*."

He laughed. "Nah, that's just wishful thinking."

She got quiet then. He couldn't see her face because she was leaning back against his arm. He'd bet anything she had that look again—the one she always got when she was thinking about sex, which she seemed to do a lot. She had zero aptitude when it came to masking her emotions. Everything she was thinking about was right there, written plainly across her face. He could read her like a book, which was why it drove him crazy when she looked at him that way.

She'd picked up his free hand and was tracing his knuckles with her index finger. She had pretty hands. Her fingernails were always some shade of pink or red, and whatever it was always matched her toenails. Today was something orangey—the same color as her rum punch.

"This must be weird for you, huh?" she asked.

"How do you mean?"

"I mean, I keep contradicting myself. Sometimes I kiss you, and sometimes I want you to back off. You must think I'm a tease."

He took a sip of beer as he considered how to respond. He didn't think she was a tease. He *did* think she had some serious hang-ups about sex. And that maybe alcohol helped her avoid dealing with them.

Probably not a message she really wanted to hear.

She shifted to face him. Her mouth was inches from his. Her hair was mostly in a ponytail, but the breeze blew little strands of it against her cheek.

"Is that what you think?" she asked softly.

Fuck it. He bent his head down and kissed her. He kept it gentle at first, but then she opened her mouth to him and his control ended. She tasted like rum and cherries, and her mouth was so sweet and hot. Her hands slid up his neck, and he felt her fingers tangling in his hair. Heat shot through him. Did she really want this? Because in a minute there'd be no going back. He put his beer aside and, still kissing her, lifted her onto his lap. She nestled against him, and he knew the instant she felt him because she froze.

He eased back and looked into her eyes. She was having doubts again. He wanted to be angry, but knowing her the way he did, he didn't want to push. Even if he coaxed her through it, she'd probably hate him afterward.

"To answer your question, I don't think you know what you want," he said.

She didn't answer—just sat there breathing heavily. He shifted her off his lap and stood up.

"It'll be dark soon," he said. "I'd better get you home."

Kate trekked across her yard in the dark and mounted the steps to her front door. She'd forgotten to buy lightbulbs again, and she could barely see as she fumbled with her keys. Her key chain hit the concrete with a jangle.

"Crap," she muttered, setting down her backpack and her plastic bag of take-out food to grope around in the dark.

"Hi."

She gasped and fell backward onto her butt.

"Calm down. It's just me."

Mike Rowe. His shadowy silhouette stood on her sidewalk.

She scrambled to her feet. "You nearly gave me a heart attack! What's with the stealth approach?"

"I got your message," he said, climbing her steps. "You said you had something to show me."

She finally located her keys and scooped up all her stuff.

"Your exterior light is out," he observed.

"No kidding? I hadn't noticed." She unlocked the door and shoved it open, then stomped into the house and dumped her stuff on the coffee table. Then she turned to face the man who'd just scared the tar out of her. He was ominously attired in a starched white dress shirt, pale blue tie, and khaki slacks. In his right hand he held some sort of pole.

"Sorry if I startled you."

"Forget it." She nodded at the thing in his hand. "What's that?"

"It's a brace for your sliding glass door." He handed it to her. "So someone can't just pop it open and walk in."

She looked down at the object, bewildered.

"I also made a list of good security companies." He took a slip of paper from his pocket and passed it to her. "It shouldn't take long to get someone out to install something."

"Okay." She stared down at his neat block handwriting and didn't quite know what to say. It seemed Agent Rowe was a little paranoid. She looked up into his eyes and saw the earnestness there overlaid with concern.

Kate put the door brace on the coffee table. "You've seen some bad things as an FBI agent, huh?"

He gave her a long look, and that was answer enough.

Then he glanced away and cleared his throat. "So tell me about this package," he said.

The package. Right. She retrieved her backpack from the table and pulled out a padded brown envelope.

"It's a videotape," she explained. "Of a Public Storage facility off Loop 620 where a unit was vandalized recently."

"Sounds like something for the Austin PD."

"No, you want this. Trust me. I watched the tape at work today, and I think it's your suspects. I couldn't swear to it, but I'm reasonably sure."

He took the envelope and gave her a steely look. "What else do you know about this?"

"Nothing. Oh, except the unit belongs to Robert Strickland's ex-wife."

"Kind of an important detail, don't you think?"

"I'll lend you this tape on one condition."

He smirked. "You've just handed me a piece of evidence in a federal investigation. I don't have to agree to any conditions."

She crossed her arms.

"Okay, I'm listening."

"If you ID these guys, I need you to tell me who they are." McAllister had been adamant on this point. He never would have lent her the tape if she hadn't agreed. "I mean it. The person who gave me this really needs to know their names."

"Cecelia Wells gave you this, didn't she?"

"No."

He shot her a baleful look.

"Look, it wasn't her, okay? Just promise me you'll get me IDs. Please?" McAllister was helping her out with this lead, and she needed to keep the tips coming.

"I'll do my best." He reached for the doorknob.

"Hey, thanks for the door thingy," she said, stepping closer. "How much do I owe you?"

"Nothing. I was happy to do it."

Their gazes locked, and suddenly there was something

uncomfortable prickling in the air between them. He'd gone above and beyond the call of duty here, and they both knew it.

He pulled the door open. "Lock up behind me," he said sternly. "And don't forget to call one of those companies."

Whoever coined the phrase "TGIF" didn't work at a shelter. The onset of the weekend invariably meant a stream of women and children tromping into the Bluebonnet House. The worst time was usually close to midnight, when Chantal was forced to turn people away due to a lack of beds. Sometimes she could direct clients to other shelters around town, but, on a rough night, families might end up at homeless centers or even sleeping in their cars.

Celie glanced at the clock and knew it was going to be a rough night. Only 5:40, and already they were at two-thirds capacity.

"Maybe it's a full moon," Janice mused, logging the most recent arrivals into the computer. "Everybody's acting a little psycho today."

"The boy's name is 'Enrique,' not 'Eric,'" Celie said, looking over the receptionist's shoulder. "He's named after his dad."

Janice grunted her disapproval. April Ramos and her two children were back for the second time this month, which meant her estranged husband had shown up, probably looking for money. Friday was payday in a lot of households.

"How's he doing?" Janice asked.

Celie craned her neck to see into the TV room. Enrique sat cross-legged in front of the television, playing a video game with a younger boy. He'd arrived with a split lip.

"The swelling's down," she answered. "I'll go see if he needs anything."

As Celie walked around the reception counter, the phone rang. She saw Chantal's mobile number on caller ID and paused to eavesdrop as Janice took the call. Chantal had had a court appearance downtown this afternoon and had called Celie in because they were short-handed. Hopefully, the director was on her way back. Celie didn't like being one of only two staffers on duty when things were this busy.

"It's been pretty hectic," Janice reported. "Are you on your way in?"

A squeal of brakes diverted Celie's attention outside. A woman jumped out of a tan sedan and rushed across the street. Before she could make it to the sidewalk, a white pickup skidded to a halt in front of her, blocking Celie's view. A man leapt out of the truck.

"Oh, God," Celie muttered, lunging for the door. "Call 911!"

CHAPTER

11

She raced outside and down the sidewalk.

"Excuse me! Can I help you?" She sounded ridiculously perky, but she'd been trained to deffuse these situations using calm, pleasant tones.

The man dragging this woman by her long brown hair didn't look pleasant. His face was red with fury, and he was cursing a blue streak as he towed her toward his truck.

"Is there a problem here?"

"Mind your own business!" He jerked the woman closer to him, and she squeaked.

"Let's all calm down, okay?"

"Don't make trouble, Grady." The woman's voice was wobbly, and her face was streaked with mascara. "Just let me go."

Celie stepped closer. "The police are on their way, Grady."

"Yeah? Well, you tell 'em to fuck off! We're leaving!"

Celie stepped between him and the truck. "I don't think so."

"Move it, bitch—"

There was a sudden whoosh of air, and Grady landed facedown on the pavement. A shiny black combat boot pressed into his back, and T-Bone jerked his arms behind him.

"This guy bothering you ladies?" T-Bone slipped off the belt from his black cargo pants and made quick work of binding the guy's wrists. Grady yelled something, but whatever it was got muffled against the asphalt.

"Thank you," Celie said, feeling woozy now as she stared at Grady's big, meaty hands. She glanced around for the woman and spotted her leaning against the wrought-iron fence. Janice was on her way down the sidewalk to open the gate.

"Hey." T-Bone gave Celie a sharp look. "You shouldn't have done that."

"But he was—"

"I'm supposed to be on you like glue. That's my job. And if you won't let me inside your workplace, I'm going to have to ask you to take some time off."

Celie bit her lip. She'd told T-Bone to stay in his SUV in the parking lot because she didn't want to explain his presence to anyone at the shelter. Now that conversation looked unavoidable. The police would arrive soon, and everything that had just happened would be written up in some report.

Maybe she could pass T-Bone off as a boyfriend who'd been waiting to give her a lift. . . .

Grady squirmed and cursed under the boot, and T-Bone jerked him to his feet. A siren sounded in the distance. Police response times were typically slow in this part of town, but the Bluebonnet House got special consideration.

"Sounds like your ride's here." T-Bone shoved the man down the sidewalk and forced him to sit on the curb well away from the gate.

Celie's cell phone buzzed, and she yanked it out of her jeans pocket to check the screen. John McAllister. Again. She knew what he wanted, and she'd been ducking his calls all day.

She opened the phone. "Hi. This is a *really* bad time. Can we talk tomorrow?"

He didn't say anything for a moment, and she could almost hear his teeth grinding.

"Did you set up the meeting?"

She sighed. "Yes."

"When and where?"

"You don't need to worry about it." She stepped onto the sidewalk as a police cruiser rolled to a stop down the block.

"It that a *siren*?" McAllister demanded.

"Yes, but it has nothing to do with me."

"Where the hell are you?"

"At the shelter. A guy just—"

"I thought you were off this week!"

"I was, but—"

"Where's your bodyguard?"

"He's right here." Actually, he was on the corner talking to the cops as Grady sat on his butt arguing. "I can't talk right now, McAllister."

"Just tell me when and where the meeting is, and I'll let you go."

She tipped her head back and blew out a breath. "That's not necessary, okay? My bodyguard can take me—"

"Fine. But I want to be with you when you talk to the feds."

God, she did *not* have time for this discussion. And she knew a quick way to end it.

"I don't want you there, okay? This isn't a press conference."

Celie cast a desperate look at T-Bone, who motioned her over with the jerk of his head.

"I can't believe you just said that." McAllister's voice was icy. "I told you, I'm not covering this—"

"And I told *you*, I can't talk right now! I'll call you tomorrow."

Celie snapped shut her phone, and set off to handle damage control.

Rowe paced the cramped reading room, practically wearing a hole in the 1970s-era gold carpet. Cecelia Wells was late, and if he hadn't been so sure she was going to turn up with something important to the investigation, he would have left fifteen minutes ago. Rowe didn't like waiting on other people to do things, but oftentimes it was the nature of the job.

Finally, a tap sounded at the door, and it swung open. A man swaggered into the room, leading with his enormous chest. His spikey hair was white-blond, and he looked like he had enough steroids in his system to supply a cattle ranch. This would be the bodyguard.

Cecelia trailed behind him, glancing around apprehensively as the guy assessed the room. She mumbled something to him, and he stepped out, closing the door behind him.

"Thanks for meeting me here," she said, dropping her purse on the table. She wore a short-sleeved white shirt today and a skirt made of thin cotton fabric with an intricate blue-and-green pattern on it that made Rowe think of India.

"No problem," Rowe said, although it had been. He'd spent an hour and a half driving up from San Antonio to meet this woman—at her request—in a stuffy, windowless room on the fourth floor of UT's main library, and she'd been half an hour late. If this meeting didn't produce a good lead, he'd wasted his first day off in a month.

Cecelia took a seat at the scarred wooden table, and Rowe followed suit. Not for the first time, he observed that she was attractive. It didn't really factor into his investigation—it was simply a fact.

"Thanks for coming alone, too," she said.

Rowe nodded. He'd been surprised by the request because women typically developed more of a rapport with Stevenski.

She chewed her lip and looked at the table, as if uncertain where to begin.

"What prompted you to call me?" Rowe asked, guessing by the welt on her cheek that something had happened.

"I was contacted by some people who work for Saledo. I think they may be the men who killed Robert." She sounded matter-of-fact, but Rowe wasn't buying it.

"How'd they contact you, exactly?"

She took a deep breath and told him about being carjacked by a couple of thugs who had later left a threatening message on her answering machine. Rowe listened, trying to conceal his frustration. A pair of agents on Rowe's team had been assigned to keep an eye on Cecelia, but obviously they were stretched too thin. They also were supposed to keep tabs on Kate Kepler, a waitress, and a convenience-store clerk. The task was next to impossible, but Rowe's SAC wasn't supplying enough local manpower for the team to do this job right.

Cecelia continued talking, providing an impressively thorough description of her assailants. He wondered if her previous encounter with the court system had given her an eye for details, such as the body art preferences of scumbags.

". . . and so on Thursday," she was saying, "they want me to show up with two hundred thousand dollars. Which I don't have. That's why I need you to help me."

Rowe noticed her stiff posture, the tight set of her mouth.

"You're sure you don't have it?"

She blinked at him. "I'm sure."

He leaned back in his chair and folded his arms over his chest. She wanted his help. She *needed* it. In exchange, she was offering to bait some high-level drug traffickers into coming out of hiding to pick up the money. Whether they worked for Saledo or a rival like the Barriolo family, as Rowe now had reason to believe, it would be a substantive collar. Neither cartel would send street punks to pick up that kind of cash. It would have to be someone highly trusted in the organization.

Rowe watched Cecelia, letting her stew for a few moments while he picked his tactic. There were a number of things Rowe liked about this woman, but she had a propensity for lying, and she didn't do it very well.

"How do you like working at the Bluebonnet House?" he asked.

She seemed startled by this abrupt shift. "I like it fine."

"Not a great part of town, though, eh?"

She eyed him warily.

"I was over there the other day looking around. The parking lot's full of potholes, the kids' trikes are all beat up. The whole place is kind of a dump, if you ask me."

"They're not running a day spa."

He leaned forward on his elbows. "No, I guess not. Looks like they're spiffing up the place, though. New rec room, new landscaping. A new dormitory to sleep some more of those kids whose dads like to slap them around."

Cecelia bit her lip.

"The director over there. Chantal? We talked briefly. She told me everything's on the up and up. They ran a big capital campaign to raise all the money they're using."

She sat perfectly still.

"Things were pretty sluggish for a while," he continued, "but back last October everything started to turn around. Local churches began donating money, thousands of dollars—all earmarked for the Bluebonnet House—

that just dropped into their collection plates every Sunday for about two months."

Cecelia watched him, her knuckles white as she clasped her hands together.

"You wouldn't happen to know anything about that, would you?"

She swallowed but remained silent. A full minute ticked by.

"I didn't think so." Rowe leaned back finally. "Just thought I'd ask."

Her shoulders seemed to relax fractionally. She stared down at her hands for a moment, then back up at him. "I wouldn't be here if I didn't really need your help."

"I believe that."

"You get a chance to apprehend two well-connected criminals. But I can't go out there empty-handed. And if I don't go . . ." She looked down, shook her head, looked back up at him. "It's not an option. I have to go. Will you help me?"

T-Bone turned onto Rosedale Avenue and drove past a park where children were busy sliding and climbing. Celie watched them, feeling wistful and thinking how nice it would be to trade lives with one of those women sitting on the benches. She'd give anything to spend a leisurely Saturday afternoon chatting with girlfriends and watching her toddler play.

Then the park was behind them and the Expedition rolled to a stop in front of a small yellow house with pale blue shutters.

"We're here," he announced.

Celie glanced around. *This* was it? The house looked all wrong. Not only was the color scheme too feminine, the quaint little postwar bungalow actually had a wreath on the door and flower boxes beneath the windows.

"Are you sure you got the address right?" Celie asked. She'd asked T-Bone to track down McAllister's home address while she was meeting with Rowe.

"It's six seventy-two," T-Bone said, nodding at the plain white house across the street.

Celie checked the numbers on the curb. The house had a simple, well-manicured lawn. No flowers. No decorations. That made more sense.

Just then McAllister appeared in the side yard, pushing a lawn mower. He wore only gym shorts, a faded black baseball cap, and Tevas. He'd just finished emptying a load of grass clippings into a black garbage bag when he spotted the Expedition. Keeping an eye on it, he knotted the plastic yellow ties and heaved the bag over his shoulder.

Celie got out of the SUV, and he stopped.

"I shouldn't be too long," she told T-Bone. "Maybe half an hour? You can go do whatever, and I'll call you when I need a ride home."

T-Bone glanced up and down the street. "I'll wait here," he said, cutting the engine.

"Suit yourself."

Celie slammed shut the door and made her way across the thick, green lawn. McAllister watched her, his face unreadable. His biceps bulged from the weight of the Hefty bag, but he didn't seem to notice. Celie approached him, trying not to gape at the broad expanse of his chest. His muscles were slick and shiny, and her stomach tightened.

"I hope you don't mind my stopping by," she said. "I wanted to give you an update."

He looked over her shoulder, and his eyes narrowed. "Who's that?"

"My bodyguard. He took me to the meeting this afternoon."

His gaze veered back to her face. "Give me a minute," he said gruffly.

He was still angry, Celie realized as he turned his back on her and hauled the bag to the curb. She was fairly sure it was the press conference comment, but she didn't regret making it. He'd wanted to be at the meeting today, but no matter what he'd said, Celie hadn't trusted him not to be there as a reporter. Plus, even if he'd left his reporter's notebook behind, she valued her privacy too much to let him in on all the messy details of her life. The less he knew about what she'd done and what she planned to do, the more she could control the situation. The more she could control him.

Or so she hoped. Clearly, he was still ticked off, which made him difficult to predict.

She followed him as he steered the mower up the drive. He stowed it in a rickety structure that at some point probably had been a one-car garage but now served as a storage shed. Celie waited beside his Jeep, her loose cotton skirt billowing around her calves, as she watched him lock the door with a padlock. Then he turned to face her and planted his hands on his hips.

"You should have let me come with you," he said.

She couldn't see his eyes well beneath the brim of the baseball cap, but his tone told her he was seething.

God, he had an amazing build. She stood in front of him, trying to breathe normally while she struggled not to stare. But merely averting her eyes didn't help because the rest of her senses were on high alert. He smelled like fresh-cut grass and male sweat, and even the hostile timbre of his voice was seductive. Everything she'd come over to tell him flew straight out of her head, and she had to fight the urge to reach out and run her fingertips over his washboard stomach.

"Come inside," he said. "I need a drink."

He led her up a few concrete steps to the back door. The screen squeaked as he pulled it back, and then he pushed the wooden door open and held it for her.

She stepped into the house and paused a moment to let her eyes adjust to the shade. The kitchen was surprisingly spacious, but not fancy. Stand-alone appliances, linoleum floor, white walls, mint green tile counters. Very 1950s *Leave It to Beaver*. An old-fashioned telephone shelf was built into the far wall, but, instead of a phone, the nook was occupied by a pile of unopened mail.

"You really live here?" she couldn't help asking. Even without the flower boxes, it seemed so domestic.

"I'm renting." He abandoned his dirt-caked sandals on the back stoop and went straight to the fridge.

Celie had expected more of a bachelor pad, something along the lines of his red speedboat. A bachelor pad would have been easy to hate. She would have pictured him bringing other women home and been completely turned off. But this place actually felt lived in, not like some chic apartment designed to impress girls. She walked across the kitchen and peeked at the living room.

Black leather couch. Matching armchair. Expensive-looking flat-screen TV. On the floor near the front door sat a milk crate filled with brightly colored, neatly coiled ropes, probably something he used for rappelling or rock climbing.

This room was more what she'd envisioned.

But then there were the glossy wood floors, which matched the floor-to-ceiling built-in bookcases. The shelves were crammed with hardbacks, paperbacks, and yellow-spined *National Geographic*s. Celie was dying to step closer and read some of the book titles. She was curious to know what he liked.

"Thirsty?"

She whirled around. He was standing there in the light of the open refrigerator, resting a tanned forearm on the door as he leaned down and rooted around inside. The muscles in his back rippled, and Celie promptly forgot whatever he'd just asked her.

He straightened and looked at her. "I'm having water. Want some?"

Suddenly she couldn't breathe, let alone talk. What had she been thinking, avoiding him for so long? She'd never, *ever* had a chance to be with a man like him. He was perfect. Beautiful. Give the guy a slingshot and he could pass for Michelangelo's *David*. Just the thought of his putting his hands on her made her dizzy.

He closed the fridge with his elbow as he unscrewed the top to his water. By the time he got the bottle to his lips, she was nearly panting. He stopped, midswig, and lowered the bottle. "You okay?"

She needed to leave. Now. If she stayed here so much

as a minute longer, she was going to throw herself at him.

A dull roaring filled her ears, and her feet refused to move. She experienced a déjà vu taking her back to that day in the storage unit when she'd discovered the cash. She'd heard roaring then, too, as she'd stared at all that money, knowing she should stay far away from it. It didn't belong to her. She had no business taking it, and yet she couldn't resist. It was the answer to one of her problems, unexpectedly sitting right there under her nose.

She had the same feeling now. *This* man. *This* instant. God, she could really have him. She could just reach out and touch him and answer all those burning questions she'd had for years.

What was so great about sex? Why did everyone care so much about it? All her life, she'd never understood. And, if anything, she'd avoided looking for answers. She was overwhelmed with the sudden certainty that if anyone on this earth could show her, it was John McAllister.

"Celie?" Frowning, he stepped closer.

She lifted an unsteady hand and took off his baseball cap. Waves of damp brown hair fell forward, but not before she caught the spark of heat in his eyes.

"Don't do that." His voice was low, almost like a growl.

"What?" She held his cap at her side, and the warmth of his body heat seeped into her fingertips.

"Look at me that way." He leaned closer, and she smelled grass again and sweat. "Not unless you plan to do something about it this time."

She eased her head back, tipped her chin up, and

stared him straight in the eye. Everything she needed, everything she was feeling, she wanted him to see it. Time seemed to stop as she stood there with her heart racing, wondering what he would do.

Then he did exactly what she'd expected—he dipped his head down and kissed her.

CHAPTER
12

It was like a levee bursting, in her mind, in her body. She was inundated with so many sensations: his lips hard against hers, the warmth of his hands, the soft little noises that were coming from her own throat. Then there was something flat behind her shoulders, and she realized he'd backed her against the wall. The solid weight of his body pressed into her, and she stood on tiptoes and squirmed against him, trying to line things up just right.

"Jesus Christ," he muttered against her temple. The rest of it was lost, though, as she yanked his head down for another kiss. He tasted so good, and she couldn't get enough of his hips pinned against her, his tongue delving into her mouth. She skimmed her hands down his back. She loved the taut muscles, the valley of his spine, the smooth feel of his skin beneath his shorts.

He pulled back abruptly. "I need a shower," he gasped. "Give me two minutes."

She didn't want him to shower. She liked him hot and glistening and smelling like summertime. Plus, if he left her for even a moment, she might chicken out. And she wanted to do this.

He raised his eyebrows. "One minute?"

Instead of answering, she trailed a hand down her chest, unfastening the buttons of her blouse.

His gaze dropped, and he looked pained. "God, Celie. I swear, just give me thirty seconds."

But then she shrugged her shoulders, and her shirt fell to the floor, and the next thing she knew, his head was burrowed against her neck and he'd filled his hands with her breasts. She felt the scrape of his stubble against her skin as he made his way down, down. His hands cupped her hips, and she started to get alarmed, but then suddenly he lifted her up and wrapped her legs around his waist.

"You're coming with me," he said.

She clutched his neck and squealed as he stumbled into the living room. "Oh my God, put me down!" she sputtered, laughing. She was too heavy for this. He'd probably throw out his back, and she'd die of embarrassment. "McAllister! I mean it!"

"No way."

He carried her into a darkened corridor, and then through another doorway into a small bathroom. He set her down on a pedestal sink and reached into the shower to turn on the faucet.

"Takes a second to warm up," he said, breathing hard.

And before she could reply, his mouth was back on hers. His kiss was rough and demanding, and she could taste all that pent-up need. She felt a cool draft against her skin as he unhooked her bra and slid it down her arms. Then his mouth was hot on her breast, pulling and nipping, and she yelped.

His head jerked up. "Sorry."

"No, it's just . . . good."

If possible, the look in his eyes became even more heated. He kissed her neck, clutching her thighs through the thin cotton of her skirt. He eased her forward, off the sink, so she was standing again, and she felt his hands tugging at her clothes. Then suddenly fabric pooled at her feet and she was naked, right there in front of him.

"How did you . . . ?"

Before she could finish, she looked down and saw that he was naked, too. Her courage vanished. Just like that. She looked up at him and tried to speak, but no words came out.

He seemed to sense her shift in mood, because the groping stopped and he looked at her for a long moment. Then he drew her into his arms and pressed a kiss against her forehead. "It's okay," he murmured.

She felt him, like a steel rod, jutting against her. She leaned her cheek against his chest, listening to his heart hammer as she tried to relax, but her throat felt so tight she couldn't breathe. She heard the steady thrumming of the shower as the bathroom filled with steam. Why couldn't she do this? Tears stung the backs of her eyelids, and she felt mortified.

"Come on," he whispered.

And then he took her by the hand and stepped into the shower. He didn't look at her body, just her eyes, as if he knew she felt vulnerable. She took a deep breath and stepped in beside him.

He turned her so that her back was to him and the hot water sluiced into the space between them. He kissed the back of her neck, and she felt his fingers loosening her ponytail. Then he combed his hands through her hair as she stood there under the streaming water and closed her eyes.

Minutes passed as the water splashed over them. His strong hands kneaded her shoulders, and her fears seemed to swirl down the drain.

"Relax," he murmured in her ear.

She nodded, although that was the last thing she could do. His hands glided lower, slowly, over her arms and hips, over her stomach and thighs, until her body started to quiver. He circled an arm around her waist and pulled her back against him. She tipped her head back and let him touch her everywhere he wanted to, everywhere she needed him to, as steam surrounded them and the tension gathered inside her.

Finally, she turned into him and brought his mouth down to hers, and all she could think about was how much she craved this man, everything about him. The kiss went on and on until she knew they were both aching from it.

He started to step away, but she caught his arm.

"Let me get a condom," he said.

But she didn't want him to leave, and she didn't want a condom either. "Are you healthy?" she asked.

His brow furrowed. "Yeah."

"Then you don't need one."

She tried to kiss him again, but he pulled back.

"You're on the Pill?"

She nodded. It was a lie, but she couldn't bring herself not to tell it. Whatever this was, whatever chance she was taking, she didn't want to think about it too much.

She stared up at him. His hair was dark and wet and slicked back from his face, making his blue eyes stand out even more than usual. She saw something guarded in his gaze, that skepticism she'd seen so many times before. He had good instincts about people, but she did, too.

"Please?" she heard herself say. "I want to feel you."

His eyebrows tipped up at the words. He reached for her hands and fastened them around his neck. "Hold on," he said. And then he lifted her up, just as effortlessly as before, and lowered her onto him.

It was hot and painful, and she sank her teeth into his shoulder to keep from crying out. Her back pressed against the cool tile, and he moved against her, slowly, steadily, until the pain was replaced by layers and layers of pleasure.

"John, I—"

"It's okay," he said tightly.

"But . . . oh my God."

"I've got you." His arms tightened around her and his breath heated her neck, and she felt like he was touching her very soul.

She clung to his shoulders, trying to get back some kind of control, but everything was too much, too strong. He pulled his head back and looked into her eyes. She saw the tension in his face and something else, too, something raw and desperate that sent her plunging over the edge, dragging him with her.

Stunned.

That's how she felt staring at his bare backside as he stood at the linen cabinet. He turned, and she snapped her gaze back up to his face. He handed her a blue bath towel, folded guy-style in a big square. As she wrapped it around her body, he pulled another towel out for himself and slung it low around his hips. Then he took her hand and led her down the hallway and into his bedroom, leaving a trail of wet footprints behind them.

The room was sparsely furnished, and a simple black spread covered the bed. McAllister pulled her down onto it and leaned over her, propping himself up on his elbow. A smile spread slowly across his face, and she felt her cheeks flush.

She had no idea what to say. It had been sweet, and then painful, and then amazingly *good,* and the first thing that came to her mind was "thank you," but somehow that sounded all wrong.

He twisted a lock of her wet hair around his finger and his smile faded. "Tell me about your meeting with Rowe," he said.

Wow. So much for talking about making love. But maybe that's not what it had been to him. A hollow space opened up in her chest as she tried to adjust to the idea. She'd known she wouldn't be any good at this, but she'd wanted to try it anyway. She didn't regret it, but the ramifications were starting to become clear. She was going to get her heart crushed here.

He dropped his head down and kissed her collarbone. "You'd better make it quick, because I have plans for tonight, and they don't involve fighting with you about this." His wet hair tickled her throat. "So what happened? They told you they'd send an agent, right?"

Okay. Clearly, this was no big deal to him. *She* was the one who felt like the world had just spun off its axis.

"Celie?" He paused and looked up at her. "Honey, you'd better start talking, or else I'm liable to get distracted."

"Yes, they offered to send an agent."

His forehead wrinkled. "And you said no, didn't you?"

"Yes, but Rowe insisted. He said I'd be much more likely to hinder the operation than help it. He agreed to let me be on the sidelines, though."

"I knew it," he muttered. He pushed himself up and sat on the edge of the bed. "Damn it, this is exactly why I wanted to go with you. I can't believe you think this is a good idea."

She sat up on her elbows. "I can't just sit at home while all this happens without me."

"Why not?"

She scoffed. "Because it's not right. This is *my* problem. I feel guilty enough getting agents involved—"

"It's their job to get involved. They're trained."

"Yes, but what if someone gets hurt? God, as if I don't have enough guilt in my life already."

He shot her a disbelieving look. "*You* have guilt? What the hell for? You're a saint."

The hollow in her chest grew bigger. He didn't understand her at all. "Well, let's see. I feel guilty for stealing two hundred thousand dollars. I feel guilty for lying to law enforcement. I feel guilty for spending years with a man who was helping put drugs into the hands of children while I was busy *playing tennis.*"

"That wasn't your fault. Your only mistake was marrying a prick."

She sat up and plunged on, just to prove to herself how little he knew her. "I feel guilty for being jealous of my best friend. I feel guilty for contributing to the stress that caused my dad's heart attack. I feel guilty for—"

"Stop it."

"—avoiding my mother all the time."

"This is crap. You've spent your entire adult life helping other people. Why can't you accept someone else's help for a change?"

I feel guilty for lying to you. She wanted to say it, but she didn't have the nerve. He was looking at her with so much intensity, she was scared to think how he'd react.

He'd be furious. And he'd be right.

"I don't expect you to understand," she said.

He shook his head and looked away. Something out the window caught his eye, and he crossed the room to peer through the blinds.

"Oh my gosh, T-Bone!" she squeaked, realizing what he was staring at. "I told him I'd only be a minute!"

McAllister scowled at her. "His name's *T-Bone?* Are you fucking kidding me?"

She gave him a sharp look. "His name's Tom. And I need to go tell him—"

"Whoa, whoa, whoa," he said, catching her arm as she tried to leave the room to track down her clothes. "*I'll* go talk to him. I'll tell him to take a hike because you're staying with me tonight."

She froze. He wanted her to stay. Was this his usual procedure, or did he actually enjoy her company? Maybe he just wanted to make love again. Or . . . whatever he thought they'd just done. Maybe she did, too, and who cared what they called it? They didn't have to call it anything. They could just *be* together, in the moment, not analyzing everything to death.

"If I stay here, I don't want to talk about this anymore," she said. "I don't like arguing with you."

"Fine. We'll find something else to do." He looked her up and down, and she felt like he could see right through her towel. "You like hamburgers?"

"Um . . . sure."

"I've got some in the fridge. We can grill out tonight if you want." He glanced at the window. "Or maybe I can grill out, and you can stay inside. Lemme throw on some clothes and go talk to *T-Bone.*"

She took a deep breath. This was crazy. *She* was crazy. She was going to spend the night with him in his cozy little house and have incredible, decadent, no-strings-attached sex.

With her luck, she'd probably fall in love with him before the burgers came off the grill.

John woke up with a start. He'd heard a noise—

Slam.

The screen door. He sat up and glanced at the empty space beside him in bed.

"Celie?"

He walked through the darkened house and found her sitting on his back steps in the dark. What the hell was she doing? It had to be 3:00 in the morning.

He pushed the screen open and stepped outside.

"It's nice here," she whispered.

He sank down beside her on the stoop. All the lights were switched off, and he could hardly see her there in the shadows. But he felt her body heat.

"Not much to see." He stroked a hand down her back. She was wearing one of his old T-shirts, and, for some crazy reason, that made him happy.

"Yeah, but it's so still tonight." She sighed wistfully. "I miss being outside."

His neighbor's porch light was the only thing illuminating her face, and he couldn't see her expression well.

"You live right next to a greenbelt," he said. "Don't you ever get outdoors?"

She shrugged, and he suddenly understood what she was telling him. She didn't go outside much, and certainly not at night. Forget taking a stroll on the lakefront or exploring Austin's hike-and-bike trails. The woman was afraid to go out alone, especially after dark.

John couldn't imagine living that way. Some of his fondest memories were of taking in the view from some remote cliff side or watching the sun go down over a deserted stretch of beach.

He picked up Celie's hand, and she leaned into him, resting her cheek on his shoulder. She smelled like soap and sex, and the combination was an unbelievable turn-on.

"I want to take you out on my boat sometime."

"We just went on your boat."

"Yeah, but I mean for real. Just to relax. No distractions." He'd slipped his hand around her waist and found her skin soft and warm beneath his shirt.

"No distractions at all?"

He'd kissed her neck. "Well, maybe a few."

Celie spent the better part of Sunday hiding. She ran errands with T-Bone all morning. She spent nearly two hours in the fitness room in the afternoon. After a quick shower, she sought refuge in Dax's apartment.

"You can't do this forever, you know," Dax told her as they hung out together in his kitchen.

His apartment was the mirror image of hers, but besides the floor plan and the ivory paint, they had virtually nothing in common. Dax had taken the time to decorate his place in a theme that he described as rustic-modern. Furniture made of glass, steel, and black leather competed for attention with hand-carved wooden statues and trinkets from around the world. The walls were lined with black and white photographs of famous baseball parks.

Celie hadn't had the heart for decorating anything since her divorce. Her efforts had consisted of throwing down a new bath mat and buying a ficus.

Celie sat on Dax's leather bar stool and toyed with an African fertility totem. The statue was a short male warrior with an exceedingly large penis.

"Sweetie? Are you listening?" Dax asked. "You're going to have to face the music sometime. That man doesn't seem like the type to give up easily."

"Says who?" Celie asked, although she suspected Dax was right. "Maybe he's relieved. From everything I can gather, he values his freedom."

Dax eyed her across the chopping block in his kitchen.

He was making sangria for a barbecue he'd been invited to this afternoon. "Well, I barely know the man," he admitted, squeezing lime juice into a bowl. "But if someone spackled *my* ceiling, I'd think he had more in mind than just a one-night hookup."

"Well, what if that's all *I* want? I just barely got divorced. The last thing I need right now is a relationship."

Dax gave her a baleful look. "You can tell everybody else that, sweet pea, but I know better. You like this man. A lot. I think you're doing a preemptive dump."

"A preemptive dump." Celie ran her fingers over the smooth wooden statue. For some reason, it reminded her of McAllister.

Dax shrugged and sliced up an orange. "Sure. You expect him to drop you, so you drop him first and pretend not to care. I've done it a few times myself. It's a textbook defense mechanism."

Celie sighed. "And does it work for you?"

He plunked the orange slices into a pitcher of red wine. "That depends on who I'm dumping. If the guy's like Richard, he never calls again, and we all move on. If he's like Sebastian, one of the few guys I've dated who actually had any *backbone*, then he'll fight you on it."

Dax's phone rang, and he wiped his hands on a dish towel before turning around to answer it.

So the question was, did John McAllister have any backbone? Celie knew the answer without even having to mull it over.

"Well, funny you should ask," Dax said into the receiver. "She's sitting right here."

Celie shook her head frantically as Dax passed her the phone.

"He's like Sebastian," Dax whispered.

Celie rolled her eyes and took the receiver. "Hello?"

"Don't go anywhere," McAllister said. "I'm coming up."

13

Celie left Dax to his sangria and walked down the hall to wait for McAllister. The elevator doors dinged open, and then he was coming toward her, pinning her in place with his gaze as those long, tall legs ate up the hallway. Just seeing all that macho directed at her made her breath catch. Today he wore jeans and cowboy boots and a tight black T-shirt that seemed to match his mood. He plucked the key from her hand and unlocked the door, then pushed it open and entered her apartment.

She thought he was just being rude until she saw him glancing around and realized he was checking the place out. He went down the hallway, and a second later she heard her shower curtain being swept back. As he looked in the bedroom, Celie secured the locks and headed into the kitchen to get a soft drink from the fridge.

When she turned around, McAllister was standing beside the kitchen counter glowering at her. She braced herself to be yelled at, but then he seemed to make a last-minute effort to cool his temper. He leaned back against the counter and crossed his ankles.

"Am I missing something here?" he asked.

"What do you mean?" She popped open her Diet Coke.

"Like the part where we agree it's okay for you to take off without so much as a conversation?"

"I left you a note—"

"A fucking thank-you note?"

"It wasn't a thank-you note!" He made it sound ridiculous.

"'*McAllister: Thank you. —Cecelia.*' Did I leave something out? Oh, like how you taped it to my mirror and it took me ten minutes to find it after I woke up and I thought you might have been kidnapped!"

Celie rolled her eyes and opened one of her cabinets. She got down a glass and filled it with ice.

"Does everyone get a note, or did I just get lucky?"

She whirled to face him. What was he insinuating? She'd practically told him she hadn't been with anyone since Robert.

But then she'd also told him she was on the Pill. Being a guy, he'd probably assumed that meant she was having sex with someone. Or several someones.

She watched him for a moment, oscillating between anger over the way he was talking to her and guilt over the way she'd lied to him. She decided to go on the offensive.

"Let me ask you something," she said, crossing her arms. "Have you ever hooked up with someone"—she purposely used Dax's term because it sounded so emotionally distant—"and then left without a conversation?"

He blinked at her, and she knew that he had. She laughed. "See? I knew it. It's okay for you to treat things casually, but the minute someone else does it, you get upset." She poured her drink and bit back the rest of the things she could have said. She didn't really want this argument. "I'm just trying to simplify this for both of us."

"What the fuck does that mean?"

Again with the language.

"Look," she said, "I know you're not looking for anything serious, and neither am I, and I didn't see the point in drawing everything out." She had to force herself to meet his gaze for the next part. "We were attracted to each other long before last night, and we finally got it out of our systems. It was probably good that it happened, but I think we should move on now."

He laughed, but he didn't sound amused. "We got it out of our systems." He stepped toward her. "*That's* how you would describe last night?"

Not really. Not at all. She'd been yearning for him all day. Just thinking of all the ways he'd touched her made her light-headed. She broke eye contact and looked down at his scuffed brown boots. The boots stepped closer, and she glanced up, realizing belatedly that she'd just issued some kind of challenge, and McAllister, being McAllister, felt compelled to leap on it.

"Maybe that's not the best way to put it," she said, "but you know what I mean."

He raised his eyebrows. "No, I really don't. Why don't you explain it to me?"

She licked her lips and tried to get her thoughts together. "I just think . . ."

He took another step closer planted a hand on either side of her on the counter. "You really think you've gotten this out of your system?"

Her heart was racing. His voice was low and sultry again, just like last night after dinner, when he'd taken her back to his bedroom and lavished her with attention.

"Do you?"

She had to tilt her head back to look him in the eye. "Yes."

"Well, I sure as hell haven't."

She cleared her throat. "You haven't?"

"Not by a long shot."

Kate spotted Rowe among the sweat-drenched joggers at Town Lake. She couldn't see his face, but there was no mistaking the mile-wide shoulders and ramrod straight posture. He wore a navy blue T-shirt tucked neatly into gray athletic shorts.

Even jogging, he looked like a fed.

Kate lengthened her stride until she was just behind him. He had a nice back. And the front was good, too, judging from the looks he was getting from the women who passed him. He didn't acknowledge their glances—at least not that Kate could tell—but she knew he noticed. The man noticed everything.

Kate drafted him for fifty yards or so, until she was certain she was getting on his nerves. Then she turned on the gas and came up alongside him.

"Nice shirt," she said conversationally. She'd expected some sort of FBI logo, but instead he had U2 emblazoned across his chest. She never would have pegged him for a fan.

He didn't even look at her. "Are you stalking me, Kepler?"

"What makes you think that?"

She focused on matching his pace. She was in terrific shape, but his legs were much longer than hers.

"Four voice-mail messages in two days. Followed by an e-mail." He shot her a glare.

"And your point is?" She tried not to look too proud of herself. Tracking down the personal e-mail of an FBI agent had been an interesting challenge, and she'd relished every minute of it. Never in a million years would she tell him how she'd done it, though. She'd probably broken a few laws.

"How'd you know I'd be here?"

That part she could tell. "I went by your motel. Ran into Nick in the parking lot, and he mentioned you'd been coming here in the evenings."

Rowe's jaw tightened at this news. She couldn't tell whether he was pissed she'd tracked down his whereabouts or pissed she was now on a first-name basis with his partner. Either way, she'd accomplished her goal. Her primary source was stonewalling her, and she intended to chip away at his indifference until she got information.

For several minutes they ran in silence, arms and legs

pumping, breath huffing out in unison. Rowe gradually stepped up the pace until the jogging was a distant memory and they were engaged in a flat-out race. Kate wolfed down air and pressed to keep up. He had the legs, yes, and the stamina, but she had the spring of youth in her step. If he thought he could beat her, he was mistaken.

"Hang on." He came to an abrupt stop by a water fountain and snagged her T-shirt.

She whirled to face him, pressing her hands against the small of her back as she sucked down air. Her skin was soaked. It had to be ninety degrees out.

"You need water," he said.

She bent over and blotted her face with the tail of her shirt. "*We* need water," she corrected, trying not to wheeze.

"Ladies first."

She took a turn at the fountain. The water felt wonderful on her parched throat, and she dipped her forehead into the cool stream.

When she straightened, he was watching her.

"You ever run track?" He took a long drink.

"Four years in high school. Now I just do it for fun."

He nodded.

A woman approached the fountain with a jogging stroller, and Kate and Rowe stepped aside. Kate's breathing was under control, but it felt like lava was pumping through her veins. She'd probably overdone it with that last burst of speed.

Rowe watched her, his face inscrutable. "You don't go away, do you?"

She shielded her eyes from the evening sun and squinted at him. "No."

He muttered something and looked away. "What is it you want?"

"You promised me IDs on the Public Storage guys."

"I said I'd try."

"Did you get them?"

"The Bureau doesn't like to share information with the media in an ongoing criminal investigation."

"That's bullshit. You guys use the media all the time, especially when it comes time to make an important arrest. We're your PR department."

He didn't respond.

"Besides," she continued, "you wouldn't even have that tape if it weren't for me. Come on. Who are they?"

"People you don't want to know." He blew out a breath. "You need to stay away from this and let investigators handle it."

"Oh, really? And how are you handling it?"

"That's not your concern."

"You must have a plan."

"What? You think I'm going to tell you?"

"At least give me a hint. Otherwise I'll have to keep stalking you."

He looked her up and down, his expression sour.

"Pretty please?" She smiled sweetly and tried to activate her dimple.

"Something's happening Thursday," he finally told her. "That's all you're getting."

Score. The dimple always worked. "What kind of something? A sting operation?"

She caught a flare of irritation in his eyes, which she took to mean she'd guessed right.

"I can't say. But cool your jets until Friday morning, and I'll call you with an update."

An exclusive. This was going to be good. "Call me Thursday night. That way I've got it in before pressrun."

"We'll see." He glanced at his watch. "That's it for right now. You need a ride home?"

She was being dismissed. But at least she'd made progress. Now she had a tip and a time frame. If she tracked him down Thursday, she might even be able to get an eyewitness account of whatever happened.

"I'm parked over there." She nodded toward the gravel parking lot nearby. "Thanks for the help. I'll be waiting for your call."

She gave him a little wave and jogged off.

John lay in Celie's bed feeling physically spent, but completely restless.

He listened to her slow, steady breathing. For hours now, she'd been sound asleep, her arm draped over his chest, her naked body nestled alongside him. Every time she shifted, her breast pressed against his rib cage. He looked down at her. She was soft, she was beautiful, she was the sweetest woman he'd ever been with.

And he had no idea what the hell he was doing here.

He'd talked his way into her bed, and now here he was, feeling like shit. He couldn't explain it, but something was off. His instincts were buzzing, and he knew he should be listening to them.

Celie sighed heavily and tugged the sheet up. He used

the opportunity to ease away from her and slip out of bed. Soundlessly, he crept from the room.

Her apartment was silent except for the faint hum of the air-conditioning. John smelled garlic from the bag of leftovers they'd brought home from the Italian restaurant, the bag they'd neglected to refrigerate, he realized now, because as soon as they'd walked in the door, he'd pulled Celie into the bedroom to show her all the things he'd had on his mind during dinner.

He picked up the bag from the coffee table and deposited it in the fridge. She had a woman's fridge, filled with fat-free yogurt and salad stuff and diet soda. He had no idea why she was on a diet—he thought she looked hot—but he'd spent enough time around women to know it was pointless to try to talk them out of shit like that.

John snagged a bottle of water from the fridge, twisted off the cap, and downed it in two long gulps. He stood in front of the kitchen window for a moment, staring at the dark greenbelt below. Then he retraced his steps across the living room and hallway, pausing beside the bathroom door. A seashell nightlight glowed next to the mirror. He stepped up to the sink, leaned his palms on the counter, and stared at his shadowy reflection.

He was such a dick. He'd made it his mission in life to get her to trust him, and, now that she had, he was ready to bolt.

"Damn," he muttered, turning on the faucet. He splashed water on his face and glared up at himself. What was his problem?

For a few minutes, he just stood there, letting ugly, suspicious thoughts rattle around in his brain as he studied his reflection. And then he realized his problem—*he* didn't trust *her*. Shaking his head in disgust, he gave into temptation and pulled back the mirrored door.

The contents of Celie's medicine cabinet stared back at him.

CHAPTER

14

Rowe found Cecelia in the Bluebonnet House kitchen Tuesday afternoon, surrounded by peanut-butter sandwiches.

"Looks like I'm just in time," he said, entering the room.

She looked up, startled. "Hi."

"I thought you wrote grants around here."

She picked up a slice of wheat bread and slathered it with Skippy. "I do. But I also help fulfill them when the money comes in."

He nodded at the paper plates lined up on the counter. "Free lunch program?"

"After-school nutrition." She placed the sandwich beside some apple slices. "We just got funding from a private foundation."

Rowe leaned his hip against the stainless steel counter and looked around.

"Watch your suit," she said, reaching behind him to move a sticky peanut-butter lid.

"I just stopped by to tell you you're cleared."

Her eyebrows arched. "Cleared?"

"To participate Thursday. If you still want to."

"I do."

That's what he'd thought she'd say. Rowe didn't think it was a good idea, but she was the contact person, so they needed her nearby.

"The decoy agent wants to meet you Thursday morning to go over everything," he said. "The basic plan is for you to leave your apartment in your own vehicle and drive to the site, but by the time you arrive there, our agent will be at the wheel pretending to be you. The sharpshooters and I will be stationed on and around the bridge. At the designated time, our agent will get out of the vehicle and carry out the exchange."

"But these guys have seen me. They'll know—"

"We have no intention of letting them get that close, trust me."

But Rowe doubted she trusted much of anybody.

"And you have to wear a Kevlar vest. Even though you're not to leave the car."

She nodded. "Sounds reasonable."

"Any chance I can talk you out of this?"

She wiped her hands on her jeans and screwed the top back on the peanut butter. "Nope."

"Your bodyguard and your boyfriend are not invited."

"My boyfriend?"

Rowe just looked at her. She had to realize they'd been watching her. It was a documented fact that she'd spent the better part of the weekend behind closed doors with the reporter.

They hadn't been seen together in two days, though, a fact that had been the subject of speculation among some of the younger members of Rowe's team. Evidently, Cecelia Wells and John McAllister were the unwitting stars of a reality show whose viewing audience consisted of bored federal employees.

"Okay, so I'll come alone," she said. "Any other requirements?"

"That's it." Rowe watched her for a moment, wondering what made this woman tick. She'd put her life at risk to give a small fortune to charity. But what was in it for her? In his experience, people weren't that altruistic.

Whatever her reasons, he supported what she was doing. He'd seen far too many abused kids during the course of his career to want to discourage one of the few people trying to help. He'd told her as much during their last meeting, although she'd never actually acknowledged what she'd done with Saledo's money.

She stood before him now, searching his face. "What are the chances this thing will go off without a hitch?"

He thought about lying to her. But she'd been through a lot, and he figured she could handle it. "I'd say, slim to none."

Her eyes widened.

"But who knows?" he said, backpedaling now. "Maybe it'll go perfectly. I've just always been a pessimist."

• • •

Celie squirmed in the hard plastic chair and glanced at the clock. It had been ten minutes since she'd given her name to the receptionist. Either McAllister wasn't here at his office, or he was avoiding her.

This wasn't a good idea. She'd give it two more minutes—three, tops—and then she'd leave. She gnawed on her cuticle and watched the clock, waiting with waning hopes for McAllister's tall frame. She hadn't seen or heard from him since Monday morning when he'd left her apartment in a rush. At the time, he'd claimed he was late for work, but now that it was Wednesday, she couldn't ignore the needling certainty that there was more to his abrupt departure.

The glass door marked NEWSROOM pushed open. But, instead of McAllister, a slender brunette wearing black jeans and a DKNY T-shirt emerged. She walked straight up to Celie.

"Cecelia Wells? I'm Kate Kepler."

Kate Kepler . . . The name rang a bell, but Celie couldn't place it. She shook the woman's outstretched hand.

"I'm sorry. I'm waiting for John McAllister. Are you his . . ." Assistant? Coworker? Fling of the week?

"We work together. I heard you were looking for John, and I just thought I'd tell you he's out on assignment right now, so—" Her gaze shifted over Celie's shoulder. "Oh, wait. Here he is."

Celie turned to see McAllister breeze through the front doors. He wore a press pass around his neck and a tie, of all things. He spotted Celie, froze, and then crossed the foyer to frown down at her.

"What are you doing here?"

Celie stared up at him, confused by the blatant hostility.

"Good to meet you, Cecelia." The young reporter smiled at Celie before heading back into the newsroom.

Celie looked at McAllister again, hoping she'd misread the situation. If anything, he looked even angrier than he had at first.

"I just—" She cleared her throat. "You didn't answer your phone, so I thought I'd just—"

"I didn't want to talk to you."

The pain shocked her. She looked up into those intense blue eyes and realized he was furious.

A man brushed past them, and Celie stepped out of his way. They were standing in the middle of the lobby, and Celie noticed the receptionist seemed to be just a little too intent on her Office Depot catalogue. She was listening to every word.

"Is there somewhere else we can talk?" Celie asked.

"*Now* you want to talk? A little late, don't you think?"

"What is your problem?"

He looked away from her and shook his head.

"Fine. You want to talk? Let's go." He grabbed her hand and pulled her through the glass doors into the newsroom.

Celie let him tow her behind him, too stunned to speak. What was he *doing*? He pulled her past cubicles, desks, and ringing phones. Several interested gazes followed them through the noisy room. After passing a series of windowed offices, McAllister turned down a row of cubicles and stopped at one in the middle. He pulled the press pass off his neck, tossed it on the desk, and leaned over the short, padded wall to the next cube.

"Hey, can I borrow your chair? Thanks."

He grabbed an empty plastic chair from a startled co-worker and dragged it into his cube. He plunked himself into the desk chair and nodded at Celie.

"Sit down. Talk."

Her cheeks burned. She couldn't believe he was treating her this way. And in front of his entire office. She was sure everyone within thirty feet was eavesdropping.

Celie hated being the center of attention. She sank into the chair and tried to swallow the lump in her throat.

"I'd like to know what's wrong," she said quietly.

McAllister's phone rang, and he stared at her for a long moment. Then he reached over and snatched it up. "McAllister. . . . Yeah." He turned his back on her and punched some buttons on his computer, bringing the screen to life. "Yeah, lemme check."

Celie took a deep breath and looked down at her lap. She was wearing a thin cotton sundress in pale blue. She'd put it on this morning thinking it looked pretty and feminine, and wondering if McAllister would see it this evening. Now she felt really, really stupid. Forget a dinner date. He was so upset with her, he probably wouldn't even see her again after this.

Whatever this was.

She looked up and caught him staring at her as he talked on the phone. He broke eye contact and turned back to his computer. "Yeah," he said. "It's running tomorrow. The follow-up runs Friday." He shuffled through a stack of folders, then turned toward her. "Here. Some light reading." He tossed a file in her lap.

Celie looked down at the manila folder. She opened it up and found a stack of printouts.

"World-Renowned Baby Doc Opens Clinic in Austin."

Celie's stomach clenched. She sifted through the papers and counted one, two, three stories about her specialist, all from the *Herald* archives. The light dawned. Her bathroom cabinet was crammed with fertility drugs prescribed by this man.

The last article was entitled "Miracle Babies!" and showed a young couple surrounded by smiling triplets.

She glanced up at McAllister. He was still on the phone, but his attention was fixed on her. She tried to read his face. Mostly she read fury, with some defiance mixed in.

He'd caught her in a lie, and he looked proud of himself. The clever investigative reporter who figured everything out.

Celie closed the folder and stood up. She placed the file on his desk, beside the computer.

"Hey, let me get back to you." He finally hung up the phone and turned to face her, arms crossed. "You still want to talk?"

"Not here."

"Shit, well, that's a problem. See, I've got work to do, and I can't exactly take the afternoon off to go hang out at your place and contribute to the cause. I might be able to get you a sample for the road, though. If you'll give me a minute—"

"I'm leaving," she said, shouldering her purse. "Call me when you're ready to have a real conversation."

He scowled. "Don't wait by the phone."

She wove back through the maze of cubicles, trying

to hold her head up and pretend she didn't notice all the curious glances.

John stared through his rain-streaked windshield, thinking he'd sell his goddamn soul for a cigarette. Smoking went with drinking, and he'd had way too much of one without the other tonight.

He'd spent most of the evening at The Ale House looking for some kind of solace. But women he could stand the sight of were in short supply tonight, and Jose Cuervo had left him twisting in the wind. John had just enough alcohol in his system to make him moody, but not nearly enough to put his problems out of his mind.

"Fuck," he muttered, thunking his forehead on the steering wheel. Water drummed against the top of the Jeep, reminding him what a shitty day this had been. He was going to have a monster headache tomorrow, and his life would be in the same sorry shape it was now.

What a weird fucking night. He'd had no trouble at all resisting the amazingly stacked blonde who'd rubbed up against him at the bar, but walking out of 7 Eleven without a pack of Camels had damn near killed him. And driving all the way home without taking a fifteen-minute detour past Celie's apartment? Shit, he couldn't do it. He didn't have the willpower.

He leaned his head back against the seat and stared up at her window. With the steady drizzle, he could make out little more than a blurry rectangle of glass. But the lights were on, had been since John's arrival twenty minutes ago.

John swigged his drink. He'd switched to Gatorade,

which was helping his body. It wasn't helping his state of mind, though. His brain was torturing him, feeding him images of Celie up there getting it on with T-Bone. Girls on the rebound were vindictive. John knew because he'd caught a few himself.

But Celie wouldn't do that. At least, he didn't think she would. He watched the flickering light in the window and tried to convince himself she was simply up there watching TV, or maybe she'd fallen asleep in front of it. Or maybe she was pacing her apartment, trying to think of a way to apologize.

There was no apology in the world that would ever be good enough. What she'd done was unforgivable.

But maybe she wasn't planning to apologize at all. John stared at her apartment and felt his anger seeping back. Maybe she was up there congratulating herself for duping him. Maybe she thought he'd gotten what he deserved— the playboy had finally been played.

John knew all about his reputation, the one he'd admittedly earned after fifteen years of partying. Hell, at one time, he'd even been proud of it.

Not anymore. Now he was sick of it—fed up with the bars and the clubs and the meaningless sex. The repetition of it all disgusted him. Pamela Price's murder had slapped him with the reality that life is short. And his, in particular, amounted to shit. He wanted more out of life than a string of interchangeable women and his name on the front of some newspaper that ended up lining a kid's hamster cage.

Celie's living room window went dark. She'd switched off the television and was probably on her way to bed now, probably slipping into one of those nightshirts she liked and sliding between crisp, cool sheets.

Alone.

At least he hoped she was alone. Just the thought of her up there with someone else made him crazy.

Suddenly he didn't give a shit about the lies. He just wanted to take her to bed again and forget everything else.

As if that were possible.

Hey, babe, mind if I use a condom this time? Since you fucking lied to me about being on the Pill?

Might just spoil the mood. Especially if she told him it didn't matter anyway—she was already pregnant with his kid. Or someone else's kid; that was possible, too. She'd been seeing a world-famous baby doctor, taking a whole mess of fertility drugs. Who knew what was going on inside that body of hers?

A sudden movement caught his eye, and John's focus veered to the side of the building, where a vehicle was leaving the garage. It was a silver SUV, looked like a BMW or a Volvo.

With a woman behind the wheel. A short, blond woman who bore a striking resemblance to Celie.

"Fuckin' A," he grumbled, starting his engine and gunning the Jeep out of the parking space. He punched the gas until he was right behind the SUV, close enough to see Celie's refection illuminated by his headlights in her rearview mirror. Where was she going this time of night? And whose car was that?

He laid on the horn, and she turned to look over her shoulder. She hesitated a moment and then pulled over.

• • •

McAllister was here.

It was the worst possible moment for him to show up, and yet there was his Jeep, right in her rearview mirror. She watched in her side mirror as he climbed from the Wrangler. In a few strides, he was beside her car and rapping on the window.

She didn't have *time* for this! With a shaking finger, she jabbed the button to lower the glass.

"What the hell are you doing?" His eyes were angry and bloodshot, and droplets of water streamed down his face.

"I'm just—"

"Do you have any idea how late it is? Where's your bodyguard?"

"I'm just running a quick errand. I ran out of"— What? What on earth could she be needing at this time of night?—"ice cream."

His eyebrows shot up. "*Ice* cream? At one A.M. in a fucking rainstorm? Are you out of your mind?"

Now he was making her mad. She glanced at the clock. And late. It was 12:49. She had eleven minutes left to get to some nightclub on South Lamar. Goatee Man had just called and given her fifteen *short* minutes. And if she didn't show, he was going to kill Enrique Ramos.

"Get in!" she squeaked.

For once, he didn't argue. He rounded the Volvo and jumped into the passenger side, bringing a few gallons of water with him on his clothes. Saledo's guy had promised to kill her, too, if she didn't come alone, but she'd already called the FBI, so what did it matter? McAllister could hide in the backseat.

Celie hit the gas before he'd even closed the door. "Put on your seat belt. I'm in a hurry."

"Yes, ma'am."

She skidded to a stop at the security gate and waited for what seemed like an eternity as it slid open. Then she shot through the opening with just inches to spare on either side.

She pulled out onto the highway, and the windshield started to cloud until she could barely see. She jabbed at buttons on the control panel until she found the defogger.

McAllister watched her from the passenger seat. "Nice ride," he quipped. "Kind of a mom mobile, though, don't ya think? They throw in a free soccer ball?"

She gave him a dirty look.

"You know, the last woman I knew who had one of these got her head blown off by one of Saledo's goons."

"You're making that up."

"'Fraid not."

Just drive, she told herself. She concentrated on the road and heard the tires squeal as she whipped around a bend. The road curved left again, and she fishtailed, barely missing the guardrail. If her heart hadn't already been at full gallop, the near-miss might have rattled her.

"That's some ice cream craving," he drawled.

"We're not going for ice cream."

"No shit. Where are we going?"

She blew out a breath. This was a disaster. Who cared what she told him anymore?

"Saledo's guys called me. The meeting's tonight."

A creative stream of curses erupted from his mouth.

"That was pretty much my reaction," she said. She wended her way down Ranch Road 2222, ignoring speed limits and warning signs. Robert had died on this very highway, at the hands of the very same people she was about to meet. The same men who'd kidnapped an innocent eleven-year-old boy.

"Did you call the feds yet?"

"Yes. Rowe's meeting me at Sixth and Lamar in five minutes. He's got the bag I'm supposed to deliver."

"*You're* supposed to deliver? I thought they were sending a look-alike!"

"They were," Celie said. "But she's not here, so they're sending me."

CHAPTER

15

Silence fell over the car as he absorbed this. For nearly a minute, the swishing of the wiper blades was the only sound.

"You're not going," he said firmly. "Tell those assholes to wait."

"I can't do that. They want to meet right now."

"Where the fuck is the agent?"

Celie blew out a breath. "San Antonio. They've got a couple of female agents here in town, but one is black and the other is five-ten. It would never work."

"So tell them to *wait*. You can't just go out there—"

"They've got Enrique." Celie sucked in a breath. A sob burst out, and she clamped a hand over her mouth.

He looked at her, eyes wide. "Enrique Ramos? The kid from the shelter?"

She nodded.

"How the hell did that happen?"

"They must have picked him up somewhere after school." Her voice quivered. "Or maybe he ran off. He does that sometimes."

"Fuck," McAllister muttered and looked out the window. They were doing sixty in a thirty-five on wet streets. "Want me to drive?"

She shook her head. At least driving gave her something to do besides get hysterical. She had to keep a level head. She took a deep breath.

A red light loomed ahead, and she would have raced through it had it not been for a Lincoln Town Car crossing the intersection. She jammed her foot on the brake, and the car rabbitted as the antilock mechanism kicked in.

"So, the FBI's bringing a bag for you?" he asked.

"Yeah. I think they've got some way to track the bills or maybe the duffel or something."

"And what's the strategy?"

She cursed mentally as another sedan rolled cautiously through the intersection. "They're going to try to apprehend these two guys right after the exchange. If they can't, they're going to follow the money."

She didn't say what they were both surely thinking. Something terrible could happen before the FBI got control of the situation.

Celie's cell phone chirped, and she jumped in her seat. The light turned green as she flipped open the phone.

"Hello?"

"New plan, bitch."

"How'd you get this number?"

"Be at the Quick Stop on I-35 and Riverside. Ten minutes."

"*What?* But you said—Hello? *Hello?*" She jerked the phone away from her ear and looked at the screen. Disconnected.

She tossed it in McAllister's lap. "Call Rowe! Tell him to get to the Quick Stop on Riverside and Interstate 35." She'd never get her hands on the money in time. And what about the sharpshooters? No one had time to get in place.

"What's his number?" McAllister asked.

"I don't know." In her rush, she'd left his business card on the kitchen counter. "Can you call the police? Maybe they have it."

"I have a better idea," he said, punching some numbers into the phone.

"What?"

But he wasn't paying attention. He turned away from her and looked out the window as the hills of west Austin flew past them. "Kate? Hey, it's me. Where are you, exactly?"

Kate shook her head to make sure she'd heard right. "Where *am* I?" She glanced at the clock. "I'm in bed."

"You got the number for that FBI guy? Agent Rowe?"

Kate kicked off the covers. "Yeah." She rolled out of bed and grabbed some jeans off the floor. "What's going on? Where are you?"

"I need you to call him. Tell him South Lamar's off. Tell him the meeting's been changed to the Speedy Stop—

What?" Kate heard a woman's voice in the background. "Scratch that. The *Quick* Stop at Riverside and I-35."

Kate fumbled in the dark for a pen. Screw it. She could remember everything he'd said. "I got it. What's happening there and when?"

"He'll know," McAllister said. "And tell him to haul ass."

She stubbed her toe on the doorjamb just as the call went dead. "Damn it!"

Slumping against the door frame, she stared at the phone. "McAllister? *McAllister?*" That was *it*?

"Son of a bitch," she muttered, scrolling through her speed dial list. She found Rowe's number and pushed Connect.

Rowe was already in position at the Whole Foods parking lot on Sixth and Lamar when Kate's call came in on his phone.

Crap. That was all he needed. He decided to ignore it.

"Shouldn't you get that?" Stevenski asked from the passenger seat of the Buick.

"Nah."

But she called again, and he reconsidered. What if she'd picked up something on the scanner? The local police didn't have wind of this, as far as Rowe knew, but it was always possible someone had slipped up. If so, he needed to know that.

"Rowe," he growled into the phone.

"South Lamar is off. The new meeting place is the Quick Stop at Riverside and I-35."

"How the hell—"

"Cecelia Wells is trying to reach you. She's with John McAllister, and they just got a phone call changing the plan."

He was speechless. That damn reporter had pulled Kate into this mess.

"You're sure it was her?"

"It was McAllister. And yes, I'm sure. They said to come fast."

Christ, this was turning into a circus. And now he and his team would have to pull this thing off without getting tripped up by the goddamn media. Or the rain. Or the utter lack of planning.

"Listen up, Kate. You stay away from this."

No response.

"I mean it. You're endangering yourself and other innocent people if you get involved. Do you hear me?"

"I hear you."

Rowe put his hand over the phone and turned to Stevenski. "Call Cecelia Wells on her mobile. Tell her to meet us four blocks east of the Quick Stop. Tell her *not* to make contact until she's received our package."

Kate was babbling in his ear.

"Did you hear what I said, Kate? This is getting more dangerous by the minute. Stay out of it."

"I *said*, I hear you."

"But you're not listening."

"It's my job to report the news. Federal agents busting prominent members of the Saledo cartel is news."

Goddamn it. "I'll give you an exclusive interview. Tonight. Just stay away from the scene and let me call you."

"Sorry, Rowe. Gotta run."

• • •

John watched Celie's face in the intermittent streetlights as they sped across town. She was sitting right beside him, but her thoughts looked to be a million miles away.

"So," he asked her, "what'd the fertility clinic charge you? Thirty? Forty thousand?"

She glanced over, obviously surprised. He was an asshole for bringing it up right now, but if she didn't know he was an asshole by this point, it was high time she learned.

"I figure you've been here almost eight months," he said. "That's what? Two rounds of in vitro? Plus meds and office visits?"

She looked away and mumbled something.

"What?"

"Three," she said. "Three rounds. It came to about sixty-eight thousand."

Sixty-eight thousand dollars to get pregnant. That was some fucking determination. She must really, *really* want to be a mom. Enough to rip off a drug kingpin. Enough to risk getting in trouble with the FBI.

Enough to lie to him.

"Are you pregnant now?" It was possibly the *most* inappropriate question he could ask her at this moment, but he had to know.

She looked at him apprehensively. "I'm not sure. It isn't likely, though. I've tried everything, and my body doesn't seem to want to cooperate."

He gazed out the window and shook his head.

"I'm sorry I didn't tell you," she said. "I didn't think you'd understand."

He sure as hell *didn't* understand. He understood even

less how she could lie to him repeatedly. For an entire weekend. How she could twine herself around him *naked* and tell him—

"I wouldn't expect anything. You know, from you."

Resentment bubbled up in his throat, and he tried to swallow it down. "You try to manipulate me into conceiving a *child* with you, and you don't expect anything?"

She brought the car to a halt at a red light. They were less than a mile from the interstate. It was crazy to be having this conversation right now.

"It was something I wanted for myself. I mean, I still want it. If it ever happens." She looked at him with those big green eyes—the eyes he'd once thought were so sweet and sincere. A little knife turned in his chest.

"I know this thing we have isn't something serious for you," she continued. "I would never ask you for anything, even if by some miracle I *am* pregnant."

He stared at her. "Un-fucking-believable. You still don't get it, do you?"

"Get what?"

He wouldn't look at her now.

"Shit. It's over. It's done," he said. "Just drop it, okay?"

What was over? Their relationship? She'd kind of caught on to that already after the way he'd treated her at his office. Not to mention the past three days.

The light turned green, and she stomped on the accelerator. They had less than two minutes to get there. She suddenly had a terrifying thought.

"Oh, no! Which side of the interstate is it on? I have no idea where we're going!"

"Northwest side," McAllister grumbled. "I used to stop there for smokes."

"You're sure?"

"Yeah. It's half a mile from police headquarters, which means these guys are extremely stupid or they've got some kind of plan we don't know about."

"What kind of plan?"

"I don't know," he said. "Who knows what they're thinking?"

Celie chewed her lip and considered this complication. She didn't like the possibility of some cop—uniformed or otherwise—stopping in for coffee and jumping into the middle of things.

Her phone chirped, and McAllister grabbed it from the console. He checked the number and flipped it open.

"Yo." He looked at Celie. "That's going to make us late." Pause. "Yeah, I got it. We're almost there now."

He closed the phone and pointed up ahead. "See that apartment complex? Pull into the lot right there."

"But—"

"Do it," he ordered. "That was Stevenski. They're waiting with the money."

John watched from inside the Volvo as Celie took a black duffel from Special Agent Rowe. He spoke to her a few moments, gesturing emphatically to underscore whatever point he was making. The man looked pissed off and disheveled, and John didn't know whether it was because of the late hour or the fact that he was wearing jeans and an FBI windbreaker instead of his usual suit. Judging from Rowe's bedhead, Celie's call had probably dragged him out of a sound sleep and torpedoed his plan to get under-cover agents and a team of sharpshooters in place before the money drop. Now it was up to Rowe, his partner, and John to keep Celie safe and make sure Enrique came back unharmed. Two measly feds and a reporter who hadn't fired a pistol in well over a year. What a joke. John held Celie's .38 against his thigh, wishing he'd taken the time to visit his grandfather's ranch and shoot up beer cans sometime in the past twelve months.

He watched Celie shoulder the duffel and go up on her toes to give Rowe a hug. What the hell? She was *hugging* the guy at a time like this? Rowe said something to her, and she nodded. Evidently they'd forged some kind of connection this past week. Or maybe she was just scared out of her mind and looking for some reassurance. John sure as shit hadn't given her any.

Celie turned and walked back to the Volvo with a de-termined look on her face. She seemed unbelievably calm for a woman who was about to walk into a meeting with gun-toting killers. He looked down at Celie's pistol and hoped he'd be able to help her if everything went to shit.

Which he was fairly sure it would.

Celie's phone chirped from the console. John was about to answer it when she yanked open the door and leaned over his lap to get it herself.

"Hello?"

As she listened to the caller, she turned and looked at him. The determination was gone from her eyes, replaced by panic.

"Why there?" she asked. "Why do you keep changing things? I don't understand."

Were they moving the meeting spot again? These guys must be schizo.

Or else really smart.

"Fine, I'll be there," Celie said, "but I want to talk to Enrique first. I need to know he's okay."

Her body stiffened, and for a second John thought they'd actually put the kid on the line.

"Hello? *Hello?*"

She snapped shut the phone and hurled it to the floor.

Celie's palms were sweating. Same for her back and her neck. Perspiration trickled down between her breasts, soaking into her bra.

"It's time," she said, glancing at the clock and cutting the engine.

She'd parked the SUV at a metered space not far from the Lamar Street Bridge, the latest meeting site. Celie had a feeling this quiet little pedestrian bridge was the place they'd had in mind all along, not the heavily traveled bridge she and McAllister had scoped out earlier.

She gazed over her shoulder at the concrete structure, which stretched over Town Lake. The narrow bridge offered scenic views of downtown Austin. On a typical evening, it was a favorite destination for joggers and couples out for a stroll. Tonight, however, it was nearly deserted, due to the soggy weather and the fact that it was 1:15 in the morning. If Saledo's guys wanted a meeting without witnesses, they probably couldn't have picked a better time.

The bridge itself was landscaped and lined with lampposts. Up and down the sidewalk leading to it, Celie saw pink crape myrtles and giant stone planters filled with rosemary. When they'd first driven by, McAllister had said one of the planters would make a good vantage point from which to watch the exchange.

"Not a bad meeting spot," he said now, surveying the area from the backseat. Celie was counting on the tinted windows to conceal his presence from Saledo's men. "Pretty smart, actually. Your car's stuck on this side, and I bet they're on the other. If you wanted to tail them out of here, you'd have to drive way the hell over there before you could cross the lake. And since they've been running you all over town tonight, they're probably banking on the fact you haven't had time to get a police backup in place." He paused and looked at her. "The lighting's not bad though. It's pretty good, actually."

Celie nodded. She hadn't even noticed the lighting. She'd been too scared to do anything but think about Enrique. What if he got hurt? What if he already *was* hurt? Despite his tough-guy facade, he was just a little boy. It made Celie sick to think that she'd brought him into all this, that her mere fondness for him had put him in jeopardy. She thought back, trying to conjure up some moment at the shelter when someone could possibly have seen her talking to Enrique. It had to have been yesterday. She'd spent part of the afternoon outside, playing basketball with the middle-school kids. Whenever Celie worked at the shelter, she tried hard to spread out her attention. But Saledo's guys must have homed in on her special friendship with Enrique.

God, where was he? Celie glanced all around. "I don't see them."

"They'll show," McAllister said. "They want the money."

"I don't see Rowe or Stevenski either."

"That's good. If you can't see them, Saledo's men probably don't either." McAllister picked up her hand. "Celie, look at me."

She tore her gaze away from the bridge. McAllister's face was shadowed, but she could still read the urgency in his eyes. "Do whatever they ask. Understand? Don't try to save the day. If you get in trouble, I'll be here. Along with two trained FBI agents."

She glanced toward the bridge. The rain had subsided, but still she saw no one. They were supposed to be here by now.

"Hey." McAllister snapped her attention back to him. "I'm serious. Be totally compliant. If these guys try to lay a finger on you, they're dead, okay? No heroics."

She nodded and glanced at the .38 in his hand. She tried to take a deep breath, but her lungs didn't seem to want to open. Maybe it was the Kevlar vest Rowe had given her. She wore it cinched tightly under a pink, short -sleeved button down. She also wore denim shorts and sandals. She hoped the casual summer attire would assure them she was harmless and unarmed. They'd specifically said no weapons.

Of course, they'd also said come alone.

She licked her lips. "If something goes wrong—"

"You'll be fine. You've got three separate people with a bead on these guys."

"But if something *does* go wrong—"

"I'll be right here—"

"Just listen! If something *does* go wrong, there's a note. On my nightstand. Make sure that it gets to my mom, okay?"

"Celie—"

"And I apologize. For lying to you. It was a terrible thing to do, but I just—" She glanced at the bridge, and her heart skittered.

"*Enrique!*" She flung open the car door and jumped out.

CHAPTER

16

Rowe watched through the rifle scope as Cecelia race-walked toward the boy. Enrique Ramos looked to be uninjured and alone.

"She's moving toward the kid," Rowe muttered into the radio mounted on his flak jacket. "No sign of the suspects. Where are you?"

"Security guy's unlocking the door for me now." Stevenski answered.

At last communication, Stevenski had been on his way to the roof of a loft apartment building just south of the bridge. From there, he was hoping to have a bird's-eye view of the scene, which Rowe didn't have from his position. Rowe did, however, have proximity. He was concealed behind a wet clump of foliage about twenty yards upstream from the bridge. He adjusted the barrel of his

SSG 3000 against the notch of a tree branch and waited.

"*Fuck!*"

Rowe's shoulders tensed. "What's wrong?"

"I misjudged the angle," Stevenski said. "There are trees in the way. My visibility's for shit."

"Can you see *anything*?"

"Not from up here. I'm coming down."

"Make it quick," Rowe snapped.

"Wait. There's a black Avalanche. North side, pulled up in the grass near the bridge. Taillights are red, like the engine's running. You see our suspects yet?"

"Negative." God*damn* it. "Give Abrams's team a heads up about the vehicle. I think they're about ten minutes out, but you never know. Then get your ass somewhere useful, fast."

Celie clutched Enrique against her and tried to shield him from whoever might be hovering nearby. "Are you okay? Did they hurt you?"

"Nah, I'm good."

She stepped back to look at him. He wore his usually baggy jeans and T-shirt—both soaking wet—and his tattered Astros cap turned backward. His bony shoulders trembled under her hands.

"You sure you're all right?"

He nodded, and she could tell he was on the verge of tears.

Celie glanced around. They were standing in the middle of the bridge, right next to a lamppost, two targets illuminated for anyone to see. "We need to get you out of here. We need—"

"I'm supposed to take your bag"—he nodded bravely at her duffel—"to the other side of the bridge. Those two dudes in the truck, they're waiting for it."

"I'll take it."

He looked up at her, his brown-black eyes fearful. "No, they said *me*. You're just supposed to stand here."

"Enrique, listen to me. You see that silver SUV at the meter over there? The Volvo?"

"Yeah."

"That's my car. It's unlocked. Walk straight toward it and get inside. Then lock the doors and duck low, as low as you can, understand?"

He nodded, clearly relieved to be given an alternative to going back to his kidnappers.

"When you walk past the planter, you might see John McAllister crouched behind it. He has a gun. Don't even look at him, okay? Walk straight to the Volvo and get inside."

Enrique hesitated a second, then nodded.

"Go."

She pointed him toward the Volvo and gave a little shove. With every step, Celie felt a minute lessening of tension. Enrique was almost to safety.

Then a man stepped into his path. He snagged Enrique's arm and strode toward Celie, towing the terror-stricken boy behind him.

Who the hell was this guy? Rowe peered through the scope, trying in vain to place the mug. It wasn't one of his suspects. Juan and Guillermo Barriolo were short and stocky, not tall and lanky like the figure moving toward Cecelia.

"I've got an unidentified male subject," he told Stevenski. "Approximately six feet tall. Thin. Wearing black clothes and a baseball cap. Lightweight jacket possibly concealing a weapon. This guy is not, I repeat, *not* one of the Barriolo brothers."

"Copy that."

The subject slipped his free hand into his pocket. Was he reaching for a weapon? With his right hand, he gripped the boy's arm. People typically held a weapon with their dominant hand, and roughly 85 percent of people were right-handed.

So was he armed or not? Rowe didn't like the ambiguity.

Rowe trained the crosshairs on the base of the subject's head as he neared Cecelia. The objective was to hit the cerebellum, causing instant, painless death before the subject had time to get a shot off. Rowe had never actually done this to a live person before, but if a woman and child's lives were at stake, he wouldn't hesitate to pull the trigger.

Cecelia reached out and grabbed the boy. She tucked him behind her, shielding him with her body. Given that Rowe had loaned her his vest, it wasn't such a bad idea.

The woman had balls.

Rowe counted himself lucky. Whether she'd planned it or not, she'd separated the subject from the hostage, giving him a clear shot.

He mentally reviewed the surrounding conditions. The rain had stopped. A slight breeze blew out of the northwest, but not enough to be a factor. "I've got a shot," Rowe reported.

"Say again?"

"I've got a shot of the subject. No idea who he is, though. Possibly Saledo found out about the meet and sent someone to intercept. I don't see a weapon yet. Where are you?"

"Almost to street level," Stevenski said.

"Forget your rifle. This thing's about to escalate. I need you near the bridge."

"Got it."

But he knew Stevenski couldn't get there in time. Rowe was on his own. He forced his shoulders to relax, tried to feel connected to his weapon. Just like in training, he and the rifle were one unit; it was an extension of his body, his mind. Rowe tuned everything else out and focused on the people in the middle of the bridge. Cecelia and the boy were separated from the subject by at least three feet. It was a forty-yard shot, a cakewalk. And if the subject made one wrong move, Rowe intended to take it.

Kate watched from behind the base of a lamppost, for once in her life feeling grateful for her petite stature. She was on the north end of the bridge, which could be accessed by a curving bike ramp or a flight of concrete stairs. From her hiding spot at the top of the ramp, she had a perfect view of Cecelia Wells as she passed a bag to the tall, skinny guy in black. Kate didn't think she'd ever seen him before.

Then the intensity kicked up. They were arguing. Cecelia began stepping backward, corralling the boy behind her as she moved across the bridge and closer to Kate.

Some movement on the stairs caught Kate's attention. A man was crouched there in the shadows. He wore a dark skullcap and had a black goatee, and Kate could almost swear he was one of the guys in the Avalanche, the ones she'd watched in the surveillance video. He held a handgun poised on his knee and looked tense, as if his legs were spring-loaded.

Suddenly he jumped up and aimed the gun.

"No!"

The piercing scream was followed by a *pop*, and Celie's head whipped around. She first thought of firecrackers, but in a nanosecond her brain identified the sound.

"Get down!" she screamed, shoving Enrique to the ground.

Another *pop*, then a shriek. The shots were coming from the far side of the bridge. Celie tried to shield Enrique, pinning him facedown against the pavement. The man in black had disappeared.

Another shot, this one from the opposite direction. Bullets were flying on both ends of the bridge. They were trapped in between.

Celie rolled off Enrique and grabbed his hand, making sure to keep low. "We have to get out of here. Do you know how to swim?"

"Yeah."

She clasped his fingers. "On the count of three, we go up and over. Don't let go of me, okay?"

Enrique nodded. She saw fear in his eyes, but also trust. He *trusted* her. After everything he'd been through, he still thought she could keep him safe.

"You ready?" She tightened her grip on his hand. "One, two, *three!*"

John sprinted onto the bridge.

"Celie!" Where the hell had she gone?

One second, they'd been in plain view. Then gun-fire had erupted, and she'd dropped out of sight. John had taken a quick potshot at the man in black, but he'd sprinted into the trees.

John raced across the bridge now, eyes scanning for any sign of Celie or Enrique. He passed lampposts, planters, benches, knowing at any moment he might trip over their torn up bodies.

And then he saw her.

Kate's arm was on fire. The burning started just above her wrist and radiated up, taking over her shoulder and her neck. She sat up and clamped her left hand down over the wound, pressing her right elbow into her side and trying to stop the bleeding.

"Omigod, omigod, omigod . . ." She bit her lip and pressed harder, but the pain was spreading. The blood, too. It poured down her arm, her wrist, her hand. The warmth of it seeped through her jeans.

More sirens approached, and she cast a frantic look around. She got up and stumbled the short distance to the top of the stairs, then felt dizzy and sank back down onto the concrete.

"Hey!" Kate yelled. "I need help up here!" She leaned against the railing and waited for a paramedic.

A young cop mounted the steps, gun drawn. His eyes bugged out when he spotted her.

"He shot me," Kate said through clenched teeth. For some reason just saying the words made her eyes fill with tears. "I need—"

"Where's the shooter? Where'd he go?"

Kate nodded toward downtown. "Took off that way. Black Avalanche." Goddamn it *hurt*!

"Medic's on his way." The cop darted a worried look at her arm. "Don't move, ma'am. You have any weapons on you?"

Kate choked out a laugh. "Yeah, right."

He reached out with his free hand, like he was going to frisk her.

"I'm not armed, I'm *wounded*! Where's the ambulance?"

"They're coming, ma'am."

She watched her blood seeping between her fingers. It looked purple in the lamplight.

"Damn it, damn it, damn it." This couldn't be happening. She squeezed her eyes shut and tried to focus on something besides the burn.

"Kate?"

Her head jerked up. Nick Stevenski towered over her, hands on his hips, panting like he'd just run a marathon. "What happened back there?" He quickly unzipped his windbreaker and turned it inside out.

"I was hiding behind a lamppost," she told him. "Just over there."

"You need to elevate this. You're losing blood." Nick crouched down and gently pulled her arm away from her body. It was bent at a strange angle, and Kate had to look away so she wouldn't think about what he was doing.

"I saw the guy," she said. "From the surveillance video.

And he had this . . . this gun. . . . And he was watching Cecelia Wells. And that little boy, too." She felt Nick wrapping the windbreaker around the top of her arm. God, was she even making sense? The events felt blurry now.

"He stood up and raised the gun. Like . . . like he was going to shoot them? And I screamed and ran at him—"

Nick pressed too hard, and she shrieked.

"Sorry."

Tears streamed down her cheeks. God, where was her phone? She needed to call her dad.

"I . . . I tackled him," she stammered, "and the gun went off. And we were on the ground. And it went off *again*."

Nick gave her a reproachful look. His eyelashes were damp and his face was so close, she could smell the rain on him. She suddenly had this insane wish that he'd put his arms around her.

"You shouldn't have jumped in the middle like that," he said. "You could have been killed."

"He was about to shoot a *kid*! What would you have done?"

God, her arm hurt, like she'd been touched with a branding iron. She started to feel nauseated.

She looked at Nick. "They're okay, right?"

He didn't say anything.

"Nick?" Her voice hitched. Had one of them been *hit*?

"We don't know," he said grimly. "They're not on the bridge."

The impact smacked the breath out of her. Celie kicked and groped for the surface, all the while clenching Enrique's hand in a tight fist.

Suddenly, *sky*. And trees and lights and a glimpse of the bridge. She gasped for air and sputtered Enrique's name.

He didn't answer.

She yanked him up, flailing and thrashing in a frantic bid to keep her head above water. God, why was she *sinking*?

"Enrique, *breathe!*"

She needed a better hold, but she was terrified that if she let go his fingers, she'd lose him. Using her free hand, she grabbed a fistful of his T-shirt and pulled him up. Now his mouth was above water, but he was gurgling.

She maneuvered behind him and tried to push his shoulders up. He needed air. "Enrique, come on! Cough it out!"

He made a wet, strangled sound. The fall must have knocked the wind out of him, too. God, what if he'd hit his head on the way down?

The lake was pulling at her, sucking her under. She kept *sinking*. She choked and spit and tried to keep her head above the surface, but her body felt leaden.

Rowe's vest. Panic hit, and she gasped, instantly filling her lungs with water. Enrique's hand jerked away, and then she was alone, sinking. She pulled at her shirt, trying to yank it off so she could get rid of the vest.

"*Enrique!*"

Suddenly something wrapped around her throat. She kicked and punched. A powerful arm snaked around her waist and grabbed her, trying to pull her under. She screamed and clawed at it.

"Celie, *stop!*"

McAllister.

"Get this off!"

The shirt ripped free. She felt the Velcro pull and tug as he yanked off the vest, and cool water surrounded her. Then she was weightless, bobbing up like a cork.

McAllister hooked his arm across her chest and pulled her across the surface. The chilly water swished around her as his legs scissor-kicked and scissor-kicked, propelling them forward.

Where was Enrique? She struggled to locate him, but sky and trees and wet hair filled her field of vision. Then the world around her darkened. Her feet touched bottom. They were near the shore, shadowed by trees. McAllister grabbed hold of a low-dangling limb and heaved them both out of the water. Her butt plunked against something hard and solid. She slid down the slope of it, saw that it was a rock, and then grasped the tree branch and caught herself before she could slide back into the lake.

McAllister stood up. His jeans and T-shirt clung like a wetsuit. He'd managed to keep his boots somehow. Water slurped as he trudged through some mud to a nearby outcropping of rock.

Where Enrique sat, breathing hard, his knees tucked up against his chest.

Relief swept over her.

Enrique looked up with wide eyes as McAllister braced a hand on his shoulder and said something. Even from a distance, Celie could see the boy shaking. But he looked okay, otherwise. Wet and frightened, but breathing.

She flopped back against the rock, wincing when her head connected. For a minute, she just lay there, shivering and wheezing and trying to figure out what had just happened.

Then a shadow fell across her, obscuring even the dim purplish light reflected down from the city's cloud cover.

McAllister loomed over her, chest heaving. "You okay?"

"Yeah." She coughed up some more water and pushed herself up into a sitting position.

The distant wail of police sirens filled the air. Celie glanced around, but she didn't see any cars or lights. Just the bridge and the churning, rain-swollen lake and the trees lining the shore.

McAllister stripped off his T-shirt and handed it to her. "Put this on."

She looked down at the ball of dripping white fabric in her hands. It was smeared with muck, but at least it would cover her transparent beige bra. "Thanks."

She wrestled the shirt over her head, noticing the scrapes and cuts on her arms for the first time. She was pretty sure they'd come from the pavement when she dove for cover from the bullets. By the time she'd managed to pull on the sodden shirt, the sirens had become shrill and insistent.

McAllister planted his hands on his hips and looked up at the bridge. She couldn't believe she'd jumped from such a height. She glanced at Enrique, who was standing on the steep hillside now, soaked and shivering and waiting for guidance.

"You ready?" McAllister looked down at her and held out his hand. She nodded, and he pulled her to her bare feet. Her sandals were probably at the bottom of the lake by now. Mud oozed between Celie's toes as she picked her way over to Enrique.

"Are you all right?" She enfolded his skinny body into a hug. He'd somehow managed to swim to shore, even weighted down by his clunky basketball shoes. His skin felt cold.

"Enrique?"

She pulled back and stared down into his face. He nodded.

Together, they started hiking up the hill. It sounded like a convention of emergency vehicles up there, and she hoped one of them was an ambulance. "Let's get you checked out just to be sure."

As operations went, this one was a clusterfuck.

Two missing suspects, three missing civilians. Plus a gunshot victim on the other side of the bridge—some innocent bystander, according to the Austin police.

The one scrap of success Rowe had to show for the night was the man in black, whom he'd just finished Mirandizing. Rowe had chased him down the slippery, shadowy jogging path that paralleled the lake, finally overtaking him near the canoe docks. They'd wrestled in the mud, the guy grunting and throwing bony elbows as Rowe disarmed him and got the cuffs on. He'd been carrying a small but lethal Chiefs Special.

The perp hadn't said anything so far. Rowe wasn't even sure if he spoke English.

But he looked American. Rowe eyed him as he sat in the back of the Buick, his hands cuffed behind him. He no longer wore a cap, and Rowe saw now that his hair was light brown, his skin pale. Not likely a relative of the Barriolo brothers. Rowe would bet money he worked for Saledo and was here to intercept the cash. If so, Rowe had to wonder, how in the world had he found out about this meeting?

He wasn't just some flunkie—that was clear. As soon as he'd stepped off the bridge, the guy had had the brains to transfer the money to a bag he'd brought with him. This maneuver would have backfired if the duffel had had an exploding dye pack in it. But because it merely had a tracking device sewn into the lining, the move had effectively derailed Rowe's plan to sit back and follow the cash.

Now Rowe stripped off his slimy windbreaker and tossed it in the front of the Buick, right on top of the gray zipper bag he'd seized with the perp. He pulled his cell phone from his pocket and checked the display. Still no callback from Stevenski. He'd tried him twice now, with no response. Rowe looked across the bridge and saw the telltale white antennae of a television news crew jutting up into the sky. The media had wasted no time making the scene. At this very moment, Kate Kepler was probably phoning her story in to her news editor before the night's final pressrun.

Rowe turned toward Abrams. He and another agent had shown up ten minutes ago to help supervise the fiasco. "You got this guy?" Rowe asked him, nodding toward the Buick.

"Yeah, I got him," Abrams answered. "Hey, and I just heard from one of the uniforms. Someone spotted your missing civilians on the other side of the lake."

"Really?" Why hadn't Stevenski called?

Abrams smiled. "Yeah, sounds like they decided to take a swim."

John hiked up the hillside, scanning the faces of emergency workers and trying to locate Rowe or Stevenski. His gaze landed on a pair of paramedics loading a woman into an ambulance.

"Hey, wait!" John sprinted over to the rig. "Kate? *Kate!*"

She lifted her head up from the gurney.

"What the hell happened?" Jesus, her arms were covered with blood.

She tried to say something, but an oxygen mask blocked her mouth. She reached up with a bloody hand and tugged it down. "One of those guys shot me." She nodded toward a white bandage on her right arm.

"Holy shit, Kate!"

One of the medics glared at John. "Save it for later. We've got to get her to the hospital."

The paramedics continued to situate Kate in the back of the rig while she spoke. "It hurts like hell." Her eyes pleaded with him. "Can you call my dad? Tell him to meet me at— Where are you taking me?"

"Brackenridge," said the medic closest to Kate.

"Okay, but . . ." John raked his fingers through his hair. "What's your dad's name? What's his phone number?" He grabbed hold of the door and levered himself onto the ambulance bumper. Blood saturated Kate's clothes, but she was lucid and alert.

"Here." She twisted and turned on the gurney until she dug a cell phone out of her back pocket with her left hand. She tossed it to John. "He's on my speed dial. Wozniak, too. Call in this story, will you?"

"You've got to be kidding."

"Hey, you mind if we get moving here?" The paramedic shoved John out of the way and pulled one of the doors closed.

"I'm totally serious," Kate answered. John couldn't see her face anymore, but her voice was loud and clear. "I gave him the lowdown on the way over here, and he's delayed pressrun until we get this story in."

The second paramedic hopped down and slammed shut the other door.

John looked at the cell phone in his hand and cursed as the chartreuse rig rolled away.

CHAPTER

17

McAllister stood just outside the ambulance bay at Brackenridge Hospital. The waiting room staff had insisted he go outdoors if he needed to make a cellular call, so he was stuck in the drizzle, juggling Kate's phone as well as his own as he enviously watched hospital workers file outside to suck down nicotine during their breaks.

Life was full of surprises. Tonight, for instance, he'd learned that Kate Kepler was the only daughter of James Kepler, who, besides being a computer geek, was one of the richest men in Austin, if not in the entire state. He was notorious, too, for some sort of shady business dealings he'd been involved with about ten years back. John couldn't remember the details, but it wouldn't take him long to turn up something on the Internet.

Another surprise was that the man didn't look like a

geek at all. A few minutes ago, he'd arrived at the hospital in a silver Tesla Roadster with plates that said PLA-COM, an allusion to PlayComp, the software company he'd founded. After whipping into a handicapped space, he'd leapt out of his car and charged through the emergency room doors like some sort of angry bantamweight fighter. He'd been wearing athletic shorts and a RunTex T-shirt and an intense look on his face that said he wanted answers about his little girl, *now*.

The gum-smacking receptionist just inside—who wore pink scrubs tonight and told everyone who approached her she wasn't at liberty to discuss the status of any patients, and could you please take a seat in the waiting area?—was toast.

John punched at his keypad and once again connected with the night editor's desk at the *Austin Herald*. The guy was a friend, but tonight John was pushing the boundaries of that friendship by blowing his deadline completely out of the water.

"Hey, Pete, I've got that info for you."

"McAllister! Shit, I'm dying here! We were supposed to go to press ten minutes ago."

"Yeah, yeah, I know. They wouldn't tell me her status at reception, so I had to sneak upstairs and sweet-talk one of the nurses. Sounds like Kate's stabilized but headed to surgery."

"Stable condition. Got it." John heard keys clacking as Pete typed this new information into the computer. "Damn. What type of surgery?"

"Something with the bones in her arm. Bullet tore everything up, apparently."

"That sucks."

"Yeah," John agreed. But having been at the scene, he knew things could have turned out much worse.

"Wozniak just arrived," Pete said. "He wants IDs on the civilians involved and a quote from one of the FBI guys."

Great. It was bad enough McAllister had to call in this story at all, but if he included names, he could kiss away any chances of ever talking to Celie again. Forget about getting back in her bed, he'd be history.

Unless, of course, she was pregnant with his kid. Under that scenario, they'd be permanently intertwined for the rest of their lives. How fucked up was that? What was even more fucked up was that John was starting to believe that wouldn't be the worst thing in the world. Three days ago, he'd been so angry at her he could hardly see straight, and now here he was, worried about pissing her off.

"No can do, man," John told Pete. "One of the civilians is a minor, so we can't ID him. Other one wants us to protect her identity so this drug cartel doesn't come after her. I've got a request from the FBI to keep her name out of print."

The last part was a lie, but John felt no compunction about telling it. If Rowe *had* known John was writing a story about this, he most likely would have declined to identify the civilians involved.

Not that John didn't already know their names, but still.

"I don't think that's gonna cut it with Wozniak, man. Wait, here he comes now. . . ."

John heard shuffling as the phone was passed to

Wozniak, John's direct boss, who also happened to be higher up in the *Herald* food chain than the night editor.

"What's this caca you're feeding us, McAllister? We were supposed to go to press almost an hour ago, and we've held off for *this*?"

"I was just giving Pete an update on the gunshot victim. Kate Kepler." He threw the reminder in there as a distraction. "She's going into surgery right now, but it looks like her condition is stable. As for the identities, like I told Pete—"

"Fine. No names, but I at least need ages and occupations."

John searched his memory banks. "The kid involved is an eleven-year-old boy, middle school student, resident of Austin. The woman is thirty-one. Also lives here in town."

"This is that friend of yours, right? Where's she work?"

"She's a social worker." John would have said student, but in a college town, that would just make for a bigger headline.

John watched as a familiar Buick rolled past the ambulance bay and slid into a handicapped space beside James Kepler's Tesla.

"Great," Wozniak sneered. "Nothing like specificity in a *news* article. I just love throwing all this vague shit up on A-one. Above the fold, no less. You don't even have the name of the arrestee in here, McAllister. Do you realize that?"

Rowe climbed out of the car, and John glanced at his watch. It was 2:44. If they held this story even five minutes longer, they probably would delay the trucks that made deliveries to newsstands all over downtown. As it was, the story wasn't even appearing in the suburban edition of the *Herald*. That edition had gone out right on schedule.

Which was fine with John. The less exposure this story got, the better, as far as he was concerned.

Wozniak was still yammering in his ear.

"Hey, give me one minute, and I'll get a quote from the FBI," John interjected. "Two minutes, max."

Silence. "Have you listened to a damn thing I've said, McAllister? Time is *money*! Shel is gonna have my head on a platter!"

"I have an agent standing right here waiting to be interviewed."

John waved his hand and caught Rowe's attention just before he went through the emergency room doors. He hesitated a moment, casting a glance into the ER, then walked over.

"I'll call you right back," John told his boss.

He clicked off and met Rowe beneath the narrow overhang, where they'd at least be out of the rain. Not that it mattered. Like Rowe, John was wearing jeans and a T-shirt that were already soaked through. Unlike Rowe, though, John had bought his T-shirt off a vagrant near the hospital for ten bucks, so it had the added benefit of smelling like week-old garbage.

"Any word on Kate?" Rowe wanted to know.

John gave him a quick update and concealed his curiosity as the FBI agent actually appeared shaken by the news that Kate was in surgery. Rowe stared through the hospital doors for a moment, then glanced back at John with gray eyes that looked like ice chips.

"You shouldn't have told her about the meeting," he said.

John felt a prick of guilt. "We needed to get hold of you, and Cecelia didn't have your number. How was I supposed to know Kate would show up?"

Rowe's expression darkened. They both knew that was bullshit. Of course Kate would show up—she was a reporter.

John hated blame games. Bottom line, if Kate hadn't jumped in, Celie and Enrique might be dead. John was sorry Kate was hurt, but he wasn't sorry she'd been there.

"Look," he said, "I need a quote for the paper tomorrow. Anything to say about the man you guys arrested? You know his name or his position in the Saledo organization?"

"We haven't identified him yet."

John watched Rowe, trying to mask his surprise. He'd expected a simple "No comment," or maybe even a "No comment, asshole." John decided to press him.

"Okay, what about the rumors floating around that the two missing suspects ditched their Avalanche at a Chevron on I-35 and carjacked a green sedan?"

Rowe's brows knitted together. "We've got a BOLO for a dark green Mercury Cougar with Texas plates. I don't know the tags, but I'll get them for you as soon as I can."

John eyed him suspiciously. This was way more cooperation than he'd been expecting. "Anything else you want to tell me?"

"Yeah." Rowe glanced at the ER doors. "Somewhere in your story, you need to mention that federal agents confiscated two hundred thousand in cash. Don't leave that out."

John frowned. "What's the deal with the money?"

"Just put it in there, up near the top if you can. It's important for the safety of everyone involved that the message gets out that the money was confiscated."

"You mean for Saledo? He knows it was confiscated. His guys were right there—" John halted, realization dawning. "Unless those weren't *Saledo's* guys? They're part of some other organization?"

Rowe's stony expression was his answer.

"Son of a *bitch*! You knew this all along, didn't you? You set Celie up!" John stepped forward and jabbed a finger at Rowe's chest. "She risked her life for you guys, and now she's still on Saledo's shit list! How's she supposed to hide from him now?"

"She doesn't have to hide," Rowe said calmly. "If Saledo believes the money was confiscated by federal agents, he won't come looking for it."

"You're an asshole, you know that? That woman trusted you." At John's urging, Celie had trusted him. He never should have talked her into going to the feds for help. "You used an innocent woman just to get an arrest."

"She's not innocent," Rowe retorted. "No one forced her to steal two hundred thousand dollars. And it looks to me like you're using her, too. Or am I wrong about that?"

John's phone buzzed, and he checked the number. Wozniak. *Fuck.*

Rowe stepped back and nodded toward John's phone.

"That's probably your editor. Pass that along about the money, like I said. You guys do your jobs, and let us worry about ours."

The sun was just rising over the apartment complexes of east Austin when Celie left the Bluebonnet House for the last time.

Miraculously, she didn't cry.

She was too busy worrying about the Ramos children, whose mother had pulled another disappearing act. When Celie and an APD officer had taken Enrique home, they'd found four-year-old Britanny by herself in the apartment. Her mom had "gone out" for the evening, apparently oblivious to the fact that her son hadn't made it home from school.

It was a miserable end to a miserable ordeal, and the only upside Celie could see was that Enrique hadn't been injured.

He'd told police that after being picked up on the way home from school, he'd spent the next several hours in a cheap motel room with his abductors eating pizza and watching ESPN. Celie hoped the paramedic who'd checked him out hadn't missed anything. Some kinds of abuse didn't leave marks.

Celie walked past the gated playground, where she'd spent so many hours with the children she loved, past the basketball court and the half-finished rec room. Her feet moved over the sections of new sidewalk where, less than a month ago, she'd helped Kimmy Taylor and Brittany Ramos flatten out their tiny hands and press them into damp concrete.

Her gaze skimmed over their childish signatures, the marks they'd gleefully left there for posterity, and Celie regretted not pressing her own print into the cold, wet slab.

Had she left a mark on this place at all?

She was fairly sure that she had, but she couldn't kid herself into believing it was a good one. The mistakes of her past had caught up to her, and her very presence here had endangered the life of an innocent child. That, more than anything else she'd done, would be her undeniable legacy to the Bluebonnet House. It overshadowed Easter cupcakes and algebra tutoring and countless games of Hi Ho! Cheery-O played with kids around the kitchen table.

Coming here had been a mistake.

Celie's flip-flops snapped against the pavement now as she walked down the sidewalk. After checking Brittany and Enrique into the shelter for the night, and after a tense conversation in Chantal's office, Celie had relinquished her Bluebonnet House ID badge, trading it with Chantal for a pair of cheap rubber sandals that probably wouldn't even make the trip home.

A block away from the shelter, Dax was waiting in his white Toyota Prius, just like she'd asked him to. When he spotted her in the mirror, he leaned over and pushed open her door from the inside. Celie slid into the passenger seat.

"Thanks for coming." She gave Dax a wobbly smile. "I'm sorry I got you out of bed. I owe you one, big time."

"No problem," Dax said. "On my way out the door, I got a phone call from John McAllister."

"He called *you*?"

"He was looking for you. It was about your Volvo? He said to tell you he left it in the visitors' lot and gave the keys to the security guy, Terrance."

"Oh." Celie rubbed the bridge of her nose, wishing there was something she could do to ward off the migraine she felt coming on. Up until this moment, she hadn't realized she'd been picturing herself crawling into bed next to McAllister. In the back of her mind, she'd been hoping he could help her forget about the whole awful night they'd just endured.

Which was ridiculous, she realized now. He may have plucked her out of Town Lake, but he was still angry over the way she'd lied to him. The rift between them still existed. Otherwise, he would have come to get her himself. Or he would have stayed and waited for her at The Overlook. He knew darn well Dax would have buzzed him upstairs.

"So," Dax said. "Looks like you spent the night in a swamp."

Celie glanced down at her clothes. She was still wearing the mud-smeared shirt McAllister had given her. It had a red scuba flag on the front, which had kept her from looking like a contestant in a wet T-shirt contest while she'd talked to the cops.

She flipped down the passenger mirror and cringed when she saw her face. "Yikes."

"Johnny's a 'yikes,' too," Dax said. "After he called, I looked out my window and saw him picking up his Jeep. I'm guessing he participated in last night's mud-wrestling extravaganza?"

Celie took a deep breath and spilled the whole story, starting with Robert's stash of money and ending with the past two hours at the Bluebonnet House. Celie had made Toaster Strudels for the Ramos children in the kitchen while Chantal argued about their fate with a rep from Child Protective Services. After much discussion—which, unfortunately, Enrique and Brittany had overheard—it was agreed that the kids would stay at the Bluebonnet House until April Ramos could be located. If and when the police tracked the young mother down, CPS would make alternative arrangements for the children.

Translation: foster care. Until a responsible relative could be called in or until April got her act together enough to convince a judge she was a capable parent. According to the CPS caseworker, this wasn't the first time her kids had been left overnight without supervision.

After the caseworker left, Chantal had called Celie into her office and launched into a tirade that began with the words, "It saddens me to do this, but . . ."

"Wow," Dax said now. "Bitch of a night, huh?"

"You could say that."

Dax reached into his jeans pocket and pulled out a small prescription bottle. Her migraine meds. He handed her the container.

"I hope you don't mind," he said. "Something in your voice told me you might be needing this. I got it from your medicine cabinet." He passed her a bottle of mineral water.

Celie was speechless. Dax was, quite possibly, the kindest man she'd ever met. Didn't it figure they'd never have a shot at being a couple?

"Thanks," she managed. She would *not* cry. She hated bawling in front of other people. It was the worst way to dump all your problems into somebody's lap.

Dax stopped at an intersection, and Celie could feel him looking at her. She popped open the bottle and took one of the pills. As she replaced the cap, she noticed her doctor's name on the label and thought about McAllister's snooping. A little nosing through her bathroom, and he had discovered all her secrets: she took fertility drugs; she suffered migraines. She used acne cream and heartburn tablets. She hadn't experienced night terrors in years, but she kept prescription sleeping pills on hand for emergencies.

McAllister had pried open a door into her private life, and he obviously hadn't liked what he'd seen. Who could blame him? His reaction didn't really surprise her, but it did make her angry. He'd snooped through her stuff and then used everything he'd learned as a reason to dump her. She'd been stupid to think she could trust him. Digging up dirt on people was one of his special talents, and no one was off-limits.

Dax battled the morning traffic across central Austin. Thankfully, he didn't fill the silence with annoying platitudes. He sipped quietly from a mug of coffee and left Celie to herself.

After finishing the bottle of water, she leaned her head back. If she was lucky, the pill might stall the migraine for a little while. Most likely, she'd still spend the better part of her day in a silent bedroom with the blinds sealed shut. Celie closed her eyes and tried to do yoga breathing.

Dax turned down the stereo. "Celie?"

"What?" She opened her eyes and glanced at him. Just as she'd expected, he looked worried.

"There's something you need to see."

"Okay."

"You're not going to like it."

She almost laughed at that. What could he possibly show her that could make this morning worse than it already was? She took a deep breath. "What is it?"

Dax reached into the backseat and scooped a newspaper off the floorboard. He handed it to her. A cold sense of foreboding settled over her as she unfolded the paper and read the headline.

"Drug wars rage in Austin." Beneath the headline was a photograph of the Lamar Street Bridge swarming with emergency personnel. In the background of the picture, among all the ambulances and squad cars, a blonde woman stood beside what looked like a gray Volvo. Her back was to the camera, but any enterprising reporter could probably track down the license plate and figure out who owned the car.

Celie shook her head. She'd known this was a possibility last night, which was why she'd stayed away from the media. Or so she'd thought. "Well, at least my face didn't make the front page."

Dax shot her a disbelieving look.

"What?"

"That's it?" he asked. "I only skimmed the first few paragraphs, but I thought you'd be much more upset."

Celie glanced beneath the picture and started to read. Before she got halfway through the column, her gaze jerked back to the byline.

"Oh my God," she whispered. "He didn't."

CHAPTER
18

Rowe trained his gaze on the hospital entrance, look-ing for a young brunette with her arm in a sling. Kate was scheduled to be discharged at 10:00 A.M. today, and James Kepler's silver Tesla Roadster in the pickup driveway indicated this was still the plan.

But it was 10:45, and still no Kate.

Rowe settled lower in the Buick's front seat and ad-justed his baseball cap. If anyone he knew saw him out here like this, he'd be forced to say he was here check-ing up on a witness, which—as excuses went—was pretty damn weak. In reality, Rowe had no official business here whatsoever. Yet here he was, checking up on a witness, the witness he'd failed to protect, the witness who was, at this very moment, being transferred to a rehab hospital so she could recover from the gunshot that had wreaked havoc with her right arm. According to Kate's doctors—whom Rowe had interviewed under the flimsy pretense of tying up investigative loose ends—Kate might never recover the full use of that arm, and she certainly would have nasty scars on it for the rest of her life. On the upside, given Kate's young age and otherwise excellent health, her doctor thought her stint in rehab might be as short as a few months.

Rowe's cell buzzed. He checked the number and snapped it open. "Any updates?"

"I've got good news and bad," Stevenski said. "Which do you want to hear first?"

Rowe hated this case. "Bad."

"Okay, Zapata's team down in Michoacán has some new info. About eighteen hours ago they recorded a phone call—from a San Antonio pay phone again—informing Saledo his guy had been arrested trying to intercept the money, and his two hundred thou had been seized by the feds."

"Let me guess," Rowe said. "Saledo wasn't happy."

"No, he was pissed."

Rowe gritted his teeth. This was precisely why Rowe had been arguing with George Purnell about the need to get Cecelia Wells to a safe house. But the SAC, who suffered from a lack of funds and an even bigger lack of imagination, had said that was unnecessary. Saledo knew his money was gone, right? So why should the FBI waste resources babysitting a civilian who no longer had plans to act as bait in an important sting operation? As a token measure, Purnell had assigned an agent to keep tabs on Cecelia for a few days.

"I'm not hearing any good news," Rowe said, imagining yet another civilian casualty on his conscience.

"The good news is, Manny Saledo seems to have completely lost interest in Cecelia Wells."

"I find that difficult to believe."

The hospital doors parted, and out came Kate in a wheelchair pushed by her father. She was trailed by a hospital staffer laden with overnight bags and a floral bouquet. James Kepler rolled Kate to the curb, where his covertible sat waiting.

"Believe it," Stevenski said. "Saledo told his informant to get his ass down to Michoacán. Saledo's convinced there's a power struggle afoot, and he's gathering his guys together for a meeting."

James Kepler opened the car door and helped his daughter in, taking care not to disturb her arm, it looked like. Kate wore sunglasses, a black tank top, and white shorts that showed off her slender legs. Rowe couldn't take his eyes off her, or the sling, and he wondered once again how bad her pain was.

"What's that mean, 'power struggle.' Is there something going on we don't know about?"

Stevenski scoffed. "Of course. We don't know shit. But we *do* know that there's an elevated level of chatter among all the major families. And this isn't the first time we've heard this rumor about a power struggle. Saledo's circling the wagons, it sounds like."

In an ideal world, it wouldn't matter. Cecelia Wells would have her safe house, Enrique Ramos would have a mother who gave a shit, and Kate Kepler would have a full-time FBI bodyguard to protect her for the rest of her long life.

"So let me guess," Rowe said. "Purnell is using this

new intelligence as an excuse to nix the safe house idea for Cecelia Wells."

"You got it. The safe house is officially off the table, but he's agreed to keep surveillance for the next couple weeks until things settle down with Saledo."

Kate's dad loaded her luggage into the Tesla's minuscule trunk and got behind the wheel. The nurse gave Kate the flowers and waved good-bye as the car eased forward. Rowe watched it pull away from the hospital with a soreness in his chest.

John pushed through The Overlook's beveled glass doors and mustered a smile for the security guard behind the counter.

"Hey, Terrance, how's it going?"

This was John's fifth visit to Celie's building in two days, and he knew damn well he was making a pest of himself. His boundless knowledge of Houston Rockets trivia was the only thing keeping him in Terrance's good graces.

"She in?" John asked, as he approached the granite reception counter.

Terrance gave him a suspicious look, which John took for a yes.

"Man, people been stoppin' by all day," the guard said. "I'll tell you what I told everyone else. The girl is *not* home."

John smiled slightly. "But she is, right? Come on, Terrance. Her car's in the garage."

He frowned. "You supposed to park in the visitors' lot."

John leaned on the counter. "I did, but I can still see

her car in there. Just buzz me up, okay? I know she wants to talk to me."

Terrance tipped back his swivel chair, making his navy blue uniform strain across his belly. "She wanna talk to you so bad, how come she don't pick up the phone?"

"Hell, how should I know? Maybe she thinks I'm one of those reporters coming by to cop an interview."

"Man, you *are* a reporter. I seen your name in the paper this morning."

Damn. Now what? John hadn't heard from Celie in almost three days. In that block of time she'd been interrogated by police, fired from her job, and hounded by the media. John was getting worried. He'd tried calling Dax to get into the building, or at least get an update, but the man wasn't home.

John gave Terrance an earnest look. "Tell me one thing. Have you seen her at all today?"

Terrance frowned. "Shoot, I could get in trouble, you know. Ms. Wells told the building manager she didn't want *nobody* bother'n her."

"I won't get you in trouble."

Terrance shook his head. "You didn't hear this from me, but she just left a few minutes ago. Don't know where she was going."

"How'd she leave if her car's here?"

"Someone picked her up out front."

"Man or woman?"

"I didn't see."

"You get a look at the car?"

Terrance heaved a sigh. He probably thought John was whipped.

And he was probably right.

"One a those little hybrid things," Terrance said finally. "White."

Who drove a car like that? Not the bodyguard. Maybe one of her girlfriends? It sounded like a woman's car.

John tapped on the granite with his knuckles. "Thanks, man. Tell her I came by, okay?"

Terrance nodded, and John retraced his steps through the double doors. The instant he got outside, he was hit by a gust of hot air. He squinted up at the sun.

John had planned to spend his Saturday afternoon rappelling with some guys from work, but instead he'd devoted most of it to tracking down Celie. He'd been to the Bluebonnet House, where he now knew she no longer worked. He'd been to campus. He'd even been by the neighborhood Starbucks, but he couldn't find her.

A red 6 Series BMW rolled by and slid into a visitor's space next to John's Jeep. Andrew Stone got out and locked the car with a *chirp*. *Lone Star Monthly* probably paid better than the *Herald*, but John preferred to think Stone was indebted up to his eyeballs.

John scowled at Stone as he crossed the lot.

"What's up?" Stone tucked a pair of expensive-looking sunglasses into the pocket of his starched white shirt.

"Cecelia's not home."

Stone propped a shiny dress shoe on the curb. "That right? I just talked to her on the phone."

John gritted his teeth. No way had Celie taken a phone call from this dickhead if she was dodging reporters. Stone was full of shit.

"Yeah, well I just talked to her, too, and she was on her way out. Tell me what you want, and I'll make sure she gets the message."

The side of Stone's mouth ticked up. "I imagine I want the same thing you do."

John crossed his arms.

"You know, you're pretty smooth, McAllister. I knew I recognized her from somewhere, and then it finally hit me. The Sixth Street Rapist trial. You were sniffing around that one, too, if I remember correctly."

John didn't say anything.

Stone lifted his gaze to the upper floors of Celie's building. "She's a good little scoop, isn't she? Got a knack for getting herself in trouble. Pretty, too. Makes for a compelling human-interest story." He flipped his Beamer keys onto his palm and smirked. "But you already know all that, don't you?"

Still, John didn't say anything. Stone was baiting him, and John refused to give him a reaction.

Like smashing his fucking nose in.

"Is that your message?" John asked blandly. "I'll be sure to give it to her."

Stone smiled and nodded at the double glass doors. "Thanks, anyway, buddy. I'll give it to her myself."

Celie was walking past the Clock Tower on campus when her cell phone rang for the third time since lunch. She checked the caller ID, expecting McAllister's number to pop up again, but, to her surprise, it was her mom.

Celie answered the phone. "Hi. What's wrong?"

Her mother never called her mobile. She considered it

impolite to use cell phones in public, which pretty much negated the point of having one.

"Cecelia. Do you have any idea what day it is?"

It was Thursday, but her mother's chilly tone told her she wasn't asking the day of the week.

"I give up." Celie sighed. "What'd I forget?"

"Abby's *birthday* was yesterday. She said you didn't even call her."

Celie sat down on the low concrete wall near the student union building. "I'm sorry, Mom, I've been so busy—"

"I swear, Cecelia, sometimes you act like you're the very *center* of the universe! Is it too much to ask for you to give your sister a few minutes of your time? Or are you too busy partying up in Austin?"

Partying. Yeah, right. Then abruptly Celie realized what this was really about.

"Did Abby get anything special this year?" she asked, even though she knew she hadn't. If her sister's long-term boyfriend had finally gotten around to proposing, Celie would already have been summoned home to shop for bridesmaids' dresses.

"Don't be spiteful, Cecelia. You know how sensitive Abby is about this birthday."

"I know, Mom."

Actually, Abby wasn't sensitive about this birthday, but her mother was. There was an unwritten rule in her mom's bridge club that all daughters must be married off by the time they turned thirty, or it reflected poorly on the family.

"Cecelia?"

"I'm sorry, Mom. I'll give her a call." She glanced up to see Andrew Stone standing in front of her. He flashed her a smile and tucked his hands into the pockets of his tailored slacks.

"Mom? Sorry, but I've really got to get to class."

Celie clicked off, and Andrew took a seat beside her on the wall.

"Thought I'd find you here," he said.

"Why's that?"

"I knew you were a student, so . . ." He shrugged. "I figured you'd be around somewhere."

Sure. UT had only about fifty thousand students, so obviously if he just showed up on campus, they'd bump into each other.

He'd accessed her schedule somehow. He'd probably followed her straight out of the social work building when her last class let out.

"What can I do for you?" she asked.

"I just wanted to say hi." He smiled, and she understood why McAllister hated this guy. He seemed completely incapable of a sincere facial expression.

She stood up. "Well. Hi. I hate to rush off, but I have a seminar in five minutes, so—"

"Wait." He took her hand, and Celie felt a spurt of irritation. She didn't like men touching her without her permission.

Except McAllister.

She pulled her hand away, and he pretended not to mind.

"I've got a project I'm thinking about, and I thought I'd run it by you," he said smoothly.

"Let me guess." She zipped her cell phone into her backpack. "'Married to the Mob,' but with a Texas flair? Or wait, how about 'Fugitive from Love'?"

"I beg your pardon?" He acted confused.

"I've heard half a dozen this week. Mostly from local TV producers, though. I guess, if you interview me, I'll be a *statewide* celebrity. That's something to look forward to."

He frowned. "It wouldn't be like that. I don't work for a tabloid—"

"No offense, but they're all the same to me. My private life is private, and I'd rather not discuss it with the news media."

Andrew's eyebrow tipped up. "Last I checked, the *Herald* was a media organization."

She waited for him to finish his point. If he so much as *suggested* that she'd given McAllister some kind of special treatment . . .

"Just give it some thought, okay? I know you've been through a lot." He stood up and gave her his "sympathetic friend" look, complete with reassuring arm squeeze and furrowed brow. "You might find it cathartic to share some of your experiences. It might help bring closure to this chapter in your life."

She brushed her hair out of her face and looked at him. "I think what would bring me closure would be for you and everyone else in your profession to just leave me be."

She turned and walked away, cutting across the grass to get to the student union, where she could lose herself in the mob of students seeking snacks and coffee. She wove through clusters of people and headed down a stairwell to hide out by the vending machines. The basement of the building was a place she knew well—it provided refuge when bright light and noise threatened to bring on a headache, like the one worming its way into her skull right this minute.

Closure. What a load of bull. At least when McAllister asked a question, he was up front about it.

Celie stared at the vending machine and felt an overwhelming craving for a Snickers bar. Sometimes a quick burst of chocolate actually helped her migraines, probably because of the caffeine. On the other hand, she didn't need the calories, and she wasn't even hungry, really, so. . . .

As her thoughts turned inward, she realized a headache wasn't the only thing bothering her. A familiar cramping sensation rippled through her lower abdomen.

Of course. What else could go wrong today? As the reality of her body's message sunk in, she felt her eyes fill with tears. Where was *this* coming from? She had no idea she'd gotten her hopes up this month. She'd told herself how unlikely it was, and yet here she was with this hole in her heart.

What a day this had turned out to be, and it wasn't even over yet. No, the worst was still to come. Now she had to talk to McAllister.

John was cranky and tired when he got home from work Wednesday night. He'd put in a fourteen-hour day running between City Hall and the newsroom, and he hadn't stopped once to eat. After flinging his keys on the counter and loosening his tie, he yanked open the fridge and searched for some dinner.

"Shit," he muttered, staring at near-empty shelves. He suddenly recalled finishing off the leftover pizza last night while watching Conan O'Brien, so he settled for a Shiner.

He rolled up his sleeves as he listened to his voice-mail messages. A woman had called, but it wasn't the one he'd been hoping for. She was a grad student he'd met at the Dog & Duck Pub several months ago. Before they'd gotten too inebriated for conversation, they'd talked about their mutual interest in climbing, and she was calling to invite him to do Enchanted Rock with her this weekend. By the tone of her voice, she was inviting him to do her, too.

John erased the message.

Six days had passed since he'd received a brief phone message from Celie: *You'll be happy to know I'm not pregnant. Please respect my privacy now and leave me alone.*

It was pretty clear she didn't want to talk to him, and he'd had no luck tracking her down. She wasn't answering his calls and was doing an excellent job dodging him at her apartment building. She was so good, in fact, John had to wonder if she'd left the place at all this week. She was either pissed off and fuming or depressed as hell.

John took his liquid dinner outside and sank down on the back stoop. It was hot and humid tonight, and he instantly started to sweat. He tipped back his beer and listened to the cicadas, remembering the last time he'd sat here after dark, the night Celie had slept over. He didn't usually invite women to spend the night at his house, but then nothing with Celie had been usual.

He pulled his cell phone from his pocket and flipped it open. He didn't want to make the call. He knew how Feenie felt about him; he knew she'd give him crap. But he pictured Celie holed up in her apartment, and his fingers started dialing the numbers.

She picked up right after the first ring.

"Feenie, it's John McAllister. Sorry to call so late."

"That's all right. I'm up with Olivia."

He'd forgotten about that. He checked his watch. It was after ten. "Damn, I'm sorry."

"Forget it. What's up?"

He heard the curiosity in her voice. They hadn't talked in months, since he'd called to say good-bye before his move to Austin.

"Have you talked to Celie lately?" John asked now.

The baby whimpered on the other end of the phone.

"No. Why?"

"Fuck," he muttered. He rubbed his hand over his face.

"What's going on?" Feenie sounded alarmed. "Is she okay?"

He blew out a breath. "No, she's not. There was an incident two weeks ago. She had a run-in with some rivals of Manny Saledo. It turned out okay, but the FBI and the police got involved and, shit, it's a long story, but—"

"Is she *hurt*?"

"No, nothing like that. But she ended up getting fired from her job."

Feenie gasped. "No way!"

"Yep."

"How could they *fire* her?"

"I don't know, exactly—"

"Those ungrateful jerks! They should be building her a statue!"

John wasn't sure what to make of that, but he filed it away for later.

"Since all this happened," he continued, "I've called her about twenty times. She won't return my messages. She won't see me. I'm not sure if she's left her apartment in a while, but I'm pretty sure she's in some kind of funk."

He could sense Feenie getting the picture. *That's right, babe. She slept with me. Just like you told her not to.*

"Y'all . . . are involved?"

Involved. An interesting way to phrase it.

"I think she was hoping I could get her pregnant. But that didn't happen, and now I think she's pretty disappointed." He cleared his throat. "She left me a message about it, and she sounded, I don't know, flat. Not herself."

Silence.

"Feenie?"

"Yeah, I'm here." She sighed. "I can't believe she didn't tell me all this."

"She probably thought you'd try and talk her out of getting involved with me."

"I would have. You barely even know her, McAllister. You have no idea what she's been through."

He clenched his teeth. "Yes, as a matter of fact, I do."

Feenie, of course, was already on a soapbox. "Couldn't you find someone else to shack up with? In a city of a *million* people? Celie's already dealing with a lot right now."

"I *know* that. Shit. I don't need a lecture."

"The entire last year has been hell for her, and now—"

"That's not the only thing." He took a deep breath and tried to tamp down his temper. "She's been all over the news."

"You're kidding."

"I wrote the original article. I know how she is about her privacy, and I tried to keep her name out of the paper. But some local station put it together that she was married to a big international fugitive, Saledo's name came up, and now it's a free-for-all. I think she's freaked out."

"Well, God, I don't blame her! You sleep with her and then all her problems end up in the paper? What were you thinking?"

"Look, this isn't why I called you."

"Why *did* you call me?"

Why *had* he called? Feenie's baby cooed in the background as John thought about how to answer that. "I don't know," he admitted. It didn't make any sense, not even to him. He'd called the dead last person who would ever convince Celie to give him another chance. "I guess, you know, I'm worried about her. She's going through something, and she won't talk to me, but I think she needs to talk to someone. I know she trusts you."

The last part stung, because he was admitting Celie didn't trust *him*.

Feenie sighed. "What a mess," she said.

"I know."

"Let me see what I can do."

The buzzer sounded, and Celie slammed shut her textbook. Why couldn't he take a hint? She'd told him to leave her *alone,* for God's sake, and instead he'd become her personal stalker.

She was going to have to talk to the management. Again.

She stomped across the apartment and punched Talk on the intercom.

"I told you, Terrance. No visitors, please."

"Sorry Ms. Wells, but I've got a lady down here named Jeannie? She says—"

"Celie, it's me!" Feenie's voice came through the speaker. "I'm *dying* for a bathroom. Better buzz me up quick before I make a puddle all over this nice floor."

Feenie was in Austin. Great. "It's okay, Terrance. Send her up, please."

Celie glanced around her apartment. She'd been studying for exams all week and had scarcely taken a shower, much less picked up after herself. Soft drink cans littered the coffee table, and the floor was blanketed with books and lecture notes. Her laptop sat open on the kitchen counter next to a now-empty carton of kung pao chicken.

She started scooping up cans and tossing them in the recycle bin. Why hadn't Feenie called first? Her timing was terrible—Celie had a final tomorrow morning and a term paper due Monday.

She made a stack of books and dumped some dirty plates in the sink. She hadn't even brushed her hair today, and she'd been wearing the same T-shirt for the past forty-eight hours.

A knock sounded at the door.

Celie blew out a sigh and gave up. Feenie would just

have to ignore the mess. She crossed her apartment, undid the locks, and swung open the door.

"Surprise!" Feenie beamed at her from the hallway. She was all blond curls and twinkling blue eyes, the same as always, except for the squirming bundle in her arms.

"What on earth are you doing here?" Celie stepped back and ushered them inside, locking the door behind them.

Feenie kissed Celie's cheek and shoved Olivia into her arms. "Hold her for a sec, would you? I've *really* gotta pee!"

Celie hugged the baby to her chest. "The bathroom's just—" But Feenie had already disappeared down the hallway.

Celie's gaze dropped to Olivia, who was staring up at her with huge brown eyes. She wore a pink striped sleeper that matched the blanket swaddled around her. "Hey there, precious," Celie said. "Just look how big you're getting!"

Olivia started whimpering. Her brow furrowed and her little mouth turned down, and Celie panicked and shifted her to a shoulder. She swayed from side to side in what she hoped was a soothing motion.

"I swear, I've been dying for the last hour," Feenie called from the bathroom. "I didn't want to pull over because I kept thinking we were almost here."

Olivia wiggled, and Celie stroked her back. "It's okay," she whispered. "Mommy's coming right back." Olivia's head was covered with downy brown hair, and she smelled like baby powder. Celie kissed her brow.

"We made pretty good time," Feenie yelled over the

faucet. "Five and a half hours, door to door, with one pit stop to feed Liv."

"Is Marco with you?"

Olivia's face crumpled. Too loud. Oh, dear.

"Shh ..." she cooed, patting the baby's padded bottom. "It's okay. I didn't mean to yell." Maybe she could distract her with something. She walked to the breakfast room window, where the midafternoon sun streamed through the blinds. Olivia blinked as the rays fell across her face. It felt warmer next to the window, and her little frown disappeared.

"Sorry 'bout that," Feenie said, coming to stand beside Celie. "I feel much better now."

"She's getting so big," Celie marveled. "And look at all this hair!"

"I can't believe it either. Every day she looks more and more like Marco." Feenie stroked the baby's cheek, and she bobbed her head.

"You think she's hungry?"

"Probably," Feenie replied, gently taking Olivia from Celie's shoulder. "It's been a few hours since her last meal."

Celie glanced around the living room. The most comfortable place to sit was an oversize armchair, but she remembered Feenie always used a glider back home.

"Let me get my rocker," Celie said, heading back into her bedroom.

"Oh, don't bother with that."

"It's no bother."

The chair was buried under towels and dirty clothes, and Celie shoved everything to the floor. She dragged the rocker across the apartment and positioned it alongside an end table.

Feenie sank into the chair. "Thanks," she said, arranging Olivia in the crook of her arm. She unfastened several buttons on her chambray shirt and, in a few expert motions, had the baby latched on and feeding.

Celie averted her eyes. Feenie was a busty woman under normal circumstances, but since Olivia's birth . . . well, it was pretty astonishing.

"Can I get you something?" Celie asked. When she'd last visited Mayfield, she'd noticed Feenie's habit of keeping a tall glass of Carnation Instant Breakfast handy while she nursed. "I don't have any milk, but I can make some herbal tea."

"I'm okay," Feenie said. "Marco and I shared an orange juice a little while ago."

Celie plopped onto the couch. "Where is he, anyway?"

"Checking out your security."

"You're kidding."

"Nope. He dropped me off and said he was going to come back and see if he could manage to get up here without alerting the guard."

"He's conducting an undercover operation in my *building*?"

Feenie smiled. "I know, I know. But it's his thing. He'll give you a full report, which I'm sure he'll be more than happy to share with whoever manages this place. He likes your security fence, and he says the gates and cameras are top of the line. I think he's more concerned about the human element."

"What, like my guard?"

"Yeah. That guy Terrance is really nice, but he never even asked me to sign in or show ID or anything. Marco will have a field day with that. You're paying a premium here for security."

Celie sighed.

"Don't worry. We're booked at the Hampton Inn tonight, so we won't be in your way."

"You're not in my way. I just had no idea y'all were coming to town. You should have called me."

Feenie shrugged and gazed down at Olivia. "It was pretty spur of the moment. We didn't decide to come until last night."

"Let me guess. Someone heard about me on the news, right?" Celie leaned her head back on the couch and stared up at the ceiling. "God, my mother's probably freaking out about now."

"John McAllister called me, actually." Feenie looked at her. "He thinks you're in some kind of funk."

Unbelievable. Celie pushed herself off the sofa. "That man has a lot of nerve telling you to come up here like this—"

"He didn't tell me to come. He just said he was worried." Feenie eyes filled with concern. "Why didn't you say something, Celie? I would have been up here in a flash if I'd known you were having all this trouble."

She scoffed. That was exactly why Celie *hadn't* said anything. "I'm not having trouble."

Now Feenie looked hurt.

"Not really." God, why did McAllister have to be so damn meddlesome?

"He said you had a run-in with the Saledos."

Celie walked into the kitchen for a soft drink. "Turns out, it wasn't the Saledos. And it was minor, really." Except for someone getting shot. "The police handled it."

"And you got fired from your job?"

Celie muttered a curse. He'd told her everything. She returned to the living room and plopped down on the couch. "I'll find something else. It's no big deal."

Feenie gave her a sharp look. She knew full well how much that job had meant to her. "Okay, so I suppose now you're going to tell me you're *not* sleeping with John McAllister?"

"I'm not sleeping with John McAllister." Never again.

Feenie shook her head and gazed down at the baby. Little Olivia had her eyes closed. A lock of damp hair clung to her forehead, and she looked rosy and content. Her tiny, dimpled hand rested on her mother's breast as she nursed.

"She's really beautiful," Celie said softly.

Feenie smiled.

"You make a wonderful mother."

She tucked the blanket around the baby and gave Celie a skeptical look. "I don't know about that. I feel like a zombie half the time."

Celie watched the two of them in the rocker together, surprised to feel tenderness instead of envy. She loved Feenie like a sister, and she really, truly wanted her to be happy.

"It's not what I expected," Feenie said.

"What isn't?"

She glanced up. "Motherhood." She tipped her head to the side. "It's wonderful and all that, and I love Olivia so much, sometimes I feel like I'm gonna burst, but it's not all Kodak moments. And it doesn't solve all your problems."

"I know that." At least, Celie thought she did. She'd wanted a baby for so long, she'd almost forgotten what it felt like to want anything else.

"I mean, it's definitely the most stressful thing I've ever done," Feenie said. "Being responsible for this other person all the time. Round the clock, no excuses. And the sleep deprivation . . ." She glanced up. "It's a lot of work sometimes. And I have *help*. Marco's been an angel. He's absolutely enamored with her, but still it's hard. We bicker a lot."

"That's probably normal," Celie offered. It was, wasn't it? It never occurred to her that Feenie and Marco might be having marital stress. She'd been so absorbed with her own life lately, she'd hardly stopped to think about her friends and family.

"Don't get me wrong," Feenie said. "We're doing fine. It's just a lot, you know? The baby, the bills, the housework. I can't imagine doing it all alone."

Celie cleared her throat. "I guess McAllister told you, didn't he? That I'm still trying to get pregnant?"

Feenie glanced up warily. "Are you sure that's the best thing?"

Celie sighed. No one understood how important this was to her.

"I'm not judging you, Celie."

"Sure you are."

"I'm really not. If anyone can pull off single parent-hood, it's you. I just . . . I don't want to see you disappointed. Or overwhelmed. Why not wait until you meet the right guy and then you can get married and adopt or something? Does this really have to happen right now? And with John?"

"It's *not* happening with him. I'm not pregnant. We're not seeing each other anymore. End of story."

Feenie scoffed. "End of story. Yeah, right. If you really believe that, you don't know squat about John McAllister. When that man makes up his mind about something, look out."

"What do you mean 'look out'? What's he made his mind up about?"

Feenie shot her annoyed look. "*You*, Celie. Open your eyes!"

"My eyes *are* open, thank you very much. And I see a chronic playboy, relieved as heck to be back on the market after a whirlwind affair with a baby-obsessed basket case!"

Feenie shook her head. "Celie . . ."

"What?"

"Hon, if that's what you really see, you need to have your eyes examined."

Celie slid the Volvo into her reserved parking space and scooped plastic bags off the passenger seat. She'd just completed a bigger-than-usual Saturday morning grocery run, but she was determined to get everything upstairs in one load.

She trudged across the parking garage, the bags strangling her fingers as she neared the door. This wasn't going to work, especially with her key card tucked away in her back pocket. She started to adjust the bags, and one of the doors swung open.

"Thank you," she gushed. "I was just—"

She glanced up into John McAllister's penetrating blue eyes. He held the door open for her and used his free hand to take all her bags.

"After you," he said, nodding toward the lobby.

CHAPTER

19

C elie huffed out a breath and went inside. She should have expected this today. He didn't usually work Saturdays, so of course he'd show up at The Overlook.

Terrance stood up as Celie strode across the lobby toward the elevator bank.

"Mr. McAllister's already checked in, Ms. Wells, but he can't go up without your approval."

Celie grimaced. "He's fine. Thank you, Terrance."

The formerly friendly security guard gave her a curt nod. Marco's report had not been kind.

Carrying all her bags like they were nothing, McAllister reached over and tapped the elevator button. He wore jeans, beat-up running shoes, and a white T-shirt commemorating some beerfest in Shiner, Texas.

The elevator doors dinged open, and they rode up in

silence, Celie staring at her feet to keep from making eye contact with McAllister in the mirrored doors. The last time they'd ridden this elevator together, he had been whispering indecent suggestions in her ear the whole way. She wondered if he was thinking about that now.

Her cheeks warmed, and she hurried into the hallway as the doors slid open.

This wasn't good. He'd follow her into her apartment, help her put her groceries away, and then what? They'd either end up fighting or in bed together. Or both. It was a surefire way for her to get her heart battered.

She stopped in front of her door and rummaged through her purse for the key. She found herself wondering if she'd remembered to make the bed, and feeling grateful that she'd showered and put on a fresh knit top today instead of the stained sweatshirt she'd been living in of late. McAllister stood patiently beside her, pretending not to notice her clumsiness as she fumbled with the locks.

She would be calm. Detached. She would listen as he said whatever it was he'd come to say, and then she'd politely ask him to leave. If she asked him to go, he'd respect her request.

She just hoped she'd have the willpower to ask him.

She pushed open the door, and he brushed past her into the apartment. He went through the old routine of checking all the rooms before joining her back in the kitchen, where he set the bags down on the counter beside her purse.

"Any weird phone calls lately?" he asked.

"No."

She opened the fridge and busied herself putting food away. Today she'd had a lengthy shopping list. If she drew things out, it would take her a while to unpack. Maybe she wouldn't even have to look at him while he talked. That would definitely help.

"T-Bone still hanging around?"

"No," Celie said. "It didn't seem necessary, what with the arrests last week." It was also expensive, and she couldn't afford to keep paying him indefinitely when there was no longer a clear threat to her safety.

Less than a day after the money drop, the Barriolo brothers were apprehended at a border checkpoint. In a dazzling display of stupidity, they were driving a Mercury Cougar that had been reported stolen in Austin the previous morning. The man in black from the Lamar Street Bridge was still in custody, too. Rowe had told Celie the guy was a Saledo employee sent to Austin to intercept the cash. How he'd found out about the drop was another question, but Celie figured it was Rowe's job to answer that one.

McAllister knew all this, but he didn't say anything. He just leaned back against her counter, watching intently as Celie arranged yogurt cups on a shelf.

"What?"

"I still think you need to take precautions," he said.

"Well, Rowe agrees with you. He said they're keeping me under surveillance for the foreseeable future."

Celie didn't really think Saledo would bother with her now—Robert was dead, the cash he'd taken had supposedly been seized by federal agents, and Celie no longer possessed any money or information Saledo could use. Still, she didn't mind having the FBI looking out for her, just to be safe.

McAllister didn't seem placated, but he didn't push it.

Celie undid a six-pack of Diet Cokes and lined them up neatly beside the yogurts.

"I talked to Feenie," he announced.

"So I heard." She kept her voice cool. "Though I have no idea why you thought it necessary to drag Feenie and Marco up here with their newborn just so they could check on me. I was not in a *funk* or whatever it was you told Feenie."

"That's what she said, too. Apparently, you were just studying for finals."

"That's right." She jerked open a cabinet door and plunked some soup cans on the shelf.

"Evidently, you weren't upset about being in the media spotlight again either."

Celie shrugged and stacked the cans, making sure the labels faced out.

"And apparently, being hounded by reporters like you were after the rape trial didn't bother you at all."

Her hands stilled on the cans. She couldn't believe he'd just said that. They never talked about the trial. Not ever. After that first time he'd told her how, as a fledgling news intern, he'd witnessed her testimony, they'd totally dropped the subject.

"It didn't really bother me," she said. The furor had died down over the past few days. Some aide in the governor's office had committed suicide this week, and local media outlets had shifted their coverage and unending speculation to the latest big story.

She reached for another bag and began unloading fruits and vegetables into the refrigerator drawers.

"Feenie also told me you're not depressed," he continued. "She said that you never expected me to get you pregnant, and that you're not really looking to have a baby right now."

Her head snapped around. Feenie told him *that*? No way. She found it impossible to believe on several levels, the first being that her best friend wouldn't discuss something so personal about her behind her back.

"Feenie didn't say that," she stated.

He shrugged. "Not in so many words. Why? You don't agree with her assessment?"

Celie hesitated, sensing a trap. If she agreed, she'd be admitting a lot of private stuff that wasn't true. If she disagreed, she'd be admitting she was depressed.

She snagged another bag off the counter and unpacked some condiments into her fridge.

"Yeah, I don't buy it either," he said. "I think you're totally on the edge."

She glanced at him, which was a mistake, because now she realized he was watching her with one of those X-ray looks, one of those looks that cut straight through all her polite crapola and saw *her*, in all her screwed-up, emotionally damaged glory.

"I'm not on the *edge*," she told him.

She unloaded another bag and noticed only two more remained on the counter. As soon as they were empty, she'd be forced to give him her undivided attention. She popped open a plastic container of mini-muffins and decided to arrange them in a cookie tin. She took her time digging one out of a bottom cabinet.

McAllister didn't say anything, but she could feel him watching her. She never should have let him up here.

"So you *aren't* sad about the fact that your best friend, and your sister, and most of the women you know are having babies right now and you're not? It doesn't bother you at all?"

She lined up the mini-muffins in the tin, resenting him for making her feel like an interview subject. "Of course I'm not sad about it. It's terrific. I'm happy for them."

"Uh-huh. And although we had unprotected sex pretty much nonstop, for a whole weekend, you weren't the slightest bit disappointed when you found out you weren't pregnant?"

"I never *thought* I'd get pregnant," she lied, "so, no, I wasn't disappointed."

"Good, because I have to tell you, I was relieved as hell when I got your message."

Her chest tightened. Now why did that hurt her feelings? Of course he was relieved. What carefree single guy would *not* be relieved to find out he was off the hook?

"I mean, shit, here I was thinking we were honestly having some fun together, and I come to find out I'm just a sperm donor for you."

She shot him a look. She hated the term *sperm donor,* always had. "I never thought of you that way."

"Really?" His eyebrows arched. "That's good, because my ego was taking a real beating. See, when you came over to my house and *got naked,* I was pretty sure you were hot for me." He stroked his chin and pretended to think about it. "Yeah, you even felt like you were hot for me. And then I find out you had this hidden agenda—"

"I didn't *get naked* at your house! You make it sound

like I showed up in a trench coat or something, like some ... some slut out to seduce you!"

He hooked his thumbs through the belt loops of his jeans. "You mean you didn't plan it?"

"Of course not!" Angry now, she snapped open another plastic carton of mini-muffins and added them to the cookie tin. This wasn't going well. He was pushing her buttons, trying to get a rise out of her, and it was working.

"Whether you believe me or not, I didn't plan it," she said. "Just like all those messages you left me where you said you didn't *plan* to write that article about me for the *Herald*."

She met his gaze now and saw the faintest flicker of remorse. Good, now he was on the defensive. "You told me it just happened, because of Kate getting shot," she said. "I don't know if I believe you, but—"

"How can you not believe me?" His voice was pure exasperation. "What, you think I *knew* Kate was going to jump in front of a bullet? And what's with you doubting everything I say, like I'm some kind of pathological liar or something? You're the one who has a problem with honesty."

"I do *not* have a problem with honesty!"

"Like hell! If I hadn't opened your medicine cabinet, I'd never have known you were were on some high-tech single-mommy track! Did it ever occur to you that I *might* have a problem with the idea of women having illegitimate babies? Shit, thank God you can't get knocked up, or I'd be wandering around ten years from now not even knowing I'm the father of some kid!"

She could barely breathe. *Thank God you can't get knocked up . . .* Thank *God?* Thank God for the worst thing that ever happened to her? Thank God she'd never be able to be happy?

"You *jerk,*" she whispered.

He frowned, obviously not even realizing what he'd said that had been so cruel.

He didn't understand her. Just like Robert. Just like her mom, and her sisters, and Feenie, and Dax, and even her doctors. *No one* understood. Everyone who knew her pitied her because she was the victim of rape, the victim of violence, the victim of a lying, conniving husband. But it was much harder to accept being the victim of her own body. It was like being a victim of God. It was like being punished.

"Get out," she said.

"What, we can't even talk about this?"

"No, we can't. I need you to leave."

"No."

"*No?*"

"Not until we talk this out." He crossed his arms, and he got that expression on his face, that bulldog expression. The one that meant he intended to hang on, relentlessly, until he got his way.

"I really hate you," she muttered. She picked up a mini-muffin and threw it at him. It bounced right off his nose, and the look of shock on his face was priceless. "Are you listening? I *hate* you!"

She grabbed another muffin and hummed it at him. And another and another and another. He batted them away, staring at her the whole time like she'd lost her mind.

"I wish you'd never *come* here!" she screamed. "I wish you'd leave me *alone*!"

She lunged at him and shoved him, hard, with both fists. "I want you *out*!" He stumbled back against the counter. "Do you hear me? Get out of my house!"

"Hey, hey, hey—"

"*Out!*" She pounded on his chest.

"Cool it, Celie—"

"I will *not* cool it!" She pounded again. "I'm *sick* of cooling it! Do you have any idea what it's like to want a child so bad you're willing to stick needles in your body every day? To go to dozens and dozens of doctor appointments? To get fat? To spend your life waiting around for pee sticks to turn blue? To have everyone always ask you, 'Why's a nice girl like you not married with kids?' I'm sick of it! And it's none of your damn business if I'm depressed, or upset, or on the edge, or just plain crazy, so get *out*!"

She pounded and pounded, and then her fist hit his chin, and his head snapped back.

"Ouch!" Scowling, he stepped around her and went to the sink.

She stood in the middle of the kitchen, breathless and horrified. *I've totally lost it*, she told herself. *I actually hit another person.*

"Shit, Celie." He dabbed his jaw with a dishrag and eyed his reflection in the microwave. "Are you wearing a ring or something?"

She looked down at her hands. She was wearing the silly friendship ring Feenie had given her in high school. She'd worn it for luck to her final exam yesterday. It had a silver rose on the top, and a tiny piece of red flesh was stuck on one of the petals.

"Oh my gosh." She rushed to the sink and looked at his face, pulling the towel away so she could see the wound.

"Oh my gosh, I *cut* you!"

He glared down at her. Then he yanked her hand up and examined her ring finger. "Since when do you wear jewelry?"

"I'm so sorry—"

"Forget it."

She reached up to wipe the trickle of blood running down his chin. "I can't forget it. I—"

"It's fine. Quit fussing." He swatted her hand away and stared down at her, probably finally realizing she was a complete mental case. She bit her lip and wanted to sink through the floor.

"I'm really sorry."

"I heard you the first time."

"I don't know what got into me. You must think I'm crazy. I—"

"Jesus, shut *up!*" He pulled her against him. "I'm not hurt. Just surprised. I didn't know you were so physical."

His arms were warm and strong around her, and suddenly she was so bone tired she couldn't summon the energy to do anything but slump against him. A hot tear slid down her cheek. She blotted it away, but it was followed by another, and another, and, before she knew it, she was sniveling against his chest. Everything came gushing out—tears, hiccups, snot—she couldn't hold anything in. His arms tightened even more, and that only made it worse.

"I'm sorry." She grabbed a fistful of his damp T-shirt. "I'm so sorry."

She felt him smooth her hair. "I'm fine, okay? It's just a scratch."

"Not *that*," she choked. "I'm sorry about that, too, but"— hiccup—"I'm sorry I *lied* to you. About something so important. I don't know why I did it. I never should have used you that way."

He held her tightly, his heart thudding next to her ear.

"Hey, let's forget it, okay?" He pulled back and looked down into her face. She took a deep breath and rubbed her nose with the back of her hand and tried to get control of her emotions.

"Okay?"

She nodded.

"Good. Shit." He squeezed her again and stroked a hand down her back. "I mean, I shouldn't be complaining, right? Having a beautiful woman use me as her stud? There're probably worse forms of torture."

She choked again, half laughter, half despair.

He circled his hands around her waist and lifted her onto the counter. They were at eye level now, and she reached for a dish towel to dry her face.

"Listen," he said. "You keep saying something, and I want to make sure we understand each other. I do *not* think you're crazy."

She blew out a wobbly sigh. Of course he did.

"I mean it. You're not crazy."

"Fine," she said. "Then at least admit you think I'm neurotic."

He was so close she could see tiny silver flecks in his

blue irises. His eyes were so intelligent and gentle, and she couldn't believe she'd *hit* him.

"You're not neurotic," he said. "You're a perfectly normal person who's been through a shitload of stress."

He stroked his hands down her arms. "I think you're completely normal. Better than normal. Hell, my sister's more neurotic than you, and she's pretty much had it easy." The side of his mouth quirked up. "Although, don't tell her I said that or she'll beat me up for real."

Celie smiled.

"Seriously," he said, getting somber, "it takes a lot of guts to go through everything you have and not get bitter. To still be so caring toward other people. It's one of the things I admire about you."

"Thanks," she said, wiping her cheeks. Maybe he meant what he was saying. Maybe not. Her mind was all jumbled, but she knew it felt good to be with him like this, just talking and knowing he was listening.

He was also staring at her. His gaze kept dropping to her mouth like he intended to kiss her.

She gently pushed him back and hopped down from the counter, then walked over to her refrigerator and searched the vegetable drawer until she found a cucumber. She had the puffy eye gene. Just a few minutes of crying, and her eyes would swell up like a boxer's. She took a knife from her chopping block and sliced off two cucumber rounds.

"Are you making a salad?" he asked, incredulous.

"No. But whenever I have a crying jag, I need at least five minutes with a cucumber or I can't leave the house."

She walked into the living room with the cucumber slices.

"My mind is reeling now. You know that, right?"

She glanced over her shoulder and scowled at him. "You have a dirty mind."

"Honey, you have no idea."

She laid down on the couch and closed her eyes, then placed the chilled cucumber slices on her eyelids. "You're welcome to stay if you want, but this is pretty boring."

She expected him to either make an excuse to leave or sink down into her armchair. Instead, he picked up her feet and sat down on the end of the sofa, resting her heels on his thigh. She felt him slide off her sandals and brush a finger over her toes.

She lifted one of the cucumbers and peeked out at him. "What are you doing?"

"I love your feet."

"My feet."

"Yep."

He stroked a finger over the arch of her foot and started massaging it with the pads of his thumbs. If she'd known she'd be getting her feet rubbed today, she would have touched up her polish. Oh well. At least they were clean.

Celie replaced the cucumber slice and nestled her head against the sofa arm. What was going on here? She'd just clobbered the heck out of this man in her kitchen, and now he was giving her a foot massage. He was too weird. Or maybe she was.

"Aren't you mad at me?" she asked.

"I told you, *no*."

"Is this something you normally do after someone pitches a fit in front of you?"

"No. But I've been wanting to do this for a while now."

"It feels good," she murmured. His hands were warm and strong, and he used just enough pressure so that it didn't tickle. At least not her feet. Other parts of her body were definitely feeling ticklish.

She cleared her throat. "Do you do this for all your girlfriends?"

His hands paused for a barely perceptible instant, and then kept moving. "No."

Great. She'd gone out on a limb, and he hadn't given her what she wanted. Did he think of her as a girlfriend? A weekend distraction? Or now that she'd shattered his trust in the area of sex, was he going to stick with friendship?

The way his hands were touching her said no.

Friendship wouldn't have worked anyway. This man was like a magnet for her. She couldn't stand to be around him without completely invading his personal space. She'd handled it fairly well back in Mayfield, back before they'd crossed the line into sleeping together. But now that she knew how he could make her feel, anything resembling a platonic relationship was doomed.

Which was probably the reason he'd built such a reputation with women. He was amazing. Magic. He made her feel like she was the only women in the universe.

And when the next woman came along, whoever she was, Celie was going to get her heart broken.

Celie sighed.

"What?"

"I don't know how to do this," she told him.

"Do what?"

"Have this . . . this closeness with you and then just forget about it and move on."

She held her breath while she waited for him to say something, glad to have cucumbers covering her eyes.

But then he plucked them off her face and stared down at her. "Who said you have to forget it?"

"I don't know." She averted her gaze. "I get the impression you try to avoid long-term relationships."

He moved over on the sofa and scooped her into his lap, making her sit up and look at him. She dabbed her eyes with her shirtsleeve. This wasn't a conversation she wanted to have with swollen, red-rimmed eyes.

"Why don't we stop analyzing everything so much and just have fun together?" he suggested.

Fun. Now there was a novel concept. She couldn't suppress the beginnings of a smile. "I guess we could do that."

"Good." He dropped a kiss on her head and wrapped his arms around her. She felt his hand moving softly over her back, brushing aside her hair and tracing patterns over her spine until she felt tingly. Then he slid his other hand under her shirt, and she shivered.

It felt so good to be touched like this again. She wrapped her arms around his neck and snuggled closer.

"Celie," he whispered in her ear. "Are we done talking?"

She nodded.

"Good, because I need to take your clothes off now."

Her nerves jumped, and she made a throaty sound that he obviously took for agreement. His breath was hot against her skin as he kissed a line down her neck, lingering just above her collarbone, where he knew she was sensitive. He lifted her arms and pulled her shirt over her head and let it fall to the floor. She watched him, amazed that they were here, in this place again, when for weeks there had been this gulf between them. He leaned her back against the sofa arm and slid his big, warm hands down her sides, and her pulse raced as all that wanting she'd been trying to ignore started surging through her body. He kept his eyes on hers as he unsnapped her jeans and eased down the zipper. She lifted her hips so he could tug the jeans off, and then she lay back against the cushions, watching his eyes heat as he looked at her in her bra and panties, which unfortunately were ho-hum white lace.

"Damn, you're pretty," he breathed, slipping a strap down her shoulder. She smiled at how easy he was to please. One of these days she was going to get dressed for this and really blow his mind.

Her breast was bare and chilly, but then he started warming the very tip of it with his mouth. Her breath caught as he slipped another strap down and moved to the other side. His tongue teased her, and she felt his hand slide between her legs.

And then he was doing it again, that slow, wonderful exploration that made her absolutely mindless. He kissed her and touched her, and she moaned into his mouth and tried to press even closer. She glided her palm down the solid wall of his chest so she could feel his heart pound. Then she moved it lower and felt him shudder as she gripped the waistband of his jeans. Soon his clothes were piled on top of hers, and he was stretched out beside her, driving her crazy with his hands and his mouth and whispering things that made her blood rush. When she was just on the verge of bliss, he took a second to retrieve a condom from his pocket and cover himself.

She closed her eyes and tried not to think about it, about how she'd lied to him before and how she still, even now, wished she could do it again.

But then he pushed inside her and her breath left her, and everything faded away except him. She opened her eyes and watched him as they moved together, his eyes hazy, his arms and shoulders flexed. She couldn't believe she did this to him, that he wanted her this much, that he always seemed so desperate for her. She wanted to memorize the feeling of him and keep it with her always, no matter what happened. Sweat beaded at his temples as the tension built and built until it was too much.

"Celie . . . *God*."

Suddenly her body tightened around him, and his muscles bunched, and she lost herself in a perfect, endless moment in which the world was right and she loved him more than she'd ever loved anything in her life.

Then he lay on top of her, immobilized, and his weight there made her feel safe and good and even a little bit sad.

He propped up on an elbow and peered down into her face. He traced a finger down her cheek, and she realized she was crying.

"Sorry," she said, embarrassed. "I don't know what's wrong with me today."

"It's okay." He gazed down at her with that look of complete acceptance, and she gave in to the urge to stroke her fingers over his jaw, careful to avoid the spot where she'd cut him.

She swallowed the lump in her throat. "You know that thing I said earlier? In the kitchen? I don't really hate you. I don't know why I said that."

He brushed a wisp of hair off her forehead and looked down into her eyes. "I do."

For a long moment, they stared at each other, and she wondered if he really understood how she felt. And if he did, what did his silence mean? Her stomach fluttered with anxiety, that faint twinge of pain that comes from imagining what it feels like to be rejected. He'd said he wanted to have fun, and so here they were, having fun. Celie was having so much fun she was going to hurt herself.

He pulled back abruptly and wiped his brow with his forearm.

"Damn, this place is stuffy. Don't you ever get hot in here?"

"Not really."

He levered himself off the sofa and picked up his jeans, then walked into the bathroom and closed the door. Celie sat up and pulled a throw over herself.

When he came back a few moments later, he was wearing his jeans again. He stood beside the sofa with his hands on his hips and looked at her. "When was the last time you got outside?"

"I just got back from the store."

"No, I mean really got outside. Did something for recreation."

She thought about it. "I don't usually—"

"Do you trust me?"

The mischievous gleam in his eye put her on her guard.

"Trust you how?"

"Nope." He shook his head. "That's the whole point, you have to trust me. You don't get to know ahead of time."

"Know what?"

He laughed. "Where we're going. I want to take you somewhere, but you have to trust me."

She watched him for a second, overcome with curiosity. "Okay."

"Really?" His whole face brightened, and she immediately second-guessed her answer.

"Is it all right if my eyes are puffy when we get there?"

He grinned. "Shit, by the time we're done, puffy eyes'll be the least of your worries."

John knew he'd successfully snapped Celie out of her funk. The sniffling, tearful woman from that morning was long gone, replaced by a Celie he'd never seen before. She wore a French braid and goggles, and her body was zipped into a purple nylon jumpsuit.

"You okay?" he yelled over the roar of the airplane.

Celie nodded and darted a glance out the window. "How high are we?" she yelled.

"About ten thousand feet, give or take."

Her eyes widened.

"You're gonna do great," he assured her, clasping her hand. "First time's always the scariest."

She nodded stoically, and John felt a rush of pride. She was doing better than the two other first-timers sharing the back of the Twin Otter. Out of ten skydivers, three were virgins. Of those, one had changed her mind about jumping, and another had just heaved his breakfast all over one of the instructors.

"You're doing great," John reiterated. "Just remember everything from the lesson. And if you start to panic, your partner will handle the chute."

She nodded again. John looked over her shoulder and made eye contact with the instructor harnessed to Celie's back. Like most first-timers, Celie was doing a tandem dive, which meant an expert would be right there with her if anything went wrong. John, who was working on his class-A certification, was diving solo today.

Celie squeezed his hand, and her fingers felt like ice. "When this is over," she told him, "I want a margarita."

John grinned. "You got it." He glanced at his watch. "It's one-thirty now. In an hour, we'll be toasting your first jump."

"Okay, boys and girls," the pilot, a guy named Vincent, said over the intercom system, "two minutes to show-time."

Everyone double-checked their gear. John watched as Celie's partner cupped his hand to her ear and gave her instructions. Celie nodded and straightened her goggles. She looked at John.

"We're going to go first," she yelled over the din.

John smiled. "That's my girl."

But she didn't hear him, and soon her partner had them positioned by the opening at the rear of the plane. Celie cast one last glance over her shoulder. John gave her the thumbs-up sign. She smiled and said something, but her words were lost on the wind.

"You ready?" her instructor roared over all the noise.

Celie's chest constricted. She nodded as she looked out the hatch at the green earth peeking through tufts of clouds. The heels of her sneakers rested on the metal floor of the plane while her toes jutted into thin air. She was going to *jump* out of a *plane*!

A strange calm settled over her as she watched her instructor's hand signals: *three . . . two . . . one.*

Suddenly her feet pushed off the airplane, and she was flying.

Only it wasn't flying at all, but more like swimming inside a giant tidal wave of wind. She spread her arms wide and felt the tremendous wall of air push against her body. The force was invisible and cold, and she was shocked by the sheer *power* of it. Then everything went white for a moment, and suddenly the clouds were gone and a green-brown patchwork of farmland stretched out below.

She was screaming like a maniac, she realized, and tried to stop, tried to save her partner's eardrums. But the sound kept coming, and the wind kept coming, and the earth below her loomed bigger and bigger and she could see the landing field.

Her partner signaled her, and for a moment she panicked and couldn't remember what to do.

Then her body jerked, her breath rushed out, and she was floating.

"Oh my God!" she said, as time stood still and she sailed through the air. She pulled the ropes, like she'd done in practice, experimenting with pivots and turns. She didn't have much control, so soon she gave up and simply let herself drift on the wind. Then the landing field was coming closer—rainbow-colored windsocks fluttering, people waving and pointing. Her partner manipulated the chute, slowing their decent as they came in for the landing.

Celie bent her knees and braced herself. The ground rushed to meet her. *Impact.* She ran and stumbled, but somehow managed to keep from falling.

It was over. The ground felt hard and strange beneath her feet.

"Great jump!" her partner said, and because Celie's ears were ringing, the words sounded far away.

She pushed her goggles up. Her face was numb, and her body tingled as her partner unclipped the harness. "Oh my God!" she said inanely. "Oh my *God!*"

Other skydiving students came up to meet her, patting her on the back and telling her congratulations. Her partner laughed at her as he scooped up their chute, and she wondered if she looked as astonished as she felt. She'd never, ever experienced such a thrill. She hugged her partner, and her entire body vibrated with adrenaline.

"Where's McAllister?" She darted her gaze around, and then she remembered to look up. A green parachute floated down toward the landing field, but it was a tandem team.

On the opposite end of the field, far removed from the crowd, she saw another green parachute, a diver dressed in blue dangling beneath it.

She sprinted toward him.

He staggered to a stop, and, when he looked up, Celie was running right for him. She was grinning ear to ear as she threw herself at him, knocking him back a few steps. He caught her in his arms.

"Oh my *God!*" she shrieked.

He shoved up his goggles. "You look happy."

"It was *incredible!* I want to do it again!"

He laughed. "I should've known you'd be a junkie."

She flung her arms around his neck. "Are you okay? You looked great up there! I watched you land! It was so *cool*! How was your jump?"

Her cheeks were pink, and she had goggle marks on her face. He couldn't resist planting a big, wet kiss on her mouth. "Perfect. Fucking fantastic. I dropped right through a hole in the clouds."

She giggled. "Me, too."

He unhooked his harness and stepped out of it. Celie watched him, bouncing up and down in place. The woman was giddy.

"How soon can we go again? Can we go twice in one day?"

He smiled and looped the harness over his shoulder. "I thought you wanted a margarita."

"Oh. Yeah, I do." She gazed up at him hopefully. "Want to come back next weekend? Please?"

"Sure."

"Next time it's on me. Maybe we could get, like, a frequent-flyer discount."

"I've already got one." He gathered up his chute, compressing the air out of it and rolling it into a manageable size. They started walking back to the skydiving school, which was several hundred yards away. It consisted of a small, corrugated aluminum building beside a hangar filled with private planes. The landing strip had once been used as a practice site for military aircraft.

"Are you really getting certified? That's so great! How much does it cost?"

She peppered him with questions as they trekked back to the building. He'd never seen her so euphoric. They neared the entrance, and suddenly she took his hand and dragged him toward the back of the building.

"Where are we going?"

"I just have to do something real quick." She towed him behind a row of rusted-out storage drums.

And then she kissed him—a full-on, soul-scorching tongue kiss. Her nails sank into his neck, her breasts pressed against him, and all the blood in his body rushed straight to his groin.

"It was amazing," she murmured against his mouth. "*You're* amazing."

Shit, he should have shoved her out of an airplane months ago. He dropped all his gear and wrapped his arms around her.

She backed him clumsily against the building. Her skin still felt cold from the jump, but her mouth was hot and eager, and her hands were all over him.

"You're killing me," he said against her neck.

"I know. Can we—"

He jerked his head up as something in his peripheral vision caught his eye.

"What?" She looked dazed, breathless.

"Someone's watching. Over there by the parking lot."

She glanced over her shoulder. "Who?"

"I don't know. He's not there anymore."

"Probably my surveillance guy." She turned back to him and started kissing him some more, her hands wandering everywhere. He gripped her hips and pulled her snugly against him. They shouldn't do this here. They definitely needed to stop.

But she was into it. She wanted him *now*, he could

tell. He was so overwhelmed, he thought his knees would buckle.

"Fuck." He caught her wrists in his hands.

"What?"

He looked down at her. As much as he wanted to, he couldn't screw her against the side of a building. He needed to take her home.

"Go get changed," he told her. "I'll turn in all my gear, and we'll go back to your place."

She smiled up at him. "Yours is closer."

He kissed her mouth. "I love the way you think."

Celie shoved the jumpsuit down her legs, and only then remembered her sneakers. She toed them off, stripped away the nylon suit, and wiggled back into the pair of jeans she'd worn that morning. Her body was still shaking, and she wasn't sure whether it was the jump or McAllister or an intoxicating combination of both. Whatever it was, she felt gleeful. Alive. Happier than she'd been in months. Years.

She pulled on her T-shirt and jammed her feet into shoes. Then she turned to look in the mirror on the back of the dressing room door.

The door opened. Celie jumped back, startled, as a man stepped into the room.

"My apologies, Ms. Wells. I didn't mean to alarm you."

"Who are you?"

"I'm Special Agent Dominguez, with the FBI. I work with Agent Rowe."

"What—"

"I will explain later, but first I must get you to a safe location. You were followed here by a man working for Manuel Saledo, and I'm afraid your safety is in jeopardy."

Celie took a step back. Her gaze veered to the closed door, and she tried to remember if she had a tube of Mace in her purse.

The man held up his hands, palms out, trying to calm her. He wore an immaculate beige suit and a white, open-collared shirt. "Again, I don't mean to frighten you, but we really must leave now."

Celie took another step back and bumped against the wall of lockers. The man's dark eyes softened. He reached into the front of his jacket and produced a leather billfold, which he flipped open to reveal a shiny gold badge. Celie recognized the eagle-topped FBI shield and released the breath she'd been holding.

"We must hurry," he said, tucking the billfold away. "I'm not sure if the operative who followed you here is alone or with others."

She remembered the man McAllister had seen lurking in the parking lot. How many of Saledo's men were here?

"I need to get my friend," she said. "John McAllister?"

The agent nodded. "He's being briefed right now by one of my colleagues. We'll transport both of you to a safe location."

Celie grabbed her purse off the bench and stepped toward the door, but the agent gestured to the rear of the dressing room. Celie looked around and saw a back exit she hadn't previously noticed.

"We don't want Saledo's man to see you," he said.

Celie went through the back door and squinted in the

bright sunlight. The partial cloud cover had dissipated since their jump. She glanced around, looking for McAllister.

"This way," the agent said, leading her toward the airplane hangar. A gray Taurus was parked on the pavement just outside the hangar's open doors.

She looked around as she walked, searching for McAllister or any sign of someone suspicious. "Where are we going?"

"Just this way." He led her past the car, and her steps slowed.

"I don't understand. Where's Agent Rowe?"

"Please, Ms. Wells." He looked back at her imploringly. "We don't have much time."

She glanced over his shoulder at the small white plane sitting beside the hangar.

Her mouth went dry.

"We must hurry. Please."

The man stepped toward her, and temper flashed in his eyes. She tried to lunge away from him, but he caught her arm. He leaned close, clenching her arm in a vice, and she felt like the earth was falling out from under her feet.

"See that plane?" he growled.

She nodded, staring past him at the sleek little jet.

"Your boyfriend is sitting inside it with a gun pointed at his head. Join him now, or you will see his brains splattered all over that window."

John exited the men's dressing room and plunked his diving gear on the counter near the front door. The woman who'd rung up their bill earlier checked in his equipment.

"You two have fun?" she asked John.

"You bet. We'll probably be back next weekend."

A bell jingled, and John turned to see the pilot coming in the door. He peeled off his leather bomber jacket.

"Your friend going home?"

John saw his puzzled expression reflected in Vincent's mirrored shades. "My friend?"

"That girl you were with? The one who just left?"

"*What?*" John rushed to the door and peered through the glass. His Jeep was right there in the parking lot.

"She just took off." Vincent removed his sunglasses and frowned at him. "What, you didn't know she was leaving?"

"*Where?*" John shoved open the door and ran into the parking lot. He didn't see any cars on the long gravel road to the main highway.

"No, man." Vincent was right behind him. "She took *off*. In the Cessna."

John's stomach dropped. "She left in a *plane*?"

"Yeah, not five minutes ago. Some guy was with her."

CHAPTER

21

"Tell me you're kidding."

But he wasn't kidding. John could tell by the perplexed look on Vincent's face that he was completely serious.

John grabbed his arm. "Who was she with? Was she hurt? How long ago did she leave?"

"Damn, man . . ." Vincent glanced at his watch. "I dunno. Three minutes? Four? She looked fine to me—"

John looked over Vincent's shoulder and saw the man from the parking lot standing near the airplane hangar. He was gesturing at the runway and talking to someone.

John charged toward him. He must have sensed John coming because his head whipped around and his eyes widened.

"Where'd she go?" John demanded.

"I don't know, I—"

"*Bullshit!*" John shoved him with both hands, and he tripped backward and landed on his ass.

"Hey!"

John straddled his chest and jerked his head up by the collar of his golf shirt. "Where the fuck did she go?"

"I don't—"

John socked him in the jaw, hard enough that his knuckles stung. Someone grabbed John's arms and yanked him to his feet.

"Hey, take it easy." It was Vincent and the man who had been standing nearby.

John tried to shake them off. "I saw you watching us! Who do you work for? Who'd you tell we were here?"

The guy scrambled up and glared at John. He held his lip, which was bleeding now, as he reached into the pocket of his jeans and pulled out a billfold. He flipped it open, revealing a gold badge.

"Trent Abrams, FBI." He spat blood on the pavement and scowled at John.

John stared at him. "What the hell—"

"I work with Rowe and Stevenski. I was assigned to keep tabs on Cecelia Wells, which I was doing fine until she went into the women's dressing room. Now she's not there. A plane just took off, and I think she might have been on it."

"She was," said the man holding John's right arm. He and Vincent loosened their grip. "I saw her get in."

John shook off the restraints and stomped toward the empty runway. He turned to Vincent. "Can you follow it? The Cessna?"

He looked him up and down, his expression wary. "If I knew where it was going, I could."

"How do we find out?" John heard the desperation in his voice. He looked at the agent. "Do you know?"

"No." He jerked a phone out of his pocket and started dialing. "Rowe? It's Abrams. I've got a problem. . . ."

John turned to Vincent. "Can we track them somehow?"

"It's not easy," he answered. "This is a public airstrip. We might be able to find a pilot around here who had his radio on, might have overheard the Cessna pilot relay what he was doing right after take-off, but that won't tell us his final destination."

"Doesn't he have to file a flight plan? Something?"

"Nah, man," Vincent said. "Doesn't work that way. This is an uncontrolled airstrip. People announce their intentions on the radio, follow certain right-of-way rules, and that's pretty much it."

"*Fuck!*" John's heart was racing. Every minute that ticked by was one more minute of Celie in the presence of some drug trafficking dirtbag who probably planned to kill her.

John had to choke down the bile in his throat. He looked up at Vincent. "I'll pay you five thousand dollars if you'll just get me in the air."

"It's not that simple. I can't—"

"Ten thousand. I know they're going to Mexico. We can at least head south. As soon as we're airborne, I'll get on my cell phone and figure out where they're landing." He had no idea how he'd do this, or if his phone would even work at that altitude, but he had to get up there.

The pilot turned and looked glumly down the airstrip. "I don't know, man."

John was going to be sick. If Vincent refused to help him, he'd have no way to get to Celie. The Mexican border was at least five hours away by car, even speeding, and then who knew where they were going?

"Fifteen thousand."

"That's not the problem. I—"

"You've got to help me!" John turned to the guy standing next to the FBI agent. He had no fucking clue who he was. "You know how to fly a plane? Can you get me to Mexico?"

"If I might say something—"

"Shit, I'll *take* you," Vincent said, interrupting Abrams. "We just have to find out where the hell we're *going*."

"I might be able to find out," Abrams offered.

"How?" John fixed his attention on the young agent. He had light brown hair and doe eyes. He barely looked old enough to drive, but if he could help find Celie, John would bow down and kiss his feet.

Abrams cleared his throat. "Homeland Security's got a Customs and Border Protection division that has drones and surveillance planes patrolling the border. I can contact my SAC in San Antonio and have him ask CBP to get a fix on any low-flying aircraft that go across, find out where they're heading."

"You can do that?" John raked a hand through his hair.

"I can try."

"Try. Right now." The agent's eyes narrowed, and John hurried to add some diplomacy. "Please? It's a good idea.

Please get on the phone and call whoever in San Antonio."

John turned to Vincent. "Can you get me in the air?"

Celie sat in the airplane, her fear like a snake coiled in her stomach. She looked across the aisle at the man who'd abducted her. Despite his neatly tailored clothes and manicured fingernails, he somehow managed to look even more threatening than the armed thugs who had carjacked her.

He glanced at Celie. It was the eyes, definitely. Cold. Calculating. Like someone who had seen or done terrible things and wasn't easily moved to sympathy. Celie's palms started to sweat.

"Where are we going?" she asked, trying to keep her voice level.

He watched her for a moment, and she decided he wasn't going to answer the question. She'd already asked this and many other questions several times since they'd boarded the plane, but he hadn't responded. He hadn't said anything, in fact, except to address the pilot in rapid Spanish.

"We are going to see someone," he answered unexpectedly. "Someone who's eager to meet you."

"Who?"

He smiled. "My uncle. Manuel Saledo. You may have heard of him?"

Celie tried not to react. She turned and looked out the window, down at the flat Texas farmland gliding below them. At least she thought it was Texas. For all she knew, they could be over Mexico by now. She'd lost all sense of time.

"Why does your uncle want to meet me?" she asked,

still facing the window. If he'd just wanted her dead, he could have accomplished that back in Texas.

The man didn't answer, and Celie stole a glance at him. He was tearing the cellophane off a pack of Marlboro Reds as he seemed to consider the question. He offered her a cigarette, and she shook her head.

"You never know with him." He took out a gold lighter and held the flame to the end of his cigarette. He shifted in his seat, as if settling in for a conversation with a friend, and blew out a stream of smoke. "Maybe he wants to meet one of the few women who's ever crossed him."

"How did I cross him?"

"You stole his money."

"My ex-husband stole his money."

He grinned, displaying a mouth full of perfectly straight white teeth. Between the flawless English and the orthodontics, Celie guessed Manny Saledo's nephew had had a privileged upbringing.

"I, for one, appreciate what you did. I have a sense of humor about these things, and the money is negligible." He took another drag. "My uncle, however, is not amused. He is a proud man. Many would say arrogant. Some people believe his arrogance will be his undoing."

Celie watched him, wondering why he was telling her all this.

He leaned toward her, and she felt a spasm between her shoulder blades. "A word of advice. Do not lie to my uncle. He becomes angry when people do that. Not a nice thing to watch."

Celie looked out the window again. Tears burned her eyes. The fear in her stomach seemed to be slithering through her entire body now. It traveled up her neck and sunk its fangs into her skull. Celie needed an Imitrex, but her purse was up near the cockpit. That was three rows ahead, beyond three oversize leather seats just like the one she was sitting in.

"How long until we land?" Celie asked, knowing that every minute they stayed in the air diminished her chances of being rescued. The chances were already low, she figured, unless she could determine where she was when they landed and find a phone.

"Don't worry," Saledo's nephew said pleasantly. "We're almost there."

John was still on the ground.

Celie had been whisked away in an airplane fifty-two minutes ago and John was still on the fucking *ground*. Worse, he wasn't anywhere *near* an airplane. He was stuck in the fucking office of the fucking skydiving school watching a fucking idiot talk on the phone.

"Can we go yet?" John asked Vincent. "Because if I have to stand here another minute, I'm gonna fucking kill someone." John stared at Abrams as he said this, and he knew Vincent could tell he wasn't joking.

"Dude, McAllister. This isn't helping." Vincent stepped between John and the agent, who had been yapping away on his phone for nearly an hour and *still* hadn't managed to figure out where the hell Celie's plane had gone.

During the wait, Vincent had spoken with the skydiving school's owner, who had agreed to rent them his personal plane and his favorite pilot, which was good, John supposed. But Vincent had insisted that taking off without a destination would be a waste of time and fuel. So

John was stuck on the ground with his pilot and the FBI agent, all of them pacing the office, a huge map of North America spread out before them on the desk—a map that had provided exactly zero leads as to Celie's whereabouts.

John shot Vincent a glare. "It's been almost an hour. A fucking *hour*, and he's come up with nothing! You've got to get me airborne, or I swear I'm gonna lose it. Right this minute Celie could be—"

John's cell phone vibrated, and he snapped it open.

"I've got something for you," Marco Juarez said.

John nearly wept. "What is it?"

"I may have a location. Hang on a sec while I double-check my map, okay?"

"Sure," John said, feeling numb all of a sudden. They had a lead. He'd called Marco in a desperate effort to learn something—anything—that might narrow down the list of possible destinations for the Cessna. John knew if anyone could come through for him, it would be Marco. Manny Saledo had played a role in the murder of Marco's sister several years back, and the PI had spent a good chunk of time and energy since then investigating Saledo and his network.

"Okay," Marco said, "this is a little thin, but I think it will help."

"I'm listening."

"I've got four known locations for homes owned by Saledo in Mexico. The first is in Michoacán. It's the head-quarters for the family business. The second—"

"Shit, hold on." John glanced around the crowded office, searching frantically for a pen.

"—is an apartment in Mexico City."

John snagged a dry-erase marker off the desk and started scribbling on a phone book. "Okay, keep going."

"The third is new. It's on the Pacific, a place called Costa Careyes. The resort is small, and I hear there's not even an airstrip nearby, so I doubt that's where they're going. The last place is your best bet, I think. It's a hacienda in Nuevo Leon, northeast of Monterrey."

"So they're landing in Monterrey?"

"Doubtful. The city's about a forty-five-minute drive. Plus, I just talked to someone at the main airport there, and he says Saledo's planes don't go through there because he's got a private airfield right on his property."

"Okay," John said, getting excited. "That sounds promising. But why not the first two? Why wouldn't he take her to the headquarters?"

"He might. But it's pretty far south. Plus, American and Mexican law enforcement typically keep an eye on the place, if not a full crew staked out there. Manny got wise to that, so he started moving around more, running things from lower-profile locations."

"Nuevo Leon," John said, racking his brain. "That's just over the border, right?"

"Right. The state's traversed by a couple major highways. A lot of product moves through there on its way north."

"Hey," Abrams cut in. "We've got a low-flying plane recently spotted, slipping over the border heading toward . . ."

John waited, his heart thundering in his chest, as the agent listened to his phone.

"Are you sure?" Abrams turned toward John. "It looks like they're going to Monterrey."

CHAPTER

22

Celie followed Saledo's nephew from the landing strip to a high adobe wall. When the plane had flown over this spot, Celie had taken in every detail of the landscape—the arid flatlands, the craggy cliffs jutting up to the west, the strip of green scrub bushes stretching from north to south, where she guessed there might be a river or stream. Celie longed to make a break for it, but the trio of men standing alongside the landing strip had convinced her not to risk it.

Or rather, their machine guns had.

Celie turned her gaze toward the steep hillside up ahead of her. Atop it sat a hulking adobe house, its warm brown color so close to that of the surrounding rock, it almost blended in. The house was tall, with at least four levels and ornate wrought-iron balconies outside the many windows. A road zigzagged down from the top of the hill, its route announced by the startlingly yellow Hummer making its way through all the switchbacks right now. Celie wondered if this vehicle would transport her up to the main house.

And was Manny Saledo at the wheel?

The nephew stopped in front of a rough-hewn wooden gate and punched a code into a keypad mounted on the wall. The gate, which looked deceptively rustic, made a clicking noise and swung back on an electronic arm. Soon the Hummer ground to a stop right beside Celie. Saledo's nephew opened the back door.

"Please," he said, gesturing for her to get in.

She glanced over her shoulder at the airfield, willing a helicopter full of paratroopers to drop down from the sky. But the landing strip was just as empty as the azure sky above it.

Celie climbed inside the monstrous car. As she scooted across the seat, she realized her purse was still on the plane.

"We forgot my purse. Could I get it, please? It has my medicine in it."

The nephew got in beside her, not acknowledging that she'd said a word. He pulled the door shut and snapped a command at the driver, who Celie noticed was only a boy. The child couldn't have been more than thirteen.

Instead of heading up toward the house, they cut across a field. The Hummer bulldozed over sagebrush and giant prickly pear cacti and spiky plants that looked like agave. They drove over a cattle guard and through an opening in a barbed-wire fence before continuing down a bumpy incline. They lurched over a dried-up creek bed, and Celie had to grip the handle beside the door to keep from careening to the other side of the vehicle. A smile played on the boy's lips, and he seemed to think this was a game.

Saledo's nephew barked out another order, and soon the Hummer rolled to a stop. Celie looked through the windshield and saw a short, portly man striding toward them, a shotgun slung over his shoulders like a yoke.

The nephew popped open his door and jerked his head to the side, signaling for Celie to follow him.

She couldn't move. Her body was cemented to the seat as the man with the shotgun came closer.

The nephew reached a hand inside the door and beckoned her to get out. "Come on. My uncle wants to meet you."

This was an order, not a request. Celie slid across the seat and stumbled out. She stood up and found herself standing eye to eye with a balding, middle-aged man.

This was Manny Saledo?

With his faded blue jeans and western-style shirt, he was the polar opposite of his nephew. He had a strong nose and big jowls and a gut that hung over the top of his gold belt buckle. His black, ostrich-skin boots were caked with reddish-brown mud.

A discussion ensued between the two Saledos, and, although Celie couldn't understand a word of it, she knew it was about her. She scanned the landscape around her and noticed a pair of boys off in the distance. They were separated by about fifty feet or so, and each stood beside a skeet-shooting machine.

Finally, the nephew turned to her. "My uncle says

you surprise him. He was expecting a blonde Amazon, I think."

Celie's eyes widened, and she looked at Saledo. What on earth had he heard about her?

She stood there, trying to look meek and harmless, hoping Saledo would realize she was no threat to him, that this was all some huge mistake.

Saledo said something to his nephew, and then turned his back. Suddenly his great baritone voice boomed across the field. The boys jumped into action, and a clay pigeon shot into the air. In a lightning flash, Saledo raised his shotgun, fired, then swung the weapon toward a second pigeon coming from the opposite side. He reduced both targets to dust.

Celie watched him, slack-jawed, as he did this again and again. She felt the nephew's eyes on her, and she clamped her lips together in a vain effort to hide her terror.

Saledo abruptly turned to face her. He wasn't even breathing hard.

"Do you speak Spanish?" he asked in a heavily accented voice.

"I'm sorry, I don't."

"We have a word, *respeto*. In English you say 'respect.'"

Celie nodded dumbly.

"Your husband, Robert, he did not know this word."

Saledo's voice thundered again, and two pigeons went flying almost simultaneously. He shattered both of them with ease. Then he turned back to Celie.

"Years ago, your husband came here as my guest. He and his friend"—he turned to his nephew—"*como se llama?*"

"Josh Garland."

"*Sí, sí.* Josh Garland." He looked back at Celie. "Your husband and Josh Garland spent a weekend here. We hunted dove together. I shared my food, my horses, my women. In my culture, such hospitality is a signal of respect."

Celie's throat felt like sandpaper. She knew she should say something, but her mouth wouldn't form any words.

"Stealing from a man, this is *falta de respeto.* Disrespect." He held his gun pointed down, casually, as if it weighed nothing. "Your husband stole from me. And then you stole from me."

"I didn't—"

"No talking!" He stepped toward her, glowering. "Just listening!"

Celie glanced at the nephew, looking for help. He smiled vaguely, like he was enjoying himself.

"I'm sorry," she said, and this seemed to have a calming effect.

"In my business," Saledo continued, "respect is everything. It is a currency. And when one man shows disrespect, you lose some of that currency. Then another will do the same, and another. If I allow this to happen, I become a poor man. It is like . . . it is like dominoes. One domino can make all the others fall. That is why you are here. Do you understand?"

Celie bit her lip, swallowed. It was time to make her case, but she needed to do it in a way that wouldn't anger him.

"I think there's been a misunderstanding. Robert Strickland isn't even my husband. He *wasn't.* Before he died. We were divorced. And I never—"

"*Basta!*" Saledo held up a hand. "We will finish this later."

Celie wanted to protest, but she could see his temper rising. He took another step closer, and she caught a sour whiff of perspiration. She tried not to cringe.

"Tonight," he said, "You will pay for your husband's disrespect. And when that is paid for, you will pay for yours."

Vincent brought the plane down smoothly, and if it hadn't been for John's churning stomach, he would have congratulated him on an impressive landing.

As it was, he barely managed to get out of his seat without puking.

Two hours and thirty-eight minutes had passed now, and John was so wound up he could hardly think. As soon as his feet hit the tarmac, he jogged across the pavement toward the primitive airport, searching for any indication of a car for hire—a taxi, a bus, a freaking rickshaw. There was nothing. The airport—if you could even call it that— was located on the northeast outskirts of Monterrey, closer to Saledo's property than the main airport in the city. Not only was the place a shithole, it was practically deserted except for someone tinkering with the engine of a single-prop plane. The plane sat in a neat row of other single- and twin-engine aircraft parked along the apron near the main building. Logos for several charter airlines had been painted on the building's cinder-block walls; no one seemed to be manning those operations.

The door to the main building opened, and a uniformed man stepped outside, shielding his eyes from the glare reflected off the tarmac. Abrams flagged his attention. The agent was in charge of dealing with local officials, somehow convincing them to allow three Americans into the country without proper documentation. John wasn't sure whether Abrams intended to accomplish this with his FBI shield or with money, but he didn't give a rat's ass as long as the fed did it quickly.

A dinged white pickup pulled onto the tarmac and stopped near the airport's main entrance. A young man in blue coveralls hopped out of the truck.

"Hey," John called, rushing toward him. "Is that your truck?"

John peered into the pickup. The driver looked like some kind of aging cowboy, with a ten-gallon hat, a faded plaid shirt, and a face like cowhide.

John switched to Spanish. "Is this truck for hire?"

Both men eyed John silently, so he promptly produced some twenty-dollar bills. The skydiving school had taken plastic, but somehow John doubted that would work here.

"I need a ride. To a place maybe twenty miles from here. Can you take me?"

"Where?"

"A private house," John said. "Out Highway 85, near Rio San Pablo." Abrams had confirmed Marco's information that Saledo had a house out that way, and John just hoped they didn't have trouble finding it. Having traveled extensively in Mexico, though, John knew getting directions and actually finding a place were two entirely different things.

"Rancho Saledo," the old man stated.

John nodded, wondering if this changed things. For all he knew, Saledo was hated by the locals. It was also possible he employed a good many of them, in which case he might be a hero.

The cowboy's gaze flicked over John's shoulder. John turned to see Abrams jogging toward him. Evidently, Vincent had decided to stay behind and keep an eye on his boss's plane.

"Two passengers," John said, pulling another few bills from his wallet.

The cowboy nodded, and John climbed into the cab.

Celie stood by the window of the sparsely furnished room and tried to formulate a plan. She couldn't stay here. It simply wasn't an option. The moment she'd entered these quarters, she'd been overcome with the certainty that someone had died here.

Or possibly several people. She didn't know for sure, but there was something about the spare furnishings—a chair, a cot, a table—that made her blood run cold. Or maybe it was the machine gun–wielding guard stationed outside her door.

The only thing Celie could stand to look at was the window, but if she got too close, it spooked her, too. The view was spectacular, but it was a four-story drop to the rocky ground below. And just beyond *that* was the steeply sloping hillside leading to the scrubby plain surrounding the compound.

She was trapped here, and she got the distinct impression she wasn't the first Saledo houseguest to be put in this position.

Suddenly a woman entered carrying a wooden tray. When Saledo's nephew had led Celie through the spacious kitchen to the back staircase, this woman had been standing at the stainless steel sink. She was young, with a voluptuous figure and shiny black hair that hung to her waist. She didn't look at Celie as she set the tray on the table. She wore a simple outfit of tight black jeans and a black sweater, and no jewelry. Celie doubted she was a family member. Surely a man who collected oil paintings, bronze sculptures, and expensive electronics would provide his female relatives with better footwear than faded black Keds.

"*Gracias*," Celie said, utilizing twenty percent of her Spanish vocabulary.

The woman nodded meekly, and turned to leave.

"Wait!" Celie stepped toward her.

The woman darted an anxious glance at the guard standing outside, and Celie lowered her voice to a whisper. "Do you speak English?"

She nodded slightly.

"Can you help me?"

The woman bit her lip and gave a slight shake of her head.

Celie looked down at the tray she'd delivered. It contained a white ceramic pitcher, a matching cup and saucer with the cup flipped down, and a custard bowl filled with sugar packets. There was also bowl of brown soup covered in plastic wrap. Celie's stomach lurched. She hadn't eaten anything since a yogurt that morning, and it was almost evening.

"Would you mind pouring that?" she improvised,

pointing to the pitcher. She needed to keep the woman in her room. She was the only other female Celie had seen since her arrival, and the only person besides Saledo's nephew who hadn't been armed with a big gun.

The woman cast a glance at the guard and stepped closer to the table. The guard—also clad in black—was staring straight ahead, military style, but Celie had no doubt he was listening to every word. She didn't know whether he spoke English.

"Please," Celie whispered. "Is there a way out of here?"

She looked at Celie, and her eyes filled with pity. That, more than anything Saledo had said, told Celie what lay in store for her.

The woman's gaze slinked toward the window, and she nodded.

The window? *That* was the best way out? Even if it hadn't been locked, it was thirty or forty feet off the ground. Celie looked toward it and tipped her head fractionally, making sure she understood. The woman nodded.

Her black hair fell in a curtain around her face as she poured the coffee. Celie watched, thinking about what she'd just learned.

The window was her best hope. But even if she managed to get through the glass undetected, she'd probably break her leg. She glanced around the room and noted that there were no drapes or bed linens or anything else that could be used to make a rope.

The woman uncovered the soup, and Celie realized she was using her other hand to arrange the sugar packets end to end in a straight line.

She was trying to say something. She traced an invisible *R* on the table.

Was she signaling a rope? A road? A river?

"Follow the river?" Celie said, barely audibly.

The woman nodded.

"Which way?" Celie had seen from the air that Saledo's property was connected to a highway by a long dirt road. But Celie had no idea how far it was to the nearest town. She could be out there for days, wandering around the unforgiving terrain and getting lost.

Or, even more terrifying, getting found.

With one hand, the woman made a noisy production of arranging the flatware on the napkin. With her other hand, she dipped a finger in the coffee and made a cross. Was there a church nearby? But she added an N on top, and Celie realized she was drawing a compass. She pointed to the bottom.

Go south.

"How far?" Celie whispered.

The guard shifted in the hallway. The woman hurried to leave the room, holding both hands behind her back and flashing a number—ten, twenty, thirty, forty.

Forty what? Miles? Kilometers? How would she ever walk that far? Suddenly the door slammed shut, and she was alone, once again, in the creepy little room.

Celie looked down at the soup tray, no longer hungry in the least. She went into the small adjoining bathroom and turned on the faucet. After splashing water on her face, she turned around and studied the tiny shower stall. It was bare. There wasn't even a shower curtain that could be made into something useful.

How was she going to get out of this place? The window was too high to hazard a jump, and then she'd have to walk or hitchhike either forty kilometers or forty miles to the nearest town.

Celie leaned against the sink, staring at the shower stall as all her most deep-seated fears paraded through in her head. Being tortured by Manny Saledo. Jumping to her death. Wandering alone in the pitch-black desert looking for help. Climbing into a truck with some strange man who might or might not deliver her safely back to civilization.

She weighed each possibility, and her gaze skimmed over the tile, fastening on the rust pattern she saw in the grout. Was that . . . ?

Blood.

Yes, it was. About four feet off the ground was a red-black stain where someone's blood had spilled. The tile had been wiped clean since then, but whoever did it hadn't managed to clean the grout.

Feeling woozy, Celie stepped out of the bathroom. She sank down onto the cot and tried to think, but as she glanced around her surroundings, her mind refused to work. She doubted the moves she'd learned in her self-defense class would pose much of a challenge for a muscle-bound guard with a machine gun. She glanced at the crack under the door.

The shadow of his boots had disappeared.

Slowly, silently, she crept to the door and crouched down to double-check. She pressed her cheek against the dusty floor. Through the half-inch gap, she saw the empty hallway. He was gone.

Her stomach clenched. This was her chance. She rose to her feet and quietly tried the doorknob. Locked.

Had he gone for a bathroom break? Food? Wherever it was, he'd most likely be back soon. She scanned the room desperately, praying for a bolt of inspiration.

Her gaze landed on the wooden chair. It looked sturdy. She stared at it a moment, thinking, calculating, considering the odds. Then she made up her mind. Hands shaking, she yanked off her shoes. She took one final glance at the crack under the door. Still no shadow. Still no sound. She took a deep breath and unzipped her jeans.

CHAPTER

23

Rowe already hated this operation, and it had barely started. From the moment his cell phone had started humming several hours ago, he'd been informed of one bad decision after another, all culminating in an ill-conceived plan to confront one of the most dangerous drug kingpins in Mexico.

Rowe blamed Abrams. If the rookie agent had been doing his job in the first place, Rowe wouldn't be here right now, crammed into a helicopter with guys from an alphabet soup of Mexican and American law enforcement agencies, hovering above a Pemex station not twenty miles south of Saledo's compound.

The helo started descending about fifty yards north of the gas station. Rowe looked out the window and saw two pickups parked at the station, but neither looked to be filling up, and Rowe surmised that the trucks represented one of this operation's major flaws. Not only had Abrams botched the surveillance of Cecelia Wells and let her get kidnapped out from under his nose, he'd compounded the problem by allowing at least three civilians to involve themselves in the rescue effort. Rowe had never met Vincent Somebody-or-other, the pilot who had ferried Abrams down here, but he'd met John McAllister and Marco Juarez. Rowe felt certain the two hotshots would somehow derail this op, which was already shaping up to be a train wreck.

The helo touched down, and Abrams approached, shielding his eyes from the tornado of dust swirling around. He climbed inside and took a seat next to the SAC. Rowe watched him begin briefing the man, obviously eager to smooth things over and convince the boss he wasn't a complete moron.

Good luck.

Rowe shook his head as the helicopter lifted off and veered toward its destination. They were approaching from the south, hoping to use the element of surprise. Mexican authorities, who—like their American counterparts—had been monitoring Saledo in an effort to build an irrefutable case against him and his network, had predicted the compound would be staffed by a few household servants and between five and ten heavily armed guards. That was the bad news.

The good news was, Saledo had just arrived here by private plane yesterday, and so his typical entourage of relatives and girlfriends hadn't caught up to him yet, which meant collateral damage might be kept to a minimum.

That was about the only good news. In Rowe's opinion, rushing into an armed confrontation, with scant intelligence, at night on the target's home turf, was a bad idea. Rowe had wanted to wait, but apparently the top brass of several of the agencies involved had a hard-on for Saledo right *now* and were using the kidnapping of Cecelia Wells as catalyst for a major arrest.

Rowe suspected egos were involved, too. The Americans couldn't sit idly by while one of their civilians—particularly a young woman—was kidnapped and dragged off to be murdered by a Mexican drug lord. And the Mexican authorities were under pressure to take a stand against one of their most notorious criminals, a man they supposedly wanted to bring to justice, yet had never mustered the political will to punish with more than a slap on the wrist.

Poor planning, civilian yahoos, and oversize cop egos. This operation was doomed.

Rowe looked to his immediate right, where Stevenski was fastening a flak jacket over his shirt. Rowe noticed the tremor in his partner's hands and the sheen of sweat covering his face. This was one of his first raids.

He glanced up at Rowe. "You ready?"

Rowe checked his sidearm. "Yep."

The AFI—Mexico's FBI equivalent—was running the show, so their guys were bringing the big guns. Rowe shouldn't technically be carrying a firearm at all, but the the head of the Monterrey legat had a beer-drinking relationship with the AFI commander, and so everyone had agreed not to notice the Americans were packing today. Rowe felt grateful for this bit of luck because he never felt right without his gun.

The Mexican SWAT team would insert from the air, the commandos fast-roping down, while the helo containing the Americans landed at the base of the property. Assuming the SWAT guys could quickly disarm Saledo and his guards—which Rowe didn't—American agents would be allowed to participate in the search for Cecelia Wells. Rowe's boss had pushed hard for this arrangement, apparently not trusting his AFI counterparts to take adequate care of the hostage.

Rowe thought about Cecelia Wells. Having known the woman for more than a year, he'd developed an affection for her, not to mention a respect. She had more courage than most men Rowe knew, and, besides that, she had heart. Rowe didn't know many people who fit that bill.

"When we find the hostage," Stevenski said, "you should take the lead. She trusts you most, I think."

Rowe agreed, knowing as well as Stevenski did that this whole plan was based on a pretty shaky assumption.

If and when they found Cecelia Wells, she might already be dead.

The sun was hovering over the western cliffs when Marco's Chevy Silverado made the turn onto Saledo's road. John watched the desert landscape fly by, still angry beyond words that the feds had gone ahead without him. John had asked the man in the white pickup to pull over at a Pemex station to meet up with Marco Juarez, whose knowledge of the area and skill talking to the locals would help them make a plan to sneak into the compound. But no sooner had Marco shown up than a chopper had arrived to whisk Abrams away, leaving John and Marco in the dust. Now instead of participating in Celie's rescue, they were stuck waiting to observe the aftermath.

"Thanks for coming," John said.

Marco shot him a look. He wore sweatpants and sneakers, and John strongly suspected he'd caught him at the gym this afternoon when he'd called. Given that Mayfield was probably two hundred miles from here, Marco had to have jumped right in his truck and hauled ass.

"This is my wife's best friend," Marco said. "If I don't move mountains to get her back, Feenie will never speak to me again."

Marco didn't smile, and John knew he was only half kidding. John had known Marco nearly three years now, and his black eyes and perennial black leather jacket were reflective of his personality. This evening he looked like a thunderhead.

John stared out the window, and his stomach knotted. He believed Celie was alive—he had to believe that—but he couldn't convince himself she was unharmed. And who knew what would happen when the feds and the Mexicans stormed in there, guns blazing?

"She's resourceful," Marco said.

John looked at him.

"If there's a way to get out of there, she'll find it. And if there's not a way out, she'll focus on survival. She's good at that."

A lump rose in John's throat, and he stared out the window. He couldn't verbalize what he was feeling right now, but it had to do with searing pain and the certainty that if anything permanent happened to Celie, he'd be dead inside.

He shifted his attention to the windshield, looking for some sign of a residence up ahead. The chopper was probably just now arriving.

"There it is," Marco said, nodding toward a cliff where, in the evening light, John discerned the outline of a house.

Below it, probably a hundred feet down, John saw a flash of machine gun fire.

"Holy shit," he muttered, going cold.

Marco reached into his leather jacket and pulled out a gun.

"I've got a backup in the glove box," he told John. "Better help yourself."

Rowe crouched behind the fountain in the courtyard, waiting for his cue. Suddenly the double doors flung open, and an armored member of the Mexican SWAT team gave him the signal.

Rowe ducked in first. Stevenski followed. They made their way up the central staircase, searching for the bedroom wing where they expected to find the hostage. Rowe's nostrils stung as the acrid scent of smoke drifted toward him. Stun grenades had been used to help distract and disable Saledo's guards, most of whom had been neutralized in the first-floor media room. Now the Americans were conducting a room-to-room sweep looking for the hostage.

Rowe and Stevenski did a brisk search of the second floor.

"Next floor," Rowe ordered, heading up another flight of stairs. They passed a commando giving one of Saledo's men an armed escort downstairs.

Stevenski said something in Spanish, and the commando shook his head.

"What was that?" Rowe asked.

"Still no sign of Saledo, the nephew, or Cecelia."

They combed every inch of the third floor. Nothing. They stopped at the top of the stairs.

"I could swear I counted four stories from the outside," Stevenski said.

"Then there must be another staircase."

"Maybe in the back? Near the kitchen?"

Rowe had no idea, but it sounded good to him. They quickly descended the curving staircase and cut through the living room. A Mexican commando stood beside the door to the kitchen. Stevenski said something to him and entered, nearly tripping over the bullet-ridden body of a young woman just inside the doorway.

"Shit." Stevenski stepped past her.

Rowe stared down at the woman. With her long black hair and startled eyes, she looked young and innocent— like she'd been caught in the crossfire. Rowe prayed Cecelia Wells hadn't suffered the same fate.

Rowe spotted the AFI commander at the back of the kitchen talking to two of his men. Several of Saledo's people kneeled on the floor nearby with their hands cuffed. Rowe approached the commander, glad the man's English was better than Rowe's Spanish.

"Sir," he said, "we've swept three levels, but four are visible from outside. Any chance we missed a stairwell?"

The commander's bushy black eyebrows tipped up.

"Fourth floor looks to be above the kitchen," Stevenski added.

All eyes turned toward the ceiling. For an instant everything was silent, and then the commander barked something at his men. They leapt into motion, pulling open all the doors in sight—pantries, walk-in closets, broom cabinets, but no stairwells.

A shadow moved behind the commander.

"*Down!*" Rowe yelled, and an armed man burst through the doorway. Time stretched out as Rowe reached for his gun, and a truck seemed to slam into his chest. He hurtled backward, smacking his skull against a wall, as gunshots reverberated all around him. The gunman staggered backward, red splotches blooming on his shirt. An instant later, half his head disappeared in a mist of red.

Stevenski stood off to the side, chest heaving, his gun poised to shoot again.

"You're hit!" He rushed over to Rowe. His voice echoed through Rowe's brain, but it sounded very far away. "Are you okay? *Rowe?*"

Rowe tried to say something, but the force had pummeled his lungs.

This is how Kate felt. He let his head fall back and stared up at the ceiling, trying desperately to breathe.

John and Marco hopped out of the Chevy and took cover next to the adobe wall. The gate was open, and a guard lay beside it, having fallen dead right on top of his machine gun. John saw Marco eyeing the weapon.

"Have at it," John told him. "I've never used one before."

Marco moved to retrieve the gun, just as a Hummer halted inside the gate and members of the Mexican SWAT team jumped out. Marco shouted out warnings in Spanish so he wouldn't be mistaken for a target, and then he stood up. John didn't catch the rapid-fire exchange of Spanish.

"They killed Saledo," Marco reported, "and the guards who aren't dead have surrendered."

Several commandos tromped through the gate. Marco spoke with them for a moment, and then they fanned out around the perimeter of the compound.

"No one's found Celie yet," Marco said.

"Shit." John had caught something about a hostage, but they'd been talking so fast. "Where are they going now?"

"Searching for Saledo's nephew. He's second in command."

"First, now, if his uncle's dead," John pointed out.

"One of the guards says he was here, but he left just before the raid. They're checking Saledo's vehicles."

Another Hummer rolled to a stop behind the first one. Several Americans got out, including Stevenski, who had Rowe leaning on his shoulder. Rowe looked injured, but John didn't see any blood.

John strode up to them. "Where's Celie?"

Rowe shook his head and slouched against the wall, wheezing.

"Didn't find her," Stevenski said as Rowe loosened his Kevlar vest.

John saw two silver patches where bullets had smashed into Rowe's chest. A few inches higher, and the agent would be dead.

"You need to lie down?" Stevenski asked, clearly shaken by his partner's near-miss.

"Think I cracked a rib." Rowe coughed and shook his head. "Could have been worse."

"I'm going up to look for Celie," John announced, starting toward the gate.

"Hold on," Stevenski said. "I don't think she's up there."

John's stomach rolled. "Why not?"

"I searched the servants' quarters, fourth floor above the kitchen. Found a room with the window busted out. Looked like someone jumped."

"From the *fourth* floor?"

"Apparently. There's no one under the window, so who-ever did it survived, I think."

She was alive. Maybe.

"Where's the window?" John asked.

Stevenski turned and looked up at the house, like he was trying to orient himself. "Let's see, back side—"

"Show me."

Celie hobbled across the field, swiping at branches and sticks, trying to ignore her left ankle and focus instead on her goal. She had to find cover. Soon. She could worry about her injuries tonight, from the relative safety of some kind of hiding spot.

She glanced over her shoulder to the west. The sun had dropped behind the distant ridge, and it wouldn't be long before nightfall. She needed to reach the strip of trees she'd seen earlier from the air, which she assumed marked the course of the river.

She limped on, her shoulders hunched forward to keep her silhouette from standing out against the cacti and brush. If one of Saledo's men spotted her out here, the chase would be over before it even began. Celie could barely walk on her ankle, much less run.

She examined the gash on her arm. She'd cut it heaving the chair into the window, and she could feel a glass shard embedded in her skin. She'd tied a sock around it to stop the bleeding and keep from leaving a trail, but she hadn't had time to dig the glass out yet.

At least an hour had gone by since she'd escaped, meaning a search was probably under way. She didn't know. She'd traveled over several rises, and she couldn't see the house anymore. But that didn't mean people couldn't see her. Especially if they were combing these fields in a Humvee with a pair of binoculars.

Celie shivered, despite the warmth of the evening, probably because she was wearing only underpants on her lower half. Her blue jeans were back at Saledo's, one ankle still tied around the decorative iron balcony beneath her window. She'd used the pants as a makeshift rope to shorten the drop between the window and the ground.

She paused to pluck some sticker burrs from her calves. She felt queasy, light-headed, and she didn't know whether that was from pain or hunger. After deciding to make a break for it, Celie had wolfed down every morsel of food on her tray, but that had only amounted to a bowl of soup and two saltine crackers. Now her throat felt parched, and she wished she'd thought to drink more of the coffee. Maybe she should have improvised some kind of canteen, but she hadn't had time. Besides the clothes on her back, she had only her Nikes and the four sugar packets she'd tucked into her shoelaces.

She tripped over something and threw out her hands to catch herself.

"*Ouch!*"

Pain shot up her right arm. A prickly pear cactus had broken her fall.

She looked around frantically and bit her lip to keep from bursting into tears. The last smidgen of daylight was almost gone. She had glass in her arm, a twisted ankle, and now a palm loaded with cactus needles. And she still hadn't made it to the riverbank. She was out in the open. Alone, unarmed, and exposed. If Saledo's men or, God forbid, some kind of helicopter started combing the area, she was a sitting duck. She'd thought she'd heard a helicopter earlier, but the sound hadn't lasted, and she'd chalked it up to her paranoid imagination. Still, it was possible. Saledo had an airstrip and who knew how many expensive toys at his disposal.

She looked ahead and could barely see anything now. Her throat tightened as her predicament sank in. Shelter or no, darkness was falling around her.

Marco halted the Silverado on the south end of Saledo's landing strip. He and John had spent the past ten minutes driving up and down the private road, looking for Celie.

"Maybe she made it out to the highway," Marco said, "then hitched a ride into town."

John looked out the window, dismayed to see the last purple glow of daylight fading behind the cliffs to the west. They had five minutes, max, before the countryside went completely dark.

"No way," John said. "She doesn't trust strangers, and she wouldn't have wanted to be wandering along some highway half naked after dark."

"You think she could have stolen a car? Maybe one of Saledo's?"

"Shit, I don't see how. But I guess it's possible." John looked out the window, his shoulders tensing at the thought of Celie out in that vast rugged terrain after dark. To the east, he knew a river ran more or less parallel to the highway, about forty miles into the city of Monterrey.

"I think she's out there," he told Marco. "She would have wanted to avoid roads and people, especially since anyone she'd bump into near here could be working for Saledo. I think she headed away from the house, probably toward the river, where she'd have some tree cover. I'm going to go look."

"That's got to be at least two miles," Marco pointed out. "And you don't have any daylight left."

John opened the door. "Neither does she. You got a flashlight?"

Marco got out of the truck and went around to the built-in toolbox just behind the cab. He unlocked it and scrounged around inside, tossing John whatever supplies he could find: a MagLite, a wadded poncho, a first aid kit.

"Shit, where am I going to put all this?"

Marco produced a bag with a shoulder strap. He ducked inside the truck cab, and John watched him unzip the bag, pull out a stack of diapers, and toss them to the floor. Then he popped open the glove box, grabbed a PowerBar and a mini–Swiss Army knife, and shoved them into the pack. In the glow of the interior light, John saw that the bag had pale blue rabbits printed all over it.

He shoved the pack at John. "Here. I don't have any water left, and I wouldn't drink out of that river if I were you."

John pulled the strap over his head, positioning it across his chest so the pack rested on his lower back, out of his way. He tested the flashlight. It worked.

"I'll check out the gas stations and rest stops along the highway, see if I can turn up anything," Marco said. "You got your cell phone?"

"It doesn't work down here."

"Damn. Take mine. I'm almost out of juice, though, so don't keep it on. Tomorrow at daybreak, I'll come back here and wait. If I don't see you after half an hour, I'll come back at noon and again at six."

John glanced up at the sky. He wasn't sure what kind of moon would be out tonight, but it hadn't risen yet. If Celie was out there, the world around her was black as tar.

"Contact Stevenski," John said. "Maybe he can get someone looking on the outskirts of Monterrey, in case she made it there by car."

"Will do."

John looked east, the direction he hoped like hell Celie had gone. "Okay, I'm outta here."

"They never located the nephew," Marco reminded him. "He could be out there, too."

John patted the Glock tucked into the back of his jeans. "Yeah, I know."

• • •

Celie stumbled over the uneven ground, wishing desperately for some light. A half-moon had peeked through the clouds a few times to cast a faint, silvery glow over everything, but mostly it stayed hidden. Celie was trapped in the darkness, holding her arms out in front so she could feel for obstacles. She kept tripping over stones and bumping into bushes, and she'd even managed to stab her shins on an agave plant. She'd been walking east for what felt like ages, listening for the sound of a river. If she could hide out among those trees until morning, she'd have cover from anyone who came after her while she followed the river's path in the daylight. She was counting on some civilization eventually, too. She'd seen cattle on Saledo's property. Maybe there would be a ranch nearby where she could borrow a phone or get a ride to a police station.

The bushes rustled behind her, and she froze. She stood motionless as the noise approached. It sounded low to the ground, like an animal. Celie didn't know what kind of wildlife lived around here and didn't want to find out.

After a few moments, whatever it was moved off, and she continued her trek. Her pace was slow, but she had to keep moving. She needed to put as much space as possible between herself and Saledo's men before morning.

She felt her way through the darkness with her feet and hands. Her senses had become heightened, like those of a blind person, she imagined. The earth sloped down here, then up. The ground cover was thick here, then non-existent. Just the weight of the air told her whether she was in the midst of scrub brushes or out in the open. It seemed like ten hours had passed since she'd escaped the house, but she wondered if it was even midnight. Her muscles were so worn out, she felt as though she hadn't slept in days.

Her ankle was throbbing, and she decided to allow herself a short break. When the clouds thinned, she strained her eyes in the moonlight, looking for a rock to sit on. She found one the size of a footstool and lowered herself onto it. Her throat was parched, so she loosened her shoelaces and ate two of the sugar packets. That got her saliva flowing, but the sugar coated her throat and made it itchy.

Celie felt her ankle. It was the size of a ham. She didn't dare take her shoe off, or she'd never get it on again, and going barefoot out here would shred her feet in no time. She rubbed the tight, hard skin. The four-story drop— probably three stories, given that she'd dangled from the end of her jeans before letting go—had probably resulted in at least a sprain, if not a fracture. Whatever it was, it hurt like the devil.

Or, as McAllister would say, like a *motherfucker*.

Tears sprang into Celie's eyes, and she tried to blink them back. She wondered where he was right now, if he even knew she was in Mexico. She wished she had a cell phone so she could tell him she was alive. He was probably torturing himself, imagining her in a ditch somewhere with a bullet in her brain.

It had very nearly happened.

Wherever he was, Celie knew he was searching. She knew, deep down in her soul, he would do anything to find her, just as she knew, deep down in her soul, she would do anything to stay alive until he did. It was a pact.

They'd never spoken about it, but Celie knew it was there. She wished now that she'd been brave enough to let him know her real feelings. If she ever saw him again, she was going to lay her heart bare and tell him she loved him. Even rejection couldn't be as bad as leaving a thing like that unsaid.

Something howled in the distance, and it took her a second to realize it was a coyote. Of course. Because murdering henchmen and fractured bones and cactus needles and dehydration weren't enough to worry about.

Celie climbed to her feet, swiped away her tears, and got moving.

The beam from John's flashlight swept from side to side as he trudged across the field. He'd been out here for more than four hours and hadn't seen any sign of Celie, not even a footprint.

His watch beeped, and he stopped to reprogram it. For one solid minute, he called her name, then paused to listen for an answer. He'd been doing this for hours, and his voice was nearly gone, but it hadn't helped worth shit. The only sound out here was the wind moving over the crappy thornbushes and the occasional coyote.

"*Fuck!*"

His strategy wasn't working. When he'd first set out, he'd cut a direct line to the row of trees near the river. Because of the darkness and his ongoing flashlight sweeps, the journey had taken him more than an hour. As soon as he got close enough to hear the water running, he'd started using a grid system. He would parallel the river for five minutes, call Celie's name for one, then turn west and walk ten minutes that direction, then call her name again. Then he'd reset his watch and walk five minutes south, call her name, then head back to the river again. It was tedious as shit, but this whole thing was a needle in a haystack, and this was the only method that made any sense. John refused to wander around out here like a dumbfuck when he knew from both his climbing and his scuba training that search-and-rescue efforts had almost no chance of success when people moved around haphazardly, missing big swaths of land and covering the same ground over and over.

John looked up at the sky, where a half-moon had risen in the east. Unfortunately, it was cloudy tonight, and he'd been able to use it for guidance only sporadically.

Something moved in front of him, and John swung the flashlight beam toward it.

An armadillo. Rooting around at the base of a plant.

John stopped, paused the timer on his watch, and took a second to catch his breath. The armadillo kept rooting, oblivious to his light.

John mopped the sweat off his brow with his T-shirt. He needed a drink. And not the alcoholic kind—more like a tanker full of Gatorade. He bent over and touched his toes, trying to limber up his stiff muscles. His flashlight shined down on some pebbles on the ground. He selected a couple, dusted them off, and popped them in his mouth. He spat out some dirt and swished the rocks around, relieving his cotton mouth. What he really needed was water, but he didn't want to take the time necessary to mine the juice out of a cactus ear.

John reset his watch and resumed his course. In the

distance, several miles to the northwest, he guessed, he heard the faint thrumming of chopper blades as another helicopter landed at Saledo's. Half a dozen law enforcement agencies were probably taking the house apart by now, processing the scene and cataloguing evidence. They'd probably already dispatched a team of agents to search for Saledo's nephew, too—probably put out an APB and stationed guys at the airport. Some murdering shithead gets loose, and law enforcement pulls out all the stops. Meanwhile, an innocent woman is lost in the wilderness, running for her life from the sick fuck, and she doesn't even merit a canine unit. Just like back in Austin, all the authorities cared about was a high-profile arrest. No one gave a shit what happened to Celie.

No one except him.

Okay, Feenie and Marco, too. They cared, but not the way he did. Not to the extent that every step farther into the darkness was making his heart bleed.

God*damn* it.

John spit out the pebbles and wiped the sweat off his forehead. Why hadn't he told her? He'd had years to do it, and he'd failed. He'd never let her know how he felt. He'd never told her that sometime between that day ten years ago, when he'd watched her swear to tell the truth, the whole truth, and nothing but the truth . . . and then proceed to hold her head up and recount her worst nightmare in front of her attacker and a room full of strangers, sometime between then and yesterday, when she'd raced up to him in her purple jumpsuit and dragged him off to kiss him and tell him he was amazing, he'd fallen in love with her.

Shit, he was stupid. He was a fucking idiot for not realizing how precious she was and holding on when he'd had the chance. He'd let her go, again and again, and now that he finally knew he loved her, she might be gone.

John's watch beeped, and he checked the time. One fifty-five. In less than four hours, Marco would be returning to Saledo's airstrip, and John hadn't found shit.

He moved to reset the timer, and his flashlight beam reflected off something.

A shoe. With a Nike swoosh. A *shoe* sitting by itself in the dirt.

He swept the light around, trying to look everywhere at once. The flashlight beam landed on an arm, a leg, a *body* curled up on the ground.

"*Celie?*"

She bolted upright, and his world tilted. He trained the light on her face. She squinted, and then her eyes widened as he approached. She probably couldn't see him past the glare.

"It's okay." His voice shook. He knelt beside her and touched her arm. "It's all right, baby, it's me."

CHAPTER

24

She was hallucinating. She had to be.

But he was right there, touching her arm.

She put her hand over his just to make sure. A flashlight shined up from beside him, making his face look ghoulish, but it was *him*.

"Oh my God. Oh my *God*, how did you *find* me?"

He stared at her, wordless, and for a minute she thought she'd dreamed it.

But then his hands were on her. Touching her face, her hair, her arms and legs. "Are you injured?"

"I'm fine." No she wasn't. "I'm okay, I just hurt myself trying to get away."

He was turning her arm, examining the cut. He picked up the flashlight and shined it down on the gash. In the harsh light, it looked disgusting—dried blood, pus, dirt, and dead bugs stuck in the mire.

"Fuck, what's this?"

"I cut it—*ouch!*"

He'd bumped against her leg, jostling her ankle.

"What? What'd I do?"

"My ankle. I think it's sprained."

The flashlight beam shifted to her ankle, all purple and swollen.

"Holy fuck. Is it broken?"

"I don't know." She didn't even care anymore, not really. He was here. She was going to be okay.

"Does it hurt?"

"Some," she said. "I finally stopped to elevate it on a rock and took my shoe off to relieve the pressure. I guess I fell asleep."

"Hold this," he said, handing her the flashlight.

Celie shined the light on him. He pulled a strap over his head and unzipped something. He started shuffling through some kind of fanny pack or . . .

"Is that a diaper bag?" She eyed the bunny rabbits all over it.

His hands stilled. "Yeah, I guess so. I didn't really notice. Marco threw all this shit in here—"

"Marco *Juarez*? He's here?"

"Him. And Rowe. And Stevenski. A whole chopper full of cops dropped down on Saledo's tonight. Must've just missed you."

She felt numb. "I can't believe it. I can't believe you all came here."

McAllister stopped rummaging and stared at her for a long moment. It looked like he was about to say something, but then he looked down, shook his head.

"What?"

He didn't answer. He just took her arm in his hands and carefully turned it over. "Aim the light there."

She did.

He took out the first-aid kit and tore open an antiseptic towelette. She tried not to wince while he cleaned her wound, dislodging a sliver of glass with his thumbs and gently wiping the blood away, the whole time staring down and avoiding her gaze. He got the gash cleaned up, but still he kept his head bowed, looking down at it. Even clean, it was pretty nasty. She probably should have had stitches, but by now it was too late.

His shoulders shook.

She dipped her head, trying to get a look at his face. She moved the flashlight beam, but he put his hand over hers and switched off the light.

They sat there together in the pitch-dark. Soft, strangled sounds were coming from his throat.

She wrapped her arms around him, and his big, wide shoulders quaked. "It's okay," she whispered. "I'm okay."

His body tensed. He sniffled and pulled back. "Shit," he said hoarsely. "I'm sorry."

"Don't be sorry." She touched his face, running her fingertips over his wet cheeks. "I love you."

He pulled her against him and squeezed her so tightly, she could barely breathe. "I love you, too," he said.

She turned her head and kissed his chest. His body was warm and solid under his sweat-soaked shirt, and she realized how cold she'd been up to now.

"Thanks for coming."

He snorted. He started laughing, his shoulders shaking now for an entirely different reason.

"What?" she asked, pulling away from him.

"Shit, Celie." He pulled her back, still laughing, and kissed her forehead. "Sometimes you kill me."

McAllister had just finished digging the cactus needles out of her palm when the flashlight flickered and faded off. She pressed the button a few times and tapped it against the ground, but it was dead.

He cursed the flashlight company, then the battery company, then the Mexican countryside.

Celie smiled in the darkness. She was leaning against a boulder and sitting on top of a spread-out poncho with her ankle propped up. McAllister had scouted out this spot with the aid of the flashlight, and it was more comfortable than the patch of dirt where she had collapsed a few hours back.

"Did Marco put any batteries in that bag?" he asked.

While McAllister played doctor, Celie had inventoried everything. They had a dead cellular phone, one Power-Bar, a first-aid kit, a tube of diaper cream, a pocket knife, Wet Wipes, and two sample packs of Enfamil. What they didn't have were spare batteries.

Or water.

"No," she reported.

"Shit. There goes our chance of getting out of here tonight."

"I didn't know we had one."

His face glowed green in the light of his watch as he checked the time. "In three hours, Marco will be looking for us on Saledo's road. I was hoping we'd get moving back that direction soon."

"I hate to break it to you, but I don't think my ankle's up for that hike." She didn't want to tell him how much it hurt, but it really did.

"I was planning to carry you. You know, piggyback."

She bit her lip, trying to keep her emotions from spilling over. He'd already been subjected to one of her crying jags yesterday.

She cleared her throat. "I don't think that's going to work without a flashlight."

"Yeah." He heaved a sigh. "If the clouds dissipate, we can use the moon."

When the moon was visible, it cast enough light to travel by—barely. Problem was, it kept going into hiding for long stretches.

"Why don't we just rest?" Celie suggested. "When the sun comes up, we'll get going. Maybe by then Marco will have rustled up some help."

John didn't say anything, and Celie knew he wasn't happy. He was worried about her injuries. Plus, they were both hungry and getting dehydrated.

"Okay," he said. "But I need you to eat that PowerBar."

He'd already offered it to her, but she'd said she didn't want it.

"Let's split it," she said now.

While she unwrapped it and broke it in half, he got up and wandered a few yards away. She thought he was relieving himself, but then he came back and set something down on the ground.

"What are you doing?"

"Have you ever eaten prickly pear?"

"No."

"You're in for a treat," he said. "I'll pluck the needles out of these, carve up the meat inside. You just chew it and get all the juice out."

"Hmm . . . Can you make me a margarita, too?"

He chuckled and sat down beside her. He went to work on the cactus with the knife, and a few minutes later, she'd washed down half of the PowerBar with a dozen mouthfuls of slightly sweet liquid.

"Yum," she said.

"Told you."

She felt him stand up beside her. "What now?"

"We need to get you more comfortable." He eased himself down between her and the rock while taking care not to jar her injuries. He nestled her bottom between his legs and gently pulled her back so that her head fit against his chest.

"Thanks," she said. "This is much better."

For a few minutes they were still and quiet, and the breeze was the only sound.

"Are you really okay?" he asked softly. "He didn't hurt you, did he?"

"I would have told you."

She felt his chest rise and fall, his relief tangible.

"Good." He stroked her hair away from her face.

"I think he was going to." She told him about her interchange with Saledo during the skeet shooting. She felt better telling someone, especially now that Saledo was good and dead.

"What do you think happened to his nephew?"

"I don't know," McAllister said. "Since we haven't seen any choppers or signs of a search party, the cops must have reason to believe he's out of the area. Or maybe they've apprehended him."

"You think they got him?"

He hesitated a moment. "In all honesty? No. My guess is, he hightailed it way the hell away from here. He's probably in hiding."

"You think he'll stay there?"

"Maybe. I doubt it, though. There's a power vacuum now, and someone's got to fill it."

Not a great prospect. Celie wondered if Special Agent Rowe ever felt discouraged by the endless nature of it all. The minute they caught one criminal, another popped up to take his place.

"I'm worried now," McAllister said, his voice low. "He could come after you someday."

Celie had been thinking about that earlier tonight. "I don't think he will."

"What, you spend the afternoon with the guy and suddenly you can predict his behavior?"

"No, it's just . . ." She had nothing concrete, only a feeling. "I think he likes me. I know that sounds strange, but I think he admires that I took something from his uncle. I don't think he respected the man very much."

Celie nestled her head against John's chest. They sat that way for a while, just breathing together in the blackness, and then she spoke up.

"I can't believe Marco came down here."

"Feenie sent him."

"I can't believe Feenie sent him."

"She loves you." He kissed the top of her head. "Same as me."

She smiled in the dark and felt his warm hands glide over her thighs. Her legs were still bare, but he was keeping the chill away.

He cleared his throat. "I've been thinking," he said. "If you want to keep trying to get pregnant, I could help out with that."

A few seconds ticked by. "I thought you didn't believe in having babies out of wedlock?"

"I don't."

She absorbed that for a moment, feeling torn. She needed to tell him something, but just thinking about it made her ache.

"When I first started spending time with you," she said, "I had this notion that you could work some kind of miracle on me."

"How's that?"

"You're just so, I don't know, manly, I guess. It doesn't make any sense, but I thought all that testosterone might kick my body into gear or something."

His hands stroked her skin in a way that was a little bit sexual and a lot comforting. "That doesn't sound very scientific," he said finally.

"It isn't." She swallowed. "You know, odds are, I'll never be able to have a baby. I don't know if that matters to you or not, but you need to know."

"I know." He took her hands in his and gently settled them in her lap, making sure not to bump her bandaged arm. "Have you ever thought about adoption?"

"I wanted to exhaust the other possibilities first."

"You know what I think?" His breath felt warm against her ear. "I think you're going to be a mother someday. And wherever your child comes from, you're going to love it, and nurture it, and take good care of it, just like you do every kid who gets the privilege of knowing you."

She didn't say anything.

"You gave all that money to the Bluebonnet House, didn't you?"

She took a deep breath, blew it out. "Not all of it. But a lot. Did Marco tell you?"

"I put it together after something Feenie said."

"Oh."

"It was a gutsy, generous thing to do," he said. "But please don't do it again."

"I don't see what's so generous about it. It was never really my money in the first place."

"Still," he said. "Promise me that's the last time you do something like that. If we're going to make this work, I need to know you're not out pissing off dangerous people and getting yourself in life-threatening situations all the time."

"Let's talk about something else."

"Like what?"

"Like us. I have a few questions."

He folded his arms over her chest and pulled her closer. "Okay, let's hear 'em."

She swallowed. Chewed her lip. Wondered whether this was crazy. Maybe she should stop giving in to her impulses.

"What you said a minute ago." She turned to look at him. "Did you mean you want to get married?"

"Celie." His breath tickled her ear.

"What?"

"I'm dying to marry you."

Her eyes filled with tears. "Really?"

"Really," he murmured.

And then he kissed her. His mouth was hot and tender against hers, and she wished she wasn't such a physical wreck. She wanted to mark this moment. She wanted to show him how happy she was.

She pulled away and looked at him. "When all this is over, will you take me camping? I want us to make love under the stars."

"Hmm . . . is that a fact?" His voice had that sultry drawl to it. "What about tonight?"

"I don't think my ankle—"

"See now, you haven't been paying attention." His hands stroked over her, warm and strong. "Your ankle's not the most important part."

In the morning light, the prickly pears didn't look nearly as menacing. With their dewy yellow flowers, they actually looked beautiful.

"Gosh, this is pretty," Celie said, looking out over the softly lit landscape dotted with green mesquite and silvery sagebrush.

McAllister grunted agreement.

She kissed his cheek. "Guess you're not too interested in the scenery, huh?"

"Not really."

For the past hour, at his insistence, he'd been carrying her, piggyback, toward the distant golden ridge that marked Rancho Saledo. It had to be three or four miles away, but it was amazing how fast they could move in the daylight on McAllister's long, healthy legs. They were making good time. Even if Marco wasn't waiting for them, the road to the house was sure to be busy with cops today.

"You okay?" she asked once again. She'd never been one of those featherweight girls men could carry around like it was nothing.

"I'm just making a list," he huffed.

"Is it a list of all the things you're going to eat for lunch when we get out of here?"

"No, this is better. It's a list of all the ways you can pay me back for hauling you out of the desert on my back."

"Oh. Yeah, I guess I owe you one, huh?"

"Yep."

"You take checks?"

"I've always been partial to sexual favors."

She kissed his cheek again. "How's that?"

"It's a start. What I really need is—" And then he halted. "Well, son of a bitch."

Up in the distance, Celie saw a tiny cloud of dust moving across the landscape, angling toward them. The reddish-brown cloud got bigger and bigger, and she made out something dark moving in front of it.

"Looks like some kind of a comet," she said, feeling her heart lift.

"I was thinking more like a black Chevy pickup."

"How'd he find us out here?"

"Hell if I know." McAllister broke into a trot. "You can ask him over a round of margaritas."

Despite every rational argument that his brain could come up with, Rowe found himself standing in front of Kate

Kepler's door. He knew he shouldn't be here. He knew this was a bad idea. But despite everything he knew, he'd had a nagging feeling for the past few days—ever since he'd been shot, to be precise—that he needed to see her, that he couldn't stay away.

And so, in defiance of all logic, here he was.

He rang the bell, mildly encouraged that her phony rock had disappeared. His encouragement was short-lived, though, as he glanced next door and observed that her shirtless, dope-smoking neighbor had multiplied. Now three of them lounged on the back deck in chairs that looked like they'd been salvaged from apartment Dumpsters.

Rowe rang the bell again, guessing the first ring hadn't been heard over the din of music playing inside. Still no answer. He tried the door and found it unlocked.

Rowe stepped inside, half expecting to see Kate sprawled out on the sofa watching MTV. But the sofa was empty. He glanced around the room and noticed the tired balloon bouquets and vases filled with wilted flowers. The music was coming from the bedroom.

"Hello? Kate?"

The volume decreased.

"Kate, it's Mike Rowe."

"I'm in the bedroom," she called.

Rowe walked down the short hallway, his dread increasing with every step. He saw the corner of an unmade bed, some laundry strewn about the floor, a lacy purple bra dangling from the doorknob.

This was a mistake.

He stepped into the doorway and found her seated

cross-legged on the carpet. A hand-held device and an array of components sat on the floor in front of her. She gazed up at him curiously.

"Hey, what's up?" She wore a black halter top and denim cutoffs. Her feet were bare.

Rowe glanced at the sling. He imagined her getting dressed this morning, and decided she'd probably stepped into the shirt and shimmied it over her hips.

He cleared his throat. "I heard you'd been discharged."

"Yeah, so?"

His gaze dropped to the thin, lifeless fingers protruding from the sling. She noticed him noticing, and shifted self-consciously.

"So, I wanted to see how you were doing."

She bent her head down over the device, which looked like an iPhone, and started tapping away with her left index finger. "If you're here to gloat, I'm not in the mood," she said.

"Gloat?"

She looked up at him, her expression hostile. "Yeah, lord it over me how smart you are, how you told me to stay away from the scene, and how it serves me right, getting my arm shot up."

Rowe leaned against the doorjamb and slipped his hands in his pockets. He always felt overdressed around her, even in khakis and a golf shirt. "I don't think it serves you right."

She eyed him warily.

"I do wish you'd listened—"

"I knew it." She shook her head and looked down. "You can save the lecture. My dad's been at it for two weeks."

Rowe watched, intrigued, as she mumbled something into the device.

"Is that a phone?" he asked.

"Sort of. It's a computer, too, with voice recognition. If I can ever get it to *work*." She blew out an exasperated breath and gazed up at him. "I'm on a freaking leave of absence until I can prove to my prick editor I can do my job one-handed. You want to help?"

"Sure."

"Hand me that box."

Rowe stepped into the room and looked around. A cardboard box sat on her dresser, and he passed it to her. She poked through all the foam packaging until she found a cellophane bag, which she tore open one-handed. She shook out a black earpiece.

"You're pretty good with your left hand," he said.

"I've been practicing."

The sole chair in the room was piled with laundry, so he sat on the end of the bed. "I heard you got a private specialist. How's the therapy going?"

"Slow."

His gaze shifted to the vase of shriveled red roses beside the computer monitor on her desk. A card lying nearby bore Kate's name. In Nick Stevenski's handwriting. Rowe stared at the envelope for a moment, thinking he might be mistaken. But he knew his partner's scrawl because he was constantly trying to decipher it on reports. The handwriting belonged to the man who, less than forty-eight hours ago, had saved Rowe's life. Rowe looked at Kate, who was too immersed in her project to catch his snooping.

He noticed the PlayComp logo on the box in front of her. "I thought your dad's company made games," he said.

"And gaming systems. This is just a prototype. It's supposed to do everything—phone calls, gaming, Web surfing. It's designed for kids, which is good because I've got small hands."

Rowe watched her for a long moment. She did, indeed, have small hands. Slender arms and shoulders, too. But she was muscular. She had been a vision of health before the shooting, and Rowe guessed she felt frustrated now by her new limitations. He felt frustrated, too. And angry at himself for failing to keep her safe.

She tried to plug in the earpiece, but the cord was tangled.

"Here." He crouched down, wincing as a bolt of white-hot pain zinged through his side. Saledo's bullets had cracked two ribs. He looked to see if Kate had noticed, but she seemed oblivious.

He unknotted the cord and passed her the earpiece. Then he sat on the bed again.

"So you can compose articles on that thing?"

"That's the plan," she said. "I've got it loaded with software that's supposed to translate my voice into a text document. I can also use it to record interviews and stuff so I won't need to take notes."

"Sounds like you've got it all figured out."

She shrugged. "Maybe. Maybe not. I still don't know if I'll get my old job back."

"Why not?"

She looked up, and he saw the flicker of fear in her

eyes. "Maybe they think I'm a liability. Maybe they're just afraid to fire me because of who my dad is." She sounded matter-of-fact, but Rowe thought this was the crux of her insecurity. Because of her dad, she had to work twice as hard to prove she was talented and competent, not just some spoiled rich girl.

Rowe watched her work and reminded himself that he had about a thousand things he needed to be doing right now besides sitting in Kate Kepler's bedroom.

"Why are you really here?" she asked, looking up at him.

He stared into those deep brown eyes. She was beautiful, and smart, and he shouldn't have come. He stood up and pulled an envelope from his pocket.

"Here," he said, handing it to her.

"What's this?"

"A pair of tickets to see U2. They're coming to Houston in a few weeks."

Her head snapped up. "I love U2!"

"I know."

"You must have spent a fortune!"

He shrugged. "It's no big deal. Anyway, you spent your birthday in the hospital, so I thought you might like to treat yourself. Enjoy."

She glanced down at the envelope, then back up at him, puzzled. "Don't you want to go?"

"No, they're for you." He stepped toward the door. "Take a friend." *Anyone but Stevenski.*

"Wait!" She caught her elbow on the bed and levered herself to her feet. "Why can't you come with me? They're your tickets."

He gazed down at her. "No, Kate. They're *your* tickets."

"But—"

"Go have fun." He looked her up and down, forming a picture of her in his mind. "Happy birthday. I'm sorry you had to spend it in the hospital."

CHAPTER

25

Konakovo, Russia
Sixteen months later

John didn't care what anyone said about global warming, this place was fucking *cold*. And it was barely fall, for Christ's sake.

Their guide turned off the narrow road and meandered up a bumpy driveway. After a few moments, he halted the car in front of a gray prefab building.

"Shit, is this it?"

"This is it," the guide replied.

They'd been driving for hours through endless stretches of barren countryside and countless industrial towns. John peered out the window of the cramped Opel sedan. They'd seen plenty of unattractive buildings over the past few days, but this was the winner, hands down. The two-story concrete structure was depressing as hell. John couldn't believe nearly fifty kids were warehoused here.

He turned to Celie. She was shivering in her down coat beside him, but he didn't think it had to do with the cold or the lack of heat in the rental car.

"You okay?" he asked.

She leaned over his lap and gazed out the window. Then she sank back against the seat and took a deep breath. "I'm okay."

"You sure?"

"I'm sure. Let's go."

They got out of the car, and John held Celie's hand as they walked up the sidewalk. Their guide—who was also doubling as a translator—led the way as they darted curious glances around the grounds. John knew Celie's thoughts must be similar to his own. How could children live in this place? There wasn't a single toy or piece of play equipment anywhere. The sole decoration was a pot of bright yellow tulips by the building's front door, and the flowers were the most depressing feature of all because they were so obviously fake.

They entered the orphanage and within minutes found themselves seated in a drafty office, staring across the desk at a stout woman with wispy gray hair. She had kind brown eyes, but they did little to soften her message.

"There has been a mistake. Our last eligible baby was placed last week. *Sozhaleyu.*"

"Come again?" John looked at the translator as Celie deflated beside him.

"No babies for adopting," the translator said.

"No, I caught that part." John took Celie's limp hand. "I mean, how could this happen? At the hearing they told us to come here—"

The director interrupted him and spoke to the translator in brisk Russian. John struggled to follow the body language as Celie stood up.

"I need some air," she said.

"Hey, just wait. We'll work this out."

She put on her coat. "I can't sit here."

John recognized the look in her eyes. She'd had it since yesterday after the hearing, after the judge had told her the baby they'd traveled thousands of miles to meet for the first time had been matched with another couple. She looked bereft.

"Celie, we'll work this out." He clasped her hand. "I promise, we will." But as he said the words, he wasn't so sure. This entire trip had been one snafu after another, beginning with the ice storm in Helsinki that had grounded their connection for twenty-four hours and caused them to miss their original court date.

Celie nodded halfheartedly and slipped out of the room. As soon as she was gone, John turned to the director.

"Listen here," he said. "I don't know what happened, but we need to fix this. We were told you could help us."

She gave him a pitying look.

"Our paperwork's all in order." He turned to the translator. "Tell her. We've been approved for months."

More Russian back and forth as John tried to tamp down his frustration. The director looked at him. "That is not the problem. Your dossier, it says you want a baby."

She turned and spoke to the guide in Russian, and he translated. "She says the newborns are still on the list for Russian families. The other children here are older. Or they are *baleznenniy*."

"What's that?"

"They have medical conditions."

John gritted his teeth. He'd heard all this before. They had fetal alcohol syndrome or mercury poisoning or some other health issue that made them damaged goods. Just the concept sent Celie into fits. He tried to summon some patience as he looked at the director.

"We're okay with a special-needs baby. It's all in our file. Did you even read it?"

"*Da*," she said. "I'm sorry. We have no baby for you."

John glanced at the door, glad Celie wasn't present to hear those words. He knew he needed to be with her.

"Excuse me," he said, standing up. "I need to go find my wife."

Celie stood in the doorway of the nursery gazing wistfully at the row of cribs. The babies were quiet, unnaturally so. A room filled with babies should be noisy, but this one wasn't.

Celie knew she wasn't supposed to be in here. This wing clearly wasn't open to the public because none of the children here were wearing diapers. Instead, they lay in their little beds, naked from the waist down until it was time for an overworked staffer to come in and change the bedding. Celie stared at the soiled sheets and wondered how often that happened.

She turned her back on the miserable room and wiped

her cheeks. She couldn't stand this anymore. All the restrictions, all the red tape. Why did this have to be so difficult? All she wanted was to love a child.

She turned down the hallway and wended her way back through the corridors toward the director's office. John would be worried. He'd be wearing that look again, that grave, concerned look. He'd been wearing it ever since the hearing yesterday.

She neared the main hallway just as he emerged from the office. She started to say something, but a high-pitched giggle caught her attention.

A little girl stood atop the staircase. She was smiling. Celie smiled back, mesmerized by her beautiful face. She was thin—much too thin for a toddler—but her laughter drifted down the staircase and filled Celie's ears.

"Hello." Celie moved up the stairs, transfixed by her sunny smile.

Another giggle.

"What's your name?" Celie struggled to remember the Russian she'd practiced on the plane. "*Kak vas zavoot?*"

The girl's smile widened.

"Celie?"

She glanced down the stairs and saw John looking up at her, his brow furrowed with worry.

"Just a minute." Celie mounted the steps, taking in every detail about the girl. She had smooth, ivory skin, and ice blue eyes set slightly too far apart. Given her long brown hair and toothy grin, Celie put her at three years old. A thin, heartbreakingly small three years old. She wore purple cords that drooped around her waist, a dingy white sweater, and scuffed sneakers without socks.

Celie sat down beside her. "Hi," she said. "*Privyet.*"

The girl plunked herself down on the top step and smiled up at her.

"*Kak vas zavoot?*" Celie repeated. Her Russian must be terrible, because the girl simply laughed. But then she reached down and touched the faux fur on the cuff of Celie's coat. Her tiny hand stroked it, like it was a kitten, and then came to a rest in Celie's palm.

Celie squeezed gently.

At the base of the stairs she heard her husband's voice, and the translator's, and the orphanage director's. She heard the words "fetal alcohol syndrome" and "irreversible damage." She heard the translator say "attorney" and "waiver" and "special hearing." But those words lost all meaning for Celie as she stared into this child's face.

Celie looked down the narrow staircase and made eye contact with John. Through a veil of tears she sent him a message.

It's her, she said with her eyes.

And he nodded because he understood.

Turn the page for a look at
Laura Griffin's exciting new novel

THREAD OF FEAR,
featuring forensic artist Fiona Glass.

Available from Pocket Books

The homes of missing children are charged with a peculiar energy. Parents wait for their sons and daughters thinking unthinkable thoughts, and their desperation is like a current in the room. Their energy is powerful, galvanizing scores of perfect strangers to tromp through woods and pass out fliers and tie ribbons. But it doesn't last forever, and as the days and weeks and months tick by, the energy fades.

Fiona knew the odds. She knew that in all likelihood she could visit Shelby's house a year from now and the energy would be gone completely, snuffed out forever by a single phone call.

She surveyed the Sherwood home as she walked up the driveway. The concrete path leading to the front entrance had been cordoned off by crime-scene tape, the doorbell and doorjamb presumably dusted for fingerprints by hopeful investigators. The yard had no landscaping to speak of, save for a leafless gray sapling whose slender trunk had been wrapped with a big yellow bow.

A handful of B-team reporters kept an eye on things while their colleagues covered the press conference downtown. Most waited for something to happen in the comfort of their vans, but a few milled around on the sidewalk, talking and smoking. Sullivan ignored their inquisitive glances as he sauntered up the drive with Fiona at his side. There was nothing going on here, his gait seemed to say, nothing new to report.

"Another member of our CARD team's on the way over," Sullivan said, his voice low. "She's in charge of releasing the drawing, so I'm sure she'll have some questions for you after the interview."

"You're with CARD?"

"Yep. They put four of us on this one."

"Good for them," Fiona said, impressed. The FBI's Child Abduction Rapid Deployment team was an elite group, and she was surprised Sullivan hadn't mentioned he was part of it before now.

They mounted the back steps. A forgotten Christmas wreath made of plastic holly decorated the Sherwoods' door. Sullivan rapped lightly on the windowpane beneath it as Fiona stood behind him on the stoop, stealing glimpses of the backyard through weathered slats of fence. She saw a sliver of patio, some yellowed grass, a red-and-blue plastic playscape.

Her icy fingers tightened on the handles of her brown leather case. She'd left her coat in the Taurus, along with her luggage, which now contained a neatly folded pantsuit. She'd changed into jeans, white Keds, and the navy Mickey Mouse sweatshirt she'd bought in Anaheim years ago. Her prim French braid was long gone, and her hair now hung loose around her shoulders.

The door squeaked open and a thin brunette woman stood on the threshold. Matching streaks of blonde framed her angular face, and she held a cigarette behind her. She looked like an adult version of Shelby, but just barely. Fiona was startled by her young age and the fact that she'd answered her door. Most people in these situations had protective relatives standing guard.

"Afternoon, Mrs. Sherwood. This is the artist I told you about, Fiona Glass." Sullivan stepped aside to make room for Fiona beside him.

The woman nodded a greeting, her gaze wary but not unfriendly. "Y'all come on in," she said, opening the door wider.

Fiona entered the small breakfast room. It smelled of Pine-Sol, as if someone had just finished mopping. The blinds were sealed shut, and the only light shone down from a fixture above the kitchen sink. So often, it seemed, these houses were dimly lit, as if the people within had an aversion to bright lights. Fiona had observed this phenomenon enough times to think there must be some psychological explanation for it, but she wasn't a psychologist and had no idea what it might be.

A vacuum hummed to life in another part of the house. Shelby's mother leaned back against the Formica counter. She wore low-rise jeans and a long-sleeved black T-shirt. Beige woolen socks covered her feet.

"Y'all want anything?" she asked, nodding at the endless row of Bundt cakes and casseroles sitting on the counter. "It's just me and my mom and Colter. No way we can eat all this."

"I'm fine, thanks," Sullivan said. "How is he today?"

She took a long, pensive drag on her cigarette, then reached over to ash in the sink. "Pretty much the same. He asked for Froot Loops this morning, but that's been about it. He's playing in Shelby's room now. I told him you were coming."

"If it's all right with you," Fiona said gently, "I'd like to talk to him one-on-one. It seems to work better that way."

The young woman pitched her cigarette butt into the sink and gazed at Fiona for a long moment. She started to say something, then stopped herself and looked at the floor. She crossed her arms and cleared her throat before looking up at Fiona with glistening blue eyes. Again, Fiona was struck by her resemblance to Shelby.

"We can certainly leave the door open if you'd be more comfortable, Mrs. Sherwood. But I'd like to minimize distractions."

"Just call me Annie," she said, swiping at her cheeks. "And whatever you need to do is fine." She pushed off from the counter and padded out of the kitchen.

As they walked through the house, Sullivan paused briefly to show Fiona the living area just off the front door. It contained a royal blue sectional sofa, an oak wood coffee table, and a matching entertainment center. A large television inside the cabinet was tuned to CNN, but the sound was muted.

"Colter was seated there," Sullivan said, pointing to a denim beanbag chair beside the table.

"And the lighting conditions?" Fiona asked.

"The blinds were open," Annie said from the doorway. "And the overhead light was on." She flipped the wall switch to demonstrate, and the room brightened considerably.

Fiona looked from the beanbag chair to the front door.

Sullivan was right. The boy almost certainly saw something.

Annie led them to the bedroom wing of the house, which was even darker than the rest and smelled like stale cigarette smoke. "My mom's been cleaning nonstop," she said as they neared the vacuum noise that drifted from one of the back rooms. "She drove up from Albany Monday night."

Annie paused beside the first doorway. "Colter, hon. The artist lady's here to see you."

Fiona glanced into the bedroom and saw a boy with sandy blond hair sitting cross-legged on the carpet. He wore footed green Incredible Hulk pajamas, and Fiona wondered whether he was ready for bed or simply hadn't dressed today. He didn't look up from his project, a multi-layered Lego structure that appeared to be some kind of staging area for his many plastic dinosaurs.

Annie gazed at her son for a few moments before shifting her attention to Fiona. "Well. I guess we'll leave you to it."

Fiona nodded and entered the room. The lilac-painted walls matched the floral-print spread and pillow sham on Shelby's twin bed. A white wicker desk sat beneath a window, and Fiona noticed gray smudges on the windowsill where someone had dusted for latent prints. Beside the bed was a second windowsill, also smudged. Gold thumbtacks were pinned to the woodwork, each spaced about one inch apart. From every tack dangled a woven bracelet made of brightly colored embroidery thread. The intricately patterned bracelets were in various stages of completion, and Fiona stared at them a moment, thinking they were just the sort of thing she'd enjoyed making as a kid.

She chose a spot on the carpet far enough away from Colter to give him a sense of space. He still hadn't looked up from his dinosaurs or in any way acknowledged that he had a visitor.

"Hi, Colter," she said casually, mirroring his cross-legged posture on the floor. "My name's Fiona. I'd like to hang out with you for a while if it's okay."

Colter said nothing, but Fiona saw him steal a glimpse at her from beneath his cowlick.

She unzipped her leather case and pulled out a wooden board. It was four boards, actually, fitted together with brass hinges. Folded, the board measured twelve inches by twelve, the perfect size to fit inside a carry-on bag. Fiona unfolded the flaps and slid several brass fasteners into place, creating a two-foot-square work surface. Her grandfather had created the drawing board in his wood-shop last summer, and Fiona considered it a clever feat of engineering. The brass fasteners that held the pieces rigid also served as clips for photographs or other visual aids. There was a shallow groove for pencils, and a notch at the top where a light could be attached if needed.

Colter didn't look up, but his hands had stilled.

Fiona pulled out a cardboard tube and unrolled a thick sheet of vellum-finish watercolor paper. She clipped it to the board and then dug a graphite pencil from her bag, along with a small container of Play-Doh. She spotted her *FBI Facial Identification Catalogue* and placed it within easy reach on the carpet. She preferred to work without it, but sometimes it came in handy when young children or nonnative English speakers struggled to describe something they'd seen. A six-year-old boy might not know the term "receding chin," but he could point to a picture.

Fiona then rummaged through her collection of Beanie Babies and selected a soft green dragon with purple spikes on his back. It was the closest thing she had to a dinosaur, and she plopped it on top of her drawing board. She made a quick sketch of the dragon and glanced at Colter. His attention was riveted to her paper.

"What's your favorite dinosaur?" she asked him.

He tipped his head to the side, giving the question ample consideration.

"Mine's triceratops," she told him, quickly drawing one. It ended up looking more like a rhinoceros than a dinosaur, but she had Colter's attention.

"I like velociraptor," he mumbled.

Fiona's heart skipped a beat, but she nodded gamely. "I'm not sure I know that one. Is he the guy in your hand there?"

"That's pachycephalasaurus."

Whoa. So much for limited verbal skills. Fiona took a closer look at the dinosaur toys and noticed they'd been divided into camps. Her prehistoric animal trivia was rusty, but she was pretty sure he had them grouped into meat eaters and plant eaters.

Colter scooped up several of the dinos and scooted closer to Fiona. "Here," he said, dumping them on the carpet beside her. "These are the best ones."

One by one, Fiona drew each plastic toy, quizzing Colter about them as she went. He was a font of information.

"I draw people sometimes, too," she said as she shaded a T. rex. "I'd like to draw the person you saw at the door after school Monday. Do you think you could help me do that?"

Colter sat across from her on the carpet now. He bowed his head.

Fiona removed the dinosaur picture and replaced it with a clean white sheet. She brought her knees up and rested the drawing board on them so he wouldn't be distracted by it. "Will you help me, Colter?"

"I didn't see him," he muttered.

Fiona tried to keep her voice relaxed. She didn't want Colter to sense the pressure, although clearly he already did. "It's okay," she said. "Just tell me anything you can."

He sat inert.

"Colter? Do you remember someone coming to the door Monday?"

A slight nod.

"What color hair do you remember?" Asking about characteristics in the abstract was less threatening, and hair color was the trait most witnesses talked about first.

"Brown," he whispered.

Brown hair.

"Okay. What else did you see?"

The silence stretched out as Colter stared at his lap. A tear splashed onto his pajama pants, and he rubbed it in with a pudgy thumb. Fiona's chest tightened.

"He said not to tell."

"It's okay to tell me, Colter. What else do you remember?"

"He made Shelby cry." The boy's voice caught and he hunched his shoulders.

"It's okay." Her heart was breaking. "Take your time."

"He sticked his knife in my face." A sob erupted from the depths of his little body. "He said don't tell about him or he'll come cut out my tongue."

Catch up with love...
Catch up with passion...
Catch up with danger....
Catch a bestseller from Pocket Books!

Delve into the past with *New York Times* bestselling author
Julia London
The Dangers of Deceiving a Viscount
Beware! A lady's secrets will always be revealed...

Barbara Delinksy
Lake News

New York Times bestseller!

Sometimes you have to get away to find everything.

Fern Michaels
The Marriage Game

New York Times bestseller!

It's all fun and games—until someone falls in love.

Hester Browne
The Little Lady Agency

New York Times bestseller!

Why trade up if you can fix him up?

Laura Griffin
One Last Breath
Don't move. Don't breathe. Don't say a word...